Touching Stars

EMILIE RICHARDS

Touching Stars

MIRA®

MIRA®

ISBN-13: 978-0-7783-2472-0
ISBN-10:   0-7783-2472-9

TOUCHING STARS

Printed in U.S.A.

First Printing: July 2007
10 9 8 7 6 5 4 3 2 1

ACKNOWLEDGMENTS

Thanks to the knowledgeable staff and volunteers of the Office of History & Archaeology of the Maryland National Capital Park and Planning Commission, particularly archaeologists Heather Bouslog and Jim Sorensen, who invited me to dig for a week at the site of a local Civil War encampment. Thanks also to Don Housley, Jim Owens and Vivian Eicke for so patiently answering my questions and making sure I didn't destroy any precious artifacts along the way.

Thanks, as well, to the staff of the Surratt House Museum in Clinton, Maryland, for including me on the John Wilkes Booth Escape Route tour led by notable historian Michael Kauffman. The facts, so well presented along the way, became fodder for my fiction.

And last, thanks to all the contributors to *Glimpses of the Past in Shenandoah County,* published by the Woodstock Museum, Joseph B. Clower, Jr., Editor. Their reporting of a local Civil War legend inspired the historical portion of this novel.

Chapter 1

Gayle Fortman knew a number of things for certain, but three were at the top of her list. One, that life could spin out of control unless she spent all her waking hours nudging it into place. Two, that even sternly administered nudges couldn't deter fate. And three, that if fate could not be nudged, cajoled or outrun, the only other possibility was to turn and face it squarely.

But she didn't have to smile.

Gayle wasn't smiling now. This morning no one was nearby, so she had no reason to pretend she was anything but worried about what fate had in store for her.

Eric Fortman, the man to whom she'd been married for seven years and divorced from for twelve, was coming home. Eric, the father of three sons who, through the years, had seen him more frequently on their television screen than in person. Eric, her first and only love, who still managed to make the men who volunteered to take his place pale in comparison.

Eric, who had faced fate head-on, nearly died from the experience and was now in need of the family he had abandoned.

A lump formed in her throat at that thought, and she reached for the coffee mug she had set on a table at the terrace's edge, grateful as the steaming liquid dissolved this one lump of many that had resided there for the past weeks.

From an ash tree at the edge of the clearing, a bird trilled a sunrise serenade, untroubled at the lack of a larger audience. Maybe the bird, an old companion, understood one of the other things of which Gayle was certain. If she jumped out of bed in the mornings and hit the ground running, she would fall flat on her face. So every day, alone on the terrace that overlooked the North Fork of the Shenandoah River, she stood with a cup of coffee in her hands and watched as dawn's artistic fingers drizzled copper and platinum on the rippling water.

When midsummer's humidity, fueled by dewdrops and river mist, sucked the breath from her lungs, or when treacherous sheets of ice glazed the fieldstones she and Eric had so carefully laid, she stood here. Dawn was the time when she gathered her thoughts, murmured her prayers, dreamed her dreams. She wasn't rich or self-indulgent, but she gave herself these precious minutes of solitude before she headed into the kitchen of Daughter of the Stars, the bed-and-breakfast inn she owned and operated, to begin her day in earnest.

Except that this morning, with so much to sort out and prepare for, it seemed she wasn't alone after all.

Surprised, Gayle stepped forward and squinted into the pearly light. The inn sat high on a slope, protected from waters that rose and fell according to the whims of the river gods. But when the Shenandoah raged, the low water bridges that skated back and forth over the snaking length of it were quickly submerged.

Gardens planted in the alluvial soil washed downstream, and *river* became a verb. Everyone within miles of the North Fork understood what it meant to be *rivered in*.

The river was behaving this morning, but the same could not be said about a certain family member. Gayle slammed her coffee mug on the table, then she started down the terrace steps at a brisk trot. The only thing that kept her from yelling her youngest son's name was the knowledge that a shout this close to the house would wake her older ones.

"Dillon," she muttered under her breath. "Dillon…Arthur… Fortman."

The boy in the boat didn't hear her, nor had she intended for him to. He was oblivious to everything. What could he hear inside the shabby rowboat tethered to the willow that grew at the river's edge, except the singing of the current, the slapping of gentle waves against the sides of the boat?

As Gayle watched, Dillon flipped a fishing rod over his shoulder, then brought it forward, flicking his wrist to cast his line farther into the river. Despite her annoyance, she winced as the rod jerked and stuttered, and the line flopped just in front of him. She had seen her son practice this maneuver over and over, yet his movements were as awkward as if he had never held a rod. Dillon had neither the coordination nor confidence to make his cast a thing of beauty. And his thirteen-year-old body, which every day seemed to explode in new and frightening directions, was as daunting an obstacle as any she'd ever seen.

Now that she was almost to the water, the rowboat no longer looked like one of the toys her son had sailed across mud puddles as a toddler. Afraid she would startle him, she raised her voice just enough that he could hear her words.

"Dillon Fortman, what are you doing out here alone?"

He turned, and the boat wobbled alarmingly. In the early morning light his face looked pudgy and unformed, his eyes heavy-lidded.

"What are *you* doing here?"

She had too many sons to go on the defensive. Sometimes she thought it was a shame Dillon never had the chance to trap her the way his brothers had.

She reached the bank and slapped her hands on her hips for emphasis. "We have rules. One of them is that you don't go near the river alone."

"But I didn't make that rule. You made it. I didn't get to say a thing about it."

"That's right." She picked her way across uneven ground to the tree where the boat was tied. Wedging her index finger between loops of what was—to give Dillon credit—an expertly tied knot, she began to loosen it so she could pull him to shore.

"I'm fishing!"

"No, you *were* fishing. Now you're coming in."

"You ruin everything!"

She ignored him, resorting again to years of experience. She managed to untie the knot, although by the time she was able to pull the boat to shore, yesterday's manicure—one of her few indulgences—was a casualty.

"We'll go over the rules while you're my captive audience," she said as pleasantly as she could muster. "You don't come down here alone. You don't go out in the boat alone. And you don't disobey me, then try to make this my fault."

"Well, it *is* your fault, because it's a stupid rule!"

The boat was close enough to the riverbank now that he could jump out and did. She moved to the edge and handed him the rope, then stepped back so he could finish pulling the boat ashore.

"We can always discuss a rule," she said as he went through the motions, then retied the boat once it was out of the water. "But we don't discuss a rule when you're in the middle of breaking it."

"Like you have time to talk to me or anybody else!"

She waited. She was a busy woman—busier than most, it was true—but all her sons knew she would drop anything if they needed her. Dillon was no exception. When he didn't, couldn't, come up with anything else to add, she took pity on him.

"Is this about your dad coming for the summer?"

Dillon was as tall as she was. At five foot five, she'd had little hope of remaining taller than her boys. Their father was a strapping six foot one, broad shouldered and raw boned. Eighteen-year-old Jared, their oldest son, was nearly as tall as Eric. At sixteen, Noah was not yet six feet, although he still looked down at Gayle from a superior height. Dillon was already taller than either of his brothers had been at the same age. Gayle hoped he would grow to be the tallest. He needed some way in which he towered over the others.

For the moment Dillon was just tall enough to gaze straight into her eyes. She saw that his were mud-brown with anger. His forehead was crinkled, and he was breathing loudly through his nose, like a bull about to charge.

"It doesn't matter." He cut his hand through the air, narrowly missing her shoulder.

"Well, it does. I'd like to know what you're doing out here." She sighed and her voice dropped appreciably. "How was the fishing?"

"Do you see any fish?"

Sadly, she didn't. "A worm waster, huh?"

The forehead crinkles deepened. "Just because I said something cute when I was three doesn't mean I have to hear about it the rest of my life."

"Personally 'worm waster' makes me smile, and these days I need all the smiles I can get." She took a risk, a calculated one, and put her arm around his shoulder for a quick squeeze. He did not pull away.

"Your dad likes fresh river bass," she said.

"Yeah."

There was nothing else to say. As she had suspected, her son had sneaked out in the darkness, before the fish were even fully awake, hoping he could go back to the house with a string of freshly caught bass or sunfish. He had braved a river he feared, a sport that bored him, the state's warnings about PCB and mercury contamination in fish caught in these waters, and, finally, his mother's wrath. All in search of Eric Fortman's elusive love.

"Your dad likes fresh bass, but he'd be sorry to lose you over pursuit of them," she said as they started back toward the house.

"I can swim."

Dillon *could* swim. A little. She had made certain that despite his debilitating fear of the water, he learned to keep himself afloat. But her youngest son was a long way from being a *swimmer*. When the water was rough he was given to panic, to hyperventilation and cramps and erratic splashing. If he fell into the river when no one was watching, if he thought he was being carried away by the current despite his efforts, it was possible he might panic and drown.

Dillon did not need a reminder. He knew.

"Your dad also likes chocolate-chip muffins," she said when they were halfway to the house. "And the state of Virginia doesn't dictate how many we can safely eat in a month. Want to help me make some?"

"It's not the same thing."

"True. Muffins taste better for breakfast."

"I just wanted to show him I can fish!"

"Maybe the two of you can fish together when your dad's feeling a little stronger."

"Do you think he'll want to?"

The question was a good one. None of them knew exactly what Eric would feel like doing this summer. Her ex-husband's life had been turned upside down. His health had suffered. In their brief phone calls he had tried to be the take-charge Eric she'd known and loved so long ago. But he had sounded like an actor playing that part, a bit player who had only managed to memorize the lines.

"I know he'll want to spend time with you." She smiled the lie into truth—or at least the nearest neutral zone. She did not know if Eric wanted to spend time with Dillon. Dillon was a stranger to him, the son he knew the least. The son he hadn't wanted.

The son who needed him the most.

"I don't know why he can't stay in the carriage house with us," Dillon said.

"Because no matter how I juggled sons or space, I couldn't find room for him."

"He could have slept in my room, with me and Noah."

"Your dad needs a room all his own, and the Lone Star room in the inn is one of the nicest. He'll just be yards away. You know you can see him any time you like."

"But we'll have to be quiet because of the guests."

"Your dad will be welcome in our house, Dillon, any time he wants to come over. You know that. Don't make trouble where there is none, okay?"

He pouted. As always, she was struck by how much this son resembled his father. Same dark gold hair, same deep brown eyes, even the same slightly off-kilter nose. Jared was the most like

Eric in personality, but when Dillon had finished growing, he was going to be a nearly exact physical replica. The irony wasn't lost on her.

They were almost to the terrace before he spoke again. "It's going to be, like, weird for you, isn't it?"

"A little." She stopped and put her hand on his shoulder, pleased he could see beyond his own turmoil. At thirteen, Dillon wasn't particularly talented at understanding how other people felt. "It's going to be a little weird for everybody. Your dad included. But you kids don't have to worry about your dad or me. We're grown-ups, and we've stayed friends. You just take care of yourself."

"Everything's changing."

"Not everything."

Dillon fidgeted, shifting his weight. His hands were balled into fists. "Dad's coming. Jared's graduating from high school."

"Life just keeps moving, and we either move with it or watch it pass right by."

"So? Do we have to like it?"

She wished, as she did at least a dozen times a day, that she could make this child's life easier. "No. We just have to accept reality."

"I'm going back to bed."

"Good luck on that. We may not have guests this week, but I bet your brothers will be up shortly."

As if to prove it, the door opened and Jared, in athletic shorts and a T-shirt, stepped out, followed by Noah in navy-blue sweats. Normally getting her sons out of bed when they didn't have school or work to do was like prying dinosaur bones from a tar pit. But this was no ordinary day.

She hadn't had time to mentally prepare for everything to come. For a moment she felt like hopping in the rowboat and floating downstream as far as she could go. But panic was a luxury she couldn't afford.

"Chocolate-chip muffins," she said, willing her voice to be steady. "How about scrambled eggs and apple sausage to go with them?"

"It's just us, remember?" Dillon said.

She raised her hand to welcome Jared and Noah. "'Just us' is plenty good enough for a special breakfast."

As they walked to join the others, she thought that this would be the last time for a long time that they would eat breakfast as a family. Tomorrow Eric would eat it with them. Not quite family, at least not *her* family. Not any longer.

Two parents, no longer married. Three sons shared. And a history of trying so hard to make things work out. First the marriage, then the divorce, and now the recovery.

"I'm glad Dad's coming," Dillon said.

"I know you are." She patted his shoulder. But she didn't lie and say that she was glad, as well.

Ariel Kensington was a star on the rise, but she wasn't a traditional beauty. Her blue eyes were just a hair too widely spaced, and her chin had a pronounced point that worked better on Reese Witherspoon. Off camera, Ariel's head almost seemed out of proportion to her body, as if on some heavenly assembly line the angels had run out of the proper model and found a substitute one size larger. The head was covered with black curls that refused to acknowledge that straight hair was the style of the day. Somehow all these flaws gave her a more powerful presence on camera. And the size of the head fit the size of the smile, which lit up any room she entered. Eric had met Ariel two years before, at a dinner at Washington's National Press Club, and a week later they had become lovers.

Now she was his chauffeur. She was taking him to the inn where his sons waited and his ex-wife was probably wondering what she was getting into.

"You could still come to L.A. and stay with me." Ariel switched lanes on I-81 heading south to Toms Brook. "My place is a postage stamp, but we could manage."

Eric realized he had been staring at Ariel's profile. Maybe he was trying to memorize it in case he was ever falling through space again. In those moments and the many beyond, he had tried and failed to conjure up an adequate picture of her in his head.

He turned away. "We've been over this. This is better."

She didn't argue. Both of them knew their relationship hadn't progressed enough for 24/7 intimacy. Neither had asked for any kind of commitment, nor, he imagined, had Ariel thought about the next step any more than he had. He had tried marriage, found wedded bliss was one of the few things he did badly, and decided not to fail again. Ariel was married to the next step on the career ladder.

"Do you know every sentence you utter has an edge to it?" She glanced at him. "That's new."

"You thought maybe I hadn't changed?"

"I just wonder if you know how angry you sound all the time. How will your boys react?"

"I'm not angry at them. I'm not angry at you."

"Eric, on the list of things you're angry about, what's at the top?"

"Is this an interview?"

"Maybe that's one of the things you're angry about. That everybody wants to know how you feel. Everybody wants—or at least *wanted*—an interview when you came back."

"You must have considered psychology before you chose journalism."

"Oh, I did, sweetie. *Dr. Kensington* had a real ring to it. Problem was, I wanted to know what made people tick, but I didn't want to take the time to make them tick faster or slower. I wanted to move on to the next story."

One of the things Eric liked most about Ariel was her honesty. It served her well on the job, too. She was gathering a reputation as a straight shooter. People often requested her when they were forced to talk to the press. She was as honest as a television journalist could be.

He decided to be just as honest. "I'm angry that this is all such a huge waste of resources."

"Fill me in."

"I've got energy, intellect, insight into world problems. I know how to use people to help me get to the bottom of things." He paused. "Or at least I used to."

"And now you've been sidelined."

That was it, of course. Sidelined. Benched. Hog-tied. Eric Fortman, charismatic, powerful, dashing television journalist. So weak, so beaten, that right now he couldn't face reporting Little League baseball scores.

"Tell me about your family," Ariel said after the silence had stretched thin.

"You've never asked for a lot of details."

"I've never been ten miles away and counting."

"What do you want to know?"

"Basics again, for starters."

"Jared's eighteen, smart enough to get a scholarship to MIT in the fall. A top athlete, charming—"

"Like his daddy."

"Not like me. He's quieter. Jared is just who he is. He never tries to prove himself."

"Watch yourself, you're giving away insecurities." She smiled and lit up her rental car with the brilliance of it.

He looked away and gazed out the window. Some fool in a black Cadillac Escalade was trying to pass on the right and getting nowhere fast. Nobody used a gas pedal like Ariel.

"Noah's more of an enigma," he said, after watching fields and trees and the occasional cow whiz by his window. The Escalade had dropped behind, as had several eighteen-wheelers. "He's…let's see…sixteen. Funny. The class clown. Very personable, the kid who picks up strays and helps his mother with the dishes. He likes art, and he's won some competitions. I've never quite figured him out."

"Do they look like you?"

"Jared a little." He paused. "And I guess Dillon will."

"Dillon's the youngest?"

"Yeah." He stopped and did a silent count. "Almost fourteen, I guess. The rebel."

"Every family needs one. Sounds like the other two had all the good stuff sewed up. Does he drive your ex crazy?"

"Gayle? Are you kidding? Dillon's her baby. She'd cut up his meat and spoon-feed it to him if he let her." But even as he said this, Eric knew it wasn't true. That was the vision he wanted to hold of his ex-wife, but it didn't begin to give her the credit she deserved.

"How do you get along with them?"

A simple question. A trick question. "Most of the time I'm not around."

"And when you are?"

"We get along fine."

"Even you and the rebel?"

"I haven't spent as much time with Dillon."

"Oh."

He heard a world of questions in that syllable. He had no answers, but he did have excuses. He listed them. "He was too young to do a lot of the things I wanted to do with the other two. And when I do spend time with the three of them, Dillon spends most of it fighting with his brothers. It's not very pleasant for anybody."

"Consequently he gets left behind," she said.

"Consequently, yes."

"Jockeying for position, I'm sure. I'd wonder who *I* was if Jared and Noah were my brothers."

"Why are you so interested?"

She sent him another of those smiles. "I'm interested in you, Eric. You don't have that figured out?"

Something eased a little inside him. And only when it did was he willing to admit how tense he had been. "It's not easy going home to them."

"Home?"

"Their home. And let's face it, it was mine for a while."

"A long time ago, right?"

"A lifetime."

"And the ex-wife? What about her?"

"Gayle's great. We get along, or at least we get along as well as two people who used to sleep together ever can. We don't fight. She doesn't ask for anything I don't want to give."

"She sounds like a paragon. Are you sure you're not still in love with her?"

"That would be a twelve-year mistake, wouldn't it? Something of a record."

Ariel slowed so that she could move into the right lane. He saw the sign for the Toms Brook exit just ahead of them. In a moment she had taken it, slowing dramatically as she did.

He gave directions, and she listened, then followed them. They were smack in the middle of rural Virginia now, magnolias bursting into bloom, grass growing tall along the roadside, daisies climbing from drainage ditches. Mountains dominated the horizon. Manageable mountains. Nothing like Afghanistan's High Hindu Kush, or the Kafar Jar Ghar mountain range in Zabul province, where he had tried and failed disastrously to chase down Taliban leaders.

"There's a part of me," Eric said, "that wishes I were coming back here as a beloved husband and father, a conquering hero to be fussed over, honored and adored. That's pathetic, isn't it?"

"Pretty natural, I'd say."

"Gayle and I have a model divorce, but this is going to test things. I'll be on their turf. At their mercy." He managed a weak smile.

"Sweetie, relax. You've already been to Iraq and Afghanistan, and this ain't neither."

"That's true. Nobody in Toms Brook wants to kill me. Nobody's going to hold a sword over my head just to entertain his friends."

"You're safe, Eric. Those people are far away. *These* people want to help you recover."

He closed his eyes for a moment, wondering which vision he would see when he did. The stifling mud-and-stone house north of Dai Chopan? Or the peaceful old inn by the river that he and Gayle had lovingly restored, one room at a time.

"I would go nuts here." Ariel made a turn onto Route 11. "The country gives me the creeps. Who do these people talk to?"

"They know each other better than you know the man in the condo next to yours. They invent reasons to get together. It's a good life."

She snorted. "So good you couldn't wait to get away."

"That good," he admitted. "I was licking wounds when Gayle and I bought the inn. She had an inheritance. I thought I'd had it with the news biz. Turns out I was wrong."

"Wounds?"

He wanted to tell her. Maybe because, after everything else, his past was almost humorously tame.

"I was forced to give up a story I was working on to a colleague. I told her there were some problems, that I was still researching and checking facts. But she rushed it into production, and when some of the information proved to be bogus, she blamed it on me. My name was still attached, and she was higher up the chain. They moved me to a nothing job at a nothing station, and I quit."

She was silent for a while, apparently absorbing everything he'd said. Then she glanced at him. "You were having an affair with her, weren't you?"

"How'd you figure that out?"

"Because why else would you put up with that kind of treatment? You knew if you squawked, the affair would come to light and your wife would find out."

"I'm not particularly proud of it. Gayle and I were separated at the time, and I probably told myself I deserved better. It was just one of those things that happened. Too many drinks after work trying to unwind. The affair didn't mean anything. Too many late nights in the same places. She was married, too. I thought that made me invulnerable."

"Fooled you, didn't she?"

"Made a fool of me, more likely."

"Did your wife find out anyway?"

"After we began talking divorce, somebody told her."

"Final nail in the coffin?"

"I think it just made the divorce a little more inevitable. When we bought the inn she thought it was a forever deal. I guess I saw it as an investment while I figured out what to do next. Then I was offered a job reporting from Bosnia. Almost out of the blue. A chance to be in the middle of the action instead of the middle of sawdust and breakfast-menu rehearsals and diapers."

"I can understand why you went."

"So could Gayle. And I could understand why she didn't want to go. Her father was in the foreign service. Gayle moved a lot. For some people it becomes a way of life. For Gayle it became a desire for roots."

"You two never thought about this before you married?"

"We thought we'd find a balance."

"Yin and yang, huh? I've never seen it work."

He wondered about that as they zipped past frame and brick houses set back from the road and through the small town center of Toms Brook, which was more of an address than a destination. No stoplight slowed their progress.

Maybe his marriage to Gayle could have worked if he had been someone else, someone better. Eric rarely beat himself up. He spent less time considering past actions than he spent trimming nose hairs. But in those troublesome bursts of navelgazing, he had come to the realization that he rarely put anyone else's needs ahead of his own. Three days when he had believed each breath might be his last had firmed up that conclusion.

And of course in the weeks since he'd been held hostage, he'd had more than a little time to consider *everything* about his life.

Ariel slowed and turned off the larger road to a narrow lane. "Okay, where do we go from here?"

He directed her, but they were silent otherwise. Ariel was assertive and pragmatic. Three days ago she had flown to D.C. to meet his plane after his long flight from Germany and taken him to the hospital for the mandatory inpatient physical performed by a doctor the network had chosen. She had helped him fill out stacks of paperwork, fended off friends both in and out of the media, and finally, last night, checked him into a suite at the Mayflower under her brother's name, then waited with him until the sleeping pill the doctor had prescribed kicked in. Early this morning she'd picked him up for the trip to the valley. No one could have done it with less fuss and more finesse.

What had she gotten out of this?

When the scenery was suddenly unfamiliar, he realized how much time had passed since he'd last been here. There were several new houses on the road leading to the inn. And the road itself, which had not been completely paved, was pristine blacktop all the way.

"There's the first sign," he said, pointing. "Daughter of the Stars, A Bed and Breakfast Inn."

"Classy."

"The place may be in the middle of nowhere, but it's a class act."

She slowed even more and took the required turn. "You'll keep in touch?"

"I plan to."

"I can be here in a day if you need me, Eric."

He kept his voice light. "I wouldn't ask you to rescue me twice in one lifetime."

"We all need occasional rescue. The people we choose to ask? That says a lot about us."

"Then it says I have good taste."

She stopped at the end of the driveway that led up to the front door. He gazed at the familiar structure. The inn sprawled in several directions, a barn-red building with white trim and black shutters. Window boxes filled with ivy, purple petunias and white geraniums graced the upstairs windows, while pots on the porch sprouted with flowers he had no names for. To one side of the house a new rose garden added gaudier splashes of color. As he opened his door, their fragrance seemed to lift him out of the car, hypnotic, sensual and welcoming.

He heard a shout from inside, and the screen door banged. Though he had grown, clearly the boy who emerged was Dillon. No one else moved with the same hyperkinetic lack of grace. His son's gold hair shone in the summer sunlight. His smile was both radiant and hesitant.

"My God, Eric, he's your clone," Ariel said softly from the driver's seat.

He heard her words, then Dillon's shout.

"Dad's here. Dad's really here!"

In that moment Eric understood the duality of his son's smile. He was filled with the radiance of homecoming, of being loved this much, of having a place in this lonely aching world that he could, at least temporarily, call home.

But in the same moment he wanted to get back into the car and beg Ariel to take him anywhere. Any place where nobody needed him.

The screen door opened again, and Gayle stepped out, followed by their two older sons, who held back. They stood behind their mother as if to say they had chosen sides, and Eric had better understand it. That they would be right there to protect her and watch over her this summer.

Gayle stepped forward first. She put her hand on Dillon's shoulder, whispered something in his ear, then stepped down off the porch and started toward Eric. When she was only a few feet away she extended her hands and grasped his. Then she leaned forward and kissed his cheek.

"Welcome home, Eric," she said. "We are all very glad to see this day."

Chapter 2

"I'm glad you're here, Dad." Jared gave his father a quick bear hug. "I'm glad you're, you know…back."

Eric knew exactly what his son meant. The word he hadn't been able to say was *alive*.

Noah danced around the word, too, but got closer. "Yeah, we're glad you made it."

Jared reached out an arm for his middle son, and he saw Noah hesitate. Then Noah leaned closer and let his father hug him. But only for a moment.

"Hey, he probably needs to sit down or something." Dillon danced from foot to foot at the edge of the group. He'd been the first to offer his arms to his father, but watching the other boys greet Eric seemed to frustrate him.

"I'm okay," Eric assured them. He held out his arm to Ariel. "Ariel, come meet everybody."

Ariel wore tight black capris and sandals with three-inch heels that showcased lethally red toenails. Her navel was adorned with a ruby that winked every time she lifted an arm. Eric saw Jared and Noah give her an admiring glance.

"What a good-looking crew," she said as she joined them. She held out her hand to Gayle before Eric could make the introduction. "Ariel Kensington."

Gayle's smile seemed genuine. "I recognize you from the series you did on natural disasters a couple of years ago on the Discovery Channel. I'm so glad you could drive Eric here, Miss Kensington."

"Ariel."

"And I'm Gayle."

Eric watched as Gayle introduced the boys. About fifty percent of marriages in the United States ended in divorce, but to his knowledge, no one had written a rulebook for moments like this. Luckily the two women didn't seem to need one. An awkward moment had been waved away by mature adults.

He hadn't seen Gayle for a year, and then only in passing. He thought she looked much the same. Her chin-length hair was the pale gold of Jared's, fine, straight and expertly layered to fall around her face. Her gray eyes were steady and serious, but her smile, although not the star caliber of Ariel's, was genuine and warm. Years ago he had fallen in love with the smile, then the woman. The smile conveyed everything about her. Integrity. Wisdom. And just a hint of the wilder woman inside. He had been captivated, and, like any good journalist, he had known she was a story worth uncovering.

Now she was telling Ariel about the inn. "Would you like a tour?" she asked after a truncated history. "You can't rush off. You must need a break from driving."

"Just a short one. I have to catch a plane out of Dulles late this afternoon, and you know airports these days. I always give myself plenty of time."

"Then a glass of tea and a quick look, and we'll have you back on the road."

"Perfect," Ariel said.

"You can't just leave Dad standing here." Dillon moved to his father's side, as if to prop him up. "He's sick. Look how skinny he is!"

The words had fallen into a conversational void, and Dillon's decibel level was always high.

Gayle flashed an apology to Eric with a glance he remembered well. Then she put her hand on Dillon's shoulder.

"Your father may need to rest, but that's his call, don't you think? I promise we aren't going to let him topple over in the driveway."

"I'm not sick." Eric's words were sharper than he had intended, but they did the job. Silence fell. He glanced at Ariel, who shrugged, and he remembered what she had said in the car about the anger in his voice.

"I'm not sick," he said in a gentler tone. "I just lost weight on this assignment. I'm planning to gain it all back."

"Well, you don't look like you used to," Dillon said with a pout. "You look older and—"

Noah dragged his brother away from Eric. "Let's go see if everything's ready in Dad's room."

"But I already—"

"No, you didn't," Noah said.

Noah was the only brown-haired son, a throwback to Eric's father or Gayle's, but his nose was hers, as was the shape of his face. He was muscular and strong, and Dillon yelped as Noah dragged him away. Noah was everybody's friend, but underneath the carefree grin, the terms were always his.

Gayle looked unhappy, but she didn't try to stop the boys. "That's one thing about Dillon. You can always count on him to tell the truth with unnecessary force. You *are* thin, Eric, but you've come to the right place. Feeding people is our specialty. And your sons make a mean waffle. No one else's compare."

He was grateful to her and not surprised. This was Gayle at her best. Facing the truth, making it feel lighter than it was, finishing on a positive note.

"Now you're making me sorry I'm not staying overnight," Ariel said.

Gayle turned to start up the steps. "I'll give you a chocolate-chip muffin as a consolation prize."

"If I stayed around here, I wouldn't fit behind the news desk."

Gayle laughed, and this, too, seemed genuine. "Ariel, if you stayed around here, you'd find there's no news to report."

The two women climbed the steps together. Eric and Jared were left below as the screen door closed.

Eric looked at his son, who was gazing into the distance. Along with her pale blond hair, Jared had inherited Gayle's straight nose and gray eyes. His forehead was broader, and his chin strong and square. There was nothing childishly soft about Jared now. Eric's oldest son was a man, and he felt a pang as he realized it. Jared had been six when Gayle and Eric divorced, the only child old enough to realize that things would somehow be different from that point on.

Eric knew this son the best and loved him the best. Other parents might not admit to favoring one child, but Eric only had one son he really understood and felt close to.

"You're really all right?" Jared asked.

"No, but there's nothing wrong that food, rest and a few pills won't cure. It's good of your mother to let me stay until the tenants move out of my condo in Atlanta. It can't be easy for her, having a full-time boarder for the summer."

"She insisted. We've been worried enough."

"There's really nothing to worry about now. But you can keep an eye on me for a while if it makes you feel better."

"It must have been hell."

One man to another. Eric heard it, and realized Jared's words and the way he said them were completely genuine. Unaccountably, he was nostalgic for the little boy who was no more.

Eric cleared his throat. "It's over. I'm glad."

"Me too."

Eric put his hand on Jared's arm. "How about a little support for the old man? Stairs aren't my friends yet."

"You got it."

"I hadn't expected to need this kind of help until I was ninety."

"We'll pretend it's preparation."

Eric laughed, rested his hand on his son's and started the climb.

The inn's Lone Star room was one of Gayle's favorites, because it had a small porch with a view of the mountains and river. Each of the eight bedrooms was named after a different star quilt and decorated in harmony with the colors of the quilt displayed there. The Lone Star room was dominated by an Amish-made Lone Star wall hanging in southwestern sunset colors.

To highlight the quilt, she had painted the walls of the room a pale gold with a caramel glaze, hung burnt-red curtains, and accented with turquoise and deep purple pillows. The furniture was dark and heavy; the bed with its sand-colored duvet sat high off the floor. The effect was pleasing and more masculine than some of the other rooms. The fact that Eric had been born in the Lone Star state gave the decision to house him here the necessary note of humor.

They were going to need all the laughter they could muster.

Gayle opened drapes and turned on lights to make the room even more welcoming. Ariel was back on the road, and Noah was keeping Dillon temporarily at bay. She and Jared were attempting to make Eric feel at home.

"You travel so light," she told him, as Jared deposited his father's two small suitcases beside the closet. "You'll have room to spare in the dressers."

Eric looked alarmingly pale. Pale, thin and, yes, as Dillon had blurted out, older. But he was still Eric. He carried himself like a prince; he hadn't quite forgotten how to smile. He had a strong, classic bone structure that was too prominent now, but still pleasing. Eric would be handsome at eighty.

"I'm sorry, Dad, but I have to go out," Jared said. "And I figured you'd need some time just to rest. I'll be back later."

"We'll have plenty of time to catch up." Eric made as if to get a suitcase and unpack, but Gayle stopped him.

"I can do that. Let me, okay? No fussing. Once you've had a few days to rest up, I'm going to put you to work."

"I don't need anything right now except some pills in the outside flap of that one." He gestured to the largest suitcase. "I'll take care of the rest of it a little at a time."

She didn't argue. She unzipped the flap and took out half a dozen containers, and set them on the table beside his bed, where the boys had put bottled water and three glasses on a tray. "We can get your prescriptions transferred to a local pharmacy."

"I picked up a bug in—" He stopped. "Nothing much to worry about. I just need to be on a couple of things for a while, including some vitamins."

"I'm heading out now." Jared made a fist and gently punched his father's arm. "See you later."

Eric smiled wanly. "You bet. Thanks for the help." He watched Jared disappear through the door before he turned.

"When did he turn into a man?"

She hesitated, then shrugged. "I guess when his father was taken hostage and nearly killed by terrorists."

"They called themselves *freedom fighters.*"

"Only it wasn't your freedom they were fighting for, was it?"

"Funny, Jared's turned into a man, while I feel like a helpless kid." Eric perched on the edge of the bed, his feet just skimming the ground. "We traded places."

"I can't even imagine what you've been through."

"I can't imagine I'm here talking about it." He looked up at her. "But let's not."

She answered by moving to the dresser and lifting a handmade basket filled with everything from cans of nuts to muffins. "What else do you need? The boys made a basket of goodies for you to snack on."

"I'll devour everything eventually, I'm sure."

"We aren't having guests this week. With Jared's graduation and party tomorrow, and your arrival, it seemed easiest. So you'll have peace and quiet to rest."

"I can imagine what losing a week of income is going to do to your budget."

She let that pass, since she couldn't disagree. "The bathroom is stocked with more toiletries than you can use in a lifetime. We change towels daily and sheets twice a week, unless you need them changed more often. No television in the rooms, but lots of books. And there's a flat screen in the guest parlor whenever you want to watch it."

"It's better than fine, Gayle. It's a gift I don't deserve, and I know it."

"It's a gift I'm happy to give the father of my sons. I want you to be here. They need to have you in reach for a while."

He looked more tired by the moment, but he stopped her before she could leave. "Where was Jared off to?"

"Graduation practice." She hesitated. "And I imagine he has to pick up Brandy so she can watch. They're inseparable."

"Brandy's the girlfriend, right?"

"She is. The first serious girlfriend. They've been together all year."

"Why do I think you don't like her?"

She was sorry her tone had given her away. "I'm not sure I understand teenage girls, never having had practice raising one and being pretty far away from those days myself. But Brandy's absolutely committed to chaining Jared to her side."

"Pretty?"

"Long black hair, a lush figure, a cute little pout when she doesn't get her way."

"You *definitely* don't like her."

Gayle considered. "Not true. She's a nice girl. She doesn't have any career aspirations, but she's helpful and sweet tempered most of the time. She just wants to be part of the family a lot sooner than I want her to be."

"The lioness protecting her cub."

"Jared has his whole life ahead of him. He's been such a star in high school, and he's going to need the stimulation of MIT. I just want so much for him. Unfortunately, he's utterly devoted to her happiness."

"I'm not sure where he learned that kind of devotion. Not from me, I guess."

She was surprised he would bring up their past so soon. She didn't know what to say.

He sighed. "That was supposed to be a joke. But it wasn't a very good one, was it?"

"You look exhausted. I'm going to stop fussing and let you get a nap. Do you need any help before I go?"

"I think I can still undress myself."

That was an image she didn't want in her head. "Or nap in your clothes. Who'll care?"

The door opened wider, and Dillon charged in. "Do you like the basket? You like chocolate, don't you? I put M&M's in there, and some chocolate-covered raisins."

"It's great," Eric said, looking, if possible, paler. "Really thoughtful."

"I can open anything you want me to."

"Not right now."

Gayle put a warning hand on Dillon's shoulder. "Your dad's tired, honey. He's going to rest. You'll have plenty of time to talk later."

Eric seemed to take pity on his son, although he looked as if it was an effort. "Just tell me quickly what you're up to these days, Dill. Before I take my nap."

Under her hand, Dillon was squirming with excitement. "There's going to be an archaeology dig at the farm next door. I think maybe I can register, even though everybody else'll be older."

"Jared and Leon are planning to be counselors," Gayle explained. "And Travis—he's the neighbor who teaches history at the high school—is considering whether to let Dillon join in."

"Leon?" Eric seemed to be surfing through his memory.

"Leon's the boy who came to live with us a while ago," she reminded him.

"It's like having another brother," Dillon said, "only he's cooler."

Gayle laughed, but her hand still anchored her son in place. "Leon's dad lives nearby. Leon moved back home last week."

"But sometimes when he goes home, he has to come back," Dillon said, "because his father drinks too much."

Gayle saw Eric's interest flagging fast. "Did you hear that Dillon won a prize as best middle-school drama student?" she asked, wanting to end on a positive note. "The principal gave it to him at the last assembly. I know he'll want to show it to you later."

"Good going, Dill," Eric said.

"I could show you now," Dillon said.

Gayle answered before Eric could. "Not now. Let's let your dad rest, what do you say? He's had quite a morning."

"If Mr. Allen lets me go to archaeology camp, I'll be digging for artifacts," Dillon said.

Eric nodded.

Gayle turned her son and escorted him to the door. "Dillon, your dad's going to need a good lunch when he wakes up. Can you take a package of chopped chicken out of the freezer? I'm going to make chicken salad."

"I'll be back later, Dad," Dillon said.

Gayle waited until he was gone. Then she turned. "I'm sorry. He's just so glad you're here."

"You don't need to be sorry. *I'm* sorry."

They both knew for what.

Eric ran a hand over his jaw, then along the side of his neck, as if he needed proof he was still in one piece. "Gayle, I'm here. I'm going to try with Dillon, I swear. I know he needs a father, and due to the luck of the draw, it looks like he ended up with me."

She didn't know what to say.

"It's just that I don't know him." Eric dropped his hand. "He's a stranger to me. And yes, that's nobody's fault but mine, so don't say it, okay?"

She felt a flash of anger. "I hope you don't think I invited you so I could tell you what a lousy father you are. You and the boys have to work out your own relationships. I'm just giving you the time to do it."

She started toward the door again, but he stopped her.

"I'm sorry. I really am. Nothing I say or do seems to come out right anymore."

She glanced over her shoulder. He looked beaten. Despite herself, she felt a stab of sympathy. "Get some rest. Right now the only thing you need to worry about is getting back on your feet."

"Thank you. For everything."

She managed a brief smile before she closed the door behind her.

Chapter 3

Jared knew there was a line beyond which the threads of reason would fray forever. Every cell in his body was screaming that he should cross it right now and forget everything barring him from having sex with Brandy Wilburn.

Only there were too many things troubling him. From what he knew, when two people had sex, it always meant two different things, no matter how much they loved each other. He was pretty sure Brandy had an agenda that was definitely not limited to physical release. If he went ahead and finished undressing her, he might be making a choice that would have lifetime ramifications.

But damn, her breasts in his hands felt warmer and softer than any dream he'd ever allowed himself.

"Jared, what is *wrong* with you?" Brandy pulled away angrily when he reluctantly shifted and put his hands behind his neck. She shoved his chest with the palms of her hands to separate them even farther. "Just tell me now. You have some deep, dark secret I don't know about?"

He snorted. "Yeah, right."

"I've seen *Brokeback Mountain!*"

"Come off it, Brandy. You *know* I want to do it. It's just…not the right time." Sunlight filtered through the canopy of trees visible through the windshield, and he wished it were night. "Or place, for that matter."

She pouted and began to button her blouse over her unfastened bra, but she took her time, glancing at him from under outrageously long dark lashes as her fingers wove in and out of buttonholes. "I don't know what *would* be the right place. Nobody's going to see us out here."

"You want to lose your virginity in the back seat of a car?"

She was silent. Okay, so maybe virginity wasn't an issue. He snorted again. He had never asked, and she had never volunteered. "I get it."

She tossed her rumpled hair over her shoulder. "So who cares? It was only once, and the guy was a jerk. This would be like a real first time. If you'd let us get down to it."

He felt as if he were going to explode, and not just sexually. For weeks now he'd felt as if there was a stranger living inside his body, somebody trying to claw his way out. "The timing sucks," he said.

"Why? I got it before. You were worried about your dad. I could see why maybe you didn't want to make love. I mean, why should you feel good when he was, like, you know… But he's home now. You're going to have a whole summer with him. What's the problem?"

"Guys usually have to talk this up. How come you're in such a freaking hurry?"

"Jared!" She sniffed and turned away.

He was contrite, but not very. He was crazy about Brandy. Just the sight of her in the halls of their high school turned him into a jabbering moron. Once he'd been talking to his physics teacher about a test score, and Brandy had come in to wait for him. And right in the middle of the conversation, he couldn't remember one thing they'd been discussing. He was that far gone.

"Look," he said, "I don't like this, either. But my life just feels up in the air or something. I don't want to make a mistake."

"Oh great, so now I'm a mistake!"

"How come you don't get this? I mean, how hard can it be? I just don't want to do it right here and now."

"You sure seemed like you did a minute ago."

"Part of me's always ready, you know that."

"I don't know why the rest of you isn't!"

He opened his door and swung his legs over the seat to step outside and adjust his jeans. So far June had been surprisingly cool, but the afternoon sun was warming the air, even through the fully leafed branches of the hardwoods in the forest just below her house. Apparently she'd decided she needed some air, too, because he heard her door slam.

He didn't get back in behind the steering wheel. He crossed his arms and leaned against his mother's sedan. He wasn't sure what Brandy would do, maybe walk back to her house in a huff, but in a little while she joined him.

"Where were you before you came to get me?" She leaned on the car beside him and folded her arms, too, as if she were imitating him.

"I had graduation practice. I told you already."

"It was supposed to be over at *two*. It was after three by the time you got to my house."

"It just took longer, that's all."

"Marijoe called me when it was over. She was already home by two."

"I had some extra stuff to do. And stuff for my party."

"You're late a lot these days, like you've got something going on the side. Is there another girl? Is that what this is about?"

"No!"

"So were you hanging out with Cray?" "Cray" was Creighton Green, who had been Jared's best friend since elementary school.

"I told you what I was doing," Jared said.

"Maybe it's been a hard day for you. Maybe that's all this is."

He wondered if every woman thought she was some kind of emotional detective. If every single one looked at somebody she loved and thought she understood, by osmosis or something, at least a part of what was wrong.

"My dad looks like a skeleton." He glanced at her. "Do you know what that means?"

"That he's sick? Or maybe that taking care of himself when he was trekking through the mountains wasn't much of a priority."

"He says he's not sick."

"I bet it's hard to see him that way."

"It makes me furious." Jared punched the air in front of him, a lightning-quick punch, like a striking snake.

"I'd be mad, too."

"He's always been this big guy. Huge. Like nothing could ever get him."

"No, my mom's huge. She weighs like a million pounds. Your dad's hot. I've seen him on TV."

He ignored that. "He's always been on the go, you know? Now he doesn't look like he has the strength to go anywhere."

"Maybe that means he'll stay around for a little while. Wasn't he the one who took off and left your mother?"

Jared didn't like to think about that, but not surprisingly, he'd been thinking about it all day. He understood the basics of his parents' divorce. His dad saw the whole world as his home. His mom saw this little corner of the Shenandoah Valley as hers. She hadn't wanted to raise her sons here and there, without roots or friends they could count on. She hadn't been willing to leave Toms Brook and the inn that meant so much to her.

So his father had simply taken off and left them all behind.

"He hurt her," Jared said. "He hurt all of us."

"Maybe you don't know everything that happened."

"I know he's the kind of man who runs out on the people he's supposed to take care of." He looked at her. "You know what I mean?"

"I know you're angry at him."

Jared wondered, but he didn't think so. His father had been gone most of his childhood. He'd watched other fathers at Boy Scout banquets and campouts, and he had wished that his dad had been there with him. He'd been angry then. And there had been plenty of times when Eric had promised to spend time with his sons and something more important had come up, at least more important to Eric. He'd been angry then, too.

But deep down Jared knew that Eric was just Eric. That he loved his oldest son as much as he loved anybody. That he would do whatever he could for the family he left behind. That he lived simply and never begrudged his ex-wife and children the money he sent them each month. He hadn't left Jared's mother for a younger, prettier woman. He hadn't left his sons because they disappointed him.

He had simply left because that was the kind of man he was. A man who let the wide world seduce him away from his commitments.

He turned away from that thought and explored another. "When my mom told us what had happened, all I could think about was how much I wished I could have been the one to save him. And that if he hadn't gone there, if he'd stayed here with us, or even just somewhere safe in the U.S., none of this ever would have happened."

"Even I know things don't work that way. Maybe if your father had stayed here, somebody would have crashed into him on the interstate, or shot him because he got in the way of a drug raid, or maybe just forgot to tell him the floor was slippery after they mopped it. Things just happen."

There was more he could have told her, more guilt, but he doubted she would understand. "You don't think we control things?"

Brandy had smooth, cushiony skin, skin that Cray insisted would sag before she was twenty-five. But looking at her now, watching the way her honey-hued face creased with laughter and her black eyes danced, Jared felt hot all over again.

"Jar-Jar," she said, "we don't control hardly a thing. You know better. All we can do is reach out and grab whatever comes our way and hang on to it. Hard. As hard as we can. Hang on for dear life."

And that, of course, was what Eric Fortman hadn't done, and what Jared's mother could and did do so well.

"And I'm right here to hang on to, if you want me," she added.

Jared couldn't tell Brandy that he wasn't ready to hang on to *any*one. There were some things it was impossible to say.

Several years ago Gayle had realized that in order to continue operating the inn at something of a profit, she had to boost her occupancy rate. Insurance costs had skyrocketed, and competitors had increased. Summer and fall were her strongest seasons, but even during those months she had too many vacant rooms.

So she had hired a consultant, who'd suggested targeted advertising and specials, like honeymoon and anniversary packages, and discounts with river outfitters on the South Fork. She had decreased the nightly rates for longer stays and hired a professional designer to produce a slicker Web site with views of every room. And to make the inn unique, she'd begun a summer entertainment series featuring local crafters. Each summer she turned over the small, light-filled morning room off the kitchen to a valley artist, who set up a studio and spent part of most mornings demonstrating his or her craft, and teaching basics to interested guests. In exchange, Gayle paid a minimal stipend and sold the artists' work in her small gift shop.

Three years ago she'd invited a jewelry maker who created fabulous millefiori beads from polymer clay. Two years ago she'd brought in a stained-glass artist. Last year she'd welcomed a weaver, who set up an antique floor loom and wove new rugs for the inn's entryway.

This year, she'd invited the quilters.

The SCC Bee was the official quilting group of the Shenandoah Community Church. Gayle was a former president of the board of deacons, and she was still heavily involved in the congregation's activities. To help support the church's prison ministry, she had asked the quilters to create a star quilt for the stairwell, a large space clearly visible from the inn's front door.

Until now she had never been able to fill the space with anything that pleased her. The size was odd, too large for a single oil painting, but a grouping looked out of place. Whatever she displayed there had to hang flat against the wall or risk being dislodged as guests made the turn.

Since she'd decorated most of the inn with quilts, another quilt was the natural choice. Unfortunately, she had never found one that really suited the spot. So this year she had asked the Bee to create a top that would fit snugly and harmonize with the colors in the reception area, then to spend the summer quilting it in the morning room. In return, she promised a sizable donation to the church.

The quilters, led by Helen Henry, who was the area's most celebrated quilter, had agreed, and the top they'd created—after their usual good-natured squabbling—was perfect for the stairwell. Using Civil War reproduction fabrics of reds and golds, blues and greens, they had designed and beautifully executed a stunning wall hanging of four traditional stars, the intricately pieced arms of each touching those of its neighbors.

Helen had pointed out that there was one star for Gayle, and one for each of her sons. Gayle didn't know if the Bee had chosen to do four stars on purpose, but she appreciated the symbolism.

The pattern was known as Touching Stars, and Gayle, who was not a quilter, could see that each diamond-pieced star was identical to the Lone Star that hung in Eric's room, only these were scaled-down, intimate versions. She had fallen in love with the pattern and the quilt top at first sight, as well as the dozens of varied star blocks the quilters had pieced and quilted to sell in her shop as potholders or table toppers. Stars had been a favorite of quilters through the centuries, and there had been many to choose from.

What could be more perfect for an inn named for the Native American legend that some believed had given the river its name? Daughter of the Stars, the Shenandoah River, where the morning stars had placed the brightest jewels from their crowns.

This afternoon, with Eric still napping, Gayle enlisted Noah to help rearrange furniture in the morning room so the quilters, who were due tomorrow, could set up the old-fashioned quilt frame that would take up the center of the room. If they desired, guests would be encouraged to quilt a few stitches. By summer's end, if not before, the quilt would be finished, bound and hung.

"This will be more interesting than the weaver," Noah said as he lifted one end of a love seat and Gayle took the other. Together they moved it under the windows looking out over the patio.

Gayle nudged her end of the seat into alignment with her knee, then stepped back to make sure it was centered. "Why?"

"Weaving is monotonous."

"Meditative."

"Whatever. But I can draw with thread. Entire landscapes."

"If you draw landscapes with thread on the Touching Stars quilt, Helen Henry will take your head off. I'm sure the top will be marked, and the quilters will follow the lines."

Noah grinned. "You know how good I am at that."

Gayle's middle son was trying to pretend that nothing in his life had changed, but she saw the shadows in his eyes. Having Eric living in the inn was going to be a big change for Noah. Although it wasn't obvious to most people, of the three boys, Noah was the one who resented his father the most. Noah had appointed himself Gayle's protector, and although she never criticized Eric in her son's presence, Noah still blamed Eric for leaving. Noah was the child who understood most fully the work that Gayle did to keep her family afloat.

At the same time, Gayle thought Noah was the son who had agonized the most after Eric's brush with death. Had Eric died in Afghanistan, Noah would never have had the opportunity to work through his feelings for his father, something that would have haunted him the rest of his days. Deep inside, she thought Noah understood this, too.

"What else do we need to do?" Noah asked.

She wanted to brush a smudge of dust from his cheek, but she knew better than to baby him. At sixteen, Noah was no longer a boy, not quite a man. In the past year childhood chubbiness had turned to muscle, and the cheerful round face had hardened into lines and planes that hinted at adulthood. He was still funny and affectionate with everyone he loved, but there was a faraway look in Noah's eyes these days.

"I think we should set the easy chair in that corner—" she pointed "—and take the coffee table into the parlor. It can go in front of the couch by the door. That should give the quilters enough room to set up the frame."

"Want me to do it now?"

She wanted to keep him with her longer. "First help me put your figurines inside the china cabinet, would you? It's going to be crowded in here, and I don't want anything to get knocked over and broken."

"Mom, some of this stuff could afford to be broken. You've kept every single carving, clay figure and sculpture I did since I was five. I'm not ever going to be famous enough that this stuff will be worth anything."

"It's not about my retirement fund. I love every one of them."

He shook his head. "Not everything I do is great. You can see that, right? You have that much objectivity?"

Now she laughed and gave in to the temptation to ruffle his dark hair, a thick, shiny mop that edged over his ears. "I am not objective about any of my boys. You're all stars in your own way."

"You need to get a grip."

Gayle opened the china cupboard and began to remove items adorning the top so she could put them inside. A rough clay figure of a little boy in a baseball cap at bat. A carving of a collie. Another of a hunter lifting a rifle. Noah's talent had been obvious right from the beginning.

She kept her tone neutral. "How are you doing with all this, Noah? You've been on a real roller coaster with this stuff about your dad."

"I wish none of it had happened."

If she had brought up this subject so directly with Jared, he wouldn't have been so forthcoming. Jared was a man's man. He believed in actions, not words. Dillon was still learning to express his feelings and didn't always understand himself or others. But Noah had been good at talking about the things that bothered him from the time he'd developed a vocabulary.

She waited, sure he would go on, and he did. "I don't want him here," Noah said at last. "I'm glad he's back on American soil. I'm really glad he wasn't killed, you know I am. And I'm sorry he still has to recover. But he left us when we needed him. And now that he needs us, he's back."

Gayle winced. Noah saw her and shrugged. "You asked."

"Are you worried about *me?*" she said. "Because I asked your dad to come, and I meant it. It's a chance for you to get to know each other a little better. You boys are going to be off into the world before long, and this might be the last summer you can all be together like this."

"We're not *together,* Mom. We haven't been *together* since I was four. This isn't a reunion. Dillon doesn't even remember what it was like to have a live-in father, and I barely do. Dad's just somebody we see once in a while. He buys gifts when he remembers and takes us places nobody else's dads can afford because he feels guilty. Not that often, but boy, when he does remember to feel guilty, he pays for it."

She was almost sorry she'd started the conversation, but Noah needed to get this off his chest.

"You asked," he said again.

"I know. And I respect how you feel. But you need to see the whole picture. Divorce is never just one person's fault."

"That's a cliché. Sometimes it is."

"When it comes down to it, your dad and I are very different people. We loved each other, and we tried. It just wasn't possible to work out our differences in a way we could live with. But it's not fair to blame him for everything. He's supported you. He's tried—"

"He tries when he remembers. It's just a fluke he'll be home for Jared's graduation. You still have to remind him about our birthdays."

She was silent. She wondered how he knew.

"I've heard you on the telephone," Noah said, answering the question she hadn't asked.

"Eric's on the road so much, I don't think he always knows what day it is."

"Don't make excuses. People remember what's important."

"Okay, I don't think birthdays *are* important to him. But the first thing he does when he gets to a new place is call me and make sure I have his contact information, in case anything goes wrong with one of you. Your rooms are filled with things he's sent from overseas. Maybe not on your birthday, but whenever he can get to it."

"We've gotten along fine without him. I know him. He's going to interfere."

She didn't know what to say to that. What was the difference between interference and parental rights? Rarely had this been an issue, because Eric hadn't been around to make decisions. But now he was in residence again, and there would be moments when the distinction became unclear.

"I want you to give him a chance." Gayle closed the cupboard door. "And I want you to remember that I'm a grown-up, and I've been taking care of myself for a very long time. I invited Eric here because he needs us, and you need him. You're going to be gone soon, Noah. This is your chance to make things right with your dad."

There was an edge to his voice now. "And I want you to remember that whatever Dad and I work out is between us."

He'd caught her in her own trap. "I guess I needed to have my say, but you're right. It's up to the two of you from here on in."

"You know, you're upset for nothing. Dad's not worrying about this stuff. He's worrying about what he'll do next, not what he's already done. He's going to get well and go on his way."

"Just don't decide you know everything so far ahead of time, okay?"

"If he causes any trouble here, all bets are off."

The French doors to the morning room were open, but the sound of knuckles rapping on glass made Gayle turn around. She expected to see Eric, but the man standing there was more familiar.

"Travis!" She smiled, relieved to see a friend, and more relieved to be finished with this conversation.

"What's going on in here?" Travis waited at the threshold. He was always careful not to intrude.

She beckoned him into the room. "Clearing out for the quilters."

Travis knew all about her choice of summer entertainment. As he crossed to stand beside them, he looked around. "They're setting up tomorrow, right?"

"Bright and early, I'm told."

He rested his hand on Noah's arm. "Doing okay? Did you find a summer job yet?"

"No, and I wouldn't have to, if you'd let me be a counselor."

Travis shook his head. "I had to set the age limit somewhere."

49

"Then set it at sixteen."

"You know I'd let you in if I could. But every rising junior would be shouting foul. Next year, I promise. It's bad enough I'm bending the rules for Dillon."

"You are?" Gayle asked. "You're going to let Dillon into archaeology camp? Even though he doesn't turn fourteen until the end of July?"

"Well, we have to talk about the terms."

Gayle beamed at him. She was too old to think in terms of best friends, but if someone had asked, she probably would have named Travis Allen. He lived in a Colonial brick farmhouse that had been in his family for four generations. The two-hundred-acre farm that went with it bordered the inn. He rented out his fields and pasture, taught history at the local high school, fended off his share of local divorcées and widows, and still had time to be Gayle's sounding board.

Travis was dark-haired and lanky, with features most accurately described as regular. Wire-rimmed glasses highlighted his greatest physical asset, heavily lashed eyes that were not quite blue, not quite green. He was in his early forties and had been married once, but his wife had died some years ago. He understood what it was like to pick up the pieces after a great loss and move on, and he understood the value of having a friend of the opposite sex to confide in. A friend who was not looking for a mate or even a date. A friend who wanted nothing more than friendship.

"Whatever it takes to get him in," she said. "Dillon is desperate to go to camp this summer with his friend Caleb."

"Here's the thing. I've got a new site I want to excavate." He hesitated. "And it's not on my property."

"It's on mine?"

"Across the river."

When Gayle and Eric had bought the inn, they had also purchased the fifteen acres directly across the river. Gayle had wanted to preserve the view, and at the time Travis's father, Yancy, had been willing to sell. Yancy had been afraid that after his death the farm would be broken into parcels for eventual development. He wanted to keep as much of the land open and pristine as he could.

Yancy was assured that the Fortmans would not develop the property nor sell to anyone who wanted to. Covenants to that effect were added to their agreement. But to everyone's surprise, when Yancy died six years ago, Travis had come home to live on his family's land. He had never asked Gayle to sell back the lost acres.

"You want to excavate the old house site?" she asked.

"One of the outbuildings. Are you interested?"

She considered. "I don't know, Travis. All those tents for the week they camp out? All that noise at night?"

"No, we'll camp where we always do, up at my place. I've got showers and toilets installed there. And your guests might enjoy coming over and seeing what we do during the day. But your view will be intact. The area where we'll be digging is behind some trees. You won't even see us. And for the most part the river will block the noise."

"And you'll let Dillon be part of it?"

"How well does he swim now?"

This was the problem with having the head of the popular archaeology camp as a friend. Travis knew too much about her family. She shrugged. "He swims."

"That has to be a condition. We can't take non-swimmers that close to the river."

"I'll make sure he's swimming even better by the time camp starts. Noah, you'll work with your brother, won't you?"

"You're kidding, right?"

"Please?"

Noah looked trapped. "I guess."

"Dillon's lived his entire life on the water," Gayle said. "He'll do fine."

"Good. Leon and Jared both expressed interest in being counselors, and they were prime campers when I had them."

"Jared won't say yes unless Brandy's part of the deal," Gayle warned.

"She already said she'd do it."

Noah added his opinion. "Brandy's good with kids. I used to help out with the fifth-grade Sunday-school class, and so did she. All the little girls loved her."

Travis listened carefully, as he always did. "That's a good reference."

"I've got stuff to do," Noah said. "I'll move the furniture later, Mom. When Jared gets back."

He said goodbye to Travis, then took off like a shot.

Travis looked down at Gayle, and his eyes were troubled. "He's okay?"

She knew exactly what he meant. "I'm hoping he will be."

"*You're* okay?"

"Well, Eric's settled in the Lone Star room, and I'm fine. I hope the boys will be, as well. It's not going to be an easy summer."

"I'm glad you don't have guests coming this week. It'll give you time to adjust."

"It's worth losing the income." She paused a beat. "Until I pay the next batch of bills."

"I brought something for Jared. I left it by the front desk."

"What's that?"

"A graduation present. He told me last month he was hoping he'd get a laptop computer from his grandparents. I got him a gift certificate for any extra software he'll need."

"You're such a good friend to all of us."

"I don't have to work hard at it."

"You might get tired of this situation before summer's end. With the boys at the camp, you're going to see a lot of this family."

"Worse things have happened."

"You'll be at the party tomorrow night?"

"I'm guessing you might need another adult to chaperone."

The presence of their favorite history teacher would encourage better behavior from the graduates. She was relieved and grateful.

She squeezed his arm lightly, then dropped her hand. "I made chocolate-chip muffins for breakfast, and I'm about to make chicken-salad sandwiches for lunch."

"I promise I never had a thought about food on my way over here."

"Yeah, yeah. I'm sure. Come with me and you can chop the celery and hard-boiled eggs."

"My timing was off. Another ten minutes and I'd have had lunch handed to me on a silver platter."

She didn't tell him, but there wasn't much she wouldn't hand Travis on her best heirloom sterling. Having an uncomplicated relationship with a good man who simply valued her friendship and that of her sons was one of the things she was counting on to get her through the summer.

"Tell you what," she said. "I'll let you use my best cutting board."

"Do I get to use one of your new Santoku knives, too?"

"Don't push your luck."

"Me? I just wait and watch until the time is right to get what I want."

"So that's your secret?"

He smiled one of his rare smiles. "Wait and watch and see."

Chapter 4

Gayle overslept on Eric's first morning at the inn. One moment she was sitting up at her usual time, peering sleepily out her window at a lightening sky. The next the sun was fully up, and the converted carriage house, where she and the boys made their home, was rumbling with the snuffling and murmuring of awakening adolescent males.

This time she leaped to her feet and peered at her alarm clock, wincing when she realized it was almost eight. She threw on a robe and padded across the Aubusson carpet she had found in an antique shop in Staunton. China, not France, was probably the country of origin, and the nap was too worn to grace the guest area. Normally the multihued roses sprinkled across the spring-green surface made her feel as if she were walking barefoot in a garden. This morning she passed over them too quickly to notice.

In the family room, Dillon and Noah were doing excellent imitations of roadkill. She hoped they were awake enough to decipher her words.

"I fell back asleep. Did either of you check on your dad this morning?"

"You always get up early," Dillon said.

"Apparently no longer true."

"Jared's making pancakes. He woke us up." Dillon looked as if Jared hadn't done a thorough job of it.

"Dad's still sleeping," Noah said.

Gayle slowly let out the breath she hadn't realized she was holding. "Well, good. I'll get dressed and help Jared. Remember, he graduates tonight."

Dillon scratched his head with all ten fingers. "I think we should wake up Dad and make sure he eats."

"He needs sleep as much as food," Gayle said.

"And stop pointing out he's skinny," Noah told his brother. "Can't you figure out he knows that better than anybody else?"

Apparently Dillon was too sleepy to take offense.

Gayle showered, then dressed quickly in blue jeans and a white cotton crewneck. She didn't bother with makeup. After slipping into loafers, she left her younger sons to finish the transition to the land of the living and headed outside.

The inn was really an assortment of buildings, and she loved them all. The bones of the house dated back to the mid-nineteenth century, but at the turn of the twentieth, the sprawling main house had sheltered the growing family of a country doctor. According to local historians, in later years the doctor and his wife had each taken in a sister, along with her husband and children, adding rooms and outbuildings to accommodate everyone.

Unfortunately, as succeeding generations had taken over the care and the property taxes, the huge old house had slipped into disrepair. Contemporary families were smaller and less likely to want to grow old together. By the time Gayle and Eric had seen the property, the house had been well beyond a fixer-upper. Instead, the sales pitch had revolved around the potential for a new house on the same site.

Gayle had never regretted the decision to ignore sage advice and renovate the old one.

In addition to the house, which had been whittled down to eight functioning bedrooms, and the carriage house, which was the family living quarters, there was a bonus room over the modern garage that Jared and Leon, when he was in residence, shared, and a garden shed—soon to be the Star Garden suite— which had been converted into an efficiency apartment for the assistant innkeepers. The shed was perched, not surprisingly, at the edge of what had once been a garden large enough to feed the doctor's family.

Until recently the apartment had been occupied by an older couple who had helped with every phase of the inn's upkeep and management. But two weeks ago they had retired to Florida. Gayle planned to incorporate the suite into her overall rental plan, but first it needed serious updating. She was subcontracting the work herself, which was progressing too slowly to suit her, and at the moment she didn't see much hope that it would be rentable until fall.

This morning, with mist rising from the river and the sky brightening, all the hard work seemed worth it. Like many owners of country inns, she knew living in a scenic area, in a house rich in history, was one of the bonuses of her profession. She was proud that she had saved the rambling old house and found a way to make it pay.

Cutting across the patio, through a well-organized storage room and into the kitchen, she found Jared frying bacon.

All the boys helped with the running of the inn. They routinely answered telephones, set tables and washed dishes. They did garden chores under protest, and more willingly helped with any chore that required use of the computer. Leon Jenkins, the high schooler who often lived with them, did an equal share. Helping had never been optional, but Gayle had been careful not to expect so much that the boys resented the inn or her.

"Hey there," she said, closing the door quietly behind her. "Happy graduation day! I'm sorry I overslept. I don't know what got into me."

He flipped a few slices, then a few more. "I was up early anyway. I figured you could use the help."

"What's going on the griddle?"

"Florida cakes."

"Yum." Florida cakes were Jared's specialty. He used a standard pancake recipe, but he replaced the milk with orange juice, added diced bananas and pecans, and sometimes, if shredded coconut was handy, sprinkled a dollop on the pancakes before he turned them. Florida cakes were a favorite with his brothers, particularly Dillon. Guests always enjoyed them, too.

"I checked on Dad," Jared said. "I didn't hear any noise from his room."

"If we don't hear him by the time everything's ready, let's take him a tray. He doesn't need to skip a meal."

"How bad off is he?" Jared removed half the bacon with a practiced hand. The cast-iron griddle spanned two burners of the six-burner commercial stove and got a daily workout.

Gayle thought about last night's dinner. After sleeping most of the afternoon, Eric had insisted on coming to the table, but it had been clear that hunger and exhaustion were at war. Much to Dillon's disappointment, he had eaten, then gone straight back to his room for the evening.

"I talked to him after we ate," Gayle said. "He assured me the doctors expect him to recover quickly. Remember, he was in Germany for more than a week, and they did every conceivable test. Then they repeated some in Washington, just to be sure. It's mostly as simple as rest and food and, once he's up to it, getting back into his daily routine a little at a time."

"It's hard to see him like this."

Gayle was surprised Jared was so forthcoming, but she wasn't surprised at the sentiment. It *was* hard to see Eric, always bursting with high spirits and in the peak of health, so thin, tired and pale. She suspected he was depressed, as well, although that wasn't something she wanted to share with her son.

"We're going to have company this morning," she warned. "So he'll probably want to stay in his room."

Jared took a handful of pecans from a plastic bin and tossed them to the cutting board beside the stove. "Who?"

"The quilters are going to set up their frame."

"Oh, yeah. Some guy from church came by earlier and dropped it off. I forgot to tell you. I helped him get it into the morning room."

"Thanks. I've also got a couple of deliveries for the party. And early in the afternoon I've got an interview."

"How are the interviews going?"

Gayle had decided to replace her live-in couple with a gardener, two part-time innkeepers and a cleaning team of three, a decision she hadn't made lightly. But by her calculations, the renovated Star Garden suite would bring in more income than its relative value as housing for another live-in couple.

She was wary about the change, but hopeful it would work if she could find the right employees. Finding a cleaning team had been easy, and they were ready to start work next week, when guests began arriving again. Unfortunately the part-timers, who would be asked to do a little of everything, were proving harder. She just hadn't found the right combination of skills and warmth, and she desperately needed help.

"I whittled the applications down to four. Nobody really jumped out at me, though. I'm still advertising."

The door opened, and Noah wandered in. "I'm going to take Dillon down the road to practice swimming after breakfast, so don't tell me I need a shower."

"Under those circumstances, I can put up with the grime."

"Funny." He made a face. "I wouldn't do it if you weren't desperate. He doesn't listen to me. You know he doesn't. I might hold him under myself."

Unfortunately, she knew Noah was right. "Give it a try until I figure out something else, would you? He knows the basics. He's just not comfortable in the water. He needs practice, and I promised Mr. Allen."

"Yeah, yeah…"

She changed the subject, knowing this one could only go downhill. "Jared, do you have a final head count for the party?"

Jared was removing the last of the bacon. "Sixty, maybe."

"Counting adults? Parents? Friends from church?"

"Best I could come up with."

She decided to finalize plans for seventy-five. Too much food was better than too little, and the family was used to leftovers. The boys had thrived on egg casseroles and oven-puffed French toast for dinner, one of the perks or hazards of B and B life, depending on whether breakfast food was a favorite.

As Jared cooked the first batch of pancakes, she ran the final menu past him. "We'll grill hot dogs and hamburgers, and set up a nachos bar. I'll buy half a dozen of those big pizzas you like from the grocery store. Macaroni and cheese, baked beans, fruit kabobs and green salad."

Jared didn't point out that everyone would have eaten before the ceremony. The party would go on into the wee hours of the morning, and his friends would be starving the moment they arrived. "Dessert?" he asked.

"Lots of it, I promise. Mr. Allen's coming," she said. "I'll put him to work at the grill."

"You'll put him to work making sure nobody brings in liquor or smokes anything they rolled themselves," Jared said.

"I'd prefer they didn't smoke at all," Gayle said. "But just make sure they don't smoke inside, okay?"

"My friends hang out here. They know the rules."

The party would be sedate by teenage standards, but kids always seemed to have fun when they came to the inn. Since Jared's wouldn't be the only party, she made a mental note to watch closely and make sure that anyone getting into a car could drive safely. She could keep an eye on them here, but she couldn't control what the kids drank at other houses.

Jared flipped the pancakes, and Gayle went for plates. Dillon arrived, but not Eric. She made her ex a tray, adding a small pot of the coffee Jared had brewed and a decanter of orange juice; then she handed it to her youngest son. "Take this to your dad, okay?"

For a moment he looked unsure. "Wake him up?"

"Just tiptoe in and put it by the bed."

"He ought to be out here with us."

Gayle couldn't fault Dillon for the sentiment. She had been nearly thirty years old before she had stopped wishing Eric wanted to be with his family.

* * *

The quilters arrived just as Gayle and Noah finished loading the breakfast dishes into the dishwasher. Gayle saw a car pull into the parking area behind the kitchen.

"You want to help set up the frame?" She dried her hands and tossed the dish towel to Noah, who made a graceful catch.

"Yeah, I'd like to see what it entails."

Jared was on the telephone with Brandy, and Dillon was outside scrubbing down picnic tables and rinsing them with a hose. She hoped he wouldn't aim the spray at Helen Henry.

By the time she stepped outside, Helen was just getting out of a station wagon from an earlier decade, assisted by Cissy Claiborne, a young woman of about twenty. Cissy and her husband, Zeke, lived in Helen's house as companions. Helen, a big-boned farm woman in her eighties, had resisted help, but a few years ago she had finally come around to the necessity. The fact that Cissy and Zeke had a newborn had cinched the deal. For a while, it wasn't clear who was going to be looking after whom.

Now the relationship was as secure as a family bond. Cissy, with a dreamy face surrounded by a cloud of strawberry-blond hair, might look as if she needed instruction and protection, but she had proved herself to be an excellent mother and a tactful companion to Helen. Gayle had grown fond of Cissy, as had most everyone else in the community.

Two more women got out of the back seat, then a third. Gayle recognized Kate Brogan, one of the younger women in the Bee, Cathy Adams, a newer member but right at home in Toms Brook after moving from the big city, and Peony Greenway, a woman in her late sixties who, like Gayle, always seemed to be on call for jobs at their church that no one else wanted to do.

"I'm glad you're here," Gayle called. "Apparently the frame already arrived. My son helped unload it this morning."

"Zeke brought it over," Cissy said.

Helen was taking stock. "This is some place you got."

"Don't tell me you've never been to the inn?" A quick search of Gayle's memory didn't turn up a time when Helen had visited.

"Didn't get out much for a long time there. Just haven't made up for it quite yet."

Gayle put her arm around Helen's shoulders for a casual hug. "Well, I'm glad you're making up for it now." She greeted the other women, then gave them a brief history of the inn as together they strolled around to the patio.

Cissy seemed the most interested, asking questions as they went. "How many guests do you have?"

"We have room for sixteen, and by early fall we'll have room for four more, including a couple of children. That's really all two wells and my sanity can handle."

Cissy asked a few more questions, and by the time they had finished a brief tour of the first floor, Gayle had shown everyone the basics as well as most of the star quilts in her collection.

"I got the idea for using them as a theme when I found a couple of old ones in the top of a closet," she said as they started back toward the morning room. "Coupled with the name of the inn, it made sense."

"What happened to those old quilts?"

"I have them carefully stored, but since they were mostly red and green I bring them out at Christmas for a brief showing. They're not that well done, but they've been here longer than I have."

"As old quilts go, sounds like yours are being treated well," Helen said.

They ended in the morning room, where Noah was waiting. Gayle introduced him to the two women who hadn't officially met him at church.

"Let me make sure Zeke got all the parts out of his pickup." Helen walked around the pile of wood with a couple of sawhorses beside it, making a silent inventory. "Looks like it's all here."

"We were going to set up a new one," Cissy said. "Like the one Ms. Henry uses at home."

"We all went and got spoiled," Helen said. "These new frames with rollers, so you don't have to baste? I like to had a heart attack the first time I saw one, on account of what my mama and her friends would have thought of it. Now, though, I figure they'd think I was touched in the head not to use the best there is. But it's harder to sit a number of people around one, that's a fact. So we're doing this the old-fashioned way."

"Authenticity," Cathy Adams said. "It'll give your guests a look at the way it used to be done. And still is by a lot of people."

For the next ten minutes, they efficiently set up the frame, working as if they'd practiced together many times. Helen supervised as they positioned poles beside square notches at the top of the sawhorses. The poles had muslin stapled along their length, and she understood why a few minutes later, when Kate and Cissy went back to the station wagon and returned with the Touching Stars quilt.

The quilt—a sandwich with the pieced top and plain backing as bread and the batting as filling—was basted every four or so inches with plain white thread and oversize stitches. The women centered it on the frame and sewed the shorter end of the quilt to the muslin stapled to the poles. Gayle glanced at Noah, who had done his share of the setting up, and saw how interested he was.

"Pretty cool, huh?" she said.

"Shows you what people can do without a lot of money," he replied.

"Now that's a fact," Helen said. "Just about anybody could find enough wood to put one of these together. Primitive, maybe, but it gets the job done. My mama made dozens of quilts on a frame like this one."

Peony and Cathy positioned the sawhorses so they were set farther apart than the finished quilt; then, carefully, Kate and Noah placed one of the poles into the square notches, where it snuggled perfectly. Peony and Cathy began to roll the other side of the quilt around the second pole, until they had it as tight as they wanted it. Then they dropped that one in the second notch.

"What are they doing now?" Noah asked Helen as the women wound folded muslin strips in and out of the sawhorse and along the side, pinning them along the other two edges of the quilt.

"That'll keep it nice and tight while we quilt. You don't pay attention to that and to keeping it straight, your quilt'll make you seasick, all wavy edges. Now, a new frame, wouldn't be no need for all this fussing. But this is the old way, when women quilted together whenever they could grab the time."

Now that the quilt was tight on the frame, Noah bent over it, examining the multiple stars that were still in view.

"This is something else," he said. "Look at all those diamonds."

"You like quilts?" Peony asked, straightening from her stint at wrapping and pinning the muslin.

"We have enough around here, I guess."

"Never enough. And once we're done, you'll have another one." Helen wandered over to the wall and stared at a series of framed objects. "Well, will you look at these?"

Gayle followed. "They're pieces of an old quilt from the homestead across the river. My neighbor, Travis Allen, gave them to me. Said they belonged over here with all my other quilts."

"How'd he come by them?"

"Back in the days when the Allens still owned the property, the house was collapsing. A couple of times hunters used the remaining shell for shelter and started campfires inside, and the roof was caving in. Travis's father decided he had to finish the job or worry about a lawsuit. There wasn't much there, but he saved what he could. He found the quilt in an old chest. The rest of it more or less disintegrated when he picked it up, but he was able to salvage these scraps. Travis gave them to me when he came home to stay."

Helen leaned closer to examine one piece. The section of quilt was about nine inches by eleven, matted on black. The colors were faded, but greens and golds were still discernible. "It's probably a piece of a star, the tip of one arm." She pointed to another piece of what looked like plain muslin, which was now a pale, splotchy blue. "And that was probably the center, where all the arms come together."

"That's what I thought, too. I had a professional frame them to protect them as much as we could. But I didn't want to tuck the scraps in a drawer. I wanted people to enjoy them before they turn to dust."

"You notice some of the fabrics we used in your quilt look like these? Most likely this was a real Civil War quilt. About that time, anyway. Not much to look at now, but it might have been a real beauty all those years ago."

Noah joined them. "Are you going to teach people how to quilt while you're here?"

"Anybody who wants a try at it's welcome."

"Noah can sew," Gayle said. "All my boys had to learn. I don't have time to do their mending. Or the talent."

"I've seen some fine quilts made by men," Helen told Noah. "It's an art form like any. You want to give it a try, I'll be glad to teach you."

"You'd better watch out, son," a voice said from the doorway. "If you get too good with a needle, some people are going to question your masculinity."

Gayle knew Eric's remark was meant as a joke. She turned to beckon Eric, clad in gray sweats, into the room to meet their guests, but Noah looked straight at his father.

He didn't smile. "I've got a pretty good idea what a real man looks like, and I know for sure he doesn't have to keep proving who he is over and over again."

If Eric realized how directly Noah had insulted him, he gave no sign. He turned to Gayle. "What's going on?"

"The church quilting bee's going to be here this summer working on this quilt for the entryway. The guests will love it. Let me introduce you."

She started with Helen, who didn't blink. Anyone who watched the news knew the story of Eric's escape from almost certain death, and his was a familiar face under better circumstances, as well. But Helen had no interest in celebrity.

"I know your sons are glad to have you here," she said, sticking out her hand for a brief handshake. "Just don't you interfere with making this one a quilter."

Eric laughed, and they shook. The other women were not quite so blasé. Cathy, who had a son in the National Guard, told Eric she appreciated what he and his colleagues went through to bring them the news. Kate and Peony told him how glad they were he was okay.

Eric managed to be charming, but Gayle could see even this minimal effort was wearing him down. As soon as the good wishes ended, she put her hand on Noah's shoulder.

"Help your dad get settled out on the porch, please. And get him something to eat if he's ready."

For the briefest moment she thought he was going to refuse. Noah, the son she could always count on to help her. His gaze flicked to his father; then he shrugged. He turned to Helen. "I'll be back for a lesson once you get started."

"I'm counting on you, boy."

Gayle watched the two Fortman men walk out together. She hoped she hadn't made a bad situation worse.

"We need to be going," Helen said. "We just wanted to get all set up."

"There's a graduation party here tonight, but I plan to lock the doors to this room. The quilt will be all ready for you next week."

The women gathered purses and said their goodbyes. Cissy lagged behind with Gayle. Once the others were far enough ahead that they couldn't hear, she put her hand on Gayle's arm to stop her.

"I have something to give you," she said.

Gayle waited as Cissy pulled a white envelope out of a tote bag. "It's my résumé. There's not a lot on it, I guess. Probably not nearly as much as I'd need for this job, but I just want you to know I'm interested."

Gayle's mind had been with Noah and Eric on the porch, and for a moment she didn't understand. Finally she realized what Cissy meant. "The job here?"

"I saw your advertisement on a bulletin board over in Woodstock."

"But you have Helen to worry about. And Reese..."

"Marian—my mother-in-law Marian—says she'll take Reese while I'm working, and she'll be in preschool over at the church five mornings a week starting in the fall. Helen, well, she doesn't need me during the day. You want the truth, I think she'd like some hours all to herself. We get along real well, but it's a lot for her to have us and Reese. Reese, well, she's not the quietest little girl the stork ever dropped down a chimney."

Gayle had to smile. Reese was a child with a well-defined personality.

Encouraged, Cissy continued. "I know I'm young, and my education, well, it's spotty. But I got my diploma and took a few college courses on the Internet. I read all the time, and I've worked on my grammar, and I like people."

Cissy was still so young, Gayle just couldn't imagine it. But she knew one thing: she owed this girl the formality of an interview. Cissy had come so far against such odds, and Gayle didn't want to discourage her.

"I'll look this over," she said. "Will you have time next week to come in and talk some more?"

"Whenever you say."

"Let's plan for that, then."

Cissy's lovely face grew lovelier as she smiled. "I do appreciate it."

"So where's everybody else?" Eric asked Noah. "I didn't mean to sleep so late and miss everyone."

Noah didn't look at him. "Jared took off a while ago. He's gone more than he's here. Dillon's around somewhere. What can I get you?"

Eric patted the rocker beside his. "Why don't you sit a little while and enjoy the view with me? I ate those great pancakes somebody left. Did you make them?"

"Jared did. He's made them for you before, but you probably don't remember."

Eric heard the barb in what on the surface sounded like a simple explanation. *He* probably didn't remember because *he* probably hadn't paid much attention at the time. Just the way he rarely paid attention to anything that was happening in the lives of his sons.

"It's cool for early summer." Eric put his hands behind his head and stared out at the river glimmering in the distance. Small talk was an effort, but he wanted to try. "The weather's as close to being perfect as I've ever seen it."

He waited for Noah to sit, and finally his patience was rewarded. But the boy didn't reply.

Eric tried another gambit. "It's going to feel odd, isn't it, to have Jared gone next year. You two are good friends."

"We fight like all brothers."

Eric glanced at Noah, who was staring into the distance. He had matured, not as remarkably as Jared, but adulthood was looming. Still, there was a natural affability that would not change with age. Under most circumstances he was both approachable and sympathetic. Eric wondered if this son was learning to discern the difference between people he should trust and people he should not.

Perhaps he was, because it was clear he didn't trust his father.

"I used to fight with my sisters, but most of the time they were right and I wasn't." Eric smiled in encouragement. "I'm sure you can't say the same thing."

"I doubt the way you grew up has much to do with the way I have."

"Well, I had both parents in residence, if that's what you mean."

"No, I mean Jared and I might fight sometimes, but we're close." Noah turned to look at his father. "He's not going to go off and pretend I don't exist."

"Wow, the arrows are coming from all directions this morning. Apparently ducking isn't an option."

"It's just a fact. You're not close to your sisters or your parents."

Or his kids. Tarred with the same brush. Eric felt more tired than he had on waking, but he realized he could at least explain this much.

"Your grandparents are very traditional people. Maybe you've noticed that?"

"On the rare occasions when I've seen them?"

"My father wanted a son worse than he wanted the next breath of air. Three daughters later, he finally got one. Me. So I was the prince of the household. It's no surprise my sisters don't like me. They resent the way they were required to kowtow, and I can't blame them. I've tried to put things right, but there's a lot of history to outlive."

"My grandparents don't treat you much like a prince these days."

"Your grandfather wanted me to stay in Texas and run his dry-cleaning chain. He's never forgiven me for disappointing him. Your grandmother doesn't cross him."

"And that's why none of them offered to take you in this summer?"

The silence stretched too long. "That would be why," Eric said at last. "But I think maybe you wish they had."

There was no time for Noah to respond. Dillon raced around the side of the house and took the steps at a run.

"Hey, Dad, you're up!"

Eric could feel what little energy he had draining away.

Dillon stopped just in front of them. "Me and Noah were going swimming, but we don't have to go. We could do something together."

Eric managed a weak smile. "Not up to that yet, champ."

"Then we could stay here. I've got stuff to show you. Noah, you can tell him all about the—"

"No, you go on," Eric said too sharply. He swallowed more of the same and tried for a gentler tone, but he could see the damage was already done. "I didn't mean to be short with you, Dillon. I'm sorry, but I'll be a lot better company in a few days, I hope. Right now I'm just not up to much. And with your brother's graduation this evening, I'm going to have to rest this afternoon."

Dillon still looked stricken, as if Eric's words had been a physical blow. Noah got to his feet. "Get your suit on, Dillon, okay? I'll be there in a minute."

"Dillon, I promise we'll spend some good time together just as soon as I'm feeling better," Eric said.

Dillon galloped back down the steps without another word.

Noah turned to his father. "You know, I remember what it was like to be thirteen. It wasn't that long ago, and you didn't have time for *me,* either. Maybe if you'd been more interested then, I'd believe you were really interested now. But I guess I just don't buy this fatherly routine. And if you wait too much longer, he won't, either."

Before Eric could answer, Noah followed his brother's path.

Chapter 5

For the first hour of Jared's graduation party, Gayle told herself that Mama's Worst Nightmare, a rock band made up of five of his fellow graduates, was passably talented. Unfortunately, their repertoire was limited, and now, after three identical sets, she was hoping all the members—particularly the lead singer, whose nasal screeching had never earned him a solo in the high-school choir—were seeking careers outside the music field.

"How are you holding up?"

Gayle turned to find Elisa Kinkade behind her. Of course she hadn't heard her friend come into the kitchen. She hadn't heard anything except one line the lead singer had shrieked into the microphone over and over again. And five minutes later she still couldn't figure out the words.

Which, most likely, was a good thing.

"I'm dying," Gayle said. "I'm going to unplug them after this song."

Elisa was the wife of Sam Kinkade, the minister of the

Shenandoah Community Church, and they had come prepared to help with the party tonight. Sam had marched straight to the grill to help Travis flip hamburgers. At Gayle's protest, he had threatened to follow her around and quote random theologians all night unless she gave in.

"The kids love it." Elisa, dark-haired and dark-eyed, looked almost young enough to be one of them.

"I'm thinking earplugs would help the situation," Gayle said. "Or tranquilizers. Strong ones." Her eyes brightened. "You could help with that."

Elisa had gone to medical school in Guatemala and was now doing a residency in Charlottesville so she could be licensed in Virginia. She gave a soft laugh and began to slice a pizza that had just come out of the oven. "There are no pills strong enough to help you sleep through this."

"I don't know what I'll do if Dillon ever starts a band. I'll make him call it Mama's Got a Shotgun."

"Where do they put all this food? I take it out, and before I can turn my back, it disappears."

The lead singer shrieked the indecipherable line one last time, the drummer banged out a final solo, and suddenly the room was quiet.

"There's hope for sanity," Gayle said.

"Maybe they'll take a long break."

"Maybe I'll throw the power switch. We can have a party in the dark, right? As long as it's quiet."

Elisa arranged the pizza slices on a platter. "I had the chance to talk to Mr. Fortman. It was odd to be face-to-face with a real man instead of a news clip."

"Everybody in the county has been so kind. Eric will probably be considered something of a folk hero here for the rest of his life."

Noah poked his head into the kitchen. "Jared says to tell you the band's packing up. They have another gig. He thought you'd want to know."

Elisa and Gayle's eyes met. They smiled simultaneously.

"Yeah, okay, they're pretty awful," Noah said. "But they're loud." He disappeared again.

"He'll be next," Elisa said. "Or rather, next after Leon. All of them graduating, and you so young."

Gayle stared at the spot where her son had been. "I had them young. I always thought it would be best that way. The boys at home while I was filled with energy and enthusiasm, then the boys leaving while I was still young enough to do the things I wanted. Eric and I would—" She stopped, appalled at what she'd almost said.

Elisa answered smoothly, as if the last fragment hadn't been uttered. "Sam and I will do it the other way. Old, tired parents with no enthusiasm."

"You know you'll be enthusiastic, both of you, once the residency is finished. You're born to be parents."

"The graduation? It was beautiful?"

Gayle thought about the moment when Jared had walked through the line to get his diploma. All the years of nurturing him, comforting him, helping with homework and trying to pitch balls he could hit. The science-fair projects and basketball games. The occasional weeks he had spent with his father, giving her a taste of what was to come.

"It was beautiful," she said. "I knew every parent who was sitting around me. Through the years, we all became friends. Eric didn't know anyone." This had seemed significant and sad to her, but she wasn't sure Eric had realized how alone he really was in the stands. People had greeted him like a celebrity, but not like the proud father of the class president.

"He had a group around him the last time I went to check on Sam," Elisa said.

"He's an entertainer by nature."

"Was he okay at graduation? Feeling strong enough to be there?"

"I don't think so, not really. But he went anyway."

"This has to be hard. For both of you."

"Having Eric here is one of the last things I can do for Jared before he leaves us for good."

"A chance to finish up business?"

"I want the boys to know they have two parents they can count on."

The door swung open, and Dillon, disheveled and sweaty, came in. "Do we have more pizza? Noah grabbed the last piece!"

"I have another plate right here, and you can have the first piece." Elisa held up the platter. "Will you take it out to the table for me?"

"Sure." He grabbed it. "Cray brought Grapevine. I'm teaching him to roll over."

"Well, *there's* a party game." Gayle wished Jared's best friend had left Grapevine, a mixed-breed puppy whose heritage remained a mystery, at home. Grapevine had never been anything but sweet tempered when she had encountered him, but with the crowds and the noise, she was less certain.

"I wish we had a dog."

It was an old complaint. Dillon knew too many of their guests had allergies, so she ignored the comment. "Come back for this after you drop off the pizza, okay?" She held up a platter of brownies.

"Man, with Jared gone, I'm going to have a lot more work to do." He left, shaking his head.

Elisa burst into laughter. "That one is a character. Don't tell anybody, but Dillon is my favorite in the coming-of-age class. I can always count on him for a smile."

Gayle had been fond of Elisa; suddenly she was fonder. "He's definitely a work in progress."

"Only because he has important places to progress."

"I think you've earned something to eat. What do you say? Shall we go out and join the others?"

"Now that the band is gone."

Managing everything but the brownies, they pushed through the swinging doors and went out to the porch. There was just enough room at one end of the long tables set up under the trees beyond the driveway for the remaining food. After Elisa left with a soft drink for Sam and Dillon dropped off the final platter, Gayle stacked empty dishes and used serving utensils in plastic crates hidden by long tablecloths. She straightened what remained.

Now that the band was packing up, someone had turned on the stereo that Jared had set up on the patio. She recognized the expressive voice of *American Idol*'s Kelly Clarkson, one of Jared's favorites. Best of all, the volume was manageable.

Popping the top of a soft drink, she made the rounds, visiting groups of partygoers. She didn't linger with the teenagers, staying just long enough to welcome them and be sure they were having a good time. From experience, she knew the presence of an adult stifled party conversation.

She kept her eyes open for unacceptable behavior, but tonight only the most serious infractions were grounds for ejection. She wondered how well she was going to cope with having a college student, or how Jared, who had been so popular and respected in this rural county, would cope with urban college life. In Cambridge he would be just one of a freshman class of top students and a stranger to New England.

At the grill, she stopped for a real visit. Sam was no longer in residence, but Travis had been joined by Noah, who handed over his barbecue tongs the moment she was in reach.

"Reverend Sam says he'll be back in a little while," he said. "Can you keep Mr. Allen company?"

The thought was pleasing. She hadn't had a chance to talk to Travis all night. She'd seen him at the graduation, sitting with the rest of the faculty, but this was nicer. She accepted the tongs, and Noah took off.

"It seems to be going well," Travis said.

"It does, doesn't it? I was afraid graduation would be overshadowed."

"By the return of the ex?"

She shuddered convincingly. "Sounds like a horror movie."

He inclined his head toward the house. "I introduced myself. He seems tired, but okay."

Gayle glimpsed Eric comfortably settled on the porch, and he wasn't lacking for company. In fact, he was more or less holding court. She guessed that even if he was exhausted, he was happy enough to be the center of attention.

"How are *you?*" she asked.

"Soaking it up. This was a good class, and these kids were the best of it. I'm going to miss them."

She thought—as she had so often—that Travis would have been a terrific father. His marriage had lasted only a few years before his wife had died of a previously undiagnosed heart condition. Like Travis, Chloe Allen had been an archaeologist, and Egypt's Valley of the Kings had been the wrong place to suffer an aortic dissection.

Gayle had always thought that Travis's marriage, as brief as it was, had spoiled him for anyone else. He displayed photographs of a curly haired, bright-eyed Chloe on his fireplace mantel, and another of the two of them in front of the pyramids, smiling into the camera without a clue that the end of their world was just around the corner. He'd had women in his life since he'd come back to the valley, but apparently no one who could measure up to his first love.

"You're the teacher they'll come back to visit," Gayle said. "There's at least one at most schools, the teacher who really wants to know how his students are doing, who actually listens when they tell him, who never forgets the important things, even if he's had hundreds of students since."

"Teaching's turning out to be a good life. None of my pottery fragments ever come back to visit me."

She laughed and nodded toward the grill. "You must be tired of that. Let's quit. Food consumption's slowing down, and I'll refrigerate anything you haven't grilled. I can't thank you enough for pitching in."

"I'll just finish what I started. But while you're feeling grateful, have you thought about the dig site?"

"I trust you completely. If you think it'll work, it will. Of course you can dig there."

"When the dust settles, we'll go over together and check it out."

"Deal."

"And along those lines? I have an idea that involves Dillon. I wonder how you'd feel about him spending a little time with me before camp starts. I have a project in mind."

Gayle's fondest hope was that Dillon and his father would finally develop a relationship this summer. But she was also realistic. Even if that were to happen, Eric and Dillon would need breaks from each other. This seemed like the answer to a prayer.

"Ask him, please. I hope he says yes to whatever it is."

"I think he will."

She left Travis with a smile and a quick pat on his arm. "I'm going to look for him right now, and I'll send him this way. Last I heard, he was training a dog."

She knew she also had to check on Eric, who might be tired of the hoopla by now and ready to vanish. She hoped she would find Dillon with him, basking in the warmth of his father's attention, but it was not to be. Eric had an audience of three adults from the church, who were sitting in chairs flanking his, and four of Jared's friends sitting at his feet. They were asking him about stories he had covered, and despite the pallor and the too-stark cheekbones, she was reminded of many times like this one, when Eric had enthralled party guests.

One of the friends, a man who had led Jared's Explorer troop, saw Gayle come up the steps and pointed to another chair, as if to question whether she wanted him to move it closer so she could sit with them. Gayle shook her head. She wasn't ready to play audience to Eric's dramatic retelling of a story he had covered. She was certain he wasn't recounting the past months in Afghanistan, since he looked more at ease than he had since his arrival. He had always been happiest when he was center stage.

Eric stopped and looked up in question.

"Just wondering how you're doing. And looking for Dillon. Have you seen him?"

"Doing fine, and no, I haven't."

She felt a flash of annoyance. Asking Eric for help would never have occurred to her. He was recovering from an ordeal she didn't have the courage to think about. But to her, keeping track of their sons didn't seem like work. It seemed natural, the kind of thing a father and mother did without thinking. She was afraid that had she asked Eric this question at any moment through the long evening, his answer would have been the same.

He didn't know where Dillon was because Dillon wasn't on his radar. Noah, and even Jared, were also off on the periphery.

"Well, if you see him, will you tell him I'm looking for him?" she asked pleasantly, and he nodded.

"So what was the inside of Yasser Arafat's compound really like?" one of the kids asked. "After they'd bulldozed it and he was, you know, still living there?"

Gayle walked through the house, where about a dozen kids had taken over the cavernous reception area. Most of them were sprawled on the comfortable chairs and sofas, chatting, while a group of six sat around the game table playing Texas Hold'em with poker chips. She could hear the television from the guest parlor around the corner. There she found another pile of teenagers raptly watching a DVD of Christopher Reeve flying through the air.

She stepped past them and opened the glass doors leading out to the patio, scanning the land going down to the river for her youngest son. She was about to hike down when she heard a commotion from the front.

She started down the patio steps and around the inn. She arrived just in time to see a blur of fur and hear the snarling of several dogs in a tangle in front of the porch. Dillon was kicking at them, risking a serious injury, and yelling at them to stop.

She heard Cray cursing at the dogs as he ran in from the other side, and saw Jared bearing down on them. Brandy, whom she had hardly seen that night, was close on Jared's heels.

"Get back, everybody!"

She heard a shout and recognized Leon's voice. She had only glimpsed her foster son when he'd arrived about an hour ago. Even from a distance, he had looked tired and glad to be back at the inn, even temporarily. They hadn't had time to catch up.

A hard stream of water cut through the air and landed in the center of the dog fight. The snarling turned to yips. In seconds the mass of canine bodies separated into three entities. Cray's half-grown pup, and two strange dogs, one that looked like a collie mix and the other a close relative of a German shepherd.

The shepherd took off and leaped into the back of a van that was parked not far away. Gayle realized the old Chevy was the one the band had used to haul their equipment. From the sidelines a boy dove for the collie, locking his arms around the dog's neck before it could disappear down the road. That dog, too, went into the van, although not under its own power. Then the van door slammed shut.

Cray was busy examining his puppy.

"I tried to stop them," Dillon said, kneeling down in what was now a mud puddle to help Cray look over the dog. "I tried! Is he okay?"

Leon was winding the hose around two hooks that rested against the house behind the flower beds.

She went over to Dillon and rested her hand on his shoulder. "Are you all right? You didn't get bitten?"

"I don't think so."

"How about standing up to let me see?"

He grumbled but got to his feet. He watched Cray examine the puppy as Gayle examined *him* to be sure none of the dogs had sunk their teeth into a leg or foot. "Is he going to be okay, Cray?" Dillon said. "I tried to stop them."

Cray, a tall boy with a brown buzz cut and cherubic round face, got to his feet. "I think he's okay. It wasn't your fault, Dill. Nightmare shouldn't have brought their dogs along. They were bound to get out of the van."

Gayle didn't point out that Cray should have left his puppy home, as well. She was too shaken to risk it.

Leon arrived, and she put her arm around him for a hug. "Quick thinking. We've missed you around here."

"I saw somebody do that once. It gets the job done." He went over to the puppy and stooped to do his own exam. "I don't see a problem, do you, Cray?"

Cray clapped Dillon on the back. "Thanks to our man here. You slowed them down, Dill, even if you couldn't stop them."

Dillon looked as if the light of heaven was shining on his blond head. His grin stretched all the way across his face.

Gayle looked up to see Eric at the edge of the crowd. He looked paler than he had before, and for a moment she wondered if he was going to pass out. She left the boys and went to him. "Dillon's fine. Don't worry."

"I wanted to get to him."

"Well, it happened pretty fast. And you're in no shape to wade into a dog fight."

His gaze snapped to hers. "Maybe not. Who's the kid who stopped it?"

"Oh, that's Leon, more or less my foster son."

"He's got a cool head."

"You'll like Leon."

"Another kid for you to mother, huh?"

Her warm feelings cooled perceptibly. "Leon *needs* a mother. Kids do."

"You'll never have enough people to take care of, will you?"

She wasn't sure if her reaction was due to the moments of fear or was just the real Gayle stepping forward, but she took Eric's arm, not a loving hold but a hard grip.

"You'd better be glad of that, Eric, or maybe you wouldn't be here this summer." Then she released his arm and went back to make sure that Cray's puppy was okay after all.

"He's a great kid." Jared watched Dillon romping with Grapevine. It was a dumb name for a dog, but Cray had found Grapevine when he was off on one of his solitary forced marches into the mountains. Someone had abandoned the puppy, who wasn't even two months old, and he had been hopelessly tangled in a web of grapevines. Cray had cut him free, then carted him down the mountainside and straight to the vet. Luckily Grapevine was a survivor.

"Dillon's nothing like you, though, is he?" Brandy asked. "He's, like, hyper or something."

"Yeah, maybe a little, but he's probably smarter than anybody else in the family. He just doesn't know how to handle it yet."

"Maybe he'll, like, grow into it."

"He will. Mom works with him all the time. He'll be okay."

Brandy examined her toenails, which this evening were painted vampire-black. She wore flip-flops studded with rhinestones, and more rhinestones snaked up the inside leg of her jeans, a trail to hidden treasure.

Very tight jeans. Jared hadn't failed to notice.

"Your dad is gorgeous."

"Yeah, that's what people say."

"He was really nice to me. Nicer than your mother is."

"My mother's never said a mean word to you or about you, Brandy."

"Maybe not, but I can tell she's afraid I'm going to take you away from her."

Jared bit off the protest that rose to his lips. *Cray's* mother was possessive. Like Gayle, she was a single mother, but unlike

Gayle, she had nothing in her life except her son. Consequently, Cray could hardly wait to get out of the house.

Jared's mother, on the other hand, had never suggested Jared cut off any options. His happiness was at stake, not hers. He knew being a mother was important to Gayle, but he suspected she was going to like being the mother of independent adults just as well.

Brandy was right about one thing, though. Gayle *was* polite to his girlfriend. Brandy was always invited to family events. But Jared thought Gayle probably didn't like her very well. Not because Brandy was trying to pry him from his mother's arms, but because Brandy wanted to lock hers around him and keep him from flying solo.

Brandy took his arm when he didn't respond. "You look a little like your dad. And I can sure see where you get all that charm."

"I'm afraid I'm too much like him." The moment he said it, Jared wished he'd continued his silence.

"How could that be a problem? He's, like, famous. He goes all over the world, and everybody knows who he is, at least people who watch the news. And he's funny and gorgeous—"

"You said that already."

Brandy dropped his arm. "You're being a jerk." She got to her feet. "I'm going to see if there's any dessert left. And maybe I'll go talk to your father. He's nicer than you are."

Jared didn't try to stop her, though he knew that was what she wanted. He watched her wiggle her hips as she walked away. Earlier she'd told him that she had a graduation present for him and all he had to do was claim it. He supposed the wiggle was rubbing the offer in his face.

He decided to lose himself in the crowd in case she came back. He made a plate of nachos, then wandered around talking to friends. He ended up at the grill, where Travis was just putting the last of the hot dogs on a platter. He wore a splattered chef's apron and somehow managed not to look silly.

"Did you know you were going to be cooking when you came tonight?" Jared asked. "You should have run for the hills."

"Of which there are plenty to run to around here." Travis turned off the grill and wiped his hands on a dish towel. "I figure cooking tonight is good practice for camp. We'll be doing plenty of it. How are you holding up? Feeling any letdown now that graduation's come and gone?"

"Nah, not really. I guess I will, huh?"

"It would be natural if you did. You've set the high school on fire. You're a leader."

"You know the problem with that?"

Travis lifted a brow in question.

"You don't know if people like you because of who you are or because of what you represent. You know, because other people think you're important."

"You can't always tell, can you?"

Jared thought about Brandy. He'd never been completely sure whether she was in love with him or the idea of who he was. The class president. Star of the basketball team. Top student. And lately, and worst of all, the son of a man who for a few days had become the nightly news instead of just the man reporting it.

He wished he had a beer. He was sorry he couldn't sneak off to another party, one where parents turned a blind eye on underage drinking.

Travis reassured him. "I think it's safe to say most people like you just because of who you are. I'm glad I got to watch you do a lot of your growing up."

"Thanks. Me too. You saw a lot more of me than my dad did."

Jared turned toward the porch. He could glimpse Eric, but there were people standing around him blocking most of Jared's view.

"I'm glad he was here to watch you graduate. For any number of reasons."

"He could have died." Jared turned back to the grill. "And it might have been my fault."

"What do you mean, your fault?"

Jared had made his announcement in an offhand way, but Travis always listened carefully. Jared supposed he had known Travis would hear his words and pick up on them. Otherwise, why would he have spoken them?

Travis came around to stand beside him. "How could your father's troubles have anything to do with you?"

"Nothing. I guess I'm being stupid."

"I doubt that."

Jared held out his plate of nachos as an offering. Travis took one. Jared was reminded of communion services at the church, where Reverend Sam asked the congregation to offer the bread to each other, like a gift from the heart.

"I wrote him, when he was in Afghanistan," Jared said. "I said something that might have made him angry."

"You must have had a reason."

Jared didn't—couldn't—answer.

"Jared, even if your father was upset by your letter, what does that have to do with what happened to him?"

Again Jared couldn't answer. There was a lump in his throat that words would not circumvent. He looked away.

Travis seemed to understand. "Tell me what you know about your dad. The big things."

Jared shrugged.

"Then shall I tell you what I see?"

Jared cleared his throat. "If you want."

"A man with a lot of confidence. One whose job is important, and one who's pretty much developed tunnel vision about it. It's a tough job, and you have to grow a tough hide to do it. That means you take a lot of criticism, you scramble over a lot of barriers. And you learn to let go of everything that keeps you from doing whatever you've set out to do."

Jared thought about that. "So?"

"So, even from the little I've seen, the man sitting up on that porch might be hurt by a letter from somebody he loves. But I think your dad probably put your letter to one side, walled it off, if you understand what I mean, to deal with later, once he got home."

"Well, he hasn't. Maybe he just forgot about me and everything I said. Because he hasn't brought it up, that's for sure."

"I doubt he's forgotten it. Maybe he's just feeling his way."

Jared wondered if Travis was right.

"You have to talk to him about whatever's bothering you," Travis said. "You have to set this straight."

"You can't talk to my dad about anything important," Jared said.

"You have to accept the possibility he's changed."

Jared wondered. And he wondered why it was so easy to talk to Travis Allen, who was just their neighbor and friend, and so impossible to talk to the man whose genes he carried.

Chapter 6

By midnight all the adults were gone except Travis. By one o'clock even he had called it a night, and most of the new graduates were gone, as well. Some had migrated to other parties; some had likely decamped to a favorite swimming hole downriver, where no adult chaperones would oversee their activities. The smartest—and possibly the dullest—exhausted from graduation and everything that had come with it, had headed home to bed. The dozen or so who remained sat around the fire pit reminiscing about their school years.

By two, Gayle turned off the outside lights, woke and evicted two girls who had fallen asleep in front of the television, and finished putting the very last of the leftovers in the refrigerator. Jared was taking Brandy home and hadn't yet returned, but except for her own boys, the property was finally free of teenagers.

She leaned against the refrigerator and closed her eyes. The kitchen smelled like pizza and chocolate, the ultimate comfort foods, and through her thin blouse the refrigerator felt cool and solidly reassuring. She was so tired she wasn't sure if she could make it across the patio to the carriage house. She wondered if anyone would find it odd if she slept on a sofa or even a rug. Not to mention that the house was filled with empty beds....

The moment that thought hit her, she realized that the house *was* filled with beds, but were they empty? Even with only a few functioning brain cells, she knew she had to drag herself upstairs and check every one of them. There was no telling who had wandered in and up during the party. She had made a serious attempt to keep an eye on that kind of traffic, but she hadn't been able to monitor every moment.

"Just...great." She pushed herself away from the refrigerator and shook her head, hoping blood would flow to her brain long enough for her to manage a quick inspection.

Out of the kitchen, she started up the inside stairwell, which by summer's end would be graced by the Touching Stars quilt. She listened as she crept quietly upstairs, but she didn't hear signs of life. Next week, when the inn opened for business again, the house would fill with overnight guests. But for now—if she was lucky—Eric had the entire main building to himself.

Trudging quietly up and down the hallway, she opened doors and peeked into rooms that were blessedly empty. The two rooms on the third floor were also vacant, the duvets unrumpled. Now she could finally go to bed herself.

Back on the second floor, she was careful to walk on the hallway runner to muffle her footsteps. As far as she knew, Eric had gone to bed around midnight. But just as she was about to start down the steps, light crept under the door of the Lone Star room, and she heard a crash.

For a moment she considered ignoring both. Eric had probably gotten up to use the bathroom, turned on a lamp and

knocked something over. She was still upset over his conde-
scending remark about Leon, and even more upset that she had
indulged in a response. What had been the point? Both of them
knew that her joy in nurturing and his lack of it had contributed
to their divorce. If Eric couldn't see that inviting him for the
summer was similar to extending a hand to Leon, then why had
she needed to point it out?

More light brightened the hallway, and she realized he had
turned on a second lamp. She heard footsteps in his room. Poised
somewhere between flight and duty, she succumbed and rapped
softly on the door.

She listened, thought she heard a muttered invitation, and
opened the door. Eric was bare chested and barefoot, wearing
nothing but sweatpants and a grimace.

"I was doing a final check of the rooms," she said, trying to
ignore the sudden image of a younger Eric disrobing for a night
together. "Are you okay?"

"I knocked over that fruit bowl Dillon brought up here."

Dillon, on a quest to fatten up his father, could not be per-
suaded that the basket he and his brothers had assembled before
Eric's arrival contained enough food. So he had filled Gayle's
favorite wooden salad bowl with a medley of fruit and installed
it on Eric's night table. This level of concern was an emotion she
could hardly discourage.

She circled the bed and stooped to pick up apples and oranges,
while Eric worked on grapes and cherries, a task she wasn't sure
her fine motor skills were up to at this hour.

"Were you having a problem sleeping?" she asked. "Maybe it's
the silence. You probably thought the party was going to go on
all night."

"I heard dogs barking."

"Really? After that awful fight the only dog left at the party was Grapevine, and Cray took *him* home an hour ago." She looked up, and saw Eric had stopped retrieving fruit. Instead, he was staring into space.

"I *heard* them," he said. "Even if they weren't there."

She went back to work, eager to get to bed. "Sound carries in strange ways in the mountains. Maybe I'm just used to dogs in the distance. Or too tired tonight to notice them."

"It's not a sound you forget."

His voice sounded strange. She glanced at him again. His hand was frozen in midair, as if he'd forgotten that a task had been planned for it.

The sight of that hand, always wide and long fingered, made whatever she'd planned to say catch in her throat and dissolve. Eric's formerly beautiful hands were like talons. The fingers seemed thin as needles, the skin rippled in distorted waves. And the hands were trembling.

She sat back on her heels. Her voice was low. "You were having a nightmare." It wasn't a question.

He looked down at his hand, then up at her. "It's nothing."

"*Nothing* wouldn't have woken you. You look like hell, Eric. What can I do?"

He went back to work, but slowly, as if he were forcing his brain to remember and guide every step. "Why are you still up?"

"I told you, I was checking rooms. It hit me that some of the kids could have slipped up here to one of the guest rooms."

"Wouldn't that have been fun to discover."

"I'm having enough trouble dealing with my own sons thinking about sex. Imagine the fun if I discovered their friends in demonstration mode."

She realized she was talking about sex with her ex-husband.

And sex had never been one of the problems in their marriage. She looked up, her cheeks warming, and saw that Eric had managed a smile.

"So they're just *thinking* about sex?"

"If they're doing anything else, they aren't sharing it with me. Last week I asked Dillon about a girl in his class, and he told me that from that moment forward I was not to discuss his love life."

"Love life?" Eric gave a low laugh. "We're really going to have our hands full with that one."

Nothing astonished her about the sentence except the plural *we*. For just a moment she considered how lovely it would be to turn over all things related to male sexuality to Eric and let him paddle through those muddy waters without her help.

"Yes, well…" She picked up the last orange. "He does look just like his dad."

"He'll need to look to somebody other than me to teach him how to deal with women. I've never understood them. You of all people should know that."

"We're getting dangerously close to joking about the dissolution of our marriage."

"What's a little humor between the perfect exes? Didn't we win some award for Best Divorce of the Twentieth Century?"

Her head snapped up. "Did we?"

He was back at work on the grapes, pinching them between his fingers and dropping them in the bowl. "Yeah, and it was a problem for a long time."

"What was?"

"All that goodwill. No knock-down drag-outs about who got what. No fights over child support or visitation rights. The boys are mine whenever I want them. I give you every penny I can spare. When we talk we have cordial conversations. If you get married again, you'll probably ask me to give you away."

"Oh, not much chance of that."

He found the last grape. They went for the last handful of cherries together, and their hands collided, his on top of hers. Both of them were perfectly still, as if viewing a moment from their past.

Gayle was the first to pull back. "I'll wash the fruit for you."

"I'll do it in the morning. Don't bother."

They were facing each other now. She cocked her head and tried to ignore the familiar chest, the ribs as prominent as corset stays. Unfortunately, she couldn't ignore where their conversation had been leading. "Why is goodwill a problem?"

"I bet it's a problem for you, too. Think about it."

"It's late, and it would be nice to have a shortcut."

"Because you didn't give me much to be angry about. So I'm stuck with everything else, right out in the open. Guilt, regret, sadness. No anger to hide behind."

She was surprised they were talking about this now, after more than a decade had passed. And in the middle of the night, to boot.

He went on. "So, for a while, I was angry about not having anything to be angry about." He smiled wanly. "You too?"

"I had a little more to work with, Eric."

He turned up his hands in defeat. "Maybe I had to dredge up a few things. Maybe I concentrated a little too much on your tendency to nurture everything that moves."

She realized he was apologizing for his comment about Leon. She gave a brief nod of recognition.

"And maybe I tried to ignore the fact that even the silk plant that somebody left in my condo died from neglect." He approximated something that looked like the old Eric grin. "Maybe I tried to make that a virtue."

"Nobody can kill a silk plant."

"One day I came home and all the leaves were on my floor in a pile. I'm not kidding."

She smiled, but it died quickly. "If somehow I left you with the impression that you're just another example of my need to serve, don't believe it. I want you here for the sake of our sons. You're not some random charity case I've taken in off the street."

"I know." He tried to smile again, but he suddenly looked too tired.

Gayle rested her hand on his arm. Despite herself, she couldn't back away and pretend he was just another boarder. Their relationship was too old and too complicated—even more complicated, she was beginning to understand, than she'd let herself recognize.

"What can I do for you?" she asked.

He hesitated. "I need to take a sleeping pill, that's all."

"Let me get it. Tell me where."

She watched him consider. Did he allow her to perform this kindness, further deepening his debt, or did he muddle through? He let out a breath, not quite a sigh, but audible. "Thanks. The bottle's in the bathroom." He hesitated. "I just need one."

She found the pills, doled out one and ran a glass of cold water from the tap. Back in the bedroom, he was sitting on the side of the bed, his long legs just touching the floor. She handed him the pill and watched him swallow it eagerly.

"Is there anything else I can do?" she asked.

He looked torn. That surprised her, since Eric rarely hesitated about anything. It was one of the reasons he had risen in his field, not carelessness, not a fool rushing in, but a man who could swiftly weigh facts, then act on them decisively and fearlessly.

"What is it?" she asked.

"It's a big favor. And I know you're dead tired."

"What is it?"

This time he did sigh. "Would you stay a little while until the pill takes effect?"

"Here? With you?"

"This is a good prescription. Once it kicks in, even if I have nightmares I won't wake up, and I won't remember them in the morning. But the pill takes a while. And if I just doze right off now, I might…"

Her voice was soft. "Nightmares are no surprise, Eric. You went through a lot."

"Knowing that doesn't seem to help."

"Go ahead, lie down. I'll stay until you look like you just can't keep your eyes open another minute."

"You're sure?"

"Go ahead, get comfortable."

He swung his legs up and settled them under a sheet, but tonight it was too warm for a blanket. The ceiling fan stirred the air, but even his sweatpants looked too hot for early summer—although she wasn't about to suggest he strip down further.

She wasn't sure where to look or what to say. She decided to tell him so. "When somebody's been through everything you have, it's hard to know what's acceptable to ask."

"Harder to know what's acceptable to talk about."

"You can talk about anything you want."

He stared up at the ceiling. "How about what a fool I was?"

"For taking the job in Afghanistan?"

"No, for staying too long when I was clearly past my usefulness. And for trusting the wrong people."

She knew only the bare bones of the story. As an ex-wife, no one had felt it necessary to communicate many details to her. "Do you want to talk about it?"

"As a journalist, one of the first things you learn is to suspect everybody. And you multiply that times ten when you're in hostile surroundings. I knew that. But I got cocky. After all that time in the country, I thought I could tell a friend from an enemy, that I had some kind of sixth sense about who was telling the truth and who wasn't. Even though I was living in a different culture, with different signals."

She waited, and when he didn't go on, she prodded him gently. "And it was harder to tell than you thought?"

"You know some of what happened from the news, I'm sure. We learned the military was planning a thrust in the south to clear out the Taliban. The rumor was that some of the Taliban leaders were holed up northeast of Kandahar, in Zabul province. I wanted to see what I could find, to initiate a dialogue with some of the less radical adherents to help viewers understand the stakes. I was warned not to go on my own, but I was sure I knew what I was doing. I had an armed guard. I had my translator, who had been with me through other tight spots, my cameraman."

This part of the story was not unfamiliar. Eric's translator had arranged an interview, but only if he left his guard behind. Safety had been guaranteed for Eric and his cameraman, Howard Short, a tough African-American father of one who had agreed to film the interview as a personal favor to Eric. Instead, they had been bound and thrown into the back of a truck and taken to the small village of Dai Chopan.

Gayle could imagine what questions her ex-husband asked himself every night. "Eric, your instincts have proved to be excellent any number of times."

"Not this time. The whole world knows we were delivered

into the hands of our captors by my translator. But not every-body knows Adib was as much my friend as Howard. I'd called in favors to get his family into safer housing, paid for his baby son's flight to Germany to have a cleft palate repaired. We'd had so many good conversations about the differences in the way our countries saw the world. He knew I was reporting the situation in his country, not cheering anybody from the sidelines."

"And he betrayed you?"

"I still don't know why. Either he was more desperate or more furious than I'd suspected. Some of his wife's family were killed in a coalition bombing in Jalalabad, and I know that deeply affected him. But I didn't see even a glimmer of regret in his eyes when he as much as signed our death warrants. We were a sac-rifice, and he didn't have any more feeling about delivering Howard and me to those men on that road out of Kandahar than if we had been lambs or goats."

"Then you think they really intended to kill you? That it wasn't some form of theater? Maybe Adib thought you would be safe, but that a point would be made before they let you go."

"You're trying to put a good spin on it, Gayle, but there isn't one. I'll never know what Adib thought. He and his family vanished. But our captors? Oh, they were going to kill us. That was never in doubt from the first moment we saw them. *When* was the only question."

Deep inside, she had thought so, too, but now her stomach knotted at the confirmation.

Eric rested his palm against his forehead, as if willing the memory away. "Howard was the one who saw our chance and made sure we took it. On our second night at the house in Dai Chopan, they decided to move us again under cover of darkness. I had picked up just enough Pashto on my own to figure that out. We were both exhausted, dehydrated. It's amazing how quickly you can decline without food or water. But we knew we had to make a break or die. The men who'd been left in charge were old, and not as fast on their feet as they should have been. They'd untied our legs so we could walk out to the truck under cover of an old Soviet assault rifle. I'd been working at the rope around my wrists all day, and it was loose enough that I was waiting to slip it off.

"As they were putting him in the truck, Howard managed to kick the weapon out of the hands of our guard. Then he head-butted him in the stomach. My guard went to help, and I managed to get the rope off my hands and grab the first guard's weapon. I used it like a club. Howard and I were able to get into the truck before reinforcements arrived and take off."

"I know the rest," she said. "They came after you, and you drove off a mountain pass." Howard Short had died in the resulting crash.

"We were out of our element. They knew those roads, and we didn't. They were gaining on us and firing at the same time. I took a curve too fast or they blew out my tire. I don't know. All I can remember is launching myself out of the cab as the truck started to flip, but Howard wasn't so lucky. I fell and slid for what seemed like minutes, banging myself up pretty badly. I stopped just inches away from going over the mountainside into forever."

"And nobody came after you?"

"There was no reason to. Our pursuers knew we were as good as dead the moment we went off the road. Only somehow I didn't die. I ended up on a ledge, maybe eighteen inches wide, with a straight drop-off below me. At first I was grateful. You don't know what grateful is until you're inches and seconds from death. Then, when I saw where I had ended up and realized that any movement I made would launch me over the side, I wished I hadn't been so lucky. I realized I was going to die there. No one would ever find me, and eventually I'd fall asleep or get a cramp I couldn't control, or I'd just—"

She put her hand on his arm. "But that's not what happened."

He was silent for a long time. "No," he said at last. "There'd been mortar fire in the area. You know the rest. The next evening, just before dark, a group of British soldiers were looking for mortar firing stakes and saw the tracks of our truck. They got out to investigate, and I still had the presence of mind to call to them. I couldn't tell who they were, but by then, even if they'd been Taliban anxious to shoot me, that would have been all right, too."

Just hours before, the network had finally called to report that Eric was missing. She had been agonizing over what to tell her sons when the second call had come to say that he had been rescued.

"I never let myself believe you were dead," she said now. "I couldn't, because then the boys would believe it. And I knew when I told them you were missing, they would need to hope for the best while they feared the worst."

"I spent my time on that mountain just trying to prepare for the inevitable. Oh, and trying to figure out how to climb straight up the side of a cliff with no handholds. And listening."

"For someone who might rescue you?"

"No. At first, just for sounds from the wreckage below. But there weren't any. Howard must have been killed instantly. We used to talk about our kids. He knew his about as well as I know mine. He wanted to get a job in the States after Afghanistan, somewhere close to Chicago, where his daughter lived. I don't know if he would have, though. He liked being right in the middle of things."

He turned his head to look at her. "Later I listened to the dogs. There must have been a pack of them somewhere out there. I heard them all through the night. Howling, snarling, fighting. Now I hear them in my nightmares. They're the sound of Afghanistan to me."

Tears welled in her eyes. "Oh, Eric. No wonder you can't sleep."

"I was afraid to sleep. You can imagine. I tried to think of all the good things in my life. Of all the blessings I'd had. As a way to prepare. I didn't want to die filled with hatred and despair. I'd brought the situation on myself, but never out of evil intent. I sought that interview because I was trying to do my job. I went in good faith, because I hoped that interview, and the next one and the next one, might be parts of the whole story of the conflict there. And how can we, as a nation, make decisions if we don't have the whole story?"

She could hear his words slowing, his voice trailing off. The pills were beginning to work. Gayle was glad.

"You've always been good at what you do," she said quietly. "The very best."

"Not anymore. Maybe I'm…just too old now. My reflexes aren't as good, my judgment…"

"You were under so much pressure. Not every decision could be a perfect decision. You erred on the side of friendship and trust. If you were going to make a mistake, that was the one to make."

"Look at all the young men in television news now. Look at the young women. So many of them reporting…from trouble spots."

"You're forty-two. You're not exactly doddering."

"No, but I'm…afraid." Eric closed his eyes. Gayle could feel him relaxing under her fingertips. "Maybe…I've lost my nerve."

"Eric, I have a friend, Kendra Taylor, who writes for the *Washington Post*. You've probably met her. You should talk to her. She understands post-traumatic stress disorder. She had some personal experience with it. Talking might help you."

"That's what they call it. Post-traumatic... Or maybe it's just...good sense. Time to quit."

She waited, but as she did, she heard his breathing slow.

Finally she whispered his name. There was no response.

She hoped the pills really could keep bad dreams away.

She stood, then, on impulse, pulled the top sheet higher and over his shoulders, resting her hand not on bare skin but on the barrier of high thread-count cotton. For just a moment she wondered what it would be like if they had never divorced and she could slide into bed beside him, throw her arm over his waist and comfort him through the night.

But they had divorced. Even a tragedy like the one Eric had so personally experienced could not change a decision that had altered their lives forever.

Chapter 7

Some bridges are masterpieces of design, such monuments to architectural and engineering skills that the bodies of water they span evaporate in significance. Others are blemishes that diminish the majesty of the waters tumbling to the sea beneath them.

Gayle had always thought that the bridges of Shenandoah County, bridges that stretched across the North Fork of the Shenandoah, across Toms Brook and the many streams and creeks that nourished the river, were graceful and picturesque. The low water bridges seemed to ride the current. They were narrow concrete paths with no railings, meant to be navigated slowly, as befitted the dignity of the Shenandoah. The suspension bridges that often accompanied them could only be traveled by foot. They swung high above the water, as slim as scaffolding enfolded by wire spiderwebs. They existed for emergencies and the exploits of adolescents. If a low water bridge flooded, residents could cross on the suspension bridges…if they dared.

One week after the graduation party, Gayle crossed the low

water bridge nearest the inn in her red Toyota Tacoma, with Dillon and his friend Caleb Mowrey squeezed in beside her. She parked a hundred yards upriver from the foundation of the old house that would be the focus of archaeology camp and watched as Travis walked across the suspension bridge just beyond the dirt road that divided their properties. The boys immediately headed for the riverbank to scout for snakes.

"Hey there! You look like you've done that before," she called.

Travis smiled down at her and playfully rattled the scaffolding. The bridge swung gracefully over the water.

Once he was on the ground, she greeted him with a glass of lemonade, fresh from a Thermos. "I'd just made this when you called."

"My timing's impeccable. I could hear you squeezing the lemons from my house." He took a long swallow.

She sipped a glass of her own and watched him. He was a serious man, but not an intense one. She liked his laid-back wisdom, his calm demeanor, and the occasional eruptions of wit. She couldn't think of anyone more suited to providing this camp for the county's middle schoolers, and she and the parents of her sons' friends knew how lucky they were.

"So, are we going to take the tour?" she asked.

"I just wanted to make sure you were comfortable with my choice of site. We're going to be looking for the farm trash pit. I know from the historical record that it was in use right up until the last resident. It should provide some interesting information and early twentieth-century artifacts without us stumbling on features that are too sensitive to let the kids anywhere near. It's close to the river, so it's been disturbed by the occasional flood, and it's probably never going to be on anybody's list of sites that need a professional dig."

"How will you know where to start?"

"Along with some legal documents from the courthouse, I have a primitive sketch of the homestead that somebody gave my father. Using that, I did a walkover and came back with my metal detector. It's a shoo-in."

He took her on a brief tour, pointing out the places where they would start the dig. Gayle could see that the kids would be well out of the way of her guests.

They settled on a grassy slope that would eventually lead them to the peak of Three Top Mountain—although neither wanted to make the climb.

"It's amazing how quickly nature erases any signs of habitation, isn't it? There's nothing here but trees," Gayle said. "Pretty much everything was cleared away when your father knocked down the house, but whatever was left is gone now."

"There's a lot of history on this spot. Farm history. Civil War history. Maybe a few flints and arrowheads buried deep. All of it just waiting to be uncovered."

"You sound like you have some insider information."

"I always do my research. There are some unusual stories connected with this site. With luck, this is going to be a successful dig."

"You're the man to organize it."

"I'm not sure how I got into this, exactly." Travis leaned back and pulled up a stalk of rye grass to nibble, the perfect picture of indolent summer in cutoffs and a faded green T-shirt.

Gayle leaned back, too, and looked up at a sky dark with clouds that, like their predecessors, probably wouldn't part with rain. "Wasn't archaeology camp your own idea?"

"Well, yeah. It was. But why did anybody take me up on it?"

"Because it's the most exciting thing going around here for middle schoolers?"

"Might be."

"So what's the problem?"

"About this time every year, something goes wrong. It's inevitable, sort of a benchmark. Every summer I think I've got it all figured out, that I can beat the pattern, and whoosh… Catastrophe."

Gayle sat up and looked for the boys. She was relieved to see they hadn't graduated to anything more exciting than skimming stones farther downriver. Caleb's dog, Rusty, was following at their heels. She settled back on her elbows.

"Okay, spill it. What's the catastrophe this year?"

"Well, last year at this time, the Commonwealth of Virginia decided what I had on my property was a bona fide campground, and therefore I had to follow all the bona fide rules. And I won't bore you with those."

"I run a B and B. Bona fide. I can imagine. Apparently you straightened that out?"

"With the help of an attorney."

"Ouch."

"The summer before that, I had to have a new septic field dug. Right before camp began."

"I don't suppose they found anything interesting? An old burial mound? The remains of a village?"

"Enough rocks to build a small house. Which the excavator kindly deposited in a heap while I was away—right where the kids were going to pitch their tents. So the first day we had a hands-on lesson in the fine art of building a stacked stone wall."

"And you told them this had something to do with archaeology?"

"It's amazing what little human critters will accept from an authority figure."

She laughed. "That's the past. So what's the present?"

"My caterer is eloping to Montana."

"You have a caterer?"

"Mary Johnston, over near Edinboro. She caters out of her home. Nothing big or fancy. She's done it since we started."

"How does that work?"

"Well, the first week, when the kids go home at night, she only does lunch. I tried making them bring their own, but half the time they'd forget. Memory is pretty selective at that age."

"From what I can tell, it revolves completely around the opposite sex."

"The start of a lifelong pattern. Anyway, Mary just brings salads, stuff for sandwiches. The kids like a selection, and they do a lot of the work themselves. Then the first Friday night, she brings stuff for a cookout. We always build a fire and have a wienie roast. But the second week, when the kids camp on my land, she shops and does the advance prep work for all the meals, finishing with the final campfire. Only now she won't be here to do it."

"I can see why you don't want to do all that shopping and preparation alone."

"It's not possible. And the counselors aren't experienced enough to be trusted with it. So now I have to find somebody fast. I've checked a couple of leads, but no go so far. Obviously I can crown this the official problem of the summer."

Gayle sifted through the names of people who might help Travis, but the answer was already clear to her. "I don't suppose you'd consider using me?"

"Think it through first." He didn't sound surprised.

She nudged him with an elbow. "This was no ordinary whining, was it? It was whining with a purpose."

"I wasn't going to ask outright. I know how much you have on your plate. But if it appeals to you…"

She sat up and checked on the boys again. When, she wondered, did a mother stop checking? How old did her sons have to be before she stopped worrying that they were heading for imminent disaster?

Travis sat up, too. "*Does* it appeal to you?"

"I've got two sons, plus Leon, involved in the camp, my son's girlfriend, my sons' friends, and the dig is on land that officially belongs to me. I'm such an obvious choice."

"Do you have time?"

She did a mental inventory of a normal day. The inn was doing a steady business, but she could only depend on it being fully booked on weekends. On the plus side, the hardest part of even a busy day was over by eleven, about the time she would need to bring food to the dig. On the minus side, she had been so busy with end of the school year activities that she had only scheduled a limited number of job interviews for additional helpers. She had hired one new employee, an older woman. But if she could find a second staffer to take on more of the administrative chores, her time could be freed up to cater for Travis.

And with Eric's room out of commission during her busiest season, she could really use the money Travis had set aside in his budget.

She gave a tentative nod, but he had a warning.

"I hate to say this, but the last day of camp happens to be on a certain person's birthday."

She was flattered Travis had remembered, although she had baked a cake on his for the past three years, so it wasn't a real surprise. "That doesn't matter."

"Seems to me it's going to be an important one."

"Hey, since when are you keeping track? It's just a birthday, even if there's a zero in it." She hoped they were finished discussing a birthday she really didn't want to celebrate. "I think I can do this. When do you have to know for sure?"

"A couple of days?"

"I've got a pretty good idea what kind of food kids like and how to make it in quantity. You were at the graduation party." She was warming up now. "And Noah can be my assistant. His nose is out of joint because he can't be a counselor this year, but this way he can be over here helping and making some money. He needs a summer job, and this beats mowing lawns in town."

"You know I'd rather have you than anybody else. We work like a team."

That was no exaggeration. In fact, sometimes, late at night, she worried that Travis would fall in love and marry again. When another woman came on the scene, friendship between a man and a woman was harder to maintain. And Gayle counted on Travis.

"So is that your only problem?" she asked. "Everything else is shaping up?"

"Thanks to Dillon."

"Okay, don't you think it's time to let me in on that secret?"

Travis turned and gave her one of the rare grins that erased the serious middle-aged teacher and colored in the charm of youth. "What secret?"

"Dillon's been gone almost every morning this past week. He's spending a lot of time at your house doing something. He comes back every day just glowing. I'm guessing he's not washing artifacts."

"I'll give you a hint. There are a couple of kids involved, including Caleb."

"Well, that doesn't help much."

"He's the one who wants to keep it a surprise. Let him."

"Whatever you're doing, it's a big help, Travis. You're building his confidence…and getting him out of the house. His relationship with his father has never been easy."

"It's not getting better?"

In her mind she ran through a summary of the past week, of Eric's quick temper, which Dillon could so easily set off, of Dillon's attempts to get attention and their frequently disastrous outcomes.

She shook her head. "Not yet. Eric's not a patient man, and since he came back from Afghanistan, he's angry and edgy."

"You know that makes sense, right?"

"Sure, and I know he's trying."

"There has to be a lot he grapples with daily. From what the news reported, it was more or less an accident coalition troops found him."

She thought about what Eric had revealed the night of graduation. He had been extraordinarily lucky. She said thank-you prayers each dawn that he had come back alive. She asked for patience and understanding, too, but none of this was easy to explain to Dillon. And day by day she watched him wilt under the full force of his father's impatience.

"How's it going with the other boys?" Travis asked.

"Noah stays away from him as much as he can. Jared seems uneasy about something. Maybe he's just not sure what to say to Eric after everything."

"I'm sure that's part of it."

Gayle heard more than a simple reassurance. She angled her body so she could see Travis better. "Do you know something about this?"

"Nothing specific."

"He confided something, didn't he?"

"Not as much as he might need to."

She was glad her son had a man he could talk to, but she was sorry he hadn't chosen to talk to her.

"Don't look like that," Travis said.

"Like what?"

"Gayle, you've got to remember you were married to Eric. The boys know you have your own baggage to carry in and out of that relationship. Sometimes they need a neutral party."

She rested her hand on his for a moment. "We're all lucky you're willing to listen to them."

"They probably have no idea how much I enjoy having them in my life."

"You should have been a father."

"Chloe and I were waiting for the right time, but we knew kids were important."

"That's part of why you do the camp, isn't it? Because you want kids to know how important they are."

He didn't usually open up about his feelings, even to her, but this time he surprised her. "Middle-schoolers are so vulnerable. They take the word of their peers about who they are. I want to set them on fire about something other than whether their jeans are the right brand or their braces are going to come off in time for the next dance. I want them to understand the difference between what somebody tells them and the truth."

"And you hope they apply that to their own lives?"

"It's a step in the right direction."

She never thought of Travis as passionate. He never fought to be heard. But there was passion in his voice when he talked about his teaching. He was a man of hidden depths.

She smiled at him. He smiled back. The sun was warm on her head, and she felt the radiance of it, the simple pleasure of being with an attractive man she admired and enjoyed.

She heard a shout upriver, and both she and Travis turned. Dillon had climbed onto the suspension bridge and was now halfway across the river. Caleb was looking on from below. Caleb was a quiet boy, an unlikely match in some ways for Dillon, but they had become friends over the past year. Caleb was older, but not by much, a loner, a wanderer.

"Come on, Caleb. It's fun up here," Dillon shouted.

Caleb showed no signs of moving.

"Not everybody's comfortable that high," Gayle said. "And Dillon isn't always very sensitive."

"I bet he'll catch on."

She wondered if Dillon would think less of Caleb if he didn't join him, but Caleb handled the situation well.

"No," he shouted back. "Somebody's got to stay with Rusty."

If Dillon suspected his friend was afraid, he didn't flaunt it.

"Caleb's good for Dillon," she said when Dillon started back down off the bridge.

"I understand the Claibornes are adopting him."

Gayle knew that Caleb was Cissy Claiborne's brother, but he lived with Cissy's in-laws, who had welcomed him into their family with enthusiasm. Gayle's sons, and Leon, too, had taken him under their respective wings and made sure Caleb was finding a place in the school community.

Suddenly Gayle raised her palm to the side of her head. "Good Lord. Cissy…"

"I'm sorry?"

"Caleb's Cissy Claiborne's brother. And I forgot to interview Cissy for a job at the inn. I don't know why I didn't think about it when Caleb came over this morning, but I've just been so busy. She gave me a résumé a full week ago. I need to call her."

"I'll let you get back to work." Travis stood and held out his hand to help her up. "You'll let me know about the catering? I promised the counselors lunch at their training session on Wednesday. It'll be a good test run."

His hand was warm from the sun, and strong. She enjoyed the sensation of letting someone help her for a change. "No matter what, I'll do that for you."

"You'll spoil me for anybody else."

She squeezed his hand before she dropped it. "Let's hope you never have to look elsewhere."

Eric was recovering. The steps were small, but the signs were unmistakable. He no longer felt as if he had to will body parts to do their job. His grip was stronger; his legs held up the rest of his body without threat of collapse. Pain now was fleeting and sleep welcome. He still had nightmares; he still took sleeping pills. But he awoke feeling rested, and always ravenous. Gayle and the boys were good cooks, and food was plentiful.

With the small steps came small annoyances. He was bored. He had a stack of reading material a foot high, but he was tired of reading. The inn was filled now with guests, and wandering the halls or watching television in the parlor invariably resulted in a conversation. And he didn't want to talk about the best area fishing spots or his favorite hike.

As if she knew he needed entertainment, Ariel called from California first thing each morning—which, luckily for him, was three hours later in Virginia. The conversation was always brisk and funny. She told him stories about the local news anchor, whose jealous wife accompanied him to the station every day on a different pretext. And the weather reporter who was directionally challenged and called east west at least once during every broadcast.

"Anyone else would get the ax, but Weather Woman's the

reason the anchor's wife comes to spy on him," Ariel had related that morning. "He's smitten, poor guy. Pretty much caught between a hurricane and a tornado."

Eric didn't want to discourage Ariel, but the television chatter only made him lonelier. He probably still had a job if he wanted one. After all, he was a national symbol of triumph—even if he had fallen into his captors' hands out of stupidity and been rescued through no efforts of his own. His agent was fielding offers. Yesterday he had called to say that so far Eric could write a book and/or produce a made-for-television movie.

In a stab at humor, Eric had said he would only take the television deal if Brad Pitt was cast for the part. His agent—whose sense of humor was hooked to dollar signs—had promised to look into it. Now he wondered if they would tap Angelina Jolie for the role of the saintly ex-wife waiting and praying at home as she doled out saccharine advice to the three teenage sons, played by the former stars of *Malcolm in the Middle*?

Under the circumstances, he knew his annoyance, his short temper, his dissatisfaction with every part of his life, were normal. After his rescue he had been so overwhelmingly grateful to be safe, he'd been sure he would never feel a shred of negativity again. He would float through life on gratitude, attend whatever church was closest, and perform daily good works in Howard's name until he was on his own deathbed.

But once he was out of danger, once the psychologists had begun to probe, the military had attempted to debrief him and the network had dug for every detail, he had slammed up against a wall of anger so thick, so tall, that he wasn't sure he could ever scale it to see what was on the other side.

He also knew that his maladjustment was showing and poor Dillon was catching the brunt of it. The child he had not wanted was not-wanted again. When he'd been frozen on that narrow ledge, thoughts of Dillon had filled more than a few hours, and regret had filled the others. But once again faced with the real child who only wanted to be loved, he was incapable of it.

This morning he had gone back to his room to read the paper after breakfast in the kitchen. But now he was feeling almost as trapped as he had in captivity.

He decided to go for a stroll around the grounds. If nothing else, he could sit outside in the sun, maybe find a spot with a cooler breeze from the river. Or maybe for once Jared had stayed home, and they could muddle through some male-bonding ritual together. Talk about sports. Throw a fishing line in the water. Try to figure out women.

Outside his room, no guests were around. The reception and dining areas were cleaned and cleared, with fresh flowers on display and oatmeal cookies in an apothecary jar on the table beside a coffee urn. He took a cookie and resisted the urge to put several more in his pocket.

Outside, he headed for the room over the three-car garage where Jared lived.

He rapped lightly on the door, but there was no response. He went back down the outside stairway and crossed to the carriage house. No one answered there, either. Everyone in the little world of Daughter of the Stars seemed to have a place to go except him.

He was on his way back to the inn when he saw Noah coming out of the former garden shed with a cardboard box. Gayle had told him that renovations were in progress so she would have a rental for families. Judging from Noah's hangdog demeanor and his scruffy jeans and shirt, he had been tapped to do some of the work this morning.

Eric crossed the distance between them. He saw Noah hesitate. Even from twenty yards away, he could see the boy gird himself for their encounter.

"It looks like your mom's got you helping out over here." Eric nodded to the building beyond. "Want to show me what you're doing?"

"Nothing interesting. Just cleaning out what was left here so the carpenters can get in next week."

"Trash, or stuff you plan to keep?"

"Stuff to keep. I'm storing it in the old fruit cellar."

"I'd offer to help but—"

"I don't need help. I've got most of it taken care of. I'm just going to see if I can make a path through the boxes after I drop this one off." He left without looking back.

Eric debated, but in the end he trailed his son across the lawn to the steps leading to the cellar, which was just below the kitchen. He followed Noah down.

Eric had expected cobwebs and the smell of mildew, the normal attributes of an old fruit cellar, but of course, Gayle hadn't allowed that. The room, about ten by twelve, was free of dust, and the air smelled fresh enough. The walls were stone, and several old metal utility shelves stood against them, along with a pile of boards and stacks of concrete blocks. Eric wandered over and saw neatly labeled boxes.

"Juice glasses, dessert plates," he read out loud.

"Mom buys in bulk so she'll always have extras in case stuff gets broken."

"Smart woman, your mom."

Noah didn't reply. He set the box in his arms on a towering pile in the corner.

"I hope that was it," Eric said. "One more and…kaboom."

"Yeah, that's it. It's just kitchen stuff, and odds and ends. We're tearing out the old kitchen and putting in something more efficient that takes up less space."

"Sounds like a big job."

"Mom says it'll be worth the cost in the long run."

Eric knew Gayle did a good job of making ends meet. If she thought the space was better used this way, it would be. He also guessed the up-front costs would set her back for a while, as would giving him one of her better rooms for the summer. He was paying her, of course, but she would only accept a percentage of the usual summer rate.

"Maybe we could organize the boxes a little," Eric said, eyeing the pile. "Instead of just pushing them into a corner."

"I don't see why."

"What if your mom needs something? How will she find it?"

"She didn't say anything about organizing them."

Eric felt a prick of enthusiasm and wanted to hang on to it, since it was an increasingly rare sensation. "Those boards and blocks in the corner were probably a shelf system at one time. We could set them up again and put boxes on them so they're not all piled together."

"I don't think she cares."

"Work with me on this, okay? What could it hurt? And it might save her some trouble."

Eric knew the last sentence would hook Noah. Noah was Gayle's champion. How could he refuse to make her life easier?

Noah still looked wary. "I've only got about half an hour."

"We can do it in less. I'll help but I'm afraid you're going to have to do the heavy lifting."

"Yeah, okay."

Ten minutes later the blocks were in place against one wall, with two-by-sixes layered across them. Eric was sweating, even though they were underground, where the temperature was ten degrees cooler. They had worked without talking, but at least there'd been no arguments or recriminations.

"You still have time to move the boxes to the shelves?" Eric asked. "I can get the lighter ones. It's good exercise. I'm supposed to be building up my strength."

"Yeah, okay."

Noah started at the top, grabbing boxes and setting them on the bottom shelves. Eric brought what he could to set beside them.

Since the silence had gone well, he tried a question. "This will be the year you start thinking about which colleges you want to apply to, won't it?"

"I guess."

"Do you have any thoughts on where you might want to go? Want to join your brother in New England somewhere?"

"I've been thinking about the University of Virginia."

Eric wasn't surprised Noah wanted to remain in Virginia. He would be an easy drive from home if he wanted to come back for weekends.

"It's a great school," Eric said, "but I hope you'll consider my alma mater. USC's another great school. And I have friends on the faculty."

"I don't want to go to school in California."

"You have to leave home sometime," Eric said, without weighing his words.

"Yeah? Well, I'm not in as much of a hurry as you were."

For a moment Eric couldn't even imagine what to say. Then anger suffused him. He threw the box he'd been carrying onto the shelf and grabbed his son's arm, digging his fingertips into the boy's soft flesh.

"You know, you may not like me, and sometimes I may not like you, but you are my son. You will not speak to me that way, do you understand?"

Noah wrenched his arm away. His eyes narrowed, and he glared at his father, but he didn't argue.

The anger left exhaustion in its wake. Eric realized that he had done more lifting than he should have this morning, and the thought brought a fresh wave of anger. Where was the man with the boundless energy and strength? The one who didn't dissolve into fits of emotion at every slight, every demand?

He turned away and started toward the door.

"You left Mom alone, with three little kids and this inn. Do you really think you can just come back and expect us to feel grateful we're finally getting your attention?"

Eric stopped, his hand on the rail. This time he waited and considered before he spoke.

"When a marriage isn't working, there are two people who have a say in what happens next. I asked your mother to come with me. She refused. And I'm not saying that anything that happened is her fault. I'm just pointing out that this was a mutual decision. I didn't skip out on her, as you well know."

"You always seem to set the rules. How does that happen? Is that what men do? We call the shots, and women get to choose whether or not to go along?"

Eric faced him. Through his exhaustion, his self-loathing, and, yes, through a haze of anger, he could still see that his answer was going to matter for years to come.

"It wasn't easy leaving all of you behind, Noah. But by then I knew it was going to be impossible to stay here. If you want to understand even one thing from this conversation, try this. I suffered, too."

"Yeah? How badly?"

Even if the question had been serious and not a taunt, Eric would not have known how to answer it.

Chapter 8

For Jared, driving Gayle's sporty red pickup was a bonus, and it was his alone, since Noah was only allowed to drive the family sedan. Jared was saving for a car, but since he wouldn't need one at school next year, there was no point in buying a junker that would take up space in the inn's parking lot while he was away. As compensation for all his help at the inn, Gayle let him drive the pickup whenever she could.

This afternoon was one of those times. Jared had promised Brandy that they would go swimming with friends. She wasn't much of an athlete, but she had a bright blue bikini, and she liked to show it off. That worked for Jared, since he liked looking at her. His government teacher called that kind of trade-off a *quid pro quo*. Whatever it was called, Jared thought he was getting the best of the deal.

When he pulled into her yard, Brandy was waiting outside. Mrs. Wilburn waved from the doorway, but she disappeared into the house before he could get out to greet her. Brandy resembled her mother, except that Mrs. Wilburn needed to lose at least a hundred pounds. She was so heavy that she tipped stiff-legged from side to side when she walked. Her legs could no longer bend properly.

Brandy was so ashamed of her mother, she was always talking about some new diet Mrs. Wilburn should try. From what Jared could tell, Mrs. Wilburn wasn't unhappy or weak willed, she simply enjoyed food. She poured gravy on her mashed potatoes and chocolate syrup on her ice cream, and relished every bite. She seemed perfectly satisfied with herself, dressing in bright colors and fixing her dark hair in an attractive style. Jared tried to get Brandy to leave her mother alone, but that was like speaking another language. Brandy just didn't understand what he was saying.

Now Brandy got into the pickup and slammed the door. "I can't believe it! I have to be home by five. We're going out for dinner. As a fam-i-ly." She rolled her eyes.

Jared pulled out of the driveway and started down the road. The Wilburns going anywhere together was actually a good thing. He was sure Mr. and Mrs. Wilburn loved their daughter, but they were gone a lot. They both worked at Mr. Wilburn's Buick dealership and had long commutes. On weekends Mr. Wilburn played golf and Mrs. Wilburn shopped, dragging Brandy along when she could catch her—which wasn't often.

"You'll probably have a good time," he said.

"You're invited."

He imagined that. Sitting in a restaurant listening to Brandy complain about every bite her mother ate.

"I'll pass." He realized he had spoken too quickly. "My grandparents are coming in tonight. I want to be there when they arrive."

"How come they weren't here for your graduation?"

"They were out of the country. Grandpa's in the foreign service. They travel all the time."

"Like your dad."

"Yeah, sort of." He pulled onto a side road and slowed, although taking bumps at high speed was the best part of driving the truck. "We're having our big Sunday dinner tomorrow afternoon, and you're invited. I'm asking Cray and Lisa, too."

"Your mom sure spends a lot of time in the kitchen. And *she* doesn't get fat!"

"She feels bad we have this big house and we don't get to use it much. So she's pretty much always closed off the dining room for Sunday dinner so we can pretend it's all ours."

"It's gotta be weird living where so many strangers are in and out."

He made another turn; then, a hundred yards later, he pulled over beside two cars and the beat-up pickup that Cray always drove, and turned off the engine.

"I hope you've got your suit on under that?"

She sent him her most provocative smile. "What there is of it."

Cray and his girlfriend, Lisa, a blonde with a narrow face and dimpled chin, were already settled on a flat rock beside the water. The actual North Fork was just beyond them, and the water here was the end of a creek that carved out a deep hole as it fed the river. Everybody knew about this place, and if anybody actually owned the property surrounding it, they never complained about the kids hanging out and swimming here. Branches draped low over the water, which was murky and mysterious, but the temperature always felt great for swimming.

Two other guys had come, as well. One, Doug, was a classmate whom Jared didn't know well, and he introduced his cousin, who had just graduated from a high school in Staunton. A junior couple, who were good friends of Lisa's, rounded out the party.

Cray sprang to his feet, did a Tarzan yell as he beat his chest and jumped into the river. Last year some hotshot kid from Strasburg had tried to dive and hit his head on a submerged tree branch. He was okay, but nobody tried diving here anymore.

Lisa slipped in to join Cray, and so did the two guys, who had brought a beach ball and were knocking it around. The juniors were too busy making out to notice.

"You want to swim?" Jared offered Brandy a hand.

"I'm going to get some sun." She slipped off her T-shirt and shorts, and kicked her flip-flops to the side of the rock.

Brandy really was beautiful, all smooth skin and curves. Maybe someday she would gain a lot of weight, like her mother, or maybe all that smooth skin would sag, as Cray predicted. But right now, Jared thought she was the most beautiful thing he'd ever seen.

He splashed when he hit the water and hoped the temperature would cool more than the heat of the sun.

Twenty minutes later he was stretched out beside Brandy, and the others were back on the rock, as well. Cray had hauled Brandy and the groping juniors into the water against their will, but no one held it against him. The guys had played with the ball, except for Doug, who had climbed back up to talk to Brandy once she got out. Now they were all out of the water on their backs, looking up at the lacy patterns of the branches.

"I wonder if they have swimming holes like this in Massachusetts," Jared said.

Brandy grunted. "Sure, if you're a polar bear. Besides, you'll be back in the summers. Right?"

He wasn't sure of anything, so he didn't answer. She sat up. "You mean you might not come back when school's not in session?"

"I haven't even left yet."

She looked bewildered for a moment; then she narrowed her eyes. "Well, not everybody's leaving Shenandoah County. Right, Doug?"

Doug, who had played halfback on the football team to no great accolades, made a noise in his throat that could have been "Right."

"Doug's staying in town. He's going to work for his father," she said. Doug's father owned one of the local drugstores.

Jared knew what Brandy was trying to do, and he was annoyed. She edged closer to where Doug was stretched out, and his annoyance grew.

Cray came to the rescue. "Well, I'm leaving. I'm joining the marines."

There was a brief silence; then Lisa shrieked, "You've got to be kidding!"

"Nope. I'll be a military man. Won't I look hot in a uniform?"

She sat up and pounded his shoulder. "Cray, that's just insane. Did you notice we're, like, at war?"

"Yeah, and I'm going to help win it."

Jared knew all about Cray's decision, so he didn't say anything. This was something his friend had talked about at length for a full year, but only to Jared. He hadn't wanted his mother to know. He'd been preparing in his own half-assed way ever since. Marching up into the mountains when the spirit moved him, doing push-ups when he remembered, shaving off all his hair to get used to looking at himself that way.

"Did you finally tell your mother?" Jared asked.

"She found out."

"Did she go ballistic?"

"Is there a stronger word?" He gave a snort. "But she can't stop me. I'm eighteen, and it's the right thing to do."

"Well, I don't think it is," Lisa said. "What about college?"

"No dough, and not enough financial aid. I don't want to work my way through and do it in eight years or something. I'd rather let the military pay for it later."

Lisa had won early admission to William and Mary, and was nobody's dope. "It's a good deal for them," she said bitterly. "There's always that chance you won't live long enough to use it."

Cray sat up. "I thought *you*, of everybody, would get it, Lisa."

She jumped to her feet and took off toward his pickup. Cray shrugged in Jared's direction and took off after her. Jared figured they wouldn't see either of them again that afternoon.

"Well, I don't blame her for being mad," Brandy said. "It's bad enough you're going off to college, Jared."

Doug, brown-haired and bullet-shaped, sat up. "We need to cleanse all that negative energy. Let's swim."

Brandy stood up. "I know, let's skinny-dip." She glanced at Jared, then away. "I dare you all."

The juniors got to their feet first. The girl might be a friend of Lisa's, but she wasn't going to be picked for Honor Society any time soon. She giggled. "You mean really? Won't somebody, you know, see us out here?"

Jared saw that the dare was actually meant for him. Was he going to let Brandy strip in front of the others? Or was he going to pay her the kind of attention she thought she deserved? He had wounded her with all the talk of leaving, and she was getting back at him.

For a moment he considered just abandoning her there to swim in the buff. Doug could take her back when they were done. He was tired of the games and the threats. But the thought of her naked in front of the other four won out.

He grabbed her by the hand, scooped up their clothes off the rock and tugged her toward the pickup.

He opened the passenger door and stood there, waiting for her to get inside.

"You know, there are only so many times a girl makes an offer," she said, her voice vibrating with anger. "Maybe you don't think I'm worth staying around for, Jared Fortman, but you aren't the only guy in this county."

"Get in, Brandy."

She shoved him hard, but afterward she got into the pickup and slipped on her clothes over her suit.

Eric wasn't sure how Dillon ended up on the roof of the garden-shed apartment. After his encounter with Noah, he had eaten lunch sitting alone on a shady bench, watching the river flow north. He fielded two cell-phone calls from colleagues who were checking on his recovery and had a casual conversation with Gayle, who made and delivered lunch before heading into town with a sullen Noah. But he was still feeling out of sorts and lonely.

He was on his way inside when he glanced at the shed and noticed his youngest son perched on the edge, legs kicking empty air. A ladder leaned against the building where Dillon had propped it, and he held a hammer in one hand and what looked like a tube of something in the other. Several shingles that lined the gutter facing the house flapped erratically in the breeze. Nailing them in place with a little roofing cement was a small job and obviously Dillon's mission.

"Hey, Dad," Dillon called. "I'm going to surprise Mom. Even if she puts on a new roof, if these fly away they could damage something else."

Eric felt himself growing dizzy looking up at his son. He averted his gaze. "Are you supposed to be up there?"

"What do you mean?"

It seemed obvious to Eric. Annoyance was becoming such a normal emotion, he didn't think twice about it. "I mean some kids ask permission before they risk life and limb. Are you allowed to get up on the roof?"

"I'm careful. I'm not planning to jump off when I'm finished or anything."

"You aren't answering my question."

"I've been up here before, and I'm careful. And I told you, it's a surprise."

Eric had faced down world leaders, but none as slippery as this. "I think you'd better get down. Your mom's not here, and if you fall off, it's on my watch."

"You don't have to worry. I'm almost fourteen. I don't need a babysitter. And besides, Mom's coming right back."

Eric started toward the apartment, his anger simmering. "When she comes back, I want her to find you standing on the ground."

Dillon didn't move. "Didn't you like to climb ladders and stuff when you were my age?"

At the moment Eric couldn't remember being any age except old, and he was feeling older by the second. "Get down, Dillon. Now."

"I know, why don't you come up instead? We could nail the shingles together and stuff. And you can see pretty far from here. There's a bird's nest in that tree over there."

Eric realized his youngest son wasn't really testing his father's authority. Dillon seemed truly perplexed, as if he was certain that if he just explained this well enough, his father would understand. Eric considered his abortive attempts to firm up a relationship with his middle son today. Noah wanted nothing to do with the father he saw as the villain in their life drama. But this son saw him as the hero. And though neither role was true, he certainly preferred the latter.

"I don't want to come up. And what are you doing home, anyway? Your mom said you were down the road with a friend."

"Yeah, but we're all done with…with what we were doing."

Eric remembered what it was like to be Dillon's age. Everything had been a test of his newly maturing body. He had perfected his Australian crawl by swimming too far out in the local lake. He had fallen from a raft in whitewater, skied down a forbidden slope, nearly trapped himself in quicksand.

He remembered the importance of mastering each of those moments, but they seemed like a century ago.

"It's not very high," Dillon called down hopefully. "I could give you a hand once you get to the top."

"What…I…want…" Eric took a deep breath. He was just inches from the ladder now, and he grasped it and looked up. The roof seemed to sway, and Dillon with it. "What I want is for you to get down. Like I told you to a little while ago. Only I want you to do it right this minute. No more talking. Get down!"

Dillon's face fell. He looked as if Eric had slapped him.

"Yeah, sure." He slid over to the ladder, grabbed it, and with one lithe motion swung himself around and onto the top rung. At the bottom he checked for the ground below him, found it with his foot and in a second had both feet on the ground again. Then, without another word, he turned and took off for the carriage house.

Eric watched him disappear into the family home.

"Strike two, Fortman." Eric hoped he didn't run into Jared in the next few hours. He was very afraid he was on the verge of his third and final out with his sons.

* * *

The moment she returned from shopping for groceries, Gayle called Cissy to set up an interview, and Cissy volunteered to come that afternoon. Considering that she had nearly forgotten the young woman, Gayle was more than willing to juggle her own schedule to accommodate her.

Cissy arrived when Gayle was in the process of checking in new guests. She quietly explored the downstairs rooms as Gayle completed the registration process and took care of payment. Experience had taught her that getting the money up front saved a number of hassles in the long run.

Gayle asked Cissy to wait a bit longer while she showed the guests upstairs. The Blazing Star was the inn's largest room, with natural maple furniture, sage-green walls and an elaborate Blazing Star quilt of peach, sky-blue and green that took up the wall farthest from the windows. She explained where they could find anything they needed, when breakfast was served, and checked once more to be certain there were no food allergies. She recommended several restaurant choices for dinner and a short hike to see the countryside. Then, the moment she sensed all questions had been answered, she wished the couple a good stay and left.

She was sidetracked in the hallway by one of the new housekeepers, a particularly meticulous woman, who had questions about the way Gayle wanted the wastebaskets cleaned—simply dumped and lined with a new plastic bag, or washed out and dried. That led to a discussion about removing and replacing the fading flowers in each room. Since Gayle had some questions herself about how well the environmentally friendly cleaning products she had discovered were working, she was gone longer than she'd expected.

She found Cissy in the morning room examining the Touching Stars quilt. Every day since the guests had returned, two quilters had arrived to quilt. So far none of the guests had tried their hands at it, but everyone had been interested in the process.

"Thinking about taking a stitch or two?" Gayle asked from the doorway.

"Ms. Henry's made a quilter out of me, but my stitches still aren't small enough to suit her."

"You're welcome to work on this one anytime."

"I like the way the rooms are laid out here," Cissy said. "If I was staying at the inn, I'd feel like I was right at home, only with somebody taking care of me, instead of me taking care of them."

"That's exactly the way I want people to feel. Like they're part of our family, only they don't have to lift a finger."

"I noticed you ask people to pay when they come in. Do you have information printed up that you send in advance? So they know?"

The question was a good one. Gayle answered as they walked back into the reception area and through it to the tiny office. Cissy followed with other, equally thoughtful questions, and Gayle was impressed. So far the only job candidate who had taken this kind of initiative was Paula, the woman Gayle had hired.

"I'm not a fan of answering machines," Gayle said at her desk, "but sometimes nobody's around to answer the telephone. So any time we see this light flashing, we call back immediately. I'd much rather have someone answering, though. I don't think it looks good for us if no one is here to catch calls. It gives guests the idea that they'll be on their own if they stay at the inn."

Cissy trailed a finger over the computer keyboard. "I can understand that."

"There's a lot of information we get and give in that first phone call. That would be one of the things you'd have to learn."

Gayle held up a laminated sheet of typing paper. "But I made a cheat sheet that we keep by the phone at all times. We all use it. It has everything." She handed it to Cissy to peruse.

"That's a good idea. I can see it would be easy to forget something or other."

Gayle gave a quick recital of the things she required. "We've got calendars all over the house, but we never take a reservation unless we're looking at this one. Double booking is an inn's worst nightmare, so this calendar is always up to date. We repeat all the information in a format that makes it impossible for guests to misunderstand. We ask if they'd like to put it on their credit card, and if not, we explain our deposit requirements." She continued to tick off the finer points as Cissy nodded.

A woman's voice drifted down the stairwell. "Miss Fortman?"

Gayle recognized the housekeeper. "There must be another question. I'm sorry, do you mind waiting a little longer?"

"I cleared the whole afternoon," Cissy said.

Gayle fled up the stairs to find out what the latest problem might be.

She was immersed in a conversation about what to do with half-used toiletries, and whether she liked the end of the toilet paper folded into a point, when the telephone rang. She was tempted to abandon the conversation and answer the line in the housekeeper's office at the hall's end, but finishing and getting back to Cissy seemed more important. They completed the newest round of instructions, and Gayle retreated downstairs.

When she entered the office Cissy was on the telephone, nodding, as she spoke. She was concentrating so hard she didn't hear Gayle approach.

"I can certainly understand why you want to visit our area,"

Cissy was saying. "And the inn's a perfect place for families to gather. Views of the mountains, the river right in our front yard. You'll love it. There's so much to do and see."

As Gayle watched, Cissy made notes on the pad Gayle always kept by the phone. "So as I understand this you'll need three rooms, and from what you've seen on the Web site you'd prefer the Blazing Star, the Mountain Star and the Seven Sisters rooms? Do you have any questions about them?" She waited before she spoke. "Good, and you noted that the Blazing Star room has a whirlpool bathtub and private porch? Yes, the porch will be a wonderful place to gather the family."

Cissy listened and made more notes.

"Yes, they're all available for those nights." As Gayle waited unseen, Cissy held up the cheat sheet she had been using and proceeded to read off the correct room rates with tax included. "Good. And you'll be checking in after three on Friday the fourteenth and checking out before noon on Monday the seventeenth of July. That will be two people in each room, correct? And you'll be putting this on your credit card."

Cissy carefully wrote down a long string of numbers, then asked for the expiration date. "I think we're about set. I'm going to have Mrs. Fortman, our innkeeper, give you a call just to finalize everything. She'll want to know if anyone in your family has allergies so she can plan your breakfasts. Just a reminder. We're a no-smoking inn and unfortunately we can't allow pets." She listened and nodded.

"It's been a pleasure talking to you, too. We'll look forward to seeing you in July."

She hung up. When she turned and saw Gayle standing there, she drew back, startled. "Oh, I'm sorry. I probably shouldn't have answered. I don't know what got into me. But I remembered what you'd said about letting it ring, and before I knew it, I'd picked it up. That information sheet of yours has everything on it, doesn't it? I took down everything so you'd have it. If I'd known you were there, I would have handed you the phone."

"I can't imagine why," Gayle said. "That was great practice for your new job. Welcome aboard."

Cissy was flushed with victory, and Gayle gave her a quick hug. By the time the girl left an hour later, they had worked out all the details of scheduling and training. Gayle was absolutely delighted. Cissy was clearly a natural. Besides, anyone who could live with Helen Henry and survive to tell the story should be a shoo-in. Gayle wondered why she hadn't hired Cissy the moment the young woman had first shown interest.

To celebrate having a full staff, she made herself a cup of tea from the urn of hot water she always kept on the sideboard in the dining room, took an apple from the bowl of fruit beside it and went out to the front porch.

Eric was sitting on the bench at the corner under a whirling ceiling fan. His eyes were closed, and he had a glass of water on the table beside him. But she didn't think he was dozing. Before she could turn around, he opened his eyes and saw her.

"Am I in the way out here?"

"Of course not." She balanced the apple in one hand and the tea in the other as she weighed her options. She decided to join him, since it was obvious she'd intended to sit on the porch.

She settled beside him on the bench. "I just hired another staffer. I'm all set for employees now. And Travis has offered me a job catering for the archaeology camp, so this was just in the nick of time."

"Catering, too? Do you have time for everything?"

"I will now. Jared and Dillon are going to be involved in the camp, and Noah can help me with the meals. I guess it's about to become a family affair."

"Have you seen Dillon since you got back from town?"

"He's over at the house playing video games with Noah. They're killing monsters. You ought to join them."

Eric folded his arms and leaned his head against the wall. "I wouldn't be welcome."

She didn't know what to say to that. "Had a bad day?" she asked at last.

"When you married me all those years ago, did you give any serious thought to what kind of father I would be?"

She tried to keep her voice light. "You mean back in the Dark Ages?"

He didn't smile. "Was it that recent? Seems to me it was more like the dawn of time."

She'd bought herself a moment or two, but no more. She dunked her tea bag and considered how best to answer. "We were awfully young, Eric. And how could either of us gauge something like that?"

"You *didn't* think about it."

"I guess I didn't see the need. You didn't torture small animals. You played piggyback with the Rileys' little boy whenever you got the chance. What was there to know?"

"I'd forgotten about little Tommy Riley. He's probably working on his MBA about now."

She didn't often think about their newlywed apartment in the Echo Park neighborhood of Los Angeles, or the families who had surrounded them. They'd all been young and poor, but on their way to greater things. She had been blissfully happy.

"What brought this on?" she asked, sticking with the lighter tone. "It's a little late to decide you're not father material, isn't it? We can't very well give the boys up for adoption. Nobody wants teenagers."

"I'm failing more miserably than usual."

She didn't ask what had happened. This wasn't about individual mistakes or rejections, and she understood that.

Instead, she tried to help. "Kids react to crises in different ways. The boys have been worried sick about you, but they handle it differently because they're very different kids. I don't know why, but Jared seems to feel guilty you were kidnapped, like he should have been there to stop it. I think Noah's afraid something like this might happen again, so he's withdrawing. And I guess for the first time in his life Dillon's aware that bad things really can happen to people he loves. So he's frantically trying to make the most out of every minute with you."

"You have them all figured out." His tone wasn't quite bitter, but it verged on it.

"It's natural that I'd understand them, isn't it? I spend a lot of time with them."

"Noah seems convinced that every bad thing in the universe from global warming to world hunger can be laid at my door."

"Noah may well blame you for some things, but I think mostly he's trying to insulate himself."

"You're putting a great spin on this." Eric smiled a little.

She was encouraged, so she went for broke. "When Noah was, oh, maybe six, he won a parakeet at the school fair. You've never seen such a love affair. He even taught him to talk. Then one day he came home from school and the parakeet had died. No telling why, because no bird's ever been taken care of that well. He was the one who found it, and he's never had a pet since. Jared kept hamsters until he was sixteen or so, and Dillon's fond of anything he can keep in an aquarium. Fish, insects—"

"Snakes?"

"I draw the line at snakes. And anything four-footed that a guest might be allergic to or afraid of."

"And your point?" His eyes were open now, and he was looking at her. She remembered that look. When Eric really paid attention, there wasn't a molecule in his body that wasn't engaged in discovering the truth. She felt warmed by the sheer force of it.

"Noah was so bereft when his bird died that he just couldn't face another loss. He makes a point of not wanting a pet. He makes fun of Dillon for his fish and his spiders. But it's really all about being a sensitive kid who's afraid of being hurt."

"So he's careful to put up the right barriers."

"That's it in a nutshell."

"Why didn't you ever tell me this before?"

She knew better than to answer. Eric hadn't been around, and both of them knew it. And she had never been sure he would show the slightest interest if she sought him out to try.

"Hang in there," she said at last.

"I guess being a parent isn't for sissies."

"I've never found it easy."

"You? You were born knowing what to do."

She shook her head. "That's where you're wrong. I never knew exactly what to do. I just kept putting one foot in front of the other and hoped I was moving in the right direction. I still do."

"And when I put one foot in front of the other, it was to run in the opposite direction."

"Maybe this summer's all about turning around." She got up and started toward the door. Then she pivoted. "Eric?"

He glanced up, and without thinking, she tossed him the apple. His reflexes were still excellent. He caught it without fuss.

"Eat it," she said. "I think you're going to need the energy."

Chapter 9

The inn was furnished with simple pieces, some antiques and some reproductions that gently suggested life as the former residents might have lived it. The quilts pulled everything together. An appreciative guest had shared her own theory about Gayle's love affair with quilts. Anyone describing a quilt—comfortable, traditional, warm, inviting—could well be describing Gayle, herself.

Gayle also collected and displayed the work of some of the many artists and crafters in the valley. The result was gracious country living with just a few whimsical touches. The carriage house was decorated much the same, but with sturdy furniture that could stand up to life with roughhousing teenage boys.

Her bedroom was a different story. At home Gayle was surrounded with males, and the inn needed a unisex approach that appealed to both men and women. But her bedroom was her own, and she made certain that when she closed the door at night, she remembered she was a woman.

The walls were a deep rose that highlighted the roses in the spring-green carpet. They were sprinkled with unabashedly feminine watercolors and lithographs—cottage gardens, dreamy landscapes and small children at play. Lace curtains were draped and bunched at the windows, and the furniture was rosewood, with ornate carving and deeply polished surfaces. She kept fresh flowers in a vase by her bed, and cut-glass perfume bottles filled with light citrusy scents on the vanity. The bathroom had a soaking tub surrounded by herbal-scented candles and lilac bath salts.

Sunday at sunrise she unwillingly abandoned her personal hideaway, but there was no hope of lingering. Today of all days she needed coffee on the terrace to gather her thoughts. Her parents had arrived last night and were sleeping in the inn, which made for a full house and two separate breakfast shifts.

Sunday-morning breakfast was always the most elaborate and therefore the most work. The menu this morning included fresh melon slices and berries, paired with cinnamon rolls made from dough prepared last evening so it could rise slowly in the refrigerator. For the main course she planned to serve a baked egg casserole with her special Creole sauce, cheese grits and country ham. No one would leave the table hungry.

Her family would be hungry by midafternoon, when she planned to serve her traditional Sunday dinner. She prided herself on those dinners, and guests who were remaining past the weekend were always warned that this would be a good time to find outside diversion.

Meals throughout the week were too often wedged between soccer games, Cub Scout pack meetings and the needs of the guests. But Sunday dinners were family time. Each boy was allowed to invite any friends he wanted. Gayle made certain that there was something on the Sunday table that each son particularly liked. There was classical music in the background; pretty, inexpensive pottery; bright linen tablecloths; laughter and conversation. She was a believer in traditions and made sure that this one persisted.

Last week the meal had been informal because of Jared's graduation party. Now she wondered how it would feel to have the first real Sunday dinner with Eric in residence. Would his isolation from his sons seem apparent to her parents? Or would everyone come together in enjoyment of the meal and company, and forget—for those hours, at least—that they were all feeling their way?

"I thought I might find you out here."

Startled, Gayle turned around to see her mother, in blue sweatpants and jacket, coming toward her from the house. Phyllis Metzger had a cup of coffee, but she didn't look quite awake. She looked soft and approachable, which was more than likely a trick of the light.

Gayle's mother was a handsome woman in her mid-sixties, sharp-featured and sharp-witted. Her hair was a bright silver, cut short and pushed back from her tanned face. She was tall and thin, and her posture was so perfect that Gayle couldn't remember a moment when her mother had sagged with exhaustion or sadness. Sagging had been discouraged in all family members, as well. Even now, Gayle felt herself straightening a little, since dawn was not an excuse for letting down.

"How did you sleep?" Gayle asked when her mother joined her.

"It's a comfortable room. The mattress should do for another year."

"Dad's still sleeping?"

"I'll have him up in time for breakfast."

Gayle bet she would. She remembered living at home. The schedule had been organized into fifteen-minute increments. There had been little room for negotiation.

"I was sorry Eric was asleep by the time we got in," Phyllis said. The Metzgers' plane into Dulles Airport had been delayed by a storm. Even Phyllis hadn't been able to negotiate with the forces of nature.

"You'll be able to catch up with him today."

"I was glad to see you welcomed him back."

Gayle heard the words her mother didn't add. *It's about time.* Phyllis had always liked Eric, although it was an unlikely pairing. Phyllis liked order. She liked people who did whatever life called them to do and despised those who dropped the ball. She valued creativity less than discipline, and personality less than intellect. Yet Eric, who had chosen a life in the hot spots of the world over a life of duty to his family, had somehow implanted himself in her mother's ironclad heart.

Phyllis had never come right out and said that Gayle was a fool to let Eric get away, but she had made the point in numerous ways.

Gayle took a sip of coffee to fortify herself. "You'll find Eric changed, Mother."

"Well, I imagine I knew that. But he'll adjust. Eric has the right stuff."

"I'm not sure the rest of us do."

As expected, Phyllis proffered no sympathy. Her preferred method of dealing with feelings had always been to pretend they didn't exist. Gayle wasn't sad, she had just stayed up too late studying. Gayle wasn't angry, she was just going through a phase. Gayle wasn't lonely, she just hadn't tried hard enough to make new friends at yet another of the many schools she had attended throughout the world.

Gayle couldn't possibly be depressed after the divorce. After all, she had made the choice to stay at the inn and raise the boys without Eric, and no one had forced her into it.

Gayle changed the subject. "Doesn't Jared look good? And haven't Noah and Dillon grown since Christmas?"

"I suppose they have. I'm sure they're delighted to have their father back with them."

"It's complicated."

"Yes, well don't make it more complicated by telling them it is," Phyllis said.

Gayle laughed softly, because what was the point of any other reaction? "Mother, what on earth are you going to do with your time now that Daddy is retiring? Who are you going to boss around besides him?"

"You always make me sound like some sort of harridan. Do I ever have a problem finding a life for myself?"

Gayle slung an arm over her mother's shoulders and squeezed, but she released her quickly, before Phyllis could pull away. "I just want you to be happy. And I'm still hoping you and Daddy will settle on the East Coast, so we'll see more of you."

"Wherever we decide to settle, you know we'll expect you to visit. You and the boys will always be welcome. And Eric, of course, if he wants to visit with them."

Or with you. Gayle heard the unspoken words.

"Eric is here to get to know his sons better," Gayle said. "But *I* know him as well as I ever need to. Don't hope this summer is anything more than it is."

"Divorce always seems like a defeat to me."

"Yes, well those millions of us who take this particular low road have each other for company, and I'm afraid the crowd's pretty thick at times."

To celebrate her parents' arrival, Gayle splurged on a rib roast. All the boys loved beef, so this was a special treat. She made

Jared's favorite mashed-potato casserole, artichokes for Noah
and homemade biscuits for Dillon. She baked lemon meringue
pie because she knew it was Eric's favorite, and a chocolate layer
cake for Leon, who was always invited whether he was in residence at the moment or not. Since her parents could be counted
on to like anything, she added her mother's specialty, seven-layer
salad, as a tribute from one cook to another.

The day was beautiful, and the morning sun had dried puddles
and damp furniture. She asked the boys to set the tables on the
terrace for thirteen, but Leon, who had come early, lagged
behind when the others went off to set up.

"Would you mind if I asked my dad to join us?" Leon looked
sheepish. Gayle, in the middle of sprinkling cheese on the
potatoes, stopped grating.

"Would he like that?" Gayle had doubts. George Jenkins,
Leon's father, had serious problems with alcohol. When he drank
he was a bully, and when his actions came back to haunt him,
he always resented the people who tried to help.

She was one of the latter. George had been a deacon on the
church board during her tenure as president. Numerous times
she had been forced to either confront him or carry his share of
the burden. Additionally, she had taken in his son when it was
clear George was failing as Leon's father. Their relationship was
tense, at best. Although George sporadically attended twelve-
step meetings and saw a counselor, he was off the wagon more
frequently than he was on it. He was sober now, but she was
almost certain Leon would be spending his senior year at the inn.

"He's not drinking," Leon said. "I don't think he'll cause a scene."

"Then by all means invite him," Gayle said. "But you go and
get him, okay?"

He disappeared, to be replaced by Eric. Gayle knew that Eric and her father had taken a walk together. Franklin Metzger was a round faced, heavyset man most often described as pleasant. He smiled easily, listened carefully, and knew what to say and how to say it. He had been the easier of her parents to talk to, and the one Gayle had most often turned to during a crisis. But he had also been busy, too often involved with an international problem that made her childish troubles seem silly and inconsequential. If anyone could understand what Eric had gone through, he would be the one.

She finished grating and set the casserole in the oven. "Did you and Dad have a nice chat?"

"Gayle, is this a banquet? Did you hire a court jester? Jugglers?"

She supposed she had overdone it. "Proving love through food. My mantra."

"If we start eating at three, we should finish by midnight. Tell me you don't do this every Sunday."

Since he didn't sound critical, she smiled. "Not quite this expansively."

"I normally eat cold pizza and watch the football game."

"We could send out for pizza and put it on ice."

"No one delivers out here."

"You'll have to cope with the banquet, then."

"Can I help?"

"I don't know. Can you cook?"

"Not any better than I used to, but I can bowl you over with my charm."

"In other words, you're good for nothing." She smiled to let him know she was teasing. More or less.

"Who's coming?"

She had told Eric he was welcome to invite friends. He had a host of contacts in D.C., and the trip was doable. But he had declined. She wasn't sure if those friendships weren't deep enough, or if he just wasn't ready to field questions about his ordeal from other professionals.

She recited the list. "Jared's bringing three friends, including Brandy. I asked Sam and Elisa, our minister and his wife. You met them at the graduation party. Dillon's friend Caleb, Noah's friend Sherry—"

"Noah has a girlfriend?"

"No, they've been friends since they played on the same soccer team in first grade. Last year they painted a mural on the lunch-room wall for their art project. If there's a romance, I haven't seen signs."

"That may not be something he'd want you to know."

She finished the list with Leon and his father. "You aren't going to like George, so don't even try. But it's important for Leon to feel he can invite his father here."

"I'll stay away from him."

After that there was a steady stream of kitchen visitors. Phyllis came in to complain about Gayle's use of taco cheese in the salad. Franklin went straight to the stove to make gravy. Jared and Cray trooped in to fill pitchers with tea and lemonade, while Brandy and Lisa stayed outside and flirted with Eric on the terrace.

Noah's friend Sherry, an athletic-looking girl with long, red, corkscrew curls, had been to enough Sunday dinners to know the score. She carried platters and casseroles outside without being asked and studiously ignored Eric, as if she knew Noah would not want her to be friendly to his father.

Sam and Elisa arrived and finished getting things to the table. Gayle was flushed with hard work and the success of finishing everything at the same time.

The good feelings didn't last. Three long tables had been set up in a *U* so that everyone could sit together. Unfortunately, by the time Sam and Elisa sat down, there were only two chairs left, directly across from George Jenkins. George had formerly been robust, but these days his eyes were sunken and his hands shook when he lifted a fork. Sam had been one of the first to confront George about his drinking, and he and Elisa had paid dearly for it. Somehow Sam still managed to be polite, even pastoral, toward George, but George would have none of it. Every comment he made dripped with sarcasm. The people sitting around them clearly felt it, particularly Leon, whose cheeks were red from embarrassment.

By the same bad luck, Sherry and Noah were seated across from Eric. Phyllis was beside Noah, and in the way a tongue prods an aching tooth, after grace, she prodded Noah to speak to his father, doing everything except openly chastising him for not being a loving son.

Sherry, normally a polite, even tactful, girl got enough of this by the time the roast was passed and asked Noah if he would mind trading places, because the sun was in her eyes. Then, once the switch had been made, she proceeded to tell Phyllis the story of her life, leaning heavily on her relationship with her father, a man who had made more than a few career sacrifices in order to give his children the life he wanted for them.

Gayle had never realized what a pit bull little Sherry could be. She was torn between dismay and admiration.

In an attempt to hold on to her Sunday-dinner fantasy, she tried to ignore the other interactions, but she was surrounded by them. Brandy and Lisa had allied themselves against their dates and were chatting over Jared and Cray's heads. Caleb seemed mystified by the tensions and didn't say a word.

Dillon, who could always be counted on to act out if he was

anxious, raised the decibel level to piercing. He hadn't been able to get a seat near his father, and in order to get Eric's attention he got louder and more boisterous as the meal continued. Eric finally got up and went over to speak to him. Gayle had no idea what he said, but Dillon stormed away from the table.

"Just great, Dad," Noah said, as Eric headed back to his seat. He got up, threw his napkin on the chair and went after his brother, followed in a moment by Sherry.

Franklin, the diplomat, caught Gayle's eye and shrugged, as if to say that compared to this, negotiations between the Israelis and Palestinians were a piece of cake.

By the time the meal ended and Gayle began to ferry platters back to the kitchen, she knew one tradition that would not go forward that summer. She had catered her last Sunday dinner.

Sam joined her as those who were left on the terrace dug into dessert. He was dark haired, with blue eyes that saw straight to the heart of most things and a natural warmth that was even more noticeable than his good looks.

"If you want to have a quick cry, there's time."

"What a disaster." Gayle swallowed convulsively but staved off the tears. "I'm so sorry, Sam. I don't know what made me think I could pull this off. I should have told Leon not to invite George."

"George isn't the real problem, is he?"

"We're a mess, aren't we? My little family?"

Sam leaned against the counter and watched her slowly setting coffee cups on a tray. She was working at ten-percent capacity, delaying her return to the terrace until August.

"It looks like a family trying to figure out who it is, with too many guests in the way," he said.

The description was good. Gayle took a clean dishcloth and

wiped each cup, as if a speck of dust might be clinging to some hidden surface.

"I just wanted everyone to be happy." She looked up. "I want the boys to feel they can have friends here on Sunday. I wanted to include Eric and my parents. I wanted you to have a chance to sit in the sun with Elisa and relax for a change."

"Your intentions were honorable. What's behind them?"

Gayle knew, although it was hard to admit. "I guess I want to prove I have the most civilized divorce in America. Eric said we won that award."

"Was that your intention right from the moment you realized your marriage was ending?"

"That was so long ago." She bit her lip; then she nodded. "Probably."

"I know you pretty well. You usually put your feelings aside and work for the greater good. It's who you are, how you think of yourself."

Gayle knew he was right. As a child, she had been taught that the way she treated others was important, but the way she felt about them? Immaterial. Still, Gayle couldn't lay the whole problem at Phyllis's door. Phyllis had never set out to make her daughter unhappy, only to make her aware of the importance of actions. And Gayle had been given plenty of chances through-out her life to change.

She gave up on the cups and faced Sam. "I'm not good at dealing with feelings. I guess that's part of who I am, too."

"I wonder, have you ever dealt with your feelings about Eric or the divorce? Really dealt with them? Or did you just plunge into being good at divorce the way you're good at everything else?"

"From the outside, doesn't it look like I've moved on?"

"Honestly?"

She nodded.

"You're a very attractive woman, Gayle. But what happens to the men who show interest? You've been divorced how long?"

"Twelve years."

"That's a long time to be alone."

"But I'm not. I've certainly gone out with men since Eric left. I have my sons. I have the inn. I'm surrounded by people all the time. I'm never alone."

"Sometimes we surround ourselves with people just so we don't have time to examine what we really need."

She realized he was also making a point about dinner. Gently and lovingly, Sam was telling her that today she had done the same thing on a smaller scale. She had surrounded her small family with other people, at least one of whom was guaranteed to cause turmoil. That way the problems the Fortmans were facing would be diluted.

She crossed to the refrigerator for a pitcher of cream and put it on the tray, adding the sugar bowl beside it before she spoke. "You know, you've got perspective on this question. Does life ever get easy? Not easier. I mean, *effortlessly* easy? Do I have something to look forward to? I could use that about now."

"There are minutes sprinkled here and there."

"I don't see any of those in my immediate future."

Sam joined her and lifted the tray to carry it out to the terrace. "Maybe not, but if you spend this summer dealing with some of the things you've swept under the rug, maybe you'll have more of those minutes for the rest of your life."

Jared knew Brandy was still angry at him. When she'd learned he was going all the way to Massachusetts for college, she had been upset enough. Now, with the reality setting in, she wanted to negotiate. But Jared knew his future was too uncertain. He had no idea what the next years of his life would require. He couldn't promise he would come home next summer, and he couldn't promise that once she was accepted to a school he would consider moving to join her. Brandy's grades were just okay. She wasn't looking at schools that would have a challenging curriculum.

Jared knew something was required of him if he wanted to smooth things over, but he wasn't sure what. He wasn't ready to end their relationship, but he wasn't ready to make promises, either.

They had dropped off Cray and Lisa, and were on their way to Brandy's house. After dinner the four friends had taken the rowboat out on the river, then hiked for a while before returning to the inn. No one had been in the best of moods. Jared wasn't exactly sure what had gone wrong at dinner, but as Sundays went, this wasn't one of his favorites.

"I wish you'd say something." Beside him in the pickup, Brandy's arms were crossed over her chest. Her tone was mutinous.

Jared turned the pickup into the Wilburns' driveway and switched off the engine. "I've said a lot. You haven't listened to much of it."

"Mostly what you said was how excited you are about going away to school."

"Brandy, my grandfather wanted to know if I was looking forward to MIT. He's paying some of my expenses. What should I have said? That I'm sorry I was admitted, and I want to stay here and wait for you to graduate?"

She opened her door and jumped down. Sighing, he did the same, going around the pickup to join her. He could see she was struggling to hold back tears.

"I'm just going to miss you, that's all." She sniffed.

He put his arms around her and pulled her hard against him,

kissing her until she was breathless. She pulled away and sent him a watery smile.

"Well, that's a little better," she said.

"You know I'm going to miss you, too. We can call and e-mail."

"Are you at least coming home for Christmas?"

He felt trapped. "I'm planning to."

"I'm going to save the money I make as a counselor. I can come up and see you."

He nodded, as if that was a terrific idea. In reality he wondered just how long Brandy would mourn before she started looking for his replacement. Senior year was a social whirl, and not having a date for the important events was going to get old quickly. By the time she saved enough money to fly to Boston, she might not remember who he was.

That last thought made him clutch her to his chest. He rested his cheek against her hair. "Do you want to watch TV or something? Or do you just want me to go home?"

"My parents won't be back until late. They said not to expect them before midnight. Keep me company."

Arms around each other's waists, they walked up the path to her house. Brandy's parents had a couple of acres on a private road. The exterior of the simple one-story house was painted tan with green shutters, but in Jared's opinion the inside was needlessly fussy. The heavy drapes looked like a queen's royal robes. The living-room furniture still looked showroom fresh, as if no one ever sat on it. Only the family room in the back seemed like a place where people lived. Despite sharing the inn with hundreds of guests each year, his mother still made the whole place feel like a home.

"Want some popcorn?" Brandy asked as he settled on the couch and reached for the remote.

"Nope, just you."

She settled beside him, and he put his arm around her.

"I'm sorry about this afternoon," she said. "I just don't want you to go. But I know you have to, Jared. I'm being selfish. Just don't forget me, okay?"

He turned her a little so he could kiss her. Her breasts were soft against his chest, and she put her arms around his neck to draw him closer.

In the corner he could hear the humming of the fifty-gallon saltwater aquarium. Outside the kitchen window a woodpecker was tapping a hole in the siding, and in the living room, a grand-father clock began to chime.

Jared was only vaguely aware of the sounds. They were a soft orchestral accompaniment to the frantic drum solo of his heart. The remote was forgotten. The room itself, with its green plaid furniture, the deer head mounted above the fireplace, the wooden plaque with the Wilburn coat of arms, faded away.

He managed to ask a question. "You're sure your parents aren't coming back until late?"

"Absolutely sure." Then, as if to sweeten the deal, she whispered the rest. "I have condoms. I don't want to get pregnant. I don't want to trap you."

He was elated. In his heightened state of arousal, this seemed like the pledge he'd been hoping for. Brandy loved him, but she didn't want to chain him to her side. She knew exactly what she was doing tonight. They would practice safe sex. Sex on *every* level would be safe tonight.

"I just love you so much," she said. "Can't I show you?"

Jared knew he was lost when no answer occurred to him except yes.

Chapter 10

On Monday morning Helen Henry handed a bright gold shopping bag tied with red ribbon to Gayle. "I figure you been so good to the church, it was about time for some of us to be good to you."

Gayle knew Helen well enough to realize the bag and ribbon were probably recycled. Helen was legendary for saving everything she thought she might use in the future. She no longer rescued other people's trash, which had once cluttered her old farmhouse, but she was still careful not to throw away anything that came her way naturally.

Gayle untied the ribbon and lifted out a long quilted strip.

"It's a table runner in the Touching Stars pattern," Helen said. "For that table in your reception area. See? We made it using light fabrics for the background, same as the light stars in the quilt. And dark fabrics for the stars, same as the background in the quilt. Sort of a negative of the one for your wall. People will see this table runner and look past it to the Touching Stars in the stairwell. I made sure it would fit there."

Gayle was touched. Helen and the church quilters had done a beautiful job on the table runner, which was pieced with fewer diamonds on each arm of the stars, for size. And they were right. It was a perfect addition to the reception area. Once the quilt was on display, one would highlight the other.

Gayle thanked her, along with Dovey Lanning and Cathy Adams, who had come with Helen to quilt this morning.

"Not much, but something," Dovey said. She was about Helen's age, with white hair pulled back in a bun and faded blue eyes that still took in everything.

"You know we call you the Quilt General, don't you?" Helen pulled out a chair and looked at the seat suspiciously, as if she wasn't absolutely sure it would hold her weight.

"Quilt General?" Gayle laughed. "Whatever for?"

"You've organized every single quilt sale we've had. You were the one printed all those tickets for the Cactus Bloom quilt raffle and counted the money. You were the one who got it advertised and got that story about it in the paper. You're the one comes through for us and makes sure everything goes according to plan. Quilt General."

Apparently Helen decided her chair would do, and she lowered herself onto it. The other women made themselves at home around the frame. Helen and Dovey both looked it over to see if anything new had been added. A few guests had finally given quilting a try. Only the worst stitches were removed. Gayle had explained that this quilt was not going to be judged at the county fair but rather was going to be something returning guests could point to next year and say, "I quilted part of that."

"So, Miss Quilt General, are you planning to take your turn?" Helen demanded.

Gayle had been waiting for this question. Helen was also legendary for making quilters out of people who hadn't had the slightest interest. Gayle had her answer all ready. "You have to promise that once I'm done, that will be that. You won't keep after me to learn to do it better."

Helen's muttered response sounded suspiciously like "Not in this lifetime," but Gayle preferred to believe the old woman meant she would not continue to insist. She wasn't too worried, since she knew that once Helen saw her primitive needleworking skills, all this would be a moot point.

She listened as Helen explained what was expected of her; then, after the quilting stitch had been demonstrated a few times, Gayle set to work.

"I can't believe what you've done with this old place," Dovey said. "I remember what it looked like twenty years ago, and I can tell you it was shameful that Doc Featherstone's descendants let it go the way they did. When I was a girl it was something of a showplace, but after the doctor died, it came down to all his children, and they could never agree which of them should keep on living here."

"That's what we were told," Gayle said.

"Nobody really wanted it, and nobody really wanted to sell. So this one lived in it, then that one, and they were always arguing about who would pay for this and who would pay for that. Most of the time *nobody* would pay until things got really bad, so the roof leaked, or windows were broke and the glass wasn't replaced fast enough. Wasn't till all his children died off that the grandchildren were able to figure out they just had to sell."

"Everyone expected us to tear it down." Gayle poked her

needle through the layers and tried to poke it back toward her again. The point came up over an inch away. And the finger underneath that was supposed to guide it already felt raw from her efforts.

"I like people who save old things," Helen said. "Nothing worse than wasting things that could be used again, and that goes triple for something like a house."

Gayle poked the needle through again, this time even farther away and definitely not close to the chalk line she was supposed to be following. She soldiered on.

"At one time the house must have been filled with laughter. When I walked through it, it didn't feel empty and sad, like some houses do. It felt like a happy house. I guess that's silly. I probably just wanted to think it had been happy, since I loved it at first sight."

"No, it *was* a happy house," Dovey said. "And that's why the family was so reluctant to sell. They had all those good memories tied up here. I guess those memories were more important than the money they could have got for it. And even when they were arguing about what to do, seems like they went on being friends. They had reunions here, I remember. Every year, as regular as a clock striking midnight."

"They still do." Gayle tried and failed at yet another attempt to get her needle back on course. "The first week of September, the Featherstone descendants take over the whole inn. And what a rowdy bunch."

"All's well that ends well," Cathy Adams said. "I like that story."

"Well, I got another story to tell," Helen said. "About that farmhouse used to be across the way."

Gayle was already fairly sure she didn't like quilting. She could not imagine why anyone chose to spend their time this way. Her left index finger felt numb, and no matter how hard she tried, she couldn't stay on course or shorten the length of her stitches. But the talk around the quilt frame? This she could get used to.

Helen took tiny, perfectly spaced stitches as she spoke. "When I was a girl, there were about as many Civil War soldiers still hanging on as there are soldiers from World War II these days. I know it all seems such a long time ago now, but it wasn't. Not really. People I knew were still affected by it, you know. Families raised by women 'cause so many of the men had died. More Americans died in that war than in others before or since. And of course the Valley took decades to get over all the crops being destroyed and Sheridan's men laying waste to anything they took a fancy to burning. You know Custer was one of them, one of the soldiers who came through here? Weren't so many Valley residents sorry when he met his end at the hands of those Indians. I'm sorry to say it, but a lot of folks here believed he got his due, and there's no mistaking it."

"All these years later, people here are still fighting the war," Gayle said.

"The odd thing about all that?" Dovey effortlessly mimicked Helen's perfect stitches. "Not everybody in Virginia was all het up about secession, you know. We were one of the last states to secede, and then only with reluctance. But after the Union came and went here more than a few times, and then Sheridan came through burning everything, weren't too many people in this part of the world who would speak up for the Union anymore. Take somebody who's sitting on the fence and give them a shove? You know what side they'll end up on, sure as can be."

Cathy Adams stitched away as she spoke, although her stitches weren't quite as perfect as the others'. "Whether there's any sense in it or not. And what sense was there in all that death and destruction? Brother against brother?"

"The woman who lived in that farmhouse across the river saw it all," Helen said. "She was a young woman when the war began. Of course she wasn't so young when I would see her here and there. By then she was older than I am now by some years. She lived in that house alone until the day she died. I think she was close to a hundred."

"Didn't she have family?" Cathy asked. "That would be unusual, I think, in an area like this one."

"She did have a son in the area. Of course, he was old by then himself. I was still a girl, but the way I recall it, she would never move away, never move in with her son or grandchildren so they could take care of her. Somebody came over every day and got her meals and made sure her house was clean, her garden taken care of. That was back before we had real phone lines here, but her family laid wires across the hills to some relative or another's house. You'd come across that wire if you were walking in that area, just lying on the ground connecting her house with one of those old-fashioned phones you had to wind up."

"Country people knew how to make do," Dovey said. "Most still do."

"I wonder if she's the one who made the star quilt I have the pieces from." Gayle tried piling stitches on her needle the way the others seemed to be able to do. The result looked like a train wreck, cars piled on cars, and no survivors.

"She was a quilter, that's certain," Helen said. "Quilting comes and goes, you know. One generation gets caught up in it, the next, well, maybe they have enough quilts already, or maybe they just grew up tired of hearing about it. But that time around the Civil War was a fertile time for quilting. She would have learned how at her mama's knee."

Helen leaned over and looked at Gayle's wobbly quilting line. "I never did see such a poor example of what a quilting stitch is supposed to look like."

"Didn't I tell you needlework's not my strength?"

"I guess I thought you were like everybody else who tells me that."

"I'm afraid I'm different."

"You might well be."

"You'll have better luck with my son."

Helen harrumphed and went back to her own section. "T'other reason I know she was a quilter? Now there's a real story. Only after that sorry work you're doing over there, I don't know if I ought to favor you with it."

Gayle laughed. "I am actually doing brilliant work. This is the best stitching I've managed. And remember? I'm the Quilt General?"

The light in Helen's eyes was warm, although her lips continued in a line that was straighter than Gayle's stitches.

"What story?" Dovey demanded. "Just get down to it."

Helen sewed a little while, as if she was pulling it all together. "Well, that farmhouse wasn't nearly as big as this house, but it wasn't a shack, either. In its time it was a nice solid house, big enough for a real family and maybe a guest or two. But by the time Mrs. Miranda Duncan—"

"That was her name?" Gayle asked.

"It was. Miranda not being a common name in her time, but my mother told me once that Mrs. Duncan told her she was named for somebody in a Shakespeare play."

"*The Tempest*," Gayle said. "I saw it performed a few years ago."

"Well, that was most likely it, then, since you recognize it. By the time she got to be old, the house was too big for one person to care for, you understand? And though her family helped, and there was even a hired man or two who came and went, the house started to show its age. And old houses, purt near abandoned like that one, well, they get a reputation, if you know what I mean."

Gayle was thinking about Travis and the dig, and trying to hang on to every word Helen told her so she could pass them on to him. "Reputation?"

"That house had stood for a very long time by then. People had lived there, died there." She punched *died* harder than the other words.

"You mean haunted?" Gayle asked.

"That's it exactly."

"So people thought Miranda Duncan was living in a haunted house?"

"They did. It was one of those stories people begin, just to have something to talk about. To my mind, nobody ever swore they saw a ghost floating around. My brothers sure never did."

"They went there?"

"You got to remember, there wasn't a lot for us to do. We didn't have television and only got radio when I was already quite a young lady. So we told a lot of stories. Made up some of them, you understand, and I'm sure this one was made up, too."

"What was made up?" Dovey demanded.

"That Miranda Duncan was touched in the head. See, some of the young people from this area used to spy on her. My brothers were older than me, and they had more leeway to come and go. They'd be out of a night doing whatever they weren't supposed to do, and they'd sneak up to her house and peek in her windows to see what she was doing. Some people said she was a witch, you know, and others said the house was haunted. Pretty soon, though, everyone just agreed that she was a little loose in her head, like old age or the war or something or other had shaken some of the good sense right out of her."

"Why? Because she didn't want to leave her home?" Gayle asked. "Even when she was too old to live alone?"

"That lent itself to the story, I suspect. But people who were spying in her windows saw her talking to herself while she sat by a fire—didn't matter if it was cold or hot outside, there was always a fire—and sewed. She was talking to herself or to somebody long gone—which was what they really wanted to think. Anyway that's what they said. Now me, I understand why a person would do that."

"Talk to the dead?" Cathy said.

"No. Talk to herself!" Helen wrinkled an already wrinkled face in a frown. "You get bored not hearing voices in a house, so you start supplying them yourself. People ever heard some of the things I've said to myself, they'd haul me off to the loony bin, and that's the truth."

"So this whole story is about an old woman living alone who just talked to herself a little." Dovey shook her head.

"If you would show just a touch of patience, Dovey Lanning," Helen said, leaning toward her friend, "I will continue."

"By all means."

Helen sat back. "Miranda Duncan finally up and died. We all do, sooner or later, after all. And when her family went in to clean out the old house, they found four hundred Devil's Puzzle blocks in her attic, and not one other block of any other kind. Every single one of them was perfect, too. Stitches so tiny they make mine look like cooked-up spaghetti. Perfectly pieced, all exactly the same size. Four hundred!" She looked over the top of her glasses.

Dovey whistled, impressed.

"It's not an easy block to piece," Helen said.

"Devil's Puzzle?" Gayle asked.

"Oh, it surely has other names, but that's what we called it around here." She traced an *X* on the quilt in front of her. "Never did know why. An *X* is used for Christ in Christmas. Can't see anything devilish about it."

"A little superstition here, a little superstition there," Gayle said with a smile.

"Yes, but four hundred of them?" Dovey said.

"You want to know what I think about that?" Helen put her needle down and flexed her hand. "I think she was so old she'd more or less forgotten all her other patterns. But she remembered that one. So she made it over and over again. Maybe she was clinging to memories, or maybe just to something she could still remember how to do."

"I bet you're right." Gayle laid down her needle, too. After all, what was the point of continuing?

"Anyway, the family gave all those blocks to somebody at our church and asked if she had a use for them. Of course she took them right to the preacher. See, she was the superstitious sort and worried the blocks had some sort of hex on them. Name of the block, after all, and all those stories about Mrs. Duncan and the old house."

"Honestly!" Cathy rolled her eyes.

"She was thinking maybe she ought to burn them or bury them or do something to stop whatever bad magic was in them."

"And your preacher went along with this?" Gayle was trying to imagine Sam keeping a straight face.

"No, the preacher told her the best thing she and her quilting friends could do was take all those blocks and make as many quilts as they could manage. He said it was a gift, and an important one. With all those tops, they'd always have quilts to give families in need. And, of course, once the Depression hit in Shenandoah County like it hit everywhere else, there was a lot of need, too. So the ladies round here had a lot of quilting bees, and Mrs. Miranda Duncan was the cause of them. And a lot of families who needed them had quilts because of her, too."

"That's one great story," Gayle said.

"I just pass on what I know." But Helen smiled.

Through the years, Eric had learned to look at the issues facing him and outline his choices. Logic was the best—and sometimes the only—barrier to seeking the most stimulating adventure. Faced with an important desk job or a year in the field facing gunfire? Gunfire would win every time. Except that with his choices logically spread out before him, sometimes he found a compromise he could live with.

This morning, as he shaved the face that was beginning to look more like the one that had first broadcast reports from Afghanistan, he outlined his choices regarding his sons.

First Jared. Clearly Jared was conflicted about his father's presence at the inn and unable to discuss his reasons. For the most part, in the ten days Eric had been living here, Jared had avoided him. Eric, who was adept at interviewing world leaders, had no idea how to find out what Jared was thinking.

Then Noah. Noah had none of his brother's hesitation. Noah didn't like his father, was still angry about Eric's choice to pursue his career instead of remaining in Toms Brook to run the inn with Noah's mother, and wasn't afraid to let Eric know it. For a kid who normally had a large dollop of his diplomat grandfather's tact, he was acting like an insufferable brat.

And finally Dillon. Eric knew that most of the problems with Dillon were his own. Unlike his older brothers, Dillon wanted desperately to have a relationship with his father. But Eric had never bonded with this son. He hadn't wanted Dillon, had begrudged Gayle's enthusiasm for this unplanned pregnancy, and had only resentfully participated in Dillon's birth.

Now, all these years later, he was facing the consequences of his own self-absorption. How many more years before Dillon was lost to him forever? Or was it months? How long before he looked into Dillon's eyes and saw disinterest or, worse, hostility. Then the damage could never be undone. It would linger, no matter how hard either of them tried to erase it. The window of opportunity was closing.

Eric wasn't certain what to do about Jared and Noah, but he did know that reaching out to Dillon would be simple in comparison. He only had to search beyond his own annoyance for common interests and dredge up the patience that had always been sadly lacking in his response to his youngest son.

In other words, he simply had to change himself from top to bottom.

His cell phone rang, and he answered it to find Ariel was making her daily call. He was warmed by her husky voice. Ariel had never known him as anybody's father. Not particularly maternal herself, she didn't care if he knew how to change a diaper or wipe a runny nose. She assumed that of course listening to the synopsis of a seventh-grade book report would be boring even if it was necessary, and that a large percentage of parenting fell into that category.

And if he wasn't the world's best father, she still thought he was a pretty terrific human being. Which was something he needed to hear at the moment.

They chatted for a while. She told her usual funny stories

about the newsroom. Weather Woman had changed her brand of shampoo to one she was highly allergic to. The resulting rash on her scalp had been so fierce that she had been unable to resist scratching during her live weather broadcast, and she had finished that night's report with her hair standing on end. Several viewers had called to see if perhaps the weather was worse than she'd indicated, since it seemed to have scared her to death.

"You sound down," Ariel said at last.

"I've hardly said a word."

"That's my point precisely."

"My sons aren't at all sure what to do with me." The moment he said it, Eric could have bitten his tongue. He liked talking to Ariel because his sons weren't the topic. And now he had introduced them into the conversation, ever after to be asked how things were going.

"I'm never sure what to do with you, either," she said easily, as if this was of no consequence.

"I'm just trying to figure out how to relate to them," he said, making the situation that much worse and not understanding why.

"Well, of course you are."

He waited. No recriminations. No suggestions. He began to relax. "Dillon wants me to be his best friend, but I have no idea how to go about it."

"Eric, he *has* friends. I'm sure he just wants you to be his father. Throw a baseball or something. Isn't that what fathers do?"

Eric wondered if he had *ever* thrown Dillon a baseball. "And that will cure a lifetime of being away from him? That is, if I can manage it without criticizing the way he uses his glove."

"Aren't you being a little hard on yourself *and* him? Isn't a big part of being a parent just showing up?"

After she went on to other things, he continued to think

about that, and he thought about it even more after he went down to the kitchen to get breakfast. Gayle was off with her parents, and she'd told him that from today on he would find his breakfast in the refrigerator, so he could warm it up at his own convenience. Dillon and Noah were sitting at the table, shoveling in mounds of French toast and sausage patties. For a moment he just stood in the doorway unnoticed and watched them shovel. They were chatting the way brothers throughout time probably had. Some sort of genetically programmed series of grunts and code between bites that each seemed to understand perfectly.

"Where do you guys put all that food?" Eric asked.

They looked up at the same moment, but their reactions couldn't have been more different. Noah looked as if he suddenly smelled something rotten in the kitchen. Dillon glowed.

"Does that taste as good as it looks?" Eric asked.

"Mom got up about dawn to make it," Dillon said.

"Well, I can't wait to dive in."

Noah got up from the table and removed his plate. "Come find me once you've got your suit on," he told his brother without looking at Eric. "We have to do this early or not at all."

"Are you two going swimming?" Eric went to the refrigerator and found the plate Gayle had left for him. He wondered how many divorced men had ex-wives who were willing to feed them.

"Uh-huh," Dillon said. "There's a swimming hole where we like to go."

"May I come, too?"

There was complete silence behind him. Eric backed out of the refrigerator and closed the door. When he faced his sons, he read their expressions. Clearly, for Noah, the smell in the kitchen had gotten worse. Dillon's glow had turned to ash.

"Okay, what'd I say wrong?" Eric asked. "Did I put my foot in my mouth again? It seemed like a simple request."

Dillon and Noah exchanged glances. Then Dillon shrugged. "You might not want to, that's all. It's pretty cold. The water, I mean. Freezing."

"I like cold water."

"Oh."

"Noah?" Eric asked. "Do you mind if I come with you? You can drive my car." The rental agency had dropped off a black Mustang convertible yesterday for Eric's use, and Eric had seen Noah eyeing it greedily.

"You and Dillon go without me." Noah looked at his brother with something like pity. "I had to be back before ten anyway. This way you can stay and, well, enjoy swimming."

"You have to come!" Dillon said.

"No, I don't. You go with Dad. I've got other things to do."

Eric knew his son really meant he had *better* things to do.

"Well, you'll be missed," Eric said.

"Yeah?" Noah's smile was light-years from genuine. "Practice makes perfect." He stowed his dishes in Gayle's huge commercial dishwasher and left the kitchen.

Dillon looked as if he'd lost his best friend. Eric reached out and ruffled his son's hair. "Hey, champ, don't worry about your brother. We'll have a great time. Just you and me."

"Maybe we ought to do something else."

"I don't want you to change your plans, and it's going to be a scorcher today. Swimming sounds perfect."

Dillon looked near to tears. "No. I don't want to."

Eric put his plate in the microwave and pushed the required buttons, which gave him the time he needed to try to look at the situation logically. Dillon wanted to spend time with him.

He'd been begging for it ever since Eric had moved in. Dillon had clearly been glad to see him that morning.

He remembered the look on Noah's face, something like pity aimed at his little brother. Pity because he was going to be forced to spend time with Eric? Or pity for something else?

The microwave dinged, and he pulled out his plate, testing the French toast with his fingertip.

"Okay, what's up?" he asked when he turned to the table, where Dillon sat with his head in his hands. "You know, you can tell me."

Dillon shook his head without looking up.

Eric remembered what it was like to be Dillon's age. Tears or any sign of weakness were always to be avoided. He felt a flash of kinship with this boy who wanted to be a man and wasn't quite there. He remembered that feeling. This was something he had once experienced, something they shared.

A tentative bond.

He set his plate across from Dillon's chair, but once he sat, he shoved it to one side and put his hand on his son's arm. "I'm trying to piece this together, Dill. The only thing I can come up with is that you and Noah were planning something fun, and I interfered. I'm sorry. I should have realized I'd chase Noah away and spoil this for you."

"No."

"I'm good at a lot of things, I guess, but reading your mind doesn't seem to be one of them."

Dillon sat up and raised his eyes to his father's. "I don't know how to swim too well. There. You can call me a sissy or whatever. I'm, like, used to it."

Eric sat quietly while images raced through his head. "Afraid of the water?" he asked at last.

"I guess."

"My God, you live on a river."

"I can swim a little!" Dillon looked away. "I just have to learn to swim better or Mr. Allen won't let me go to archaeology camp. I can just, you know, paddle and stay on top of the water. Noah's been helping me."

Eric felt an irrational burst of anger. How had Gayle let this happen? How had she allowed this boy to live on a river all his life without the necessary skills to save himself?

Dillon was apparently better at reading minds. "And don't you blame Mom. She made me take swimming lessons even when I screamed and cried. How do you think I learned to paddle around in the water?"

"Nobody bothered to tell me."

"Would it have mattered?"

Eric heard echoes of Noah in Dillon's question. How many months did he have before Dillon turned into Noah? How many weeks? Hours? Minutes?

"What do you really like to do?" Eric asked. "I promise I'm going to teach you to swim, but not today. Today I want to have fun. What shall we do? Your choice."

Dillon just stared at him, as if this stranger sitting in front of him was speaking Swahili or Urdu, as if the words had absolutely no meaning in their present form.

"Do you like to hike?" Eric prompted. "Because I'm itching to. I can't go fast or far yet, or do any climbing, but we could pack a lunch, take binoculars along the river, maybe, and see if we can spot an eagle's nest. There used to be one downstream a ways. I doubt it's there now, but we could try to find it."

"Just us?"

"Nobody else gets to come. Not even if they beg and plead. Which, under the circumstance, is unlikely."

Dillon chewed his lip. "I promised Mom I'd practice swimming today."

"I'll clear it with your mom."

Dillon's smile was like sunshine peeking from behind a dark cloud. "I'll put on jeans and shoes."

"Come back when you're ready, and we'll pack a lunch together."

Dillon threw his dishes in the dishwasher and disappeared. Eric wondered if being a father could be this simple after all. At least he was on to something. First you had to want to, then you had to try.

Chapter 11

Jared hadn't seen Brandy since they'd made love. In one brief telephone conversation, his worst fears had been confirmed. Brandy was over the moon, convinced they'd made a pledge that would take precedence over all his plans for the future. She might not expect him to miss his first year at MIT, but clearly she thought the moment something could be arranged, he would want to be wherever she was, that now she would be the center of his life and all his decisions.

Jared hadn't known what to say, so he'd made excuses not to get together. He blamed his mother, who asked him to do this or that, and truthfully, he thought Gayle *was* laying on extra work. He knew she was unhappy about his relationship with Brandy, although she never overtly interfered. But his mother had hopes for his future that didn't involve him settling in Shenandoah County before he had a chance to see the world. And she wasn't above finding excuses to keep him out of danger of a lasting and local commitment.

He should resent that, he knew. But for the most part he was simply grateful.

Now it was Wednesday, and excuses had ended. He pulled into Brandy's driveway to give her a ride to counselor training at the archaeology campsite, and she was already waiting in front of her house. She wore tight jeans and some kind of top that bared most of her shoulders. Her long hair fell nearly to her waist, and the sight of her brought back memories of Sunday night—and an all too familiar ache.

Mrs. Wilburn, wearing a loose, brightly flowered dress, came out to greet him. Brandy scrambled into the car well ahead of her mother and rolled her eyes as they waited.

Mrs. Wilburn finally arrived and leaned down to ask how his father was feeling. They chatted for a few moments until she straightened and waved them off.

"If I look like that when I'm her age, you have my permission to shoot me." Brandy tossed her head. "I'm going to stay thin and pretty for you."

Jared tried to imagine what it would be like to be married to Brandy when they were the ages her parents were now. For a moment he couldn't breathe, as if in that fantasy the older Jared reached through the mists and wrapped his hands around his throat.

"I don't know why your mom keeps you so busy." Brandy examined her nails, some of which had pictures painted on the tips. She seemed particularly fond of one with a kitten.

"The inn takes a lot of work," Jared said.

"You know, if we get married, maybe someday we can run it. Your mom's not always going to want to. Wouldn't it be nice if we could take over?"

He tried to sound merely instructive. "It looks like more fun than it is. My mom works all the time, and she doesn't have a lot to show for it."

"I bet more people would come if *I* ran it. I'd paint it a different color, make it more modern, like a real motel. But we'd have to live somewhere else. I couldn't stay there with all those strangers coming through my house."

He tried not to picture the inn painted a perky pink or yellow. "Don't you want to travel? See what's out there before you decide where you want to settle?"

"I don't see why. Oh, I'd like to maybe go on a cruise or something for my honeymoon. But what could be better than where we live?" She snuggled against him as much as the bucket seats allowed. "It's not where you live, Jar-Jar, it's who you live with."

He glanced over at her and saw the sweet, familiar contours of her cheeks, the small, ripe mouth. She winked at him.

Jared felt his body respond again in an all too familiar way. But the sinking of his heart was becoming familiar, too.

Gayle was delighted with her new assistants. Paula and Cissy had hit it off immediately, and even though they wouldn't often be working the same shift, it was clear that when they did, harmony would reign. Both were learning quickly but also bringing their personal strengths to the job. Cissy was naturally warm and accommodating, and guests had already begun to sing her praises. Paula was a whiz at organization and had suggested an improvement for the way dirty linen was replaced that would save everybody time. Gayle's concerns about taking on the catering job had diminished.

Today was more or less a dry run for camp. She had promised

Travis that she would do the counselors' training lunch, and she was using it as a chance to experiment with menus. She'd prepared a few more dishes than she needed, but she planned to study the leftovers.

"Mom, there's enough food here for the first week of camp." Noah, who had been happy enough to take the job as her assistant, was less enthused after chopping and stirring all morning.

She had decided to serve do-it-yourself tacos and several different salads. Travis used this training day as an opportunity to instill enthusiasm in his counselors, as much as to teach them what they needed to know. A good meal would help with that, she knew.

"Wait and see. I'll bet there won't be that much to pack up and bring home." Gayle loaded a bowl filled with a cold rice salad into a box lined with towels to keep it safe.

Noah finished packing cutlery and plastic glasses into another box, added packages of napkins, then sealed it by folding the flaps over the contents.

"I think we're set," Gayle said. "The pickup's outside the door. Let's pack the back and go."

With a box resting against his chest, Noah stepped outside just as Eric, in jeans and a stretched-out T-shirt, came in from the opposite door.

"Need help carrying the stuff over?"

She debated. Eric had taken Dillon swimming that morning, and from what she could tell, the two had avoided each other ever since. Eric seemed at loose ends. Maybe a trip to the site would be exactly what he needed.

"We could use the help." She gestured to the box she'd just packed. "That one's all ready. You just have to put it in the back of the truck. Maybe you'd like to see what they'll be doing."

"Sounds good." He paused. "Dillon will be okay here alone? Or is he going?"

She had to applaud him for remembering their son still needed supervision. "Cissy can keep an ear out for him. I'll talk to her."

"I take it he knows to stay away from the river?"

She ignored a stab of annoyance. "That's always been the rule."

"I wish he could swim better."

"The lesson didn't go well, I take it."

Eric looked perplexed. She supposed when somebody was good at nearly everything, failing was particularly difficult. And after a lifetime of winning, these days Eric was facing failure on a number of levels.

"He flounders around like he's dying, and nothing I did made it any better. I don't have a clue what to say to him."

Gayle was surprised he was so willing to admit that. "Thirteen-year-old boys are notoriously difficult to talk to."

"Swimming seemed like a good way to get to know him. But maybe it's not. Maybe I'm not the right person to help."

She was surprised at how quickly her annoyance flared into anger. "Well don't you dare quit on him."

"Did I say I was going to?"

"History suggests you might."

He stared at her for a moment before the stare turned to a frown. "What next, Gayle? Maybe you should point out that I don't even *have* a history with Dillon, that I didn't want him, that for a while I even thought he might not be mine."

He was fanning the flames. She struggled for a breath to cool them. "Let's not get into that now—or ever again."

Eric raked his fingers through his hair. "Maybe it goes to the heart of the matter."

"The heart of this matter is that you have three sons, and whether we planned for the third or not, he needs you. Most of all he needs you to uphold your promises, the most recent of which is that you will teach him to swim whether it's difficult or not."

She looked up and saw Noah standing in the doorway. For a moment she froze. She and Eric hadn't been speaking loudly, but how much had he heard? And how much had he understood?

"Let's get going," Noah said after a pause that deepened Gayle's embarrassment. "The sooner we get there, the sooner we can come home."

She wasn't sure Noah was a good enough actor to ignore his parents' fighting, but despite his cheerful exterior, he was deeper than others first guessed. His art was proof of this, perceptive, exploratory, and occasionally distressing.

"Your father's going to come with us, so maybe the two of you can finish carrying everything out while I give Cissy some last-minute instructions." She turned and left before either male could reply. She didn't want to hear a thing they had to say.

Five minutes later they were on the way to the site. Noah was sandwiched between his parents on the bench seat and clearly not happy about it. Thankfully they arrived without more harsh words, and Gayle went to search for Travis.

She found him under the shade of several maples. The counselors had paired off around the site and seemed to be speaking earnestly to each other. She noted that Brandy and Jared were not working together and wondered who had engineered that. Jared had his back to her, but Brandy gave a quick wave. Gayle admired the way the girl looked in a skimpy tank top and tight jeans, even while she wondered what the sight of so much bare skin did to her oldest son.

She shook off the thought and instead turned her attention to

Travis. He wore a dark blue knit shirt and khaki shorts, and looked absolutely comfortable leaning against a tree doing nothing.

"What's up?" she asked.

His eyes lit up, and he smiled. "My food lady."

"From friend and neighbor to food lady. This may not be a promotion."

"I'm forever in your debt. The kids are role playing and doing a good job of it, but I'd have had a rebellion on my hands if I didn't feed them in the next fifteen minutes."

She felt the tension in her spine release a vertebrae at a time. Travis had that effect on her. "What kind of role playing?"

"One of them gets to be a whiny camper, and the other gets to practice active listening. I make them practice at home, too, and write down a couple of conversations where the technique worked. This is a good group. They all more or less have the hang of the basics. The whining in particular."

She laughed before she could think about it; then, unaccountably, tears filled her eyes. She looked away, but Travis reached out, spread his fingers along her jaw and turned her face to his. "Hey, what's this about?"

She shook her head, almost more embarrassed than she'd been when she saw Noah in the doorway.

"This summer is bound to be hard." He dropped his hand, but his eyes were sympathetic. "You bit off a lot."

"Sam says I'm trying to create the perfect divorce."

"Is he right?"

"If I couldn't create the perfect marriage, whatever made me think I'd be more adept at ending it?"

"I hope you've factored in the reality that you've tried to do both with the same man. And that he might share just a little in the blame?"

"Some things lodge in the brain but not in the gut." She looked away. "Do me a favor, would you? Will you give Eric a mini-tour of what you're going to be doing here while Noah and I set up the tables? I want to talk to him without Eric around. Just tell me where you want them."

Travis pointed to an area well to the west of the old homesite where she could set up without disturbing anything. Then she went to tell Eric that Travis would show him around.

She and Noah set up the tables. The counselors were still practicing, although they were looking longingly toward the food.

Gayle waited for Noah to speak first, and he didn't disappoint her. "You were fighting with Dad, weren't you?" he asked, as they began to pile up plates and salsas.

"It's to be expected." Gayle managed to sound calm. "But we're okay."

"Yeah, I know. You both love us. You both want what's best for us. Yada, yada…"

She wished he wasn't quite so good at mimicking her. "Sometimes clichés are true."

"Well, I wish he weren't here. Things were better when he wasn't."

Gayle didn't know what to say. Her first instinct was to reprimand him, but for what? Speaking the truth?

She found an answer. "Life doesn't often give us second chances. You've got one with your father now. I hope you'll take advantage of it."

"Yeah? Well, I hope *you're* not looking at this as a second chance."

She took his arm to stop him from going back to the pickup. "This summer isn't about your dad and me getting back together, Noah."

"You can say one thing, even mean it, and in the end, words don't have a thing to do with the truth."

"You need to forget this and work on getting to know your father better. Whatever passes between us is about us, not about you boys."

"Whatever was passing between you today was about Dillon."

When he didn't go on, she guessed he hadn't heard the particulars. "Your dad's got a way to go before he connects with Dillon or you. But that doesn't mean he and I aren't going to have occasional disagreements about what's best. We're still your parents. Married or not, it's natural to disagree."

"Oh, come on, none of this is natural."

"Look at your friends, Noah. You know how many of them are from families like ours. And I'm afraid any kind of family life is occasionally messy and uncomfortable. Unfortunately, sometimes that's what it takes to make things come out right."

"Well, it doesn't matter, because we aren't a family anymore."

"Yes, we are." Gayle set him free. "Maybe not the kind we started out to be, but for better or worse, we're connected forever. We can't ignore it. And in lots of ways, your dad and I still care about each other."

"Yeah. Just do me a favor, okay? Don't care too much. This is just one summer to him. And we do fine without him."

Gayle watched as Noah stomped back to the pickup to get the final supplies. How well *had* they done? Whether he would admit it or not, each boy had missed having Eric in his life in a different way.

Had she missed him, too? Was that what Noah was sensing? She thought she'd gotten over Eric early in the divorce, that she'd been relieved to put her life on a different track. Now she thought about what Sam had said and wondered just how lonely she *had* been all these years. The only thing she knew for sure was that at this moment she felt as if she were the only person left standing on the earth's surface.

Eric had a hot temper, which over the years he had learned to control. Anger for him was quick and clean, a shooting star blazing a fiery trail, then disappearing—at least to the naked eye. People who didn't know him well sometimes missed the signs of it entirely.

Today was different. By the time lunch was finished, he was still angry, and Gayle seemed to know it. She'd stayed away from him since arriving at the site, spending her time talking to the counselors about food or chatting with Travis Allen, who seemed to be something more than a casual acquaintance.

He wondered if there was a romance there. If so, they were keeping it a secret. They didn't touch, didn't find excuses to brush past each other or engage in intimate whispered conversations.

And why did it matter, anyway?

"Mom said to ask if you'd help me pack up."

Eric pulled his attention back to his surroundings. Noah was planted in front of him, his stance cocksure and borderline threatening.

"No problem." Eric assessed his son. He suspected Noah wasn't finished growing. He was going to be shorter than his brothers, but probably not by much. He was bigger-boned, perhaps not as classically good-looking. But Noah had a presence Eric associated with other socially adept creative people, and Eric had known many.

At first glance Noah was approachable, warm, a good listener. Then, after a while, it became obvious that this boy, like other artists, writers and musicians before him, was sucking the marrow out of every moment. He listened because he was fascinated by life, because after each word he was putting his universe into a different order, because he was learning something that, someday, he would give back to the world in a distinctive and brighter form.

"When you're done staring at me, we should get moving." Noah sounded polite enough, but it was a taunt all the same.

"Sorry about that. I like trying to figure out who you are."

The honesty threw Noah. He looked less assured. "Instant analysis, huh? Is that how it works when you don't have much to go on?"

Eric was determined to ignore the insults. "So what do we do about cleanup? More or less what we did before, only backwards?"

Noah turned away. "Yeah, more or less."

"Let's get on with it, then."

The counselors had brought all their dishes to the closest picnic table, and Noah and Eric worked in silence to pile them in the same crates and boxes they'd carried them over in. Noah worked with efficiency. Eric guessed his son hated repetitive work, just as he himself certainly did. But Noah could perform mindless chores like this one quickly and correctly, so that he wouldn't waste a moment he didn't have to.

"I can see why your mother asked you to be her assistant." Eric heaved a box of plasticware into the back of the pickup. "You don't fool around."

"I'd rather be a counselor. Galley slave's no fun."

"I've noticed you're your mom's right-hand man at the inn, too." He'd meant it as a compliment, but Noah arched a brow, and his eyes were angry.

"Yeah? Well, somebody needs to be."

Eric thought about his answer carefully. In the end, though, he simply said what he thought.

"You don't like me very much, do you, son?"

"I don't know. I don't spend a lot of time thinking about you."

"We've had some good times together. I'm just curious. What about the vacations we took? The World Series tickets? Those scuba-diving lessons last summer?"

"*Two* summers ago. That was the last time we spent more than a day with you. And by *we,* I mean me and Jared. Dillon wasn't even invited."

"Dillon was too young for the scuba program. And considering that he doesn't swim—"

Noah stopped collecting plates and interrupted his father. "Wow, what a classic example. You chose something he couldn't do. Do you think there's a message there? We do stuff together that *you* want to do, Dad. That's the way it always is. If you want to scuba dive and we happen to have a vacation then, fine, you invite Jared and me to come."

"Noah, I thought and thought about what to do with you and Jared. I asked my friends for advice. And no, I didn't think about Dillon, because I figured I'd have plenty of time with him once you two were off on your own."

"Plenty of time?" Noah gave a bitter laugh. "That's funny. You don't have the time of day for Dillon and never have. And you're talking about plenty of time? When have you spent plenty of time with any of your sons? Even the one you like best?"

"I don't like any of you best!"

Noah just stared at him, his head slightly cocked, his eyes disbelieving.

"What should I have done?" Eric asked when he could speak without saying something he would never be able to take back.

"You could have asked us for ideas, instead of your friends. You could have included our brother."

"Maybe I made mistakes, but I spent a lot of time and money trying to entertain you."

"It doesn't matter how much money you spend. Entertainment is cheap. Like the commercial says? Taking us to the doctor, talking to our teachers, asking us how our day is when we come home from school? Priceless."

Eric heard an adult voice reciting the list, not a teenager's, and suddenly he suspected whose. "How much of that did your mother think of first?"

"What do you mean?"

"I mean, how much of your anger is fueled by her complaints about me?"

Noah took a step toward him, a menacing, angry step. "Don't you dare blame this on Mom. She *never* says anything bad about you. She pretends everything's lovey-dovey, and when you finally remember you ought to spend time with us, she's the one who gets most excited. You didn't deserve her when you were married to her, and you don't deserve what she's doing for you now."

Eric let that wash over him, because he knew if he dove in, he would lose this son forever. As angry as he was, he knew there was truth in too much of what Noah had said. He *had* been an absent and absentminded father. He *had* depended on Gayle's superior parenting skills and her desire to raise their sons. Worst of all, he had hoped that by trading a little time, a lot of spontaneous gifts and some exciting vacations, he would still be loved and respected. The way a father should be.

He also remembered what Gayle had told him about Noah. Noah was pushing him away. Noah was frightened to love him, because it was too easy for Eric to disappear forever.

As he almost had.

The fight went out of him; the anger drained. He felt more tired and more discouraged.

He shook his head slowly. "What can I do to make it up to you?"

Noah's eyes opened wider. For a moment he looked surprised and perhaps a little confused. Eric thought he even looked as if he wished he could think of a suggestion, an easy answer to make things right.

Then, like his father, he shook his head. "It's too late."

From the corner of his eye, Eric saw Gayle heading toward them. He reached for the box that Noah had filled and clutched it against his chest.

"We're not done here," he told his son. "But we both have things we should think about before we talk again."

Noah shrugged. Eric thought that, as responses went, it wasn't the worst he could have gotten.

Chapter 12

On Friday morning, Eric gunned the engine of his rental Mustang and started down an unfamiliar road. Dillon had spent the past ten minutes insisting there was no point to this trip.

"I can swim well enough. I won't drown." His argument finally lost steam, and he fell silent.

Eric concentrated on the road ahead of him and didn't answer. He was grateful that, for a change, the only thing he had to listen to was the purring of the rental's engine. He was pretty certain he'd taken a wrong turn somewhere along the way. They were climbing into foreign territory, and nobody had told him the house he was looking for was up in the mountains.

"You're not listening to me!" Dillon said.

"Right."

"So what's new?"

Eric hazarded a quick glance. Dillon's eyes were narrowed, his arms crossed over his chest. He looked as if he were plotting a murder. Eric flicked his gaze back to the road, and his hands clamped around the steering wheel. If they didn't see the turn-off soon, he was going to have to find a spot to turn around. If they had missed the right road, he didn't want to find out at the top of the mountain.

He slowed, keeping his eyes open for a place to turn around in the distance. "If we're on the right road, we'll be there soon."

"I don't even know where we're going. What's going on? Why aren't we going to the swimming hole?"

"Wait and see."

"This is dumb. You can't teach me to swim any better than I already do. Nobody can."

Eric noted a sign up ahead and slowed even more. The sign pointed to a private road and a community of houses off to the left. It was the only deterrent to sightseers. There were no gates here. With relief, he took the turn and started looking for landmarks. They passed log cabins, and expansive post-and-beam houses with windows looking out over the valley below. He almost missed the driveway and had to back up to see the sign with the owners' name.

"Well, finally." The one-lane driveway snaked out of sight, but Eric wasn't worried about meeting anyone. The owner, the former station manager who had given him his start in broadcasting, was in France for the summer. He had been delighted to let Eric and Dillon use the pool at his country place while he was away.

"What are we doing here?" Dillon's voice bounced in rhythm to the gravel under the Mustang's tires.

Eric waited until they reached their destination. "This house belongs to a friend of mine. The swimming hole's too deep and too public to make this any fun. We can relax in his pool and take our time."

"You mean splash around in the shallow end like a little baby!"

Eric turned off the engine. "Dillon, splashing around in the water isn't acting like a baby. Whining and complaining before we even get wet? That's pretty darned close."

"I feel stupid."

Eric felt a stab of sympathy. "Yeah, I'm sure you do."

"I don't want to do this."

"I know that, too. But this is important."

"Just because you told Mom—"

"This has nothing to do with your mom," Eric said a little too sharply. "Believe it or not, I have a mind of my own. And I don't want you falling in the river by accident someday and drowning. When I leave next month, I want to know you're safe. Or I'll have nightmares every single night."

"What's one more or less?"

That struck Eric funny. He laughed; then, before he knew it, he reached over and ruffled his son's hair. "Come on, champ. Won't you just give it a try?"

Dillon looked sullen, but he opened his door, and, outside, he followed Eric into the house and out through the back to a pool bordered by slate tile, and landscaped with azaleas and forsythia. Farther from the water, dogwood trees and Japanese magnolias spread their delicate branches for shade.

The house itself was small but impressive, with an open floor plan, shining wood floors and windows that took advantage of the views. But the pool and the surrounding patio and yard were extraordinary. They had climbed high enough that some of the sharp bends in the river were visible from here.

"You mean somebody owns this but doesn't live here?" Dillon sounded as if he couldn't believe such a thing.

"Someday we'll do some real traveling together, Dill, and I'll show you places where the gatehouses are bigger than this entire property."

Dillon smiled almost shyly. "It's not fair, you know. People shouldn't have a place like this if they don't use it."

"If it makes you feel better, the man who owns it is usually here a lot. And he's happy that we want to use it this summer."

Dillon's smile faltered. "What do you mean, 'this summer'?"

"I mean until you're swimming like a fish."

"Not going to happen."

"First you have to believe in yourself. You're a strong kid. There's nothing wrong with your coordination."

"You just don't understand!"

Eric considered that. Until they got past this particular hurdle, his new plan for teaching Dillon to swim wasn't going anywhere. Dillon needed to know Eric understood his fears. And Eric knew how to make that point.

Only he really didn't want to.

"Why are we just standing here?" Dillon said after a while. "Are you thinking about going home?" He sounded hopeful.

"No, but I want you to take a walk with me. I saw a trail a ways back. Let's take a hike. I want to show you something."

"This is weird. I just want to go home and forget the whole thing."

"Yeah, me too. Come on anyway."

Dillon was silent as they retraced their steps. Eric left the car where he'd parked it and started walking down the driveway. At the road, he turned back the way they'd come, and Dillon trailed along behind him.

"You want me to get tired or something?" Dillon said at last. "So I'll be too tired to fight the water and just drown?"

Eric managed a smile. "What, when I hold you under?"

"That's not funny!"

Eric stopped and pointed. "I noticed this when I was looking for the house. Looks like the community built a trail up the mountainside. We're going up."

"You know, I live around here. I hike a lot."

"I don't."

Dillon grumbled under his breath, but he started after Eric, and when Eric turned up the overgrown path, Dillon was close on his heels.

Eric forced himself to put one foot in front of the other. He was thirty yards up the steep path when vertigo finally claimed him. He shut his eyes, but even though he was standing perfectly still and knew it, some part of him was certain he was falling through space.

"Why'd you stop?" Dillon demanded.

Eric couldn't answer. He lowered himself to the path and collapsed against a tree, opening his eyes again once he was sure he was stable. He resisted the urge to cling to the trunk, but just barely. He put his head in his hands as a whirlwind roared through it.

"Dad!" Dillon sat down and tapped him on the shoulder. "What's wrong? Are you okay? This was too much, wasn't it? Why'd you want to climb right up the side of a mountain, anyway?"

Eric flung his arm out, wrist up. "Take my pulse."

"What?"

"Just do it."

Dillon put his thumb against the pulse point on Eric's wrist and pressed.

"Wow! Are you dying?"

"What do you feel?"

"It's like one big heartbeat. Can somebody's heart beat that fast?"

"You've got proof."

"Well, how come?"

"Because I'm scared sh—" He caught himself. "Scared silly."

"Of what?"

"Of being up here."

Dillon dropped his father's wrist, but his hand crept to Eric's shoulder. "How come?"

Eric took a slow, deep breath. Then another. He was sitting. He was not falling through space. If he needed to, he could slide back down to the road. Even if he fell, he wasn't going to die here. He was safe.

"You know what happened in Afghanistan, right?"

"I read everything I could find on the Internet. More than Mom told us."

He made a mental note to tell Gayle that this was the twenty-first century and parents couldn't pad or alter the truth to spare their technology-savvy children. He felt a moment of regret that the news business was part of that change.

"So what's up?" Dillon prodded.

"I spent almost twenty-four hours on that ledge, Dill. And even though I was never afraid of heights before, now they terrify me."

"Oh." Dillon was silent for a while. "Well, that makes sense."

"I thought you'd get it."

"That's why you were mad when I was up on the roof."

"Uh-huh."

"I wish you'd told me then."

"You're embarrassed you can't swim very well. I'm embarrassed by this."

"I don't know why I'm afraid of water. At least you have a reason."

Eric was encouraged that Dillon was finally talking about being afraid. He was just sorry he'd had to climb up here to start that conversation.

"You don't remember falling in or getting dunked against your will?"

"Mom says once we were at a picnic when I was really little, and somebody swam out too far in the lake and almost drowned. That might be it."

"We don't always know what causes a fear. I'm not sure it matters. But you're not alone. I just wanted you to understand. I know what it's like to be terrified, too. So that makes me the perfect person to teach you to swim. Because I won't push too hard, and I won't scare you even more. I know better."

Dillon considered. "Well, maybe. Only there's one thing."

"What would that be?"

"We have to get down to the road first. And I'm not sure you're going to make it."

"I'll make you a deal. I'll get down, by hook or by crook or on my butt if I have to. But only if you'll promise to give the swimming lessons a try. Otherwise I might just stay here until I'm ninety."

"What if I don't get better?"

"I've been reading about this the last couple of days and talking to people on the phone. We'll take it really easy. First we're going to work on making you comfortable. You already know the strokes. So we're not going to teach you to swim, we're going to teach you to love the water."

"I'd like to see you go down the hill on your butt. That would be cool."

Eric laughed. He put his arm around his son's shoulder and pulled him close for a moment. "Just don't take any pictures, okay?"

By late afternoon Gayle was beginning to wonder if she'd taken on too much. With the first campfire just an hour away, she still had to pack up the food she had prepared and finish the pasta salad, fruit platters and dip. She'd bought as many things ready-made as she could, but there was still a lot of work to do.

"How's the fruit coming?" she asked Noah.

"I never want to see another cantaloupe."

"I've felt that way." She peeked over her son's shoulder and saw he still had three to slice. "I'll do the dip if you don't think you'll have time."

"I'll get to it."

"Can we safely say you won't be going into the restaurant biz?"

"I'll paint murals and design their space. But I'm not touching the food."

Gayle heard footsteps approaching the kitchen. The door swung open and Dillon appeared. "Ta-da!"

"Hey, honey, back from your swimming lesson?" Gayle was surprised to see a smile on her son's face. This wasn't his usual reaction.

"Guess what we got!"

She didn't have time to answer before Eric poked his head inside the kitchen. "Is Noah here?"

"He is." Gayle glanced at her son, who was studiously ignoring the hubbub and continuing his cantaloupe dissection.

"I'm not sure I ought to bring this into the kitchen."

Gayle dried her hands on a dish towel and started toward the door. "What?"

"Noah?" Eric called.

Noah finally looked up. "What?"

"Come out here a minute, would you?"

By then Gayle had seen the prize. She looked at Eric in question, but he gave a quick shake of his head.

She glanced over her shoulder at her son, hoping he was on his way. She wasn't disappointed. Noah didn't look happy, but she guessed even interacting with Eric for a moment was better than slicing melons.

"What is it?" He didn't sound pleased.

Eric nudged the door wider with his shoulder, and Noah saw what he was holding in his left hand.

"What's that?"

"This is Buddy."

"Why do you have a parakeet in a cage?"

"Long story, but somebody was about to set him loose."

"What?" Noah looked incensed. "He wouldn't last an hour with the wild birds."

"We stopped at a garage sale on the way back. Seems this guy belonged to the woman's boyfriend, who took off a month ago and hasn't been seen since. She doesn't want it, and nobody else seemed to, either. She said she was just going to let him go. So Dillon and I bought him for you."

"Me? Why me?"

"Dillon says you need a pet."

"I don't." But Noah was getting closer to the parakeet and peering in the cage. "Was she mistreating him?"

"I doubt it. The cage is clean, and he had plenty of food and water. She hung him in the shade at the sale."

"But she was going to let him go."

"I think she knew a couple of suckers when she saw them. She just gave us an extra nudge."

"Still…" Noah stuck his finger into the cage and wiggled it. The little blue parakeet ran back and forth on his perch, as if considering whether to play that game or not. He chattered wildly.

"I didn't want to take a chance," Eric said. "Do you think you could give him a trial? If you decide you're not interested, we can advertise or see if any of the teachers at the elementary school would like to keep him in their classroom next year."

Noah looked up. "You've given this a lot of thought, considering you practically just picked him up on the side of the road."

"I think fast on my feet."

Noah smiled. Gayle thought it might be the first time he'd really smiled at his father in her presence. "Buddy?"

"You could change his name."

"No, that's okay. Does he talk?"

Dillon answered. "She said he does."

"Maybe he knows his name." Noah made a chirping sound. "Buddy. Buddy."

The little parakeet ran back and forth excitedly.

Noah straightened. "I guess I could try him out."

Gayle caught Eric's eye. He looked as if he'd just scooped CBS.

"Why don't you take him over to your room and settle him in?" Eric said. "She gave us what food she had. Maybe tomorrow you and I can go into town and load up on whatever you think you'll need."

Noah stepped back. "I'm not done here. I've still got stuff to do for Mom."

"I'll take over for you," Eric said. "Gayle, is that okay?"

Gayle imagined her ex slicing cantaloupe and making the yogurt dip to go with the fruit. "You can give it a try. Go on, Noah. Settle Buddy in your room."

The two boys took off together, carrying the cage as if it held precious cargo.

"Wow," she said when she and Eric were alone in the kitchen. "What a coup. You're sure you didn't hop on the interstate and find a pet store when you and Dillon were supposed to be swimming?"

"Nope, it happened just the way I said."

"I bet that was your very first garage sale."

"Me? I got used to open-air bargaining in the Mideast. I could have gotten a real deal if she'd tried to sell me a rug."

She had to laugh. "Feel like cutting cantaloupe?"

Eric washed his hands at the sink, then dove right into the job. She gave one quick glance; then, satisfied that he was following Noah's example, she took the dressing for the pasta salad from the refrigerator and started assembling the rest of the ingredients.

"Am I imagining this, or did Dillon look happy? Was that from finding Buddy or something else?"

"No, the lesson went okay. The pool was perfect. Nice and shallow. We just relaxed in the water. He practiced blowing bubbles."

"He actually let you teach him something that elementary?"

"Trust me, it wasn't easy. But we made a little progress." He paused. "And we had fun."

She was glad to hear it. She was also aware that she'd felt an unexpected pang of jealousy at the words.

"The boys need me to help them be men," he said. "I dropped that ball."

"They've had men in their life." She thought of Travis, who had served as confidant and role model.

"That's great, but a father is unique."

"What about yours?"

He pulled the trash can closer and dumped handfuls of cantaloupe rind into it. "I'd like to be closer. But I didn't live up to his expectations. I don't want my own sons to feel that way."

This time she thought her feelings were entirely appropriate. He looked up and caught her eye. She stepped over and gave him a quick hug. "This is going to take some getting used to, I guess. But you're on the right track."

When she tried to return to the counter, he held her back. "Getting used to? Because you don't believe I'm really trying to change?"

"No, because I'm used to being the *real* parent, and sharing means giving that up."

He searched her eyes. They were standing close, and she was all too aware of it. There were boundaries they needed to observe, places they really shouldn't go. She realized they were teetering too close to one right now.

"I left you with too much to deal with," Eric said. "I asked you to make the boys your whole life, to fill in for my absence. It wasn't fair, and now, after all that, I'm changing the rules."

"No, it's a good change. It might take some getting used to, but I want you to be closer to them."

He dropped his hand. "That means I might be around more often. You're okay with that?"

She really didn't know. But she nodded anyway, as if she were completely composed. As if some part of her wasn't wondering what it would be like to take two pieces of a family and rejoin them after a dozen years had passed.

As if she wasn't wondering if she could fall back in love with a new, changed Eric, this time once and for all.

"I want what's best for our sons," she said.

He smiled, not the way he did on camera, but the way he had always smiled when they were alone together.

"So do I," he said. "Let's work on that."

Chapter 13

Jared got dressed quickly. Brandy took longer. She was proud of her body and not at all modest. She walked from her bedroom into the connecting bathroom as if she had no idea he would find that disconcerting. He heard the shower go on and off; then she came back in as he was fastening his belt. Turning her nearly naked back to him, she made it clear that she wanted him to fasten her wisp of a bra. He found the clasp no easier under these circumstances than he had when he'd tried to unfasten it on their third date.

Brandy pulled her hair to the top of her head with one hand to make his job easier. "Do you like my room?"

Jared hadn't paid the slightest attention. Now he gave the smallish bedroom a cursory glance. Lavender walls, frilly white curtains, stuffed animals. "Uh-huh. Nice."

"I'll probably do something different with it now. More in line with the den-of-iniquity theme."

He had to smile. Brandy often surprised him. At times like this, he thought she was probably smarter than she let on.

She turned and put her arms around his neck. "I love you, Jar-Jar. You're the best."

He kissed her. "Love you, too."

"We'll see."

"What does that mean?"

"Well, absence makes the heart grow fonder…for somebody else."

"We can't predict the future. Let's just enjoy the summer, okay?"

"I *am* enjoying it." She smiled, then bit her lip.

"What is it?"

"Nothing important. Just, well, I didn't think we'd be doing this today. I thought…"

"What?"

"Well, like I'd have my period by now."

His heart turned to ice. Maybe he was anything but a man about town, but he knew what this meant. "You're late?"

She manufactured a pretty pout. "Don't get all bothered about it. I'm late a lot."

"We've been using condoms."

"Yeah, but the ones we used that first time were, like, old. Lisa gave them to me, and I think maybe they were some Cray got from somebody. I threw them away and got some new ones last week, just in case."

He put his hands on her shoulders and stepped back. "Now you're telling me?"

"I didn't know! Not until I told her I was late."

Jared could have kicked himself for letting Brandy take care of that part of things. He'd had the sex-education classes, read the books. Of course the condoms had been wrapped, but apparently not new, as in "right off the shelf."

She let her hair fall down her back again. "I'm not pregnant.

I'm not feeling sick or anything. This just happens sometimes. But if I was, would it be a big deal?"

"Big deal? What do you think? You're still in high school!"

"I'm not going to worry, because I'm *not* pregnant. But you know, my parents would go insane if it happened. They have no idea who I am. I'm their pretty little girl. They think I do whatever they tell me. It would really shake them up."

He tried to figure out if that would please her. She seemed to have no real opinion about it. She just seemed to find it interesting.

"This really happens sometimes?" he asked, hoping for reassurance.

"It really, really does. I shouldn't have said anything."

"You'll tell me the minute you get your period?"

"Oh yeah, you'll be able to tell. I'll eat you alive."

He relaxed a little as she slipped into tight jeans and a long-sleeved T-shirt. By the time she was selecting which sneakers to wear, he had nearly recovered.

Brandy was quiet most of the way to the campsite. He knew she was looking forward to being a counselor. The previous summer she'd flipped burgers during the day and babysat in the evenings. For her, babysitting had clearly been by far the better job.

Jared wasn't as thrilled as she was. He liked kids okay, but he wished a more exciting job had been available. He had applied to Outward Bound, where he would have had the chance to really challenge himself, but after he'd learned his father would be spending the summer in Toms Brook, he had withdrawn the application.

They parked where a line of cars were already gathered and got out. Since they were a little late, a bunch of the middle schoolers had already arrived and received their name tags. Brandy found hers, pinned it on her shirt and went to look for the campers wearing the drawing of a pottery vase like the one on her name tag. Jared's sported an arrowhead, but he wasn't as eager to find his campers. He would be stuck with them long enough.

He found Cray with some of the other counselors who, like him, seemed to be gathering either strength or courage to start their jobs.

Cray pulled him off to one side. "Hey, listen, has Brandy talked to you about…" He didn't seem to know where to go with the conversation.

"You mean that she's late?"

Cray looked relieved that Jared knew. "It's probably not anything."

"How old *were* those condoms?"

"I didn't know Lisa was going to start passing them around. This isn't my fault."

"How old?"

"I kind of borrowed them from my uncle. He doesn't know, and I'm not about to ask. They were in his bathroom." Cray paused. "But he, like, hasn't had a girlfriend for a while. Not that I know about, anyway."

"That was really stupid, man."

"You're telling me. Lisa pregnant isn't something I want to see." He noted Jared's glare and quickly added, "Or Brandy. I just figured, you know, if they were still in the package they were okay."

And they probably had been. Jared figured the odds were in his favor. But even good odds came with a flip side. One chance in a hundred was still a chance. It had to happen to somebody.

"You've got the arrowhead kids? I've got the bottles." Cray held out his name tag, which had a drawing of an old amber medicine bottle. "We're supposed to go find them. I'm going to knock a few heads together right at the start to let them know who's boss."

Jared knew Cray was just talking, probably to change the subject. He looked beyond his friend and saw that Brandy had already gathered her flock of five campers and had them sitting on the ground playing some kind of get-acquainted game. Since gathering middle schoolers into a cohesive group was like rounding up grasshoppers, Jared figured she had already worked a miracle.

Cray turned to see what he was looking at. "Brandy told Lisa all she really wants to do is be the best mom in the world to a herd of kids."

Jared's heart sank. "Let's just hope she's not getting an early start."

Cray clapped him on the shoulder.

Gayle was gratified that her side dishes were wolfed down by everyone from students to adults. For the main course they roasted hot dogs on sticks, and then they finished up with flaming marshmallows and s'mores. The students sat quietly enough while Travis explained a little about what they would be doing and what they could expect during the two-week stretch. He handed out lists of what to bring during the second week, when they would be camping on his property, and what they would need to bring each day until then. They got tentative schedules, a list of interesting sites on the Internet and a field manual.

The sun was almost down and the air was redolent with citronella from candles in metal buckets around the perimeter and bug spray on bare skin. Bats flapped and soared overhead, and bullfrogs bellowed a welcome.

"He's good."

Gayle realized Eric had joined her at the edge of the campfire.

She had already packed the car and was ready for the return journey, but Travis had asked her to stay for the next part.

"He is, isn't he?" As always, she was impressed with the way Travis treated teenagers. He specialized in a mixture of respect, humor and high expectations, which was coupled with a dose of reality. He knew how to make them listen. Of course, it helped that there was an equal mixture of girls and boys, and the girls seemed inclined to follow orders, which at least at this point was keeping the boys in line.

"He asked me to stay, too," Eric said. "Do you know what's up?"

"I know Dillon and Caleb have been working with Travis on something. I bet it has to do with that."

"I bet you're right. Dillon wanted to know if I was planning to stay, too."

"If nothing else, he's learning a little self-control. A year ago he couldn't have kept a secret to save his life."

"He showed me a videotape of that play he won the prize for. He was good. He's a natural ham."

"I wonder where he gets it?"

He laughed.

Gayle advanced a theory. "I think the world he inhabits when he's acting is less confusing than this one, and the characters' personalities and motives are laid right out for him. It's easier than trying to figure out who he is."

"If that's how he gets through adolescence, more power to him."

The kids had been sitting on logs around the fire while Travis spoke to them. Now Gayle saw that they were all getting up and moving to another area, where more logs had been set up in a semicircle looking toward the site of the old house. Gayle had assumed Travis would be using this as a teaching area.

"Let's see what they're up to." She started across the newly mown grass, and Eric joined her. They took seats toward the back. The kids had broken up into groups with their counselors and were sitting together in front of them. There was the requisite amount of shoving, giggling, primping, and offering of gum and breath mints while they waited. It was darker now, and even though she scanned the backs of heads, she couldn't locate Dillon, although she saw Jared's baseball cap, and Brandy's dark hair twisted and pinned on top of her head.

Travis stepped up to the front, and the kids quieted again. "Archaeology is only one way to find out about our past. What are some of the other ways?"

Gayle listened as different students called out answers. Books. Science. The Bible. The list grew longer.

Travis encouraged them, and every answer received appropriate respect. Finally, when the students had finished, he elaborated.

"How many of you have older relatives who have told you stories about people in your family who died before you had a chance to meet them?"

Hands went up slowly. Gayle guessed that half the students had theirs in the air by the end.

"If somebody had asked that question when we were their age, more hands would have been up," Eric said, so only Gayle would hear. "And our parents' generation? I bet every one would have gone up. Before computers and television and air-conditioning kept us all indoors and away from each other."

Travis said as much to the students. Then he went on. "I'm glad a lot of you have had that experience. Listening to stories of people who lived during years we didn't is one way to gather information, isn't it?"

"Yeah, but is it always true?" one of the boys asked. Gayle thought his name was Frank, but she wasn't certain.

"That's a very good question. In fact, it's a great question. How many of you have been told a story that you know *wasn't* true? By somebody who swore it was?"

This time, after a few moments, every hand was waving. One kid yelled, "My dad still swears there's a Santa Claus!"

"Okay then," Travis said when they stopped laughing. "So you've seen it yourselves." He waited as the kids nodded. "That's why science is important, because we have stories, but we also have ways, although they can be limited, to prove whether the stories are true or not. Right?"

The kids were nodding again.

"Well, there's a story that goes with the house that used to sit right over there." Travis turned and gestured. "There are a lot of stories, as a matter of fact, but this one occurred just after the Civil War. Or I ought to say just after Lee surrendered at Appomattox and after Lincoln was assassinated at Ford's Theater in Washington, D.C. Do any of you know the year?"

Gayle listened as the kids guessed. Eric leaned toward her as the answers flew thick and fast and, except for one boy's, wrong.

Travis continued. "I knew somebody would get it right if we just kept at it long enough. 1865 is correct. I don't think you need to memorize the date of every important thing that ever happened, but you do need some. Think of them as signposts through history. If you know the really important dates, you'll be able to figure out a lot of the others, just using common sense. I'll make sure you know them if you take my history classes in high school."

"Is it a true story?" one of the boys asked. "The story about that house?"

"I don't know," Travis said. "I got it from a couple of different sources. It's been passed down through a local family and some of their friends. But do I have proof? Not yet. I'm hoping we might find some on our dig, so we need to know about it as we work. But will it be easy?"

"Like looking for a needle in a haystack," Eric told Gayle.

Travis told the kids the same thing in different words. "But here's the thing," he added. "If we didn't know the story, we might see all the evidence and not know how to fit it together. So the story's a starting point."

"So what's the story?" a girl asked. "So we'll know."

"I had some help with that," Travis said. "I asked a friend of mine to take everything I've learned myself and write a play about it. You'll meet her when you get to the high school. Carin Webster—that's Miss Webster to you. She worked on it for several weeks with some of our campers. Tonight you get to hear the prologue. Then, as camp goes on, you'll get to hear the rest of it."

Gayle could tell the kids were interested. There was whispering, as if they were trying to guess which campers had been involved in the play. But Gayle was satisfied she knew the answer.

"So that's what Dillon and Caleb have been doing," she told Eric. "No wonder Dillon's been so excited."

"Who's this Miss Webster?"

"I haven't met her. I guess none of our kids have had her."

Travis stepped forward. "Ladies and gentlemen, I give you Dillon Fortman and Caleb Mowrey, who will take you back in time to this very place where you're sitting. It's 1865, and Sheridan and his troops have already stormed through the Shenandoah Valley to burn whatever they can. I told you about Lee and Lincoln. Now it's time to let Dillon and Caleb tell you the rest."

Travis turned and began to clap. The kids took it up. And on cue, the two boys came to stand in front, one from each side. Gayle saw they had changed their clothes. Dillon wore a collarless shirt tucked into loose jeans and covered by a vest, along with boots and a dark felt hat with a brim. Caleb was dressed similarly, although he wore a straw hat and no shoes.

Dillon took out a notebook and opened it, holding it in front of him like a tenor in the church choir. He looked confident and, if anything else, excited. Caleb looked less assured, but he folded his hands over an identical notebook and waited.

Dillon looked out at his audience, waiting for the buzz of excitement to die down. At the exact moment when it did, he began.

"My name is Robby Duncan. I don't know why I'm trying to put everything that happened this past spring on paper. I don't think anybody who finds this will believe what I'm about to say. I don't even know whether _I_ should believe it or not, so why should you? I just know that what my ma and I have been through these past weeks is worth this paper and ink and the time it will take me to tell my story. I guess you'll have to decide for yourselves if the time you spend listening is worth it to you."

Caleb opened his notebook and stepped forward. "I was born fourteen years ago, during better times, when the farm where you're sitting was a place my family could be proud of. My father, Lewis, had two wives. The first, Nellie, died soon after they married. I don't think Pa wanted to go through that again, because he waited ten years before he married for the last time. His second wife, Miranda, is my mother. I am my father and mother's only child. So I have no choice. It's left to me to tell their story."

Gayle looked down at the students and realized they had grown still as the two boys took turns narrating Robby Duncan's story. She hadn't realized that Travis had come around to the back until he joined her on the other end of the log.

She grabbed his hand and squeezed it. "Thank you," she whispered.

"My pleasure," he said, and squeezed back.

Then she gave herself up to the joy of watching Dillon and Caleb entertain their fellow campers.

Chapter 14

1865

I was a fat baby. Aunt Cora, who lives with her husband Ebenezer and his brother Ralph in a cabin close to the river's edge, once told me that I was *so* big, I like to have killed my mother getting born.

Aunt Cora has a way of putting things that leaves no doubts. "You was so fat, your skin folded up like some old pumpkin left in the field too long to make a pie. I could take a whole handful of it..." She extended her fingers like claws, and milked the air in front of me. "And you never even knowed you'd been pinched!"

When she said this, she nodded with almost every word, the loose skin under her chin flapping in demonstration. Cora isn't really my aunt. She and Uncle Eb have worked for my father's family since long before my parents were married. Now she's an old woman, or at least she seems old to me. If the truth were told, since the war began, nobody looks young anymore. When I glimpse my own narrow face in the still waters of the stock pond, my arms as thin as cornstalks poking out of shirts Aunt Cora patches for me, I glimpse the old man I will be someday.

I'm not fat anymore, but I remained round-faced and doughy almost until the day my father mounted the roan gelding he raised from a colt and rode off to join the Muhlenberg Rifles of the Tenth Virginia Infantry. I wasn't yet eleven, and despite feeling frightened, I stood at my mother's side, the Virginia sun prickling my scalp. I remember the way the air smelled, the way the dust from the gelding's hooves became a fine, punishing grit I couldn't scrub away for weeks. The way my mother's mouth tightened into a long hard line, as straight as the blade of an ax.

My father packed his own supplies, but at that last moment Ma fingered the quilt he had chosen to bring with him. She told him the pattern was called Devil's Puzzle, and she thought his choice of it appropriate. This terrible war belonged to the devil, and it remained a puzzle to her that any good man would choose to fight in it.

She would not kiss my father goodbye. He was already dead to her, she said. She would not kiss a corpse.

I tried not to cry. I knew better than to cheer. I remember tears and pride being locked inside me, fighting a battle that ended in defeat for both. When the dust settled and hoofbeats were overshadowed by the squawking of one of Pa's prize roosters, I remember Ma telling Uncle Eb to find the bird and wring his neck. We would have chicken and dumplings for supper while we still could. We did, too, but nobody was hungry.

Not long after that we were hungry almost all the time.

They say now that Lee has surrendered and the war is over, even though some soldiers are still fighting. I wonder if saying this makes it true? When I was younger, I searched for a way to make the war end. I prayed, but nothing came of it. I wished on stars and on the first toad I saw in the spring until the day we learned my father had died trying to take Culp's Hill at Gettysburg. Then I stopped wishing and praying, because if those things hadn't saved my father, why would they save anybody else?

They sure didn't save Abraham Lincoln. A lot of Unionists have been praying for their president since the war began. But early in April somebody killed him anyway. When it happened, the only thing I could think of was that maybe the man who pulled that trigger was like me. He'd stopped knowing what was real and what wasn't, what to believe and what to do. And whether anything he did would make a difference anyway.

Aunt Cora says that when men are intent on killing each other, the Lord above has to look away to keep from striking all of them dead. I think this time he didn't look away. Because even the men who are still living, the men who take the back roads of our county to avoid detection, men who stop by our farmhouse and beg for food or a place to sleep, look like dead men. I know because I have seen men laid out in their coffins, and if they have any look at all, they have that same sad surprise on their faces. Men in their coffins have copper pennies weighting their eyelids, but the eyes of the men who ask us for help are as blank and cold as copper. Uncle Eb says they have all seen hell and wonder why now they're walking through a land of cool, clear water and sweet green leaves.

Our land was not so cool or green last year, when Sheridan and his men came through, burning houses and barns, destroying fields and crops and whatever animals the Union army hadn't already stole from Valley farms. Ralph, who helps tend our fields, told me Sheridan's men burned anything that might serve as food for the Confederate army. I guess it didn't matter that those of us left at home need food, as well. Uncle Eb and Ralph saw smoke in the distance and guessed what was about to happen. We had prepared, and we hid what we could, leaving just enough so the invaders would feel they had accomplished their mission.

But no soldier crossed the river to burn our house or barn. A month earlier the barn had nearly burned to the ground anyway, the fire set by a pipe still smoldering in the hand of a deserter who had fallen asleep in our hayloft. Lucky for us a heavy rain spared us the worst. Luckier still when Sheridan's men, intent on destroying everything that could be shipped elsewhere, left us mostly alone. Too far off the Valley Pike and the Back Road, on a shallow river with so many bends and twists that ships avoid it, we were of little interest.

Now I find it curious that Sheridan's generous and unanticipated gift of the food we had expected him to steal or burn might have destroyed us anyway. Because our wealth, measured in grains of corn and the peeps of hatchling chicks, has brought brigades of strangers to our door.

Mostly they are men mustered out of service, on their way to somewhere and worried about what they will find. Saddest of all are the wounded and shattered who hardly remember their names. Like others throughout the countryside, my mother takes them in, feeding and sheltering and nursing whenever she can.

We are still poor, even if we have a little food. In return for whatever we do or give, Ma accepts help in our fields, wood chopped to keep us warm in winter, coins, coffee, tobacco or sugar to hide away. A man with nothing to offer sleeps beneath the half-charred roof of our barn. A man with something to give fares a little better, although he never receives encouragement. Ma is still young, even if she has aged five years for every year my father has been gone. Men look at her with an expression I have learned to recognize, but those who move too close find themselves staring down the barrels of Uncle Eb's shotgun.

Until April when Blackjack came to us.

The morning he rode up on his pale bay horse, we didn't know the stranger's name, of course. Uncle Eb and Ralph, too old to serve in the army but still strong enough to serve as our guardians, heard a horse and left the porch where we had been drinking Ma's coffee. We had long since run out of real coffee beans, although a time or two soldiers staying with us had a bit to share. But two years ago Ma took to roasting dandelion roots until they were as dark as dirt, then grinding them to brew and sweeten with sorghum or honey.

April on the river can be hot, the mist that rises from the water settling against our flesh like steam from Aunt Cora's Monday washtub. This year April wore her second disguise. Frost crunched under our boots in the mornings and etched spider-webs on our windows at night. The morning air was cool enough to prompt thoughts of a retreat to the kitchen, where the cookstove provided welcome warmth.

The man on the horse put those thoughts from our minds. I wrapped my wool shirt tighter around me. The shirt was an old one Pa had not taken with him, gnawed by moths and reeking of lavender and wormwood to discourage them. Ma does not like to see me wear it, but she's never told me not to.

Uncle Eb and Ralph were on the ground waiting for the stranger to arrive at our porch when Ma stepped out with the coffeepot. She paused just beyond the doorway, gazing into the distance as the stranger rode toward us.

"Not another," she said, almost to herself.

"He's alone." I stepped to the edge of the stairs and squinted into the rose-hued dawn. "He won't cause you much work."

She joined me there, coffeepot still poised in her hand, as if she was about to pour. "At least we aren't closer to town. If we were, we would have more of them."

"If Pa were alive, he would be on the road now, too."

"Yes, but he isn't."

A cold wind blew through her words. From the beginning, the idea of war had angered Ma. When Virginia had seceded to the Confederacy, she'd been angrier. When my father had reluctantly chosen to fight, her anger had turned to ice.

It seems I've always known that my mother married my father because he was the best of bad choices. Neither of them ever told me this, of course. But even as a small child I knew how to stay silent and listen, how to move quietly in shadows, how to make myself even smaller so that others forgot I existed. From this and from Aunt Cora, I pieced together the past.

My mother's parents acted on the stage until my grandfather took a job as schoolmaster in town. My mother claims her parents were rich in education and conversation but poor in every other way. When they died of putrid fever she was left with little but her clothing and their many books.

From gossip in the churchyard, I know there was a suitor, a handsome young man from the town's leading family, and Ma fell in love with him. I know that although she expected to marry him, he wed another woman. With no alternative, she took her father's place at the school, a job she did not relish, and watched as the world passed her by.

My father was nearly twenty years older than my mother, and at first he refused to court her. But Ma was golden-haired and smooth skinned, with eyes that even today are so large they seem to take in the whole world. By then her unhappiness was growing. Although a patient, warmhearted teacher with her only son, she herself has told me that teaching the children of strangers was like walking into a room with no windows.

Rejected by a man she thought she loved, orphaned by the deaths of her parents, forced into an occupation for which she had no calling, I believe my mother surveyed the limited supply of men she might marry and decided my father was the best of the lot. She is a persuasive and, if need be, a demanding woman. However it was accomplished, one year after the death of her parents, my father and mother were wed.

I once heard Aunt Cora say that my mother set her sights on my father most deliberately. Ma chose a man who would support and adore her. The Duncan farm was successful, and my father had proved himself a hard worker with a head for business. Lewis Duncan was a man known for his loyalty, faith and steadfastness.

If my mother had few thoughts of love when she repeated her wedding vows, I'm afraid that in the years that followed she had no thoughts of it at all. If my father understood this, he never gave a sign in my presence.

On that morning in April, however, thoughts of the past were fleeting. The stranger approached, leaning forward over the full, dark mane of his horse. Ma finally turned and set the coffeepot on the table beside the front door.

"Another man trying not to die, Robby. Eb may need you."

I was halfway down the steps by the time she finished. Ralph and Uncle Eb were not as strong as they liked to pretend. Each year since the war began, the fields we cultivated grew fewer and smaller as the forest at their edges devoured them. Ralph, a white-haired, stooped man with only one good eye, rested after each turn of the plow. Uncle Eb, the younger of the two brothers and the slighter, did the farm chores with no spring to his step. Every day the chores seemed to take longer.

I waited beside the others as the horse slowed to a halt just beyond us. The man in the saddle tried to straighten, but the effort cost him dearly. As we watched, he slid to one side and fell from the saddle.

We caught him just before his head hit the ground. The horse, a mare of a quality only seen these days under a uniformed officer, was streaked with sweat and glowed under the light of the rising sun. She danced away from us, uneasy at our presence. Uncle Eb caught the bridle and held her still as Ralph and I finished lowering the stranger to the ground.

"Is he dead?" my mother asked from the porch.

"Nah, still breathing," Ralph said, his fingers at the side of the man's throat. "Could change, though."

"If he dies, I suppose we'll keep his horse," she said. "If he doesn't? We can be proud we aren't yet animals ourselves. Bring him inside."

Ralph squatted and put his hands under the man's armpits. I slipped my arms under his knees, and together we lifted him from the ground. He groaned, and only then did I really take note of him. He was a young man, fine featured, with a strong, square chin and jutting brow. His dark hair waved over a broad forehead, and he had a luxuriant mustache and several days' growth of beard. His clothes were travel stained, but they seemed of good quality. There was nothing suggesting a uniform about them. Not for one side or the other.

Ma had lit a lamp in the parlor, and Ralph and I took him there. She carefully spread a quilt over the sofa, and as gently as we could, we laid him on it. She fetched a basin of water and several cloths, and proceeded to wipe his face.

"Can you hear me?" She rubbed a little harder. "Can you tell us if you're wounded?"

He became aware again all at once, gasping as if all air had abandoned his lungs. He tried to sit up, but Ralph firmly forced him down.

"You're safe," Ma said. "And the war's nearly over."

This seemed to quiet him. He lay still and stared up at her.

"How did I come to be here?" he asked at last.

"You rode nearly up to our house before you fell from your horse," I said.

His eyes followed my voice, and his gaze rested on my face. "You brought me in?"

"We did," my mother said. "Now tell us if you're wounded. We'll do what we can." She paused. "Although we'll expect you to help in return if you're able."

"Give the…devil his due."

"Hey now," Ralph said, bending over him. "That's no way to talk—"

Ma put her hand on his arm. "It's only an expression. Mr. William Shakespeare. And true enough in these times."

"I can pay. Although I daresay you'll discover that without my help." Sweat was trickling off the man's forehead, although the parlor was cool. His eyes were glazed with pain.

"You're among honest folk," Ma said. "And we'll take care of you if you tell us where to begin."

"I…I fought at Petersburg. I was wounded, then released. I thought…I thought I could make it to Winchester. My parents…"

"You're a long way from there." Ralph frowned. "And not dressed like any soldier I've seen in these parts."

"Discharged. Left all that behind."

"That horse belongs to an officer."

The stranger's expression was more grimace than smile. "No longer."

Ralph gave a short laugh. "You have a name?"

"Jack. Jack Brewer. I'm called Blackjack."

"I'm Mrs. Lewis Duncan," Ma said. "This is my son Robby, and that's our man Ralph, who makes certain all travelers stopping here move on as soon as they can."

"A move I support."

Ma wrung out her cloth and wiped his brow. "Where is your wound?"

"My leg. Broke it, and a sawbones set it right on the battlefield. But there must…be trouble."

"We'll get you upstairs. It won't be pleasant. But once you're there, we'll have a look at it and do what we can. I suspect you need rest as much as anything." She turned to me. "Robby, get Uncle Eb to help us."

I was glad to leave. The stranger was in pain, and I didn't relish what was to come. Our stairs are narrow and steep. The trip would not be easy.

Outside, I found Uncle Eb trying to tether Blackjack's horse, but with no success. As I watched, the horse reared and tried to kick him.

"She won't be tied," he shouted to me. "A wild thing, this one."

"I can put her in a stall in the barn."

"Might be best. Her rider will be here a while?"

"So it seems."

Uncle Eb has a way with horses. He whistled and clucked, and the mare finally calmed. "What did he tell you?" he asked, once the horse was under control again.

I repeated Blackjack's story.

"No," Uncle Eb said, shaking his head. "He would never have

been discharged with such a horse under him. Not even a wounded man. I'll tell you what I think. I hear tell Mosby disbanded his Rangers rather than surrender. Those who still can are on their way to join General Johnston and finish the fight."

Johnston was one of those who had not yet surrendered. Some people called him a hero. My mother called him another fool.

Uncle Eb stroked the mare's muzzle. "This Blackjack could have been wounded at Arundell, back at the beginning of the month. That's when the Rangers last fought together. If that were me, I'd make up a story, too, about heading home. No matter *where* I intended to go."

The story made some sense. The wound, the horse, and clothes a man might wear who wanted to disguise his real purpose in traveling back roads.

"He doesn't sound like he's from around here." I had already noted Blackjack's unaccented speech, which was somehow different from ours and our neighbors'.

"Well, we won't hold that against him."

"He could be almost anybody."

Uncle Eb handed me the horse's reins, and I took them gingerly. I'm not afraid of any animal, but a nervous horse bears watching.

Uncle Eb dusted his hands on his trousers. "In these times, Robby, it don't pay to look too closely at the people who come through. We'll take his gun if he has one and watch him close. But everybody's running now. Some running to, some running from. All we can do is help them on their way."

"And give the devil his due," I said.

"What's that?"

I shook my head. "Ma needs you to help her get him upstairs. I'll help, too, soon as I get the horse in the barn."

"We can manage. You go on." Uncle Eb started up the steps and disappeared into the house.

I watched him go and wondered about the man in our parlor and all the things that had brought him this far.

Chapter 15

Eric was determined to teach Noah's parakeet to talk. So far Buddy had only favored the family with chicken-on-the-chopping-block squawks. To remedy this, Eric had taken to sneaking into the boys' room when his sons were occupied else-where and patiently repeating a phrase.

Luckily for him, his sons were often forced to be early risers. This morning Noah was already at the inn helping his mother prepare lunch for the campers. Dillon was picking up the remains of the Fourth of July fireworks show the boys and some of their friends had produced last night for the inn's guests. Eric had their room to himself.

He had considered at length what to teach Buddy. He'd dis-carded the usual bird claptrap and anything remotely sentimen-tal. He wanted something to make Noah think about his life and future, but nothing too obvious. The amount of time he'd spent on his selection was appalling, but he had finally arrived at the perfect phrase.

"Up, up and away." Eric leaned over the cage, his nose nearly in pecking distance. "Up, up and away…"

Buddy ran back and forth on his perch, squawking and chattering with excitement.

"Up, up and away…"

Buddy hopped on the bars beside Eric's nose and began to peck at the cage, as if he wanted to get out. Eric knew better than to accommodate him. Noah had released Buddy a couple of times without any serious incidents, but Eric could just imagine what his son would think if his father—who hadn't been invited into his bedroom in the first place—let Buddy out of his cage and couldn't get him back in. Or, worse, if somebody opened the bedroom door and the little bird flew away.

"Up, up and away… Up, up and away."

Buddy's tiny eyes widened. He batted his head against the cage and screeched with joy.

Eric continued the lesson until he tired of it. Buddy was still raring to go but not saying a decipherable word when Eric finally closed the bedroom door behind him.

Parakeet 101 had used up fifteen minutes of his morning, but it wasn't even seven-thirty. A dream had awakened him at six, and he'd been afraid to go back to sleep. He had been suspended by a silk thread from a spiderweb. Looking down for help he'd found only a yawning chasm waiting to welcome him. The spider, a hideous thing with an all too human face, had been creeping toward him. After waking, minutes had passed in a cold sweat before he could force himself to move. He was halfway through his morning shower before he'd convinced himself the nightmare wasn't real, and he didn't have to choose between a spider's jaws and a terrifying fall through space.

Now the day stretched in front of him, an endless progression of minutes to fill. All the boys would be at camp. Gayle, well, Gayle would be doing what she always did to keep the inn running. The day promised to be a scorcher, which let out fishing, hiking or canoeing for fun.

He rejected driving into D.C. to see old friends. The first week of July was prime vacation time, and truthfully, there were few people he really cared about seeing, anyway. Exactly what would he say to them when he did visit? How would he explain the mistake he had made, a mistake that had cost a good man everything and left Eric himself so rattled he had retreated to the life he had left behind a dozen years ago?

A life that did not include risking his own repeatedly. A life in which he might have more value to his sons than he had ever had to his viewers.

A life with Gayle.

The moment that thought entered his head, he shoved it away. There were rules here, for the most part unspoken but clear nevertheless. He had come to the inn to recover, to assure his boys he was really okay and perhaps to grow closer. In all their years apart, neither he nor Gayle had ever kidded themselves that they should have stayed together.

He saw Dillon outside the carriage house in shorts and a yellow T-shirt that had probably belonged to at least one of his brothers. His youngest son was trudging toward the old garden shed where Gayle's assistants had made their home. Eric followed to see what he was up to. He knew there had been a delay in the renovations, and that Gayle was growing frustrated. Now she only hoped to have the old garden shed finished by early fall so she could christen the new Star Garden suite before the leaves changed. Fall was the inn's busiest and most lucrative season.

He stopped in the doorway and watched Dillon make his way around a poorly designed kitchen. "What's up, champ?"

Dillon turned, startled. "Mom told me to check for trash since I was picking up trash outside, anyway."

"That was some fireworks show last night."

"We do it every year. It's the only time Mom lets us have them."

Gayle had taken Eric aside to ask how he would feel about the display, afraid, he supposed, that the booms and fire bursts might stir memories of his stint in Afghanistan. Instead, the fireworks had driven home another message. He could not remember ever spending a Fourth of July with his sons. He had missed the starstruck looks of awe of his preschoolers, the first sparklers, the graduation to bottle rockets and Roman candles. By now the boys had moved on to minor pyrotechnics, limited only by their mother's good sense and the Commonwealth of Virginia.

Eric glanced around the suite, which looked almost exactly the way it had last time he'd been here. "It doesn't look like the contractors got very far."

"Mom's going to hire somebody else."

"Oh?"

Dillon found a black plastic bag tied off at the top and crossed the floor to heave it outside the door. "Yeah, they haven't even gotten the old cabinets out. They're supposed to pull out the paneling. Stuff like that. They keep making excuses or something and don't show up."

"I ripped out the inn's old kitchen in just a day. With a little help."

"You did that?"

"Your mom and I did a lot of the renovations together. You should have seen the place when we bought it."

"I guess I did, but I was a baby."

Eric grinned. "You cried all the time."

"Yeah? Well, maybe I didn't like what I saw."

This time Eric laughed. "I know I told you already, but I really liked your play the other night. I've been thinking about it. Why don't you tell me what happens next?"

"Nope. Then you wouldn't come and watch."

"You like having an audience?"

"Don't you?"

Eric hated to admit just how much.

He watched as Dillon, a trash bag under each arm, headed up toward the house. Breakfast wasn't served until eight-thirty, and if Eric didn't get there on time, his would be waiting in the refrigerator whenever he wanted it. He had an hour to kill, and he finally knew exactly how he was going to do it. He just needed a few tools.

An hour later he paused to survey his work and nearly stepped back into his ex-wife's arms.

"So this is where all the banging's been coming from."

He turned to find Gayle looking cool and fresh in a coral blouse and khaki capris paired with rope-and-leather sandals. Her gray eyes were serious as she gazed around the room.

"What do you think?" he asked.

"What do you think you're doing?"

He raised an eyebrow. "I could swear it's obvious."

"When did you hire on?"

He took a moment to read her voice and get his bearings. From years of experience, he knew Gayle never made that easy. When she thought the time was right, she explained what she was feeling, but she rarely put on much of a show. He wasn't sure her reticence had mattered to him during their marriage, except that pretending she wasn't feeling anything had been easiest. That way he could do almost anything he wanted.

Eric felt his way, lowering his voice to a level between intimacy and persuasion. "Dillon told me you were having problems with the contractors. I thought I could lend a hand here. I seem to be really good at tearing things apart."

She finally looked at him and somehow managed not to point out the parallels to their marriage.

"You've done quite a job of it," she said at last. "In a very short time."

"Was I too noisy?"

"I'll know when the guests start hauling suitcases to the car."

He flashed his most winning smile. "You couldn't really hear me from the guest rooms, could you? Maybe from the terrace, but no farther."

She looked as if she wanted to say something else, but she finally shook her head. "You've done more since you got up this morning than that worthless crew did the one afternoon they showed up to work."

"I can finish tearing out the kitchen, and the paneling, too. I thought maybe this old ceiling could go, as well. I—" He stopped himself. "Of course, if that's not what you had in mind…?"

"No, the ceiling has to go, too."

"I'd like to do this."

"Are you feeling well enough?"

"If I don't overdo." He knew how to be self-deprecating and used that skill now. "But I need something to work on, Gayle. Besides figuring out who I am and where I fit in the world, that is. And figuring out my kids."

She hesitated, and this time he thought he understood. "I owe you a lot for taking me in," he said. "This won't begin to put you in my debt. Don't give that a thought."

"I didn't."

"Oh."

"I was thinking about you figuring out your kids. One of them needs some figuring out, or straightening out or…ferreting out. I don't know which. I was going to ask Travis for help."

Eric set his sledgehammer on what was left of a counter and rubbed the palms of his hands on his jeans. "Who and what?"

"Jared."

"I thought the two of you got along like peas in a pod. He's Mr. Responsible. You can't talk to him?"

"He's also likely to keep things to himself, just like his mother. And these are things he might prefer to talk to you about."

"Things? Or the girlfriend?"

"The latter."

"Sure, no problem."

She tilted her face to his. "You're kidding, right?"

"I'm a guy, he's a guy, women are complete mysteries. We start on common ground."

For a moment she didn't reply. This close to her, he was aware of an enticing scent, something vaguely herbal or citrusy. Her skin was lightly tanned and smooth, and the faint tracing of lines around her eyes only added character. He had rarely given much thought to what Gayle did for a personal life, but standing here now, he knew that whatever she did was her choice. He was sure that even in the countryside of Shenandoah County, she did not go unnoticed.

"I have to finish feeding the guests breakfast," she said. "Jared's going to be leaving in a little while to pick up Brandy and go to the dig. There's time now, if you're willing."

Eric was glad for the break. He was already exhausted, even if he was reluctant to admit it. "I'll go find him. And thanks for giving *me* the job."

For the first time since her arrival, she smiled a little. The smile warmed her eyes to taupe. "I'll save you an extra sausage patty, Hercules."

He watched as she headed back to the house. He had always liked the way Gayle moved. She didn't bustle, didn't saunter. She had a long, confident stride with just the hint of a wiggle. The walk said a lot about the woman.

Eric found his oldest son in the room above the garage that he shared with Leon Jenkins, when Leon wasn't living at home with his father. Eric hadn't been surprised at the boys' interior-decorating scheme. The walls were painted black; the furniture was mismatched and worn; Christina Aguilera and Shakira stared down from posters on the ceiling. Clearly Gayle had abandoned hope beyond this threshold.

"So, getting ready to head off for the day?" Eric asked from the doorway.

Jared was sitting on his bed, emptying out a pair of scuffed tennis shoes. He'd had the good sense to move a wastebasket into target range.

"Were you ever a camp counselor?" he asked Eric.

"At your age I had no talent for taking care of anybody else and not a lot for taking care of myself."

"Well, I suck at it. The girls giggle, and the boys do stupid things to make them. I never acted like that."

"You're sure?"

Jared looked up. "I was fourteen a hundred years ago."

"You've always been a responsible guy and kind of serious."

Jared didn't smile. "Maybe not as responsible as I should be."

Eric could think of a thousand things that might lie behind that statement, and all of them frightened him. In the moment before he replied, he wondered which was more terrifying, going back to the Mideast or delving into the emotional life of his eighteen-year-old son.

"What's up? Your mom—" he hesitated a second too long "—and I have noticed something seems to be bothering you."

"Nothing's up." Jared dumped sand from one shoe into the wastebasket and loosened the laces. He took long enough that he could have pulled them out and restrung them.

"I'll make an educated guess here. Man to man. You're fighting with Brandy?"

Jared hunched a shoulder in the approximation of a shrug. "Not really."

Eric crossed the room and perched on the opposite bed, which was neatly made up with an army blanket. "I had a girlfriend when I was eighteen, but she wasn't nearly as pretty as yours. I imagine a lot of guys have noticed her."

"Brandy's hard to ignore. But she's all mine as long as I do what she wants."

Eric crossed one problem off the list forming in his head. "I guess it's going to be hard to leave her next year."

"She's not happy about it."

He noted that Jared hadn't said *he* wasn't happy, either. "Can she join you at MIT when she graduates?"

"She won't have the grades, and her interests run in different places."

Eric was mentally patting himself on the back. "Oh. What does she like?"

"Kids."

"She's planning to teach?"

"No, she just wants to get married and have a bunch. It's her life ambition."

Eric sat back. "And not yours, huh?"

"Sounding familiar?"

Eric hadn't tensed for the blow. He winced. "Not exactly. Your mom had an education and a lot of interests. And we were a little older. I didn't get roped into anything." He didn't add that neither Jared nor Dillon had exactly been planned babies. That was not information you passed on to the next generation.

"Mom had lived all over the world. I guess she'd had a million experiences before she got married. Brandy just wants to stay here, have kids. Marry me."

"Jared, if you go along with that, your whole life will be mapped out for you." Eric hesitated, then decided to be brutally honest. "And you don't want to be in the position I was in."

"No? What position was that?"

"Of realizing you've chosen a lifestyle you aren't cut out to live. Your mom and I went into our marriage with our eyes half-open. Neither of us saw the whole picture. By the time we did, we had three children and no workable compromise on the best way to stay married and raise you boys. And even if we were young, we were still older and more experienced than you and Brandy."

Jared was silent.

Eric realized he needed to go further, but he was walking on dangerous ground. "Someday you'll be a great dad, better than I've been. Hands down. But I guess I'm trying to tell you there's no hurry. There's a lot of world to see. This is the time for you to live out your own dreams, not somebody else's. You need to be careful."

Jared looked up. "Careful? You should talk. Why weren't *you* careful?"

"I was young. I thought I could do everything, be everything, and I—"

"Not then. Now! While you were in Afghanistan. Why did you put yourself in danger like that? How could you have let yourself be captured that way?"

Eric felt as if the conversation had taken a nosedive. For a moment he couldn't reorganize his thoughts.

"You must not have been paying attention," Jared said. "All those years you stayed safe, then, suddenly, you just let them grab you?"

"I didn't exactly let them. I mean, I didn't stand on the corner with a sign on my chest saying Take Me, I'm an Infidel and a Sucker."

"Dad, something must have been bothering you, or you wouldn't have taken that kind of a chance! And I'm pretty sure I know what it was."

Eric couldn't get a handle on the conversation. "You're going to have to speak plainly here. I'm afraid I'm really lost."

"It was my letter."

Eric stared at him. Jared had mastered his mother's stoic demeanor, but now the mask had slipped. His eyes were haunted. His cheeks were flushed. He looked as if he was trying not to cry.

"Letter..." Then he understood. "Jared, you mean the letter about your graduation?"

Jared looked away, an answer as plain as any he could have given.

Eric had never felt like a greater failure as a father. He swallowed, and the taste was bitter.

"I had no idea you thought that," he finally said. "It just never occurred to me you'd think there was some connection."

Now he remembered the letter clearly. In one of their infrequent, difficult-to-arrange phone calls to or from Afghanistan, Jared had reminded him about his graduation and asked when Eric would be arriving home. Eric had told him the truth. They would celebrate whenever he was able to get back to the States, even if he was late. But his travel arrangements and work schedule were uncertain and Jared shouldn't count on him.

Shouldn't count on him. Exactly the way Jared had never been able to count on his father being at his side for any of the important events of a child's or teenage boy's life.

A letter in his son's neat, careful handwriting had arrived two weeks later, adorned with colorful stamps, opened and resealed somewhere along the way. It was all right that Eric wasn't planning to come home to see Jared graduate. Eric was never there for anything that mattered anyway, so why should he start now? In the future, Jared wouldn't even bother his father when things were happening in his life. Then Eric wouldn't have to search for new excuses.

The letter had shaken Eric. He'd scurried around trying to make arrangements to get back in time, until the opportunity to interview the Taliban connections had landed on his doorstep. In the flurry to find a way to make the interview happen, Jared's letter had been tucked away to deal with later. And in the aftermath? In the aftermath, Eric hadn't given it another thought.

"People who are worried or upset are careless," Jared said. "I've always known that. I've always tried not to upset you. None of us want you to make a mistake. But you did this time."

Eric wished for a time machine. Not one that would take him back to a phone call he had mishandled, but one that would take him back to the day Gayle had given birth to their first son. He wished he could try all over again to be a better father, but even as he wished it, he knew that even if he could, he would probably fail in many of the same ways.

All he could do now was tell Jared the truth.

"I *was* upset." He cleared his throat. "The letter brought home to me what a loser I can be. But it never occurred to me that I couldn't make it up to you, Jared. I love you, and you love me. I'm not the world's most perfect father, but the love's always been there. And I knew that the way we really feel about each other would get us through. So no, I didn't go into that meeting distracted and worried about you. Because right or wrong, I thought things would be okay. We would talk. If I couldn't get back for graduation night, I would find a way to make it up to you. Maybe I was wrong about that, but that's what I thought."

"You're just saying that." But Jared didn't sound sure.

"No, I'm not. It's true. I started making arrangements to come home right after I heard from you, then that interview came up, the one that got me in trouble. I put the letter and the arrangements aside, and I focused on what I was about to do. Completely. Stupidly, as it turned out. But the only people who had any fault in capturing me were me, for believing a friend would never betray me, and the men who wanted to kill me. Never you. If anything, knowing you and your brothers were here waiting for me to come home helped keep me alive. It gave me that much more of a reason to escape."

"You're not just saying that to make me feel better?"

Eric shook his head. "If you want, you can be angry at me for not being more upset by your letter. But don't be angry at yourself for writing it, and don't worry that it affected anything that happened. I promise I'm being honest with you."

Jared searched his face. Then, as Eric watched, his tension seemed to ease, and he actually smiled a little. He shook his head. "You're a selfish bastard, aren't you?"

Eric sighed, then smiled, as well. He wasn't particularly good at knowing the right things to say to his sons, but this time he had calmed the waters. "Sometimes self-absorption is a good thing. You can let go of this now, right? Knowing I was selfish enough to put my work ahead of you?"

"Yeah, I guess."

"I may be selfish and a bastard, but I promise that before all the other stuff intervened, I was trying hard to make it home for your graduation."

"Well, you did make it home, after all."

"Right, only next time you write me a letter like that one, I'm going to hop on the first airplane out of wherever and not wait to get kidnapped. It will be easier on both of us."

In the past, Gayle had rarely had to struggle to figure out what she was feeling. Since Eric's arrival, those days were gone. This morning she had a choice of quandaries. Did she have any right to feel annoyed that Eric had begun demolition on the garden-shed apartment without asking her permission? After all, he had done it as a surprise, a favor. Was she overreacting to simple kindness?

And second, had she done the right thing by asking Eric to intercede with their son? Would he be sensitive, or would he go after Jared like a journalist who couldn't take no for an answer? And was this last concern really about Jared, or about sharing the rewards of parenting?

She was straightening the morning room, wondering if she'd really faced how complex this summer might turn out to be, when Eric found her again.

"I thought you had a housekeeping crew."

She looked up from gathering newspapers and piling coffee cups on a tray, and tried to evaluate his expression.

"I just wanted to clear out the debris before the quilters get here. The crew will clean the room later." She decided it was safe to continue. "Did you find Jared?"

He rubbed his chin, as if trying to decide whether to shave again. He hadn't for a few days, but on Eric, it was a look that worked.

"Did you know he blamed himself for what happened to me?" he asked.

She listened as he explained that their son had felt responsible for the kidnapping because of an angry letter. Once he finished, she was immeasurably thankful she had given him the opportunity.

"That explains a lot, but Jared never said a thing."

"I think it was just between us."

"You set him straight?"

"I think it's squared away."

She wished she could find Jared and give him a hug, but that kind of sympathy wouldn't be appreciated. The days of gathering him in her arms and kissing boo-boos had ended.

She picked up the last cup and set it on the tray. "They've all taken the events of this summer so differently."

"I've always been lousy at remembering how important rituals and holidays are."

"It's funny, too, because nobody likes a party better than you do."

She had already noted that Eric had gradually cranked up the warmth of his smiles since his arrival. Now the one he sent her heated the air.

"I know somebody who needs a party and a celebration."

"Oh, no. Don't even think it."

"Forty's a big birthday, Gayle. And I'm not so far removed from your life that I don't remember that *your* fortieth is right around the corner. As Jared duly pointed out to me, I need to start paying attention."

"My birthday is right at the end of camp, so I'll be busy anyway. The boys will give me books and CDs. They'll probably cook dinner and make me a cake. That's all I want."

"That's no way to celebrate."

"I prefer to celebrate this one by forgetting its existence."

He moved closer and put his hand on the back of her neck. He began to knead it. "You can't bury your head in the sand. I'm past forty and still alive to tell about it." He paused. "Even if it was a close call."

Eric was a physical person, a toucher. She knew there was nothing to this; still, the unexpected pleasure of being touched by a man radiated through her. She looked up and saw Noah frowning in the doorway, and she had a sudden impulse to push Eric's hand away, even though the contact was casual.

Eric dropped his hand anyway. "You're not getting off that easily," he told her.

She shook back her hair and straightened her shoulders. "I mean it, Eric, I just want to be with family."

She watched as he passed Noah going out of the room. Noah stepped back to be sure his father didn't touch him. Eric made a point of clapping his hand on Noah's shoulder briefly anyway.

Noah didn't look at Gayle. She could feel the animosity radiating from him. "I'm done with my part of lunch," he said.

She wanted to explain, but she didn't have a chance. Helen came through the door, along with Kate Brogan and Cathy Adams. The women already looked wilted by the heat and glad for the air-conditioning.

"Just the man I wanted to see." Helen wiggled a finger at Noah. "Time we started those quilt lessons, don't you think?"

Noah glanced at his mother, his expression still sullen. "I *am* done in the kitchen for now."

"Go ahead. We don't have to leave until eleven. I've got things I need to do."

"Not so fast." Helen pointed to the quilt. "Don't you want to try again?"

Gayle couldn't honestly say she didn't have the time. Both Cissy and Paula were working this morning, and several of the guests had already checked out. Noah had done the prep work for the campers' lunch. It was too hot for the gardening she'd planned. She searched for another excuse, but Helen was on to her.

"My mama always said if at first you don't succeed—"

"Try, try again," Gayle finished.

"No, if at first you don't succeed, you might not have a lick of talent, but that's not enough of an excuse to stop."

"I don't have a lick, a squint or a sniff of talent."

"Then it's up to you to show the boy he can do something better than you can. Good for his ego."

"Just show him my stitches from the last time." Gayle leaned over to point them out. "Where are they?"

"You don't think we'd leave stitches that sorry in a quilt going up on the wall, do you? Those stitches were so long, they'd like to reach out and loop themselves around the necks of anybody passing by. Death by sloppy quilting, that's what it would be."

The women laughed. Even Noah, who seemed to be trying to hold on to his bad mood, smiled a little.

"The innkeeper needs to leave her mark," Helen said.

"Fifteen minutes. That's all I have."

"Long enough for me to tell you some more about the people in that old house over yonder."

"What house?" Noah asked. Cathy had already settled him beside her, and handed him a thimble and a threaded needle.

"Where the dig is?" Gayle asked. "The old Duncan house site?"

"That'd be the one."

Gayle made a mental note to share Dillon's play with Helen. She took a chair beside her tormentor, and took the needle Helen handed her and a thimble tight enough to cut off the circulation in her fingertip.

"Now you and Noah take a good look at what I'm doing." Helen poked the needle straight down through the quilt layers, using the thimble on her middle finger. "See, my other hand's just underneath, and the minute I feel the tiniest prick I bring the tip up like this until I can feel it with my top thumb, then repeat. See how little fabric each stitch covers? See how the needle rocks?" She demonstrated.

Gayle watched. "That's exactly what I did last time."

"I wouldn't quite say exactly." Helen's eyes sparkled.

"It's harder than it looks," Noah said after trying a few stitches. "This is going to take some practice."

"You got a quilt right here to practice on any time you want. Nothing to stop you."

"Yes, ma'am. I might just do that."

"You're raising a sensible boy," Helen told Gayle. "That's what Miranda Duncan did, too. All those years after the war, when those vultures in the North took advantage of folks here in Virginia. Robby Duncan—he was her son—must have seen it all. The men who could hardly get around afterwards, the farms and houses people couldn't hang on to. He took a good look around and realized that his mother needed cash more than she needed his labor. Richmond had burned, and the city was crying out for workers to help rebuild it. So once their first harvest was in after Sheridan came through, he took off. He wasn't but a boy, but somehow he earned enough money to help his mother get the farm back on its feet."

"I like a boy who's good to his mother," Gayle said, glancing up at Noah.

Helen went on. "And when he was in his twenties somewhere, he came back for good and started his very own hardware store down in Woodstock. My daddy shopped there, and when he needed credit, Robby Duncan never said a word about it. Just wrote it up and handed over whatever Daddy needed like he'd been paid with real money."

"I guess the store's gone now," Gayle said.

"He didn't die a rich man, but he had enough to see him and his family through hard times. They went on to other things and other places."

"That's interesting. Is that what you were going to tell us?"

"That? Nothing like it. I was going to tell you a story my grandmama told me. About one year after the war ended, Mrs. Duncan did something bordering on strange. See, her husband had died in the War of Northern Aggression, and he was buried in an unmarked grave on some battlefield, so she didn't have a body she could lay to rest in her church graveyard. But she went ahead, got a plot and erected a tombstone for him, all the same. And when *she* died, she was buried underneath it."

"That wasn't so uncommon, was it?" Cathy asked. "And, Helen, up north where I grew up, we called that war the War of Southern Rebellion, just so you know."

"Call it anything you want," Helen said. "Just be sure you call it a sad day in history. And yes, it wasn't so uncommon to have a grave with no body in it. Especially in those times. But the tombstone? Now that was the oddest thing. See, other people, someone dies, they put something on the tombstone about missing them, or a bit of their life, or something from the Holy Bible. But not Mrs. Miranda Duncan. She paid a stonecutter what was a lot of money for those times, and had him carve some lines from Shakespeare."

"Shakespeare?" Gayle asked.

"Something long, too, if I recall the story right. Needed a mighty large stone. Some folks thought it was an unholy scandal, at worst, or a sign she was losing her mind from hard work and sorrow, at best. To spend good money that way on a heathenish epitaph."

"That seems harsh," Cathy said.

Helen put down her needle and flexed her hand. "It didn't much matter. Miranda Duncan never changed a thing on that stone, not in all the years she lived after that, and when she died, her son made sure her name and dates were added, but that was all. He refused to change a word. I guess he knew what she meant by it all, even if nobody else in town understood."

Gayle wondered just what quotation Miranda had chosen, and what it said about the woman and her marriage.

For a moment she tried to imagine her own headstone. Gayle Fortman, beloved mother? It seemed perfunctory, but what else could be said? She was a modern woman and had never felt she needed a man in her life in order to be whole. But somehow, this sudden picture of a solitary grave haunted her.

"Did you prick your finger again?"

Gayle realized Noah had addressed her. She pulled herself back to the present and forced a smile. "Nope, I'm okay. Perfect."

But she wondered.

Chapter 16

Jared didn't know if Brandy was pregnant or not. He hadn't asked her again, and she hadn't volunteered the information. He was perfectly aware that this was immature and irresponsible. He knew that if she was pregnant, they had to face it quickly, pull their parents into the discussion of alternatives and make a choice they could all live with. But that course of events was so terrifying to him that he had fallen back on the other alternative—pretending none of it had ever happened.

He was pretty sure Brandy would tell him when something changed. He also knew that her feelings about the situation were different than his. She hadn't tried to get pregnant. She'd handed him the condoms herself. When she'd realized the first batch was past its prime, she'd even bought new ones. But if she *had* gotten pregnant, he was pretty sure she would view it as a sign. She wanted him to stay in Virginia. She wanted to be a wife and mother, and if fate had handed those roles to her, she would gratefully accept them.

By taking on more jobs at home, he had managed not to spend much time alone with her in the week since she'd dropped the bombshell. When they had been together, she hadn't brought up the subject, and neither had he. Most of the time they'd been with Lisa and Cray, anyway. And even though both their friends knew the score, they were too smart to bring it up when Jared and Brandy were together.

This morning, after his talk with his father about the letter, Jared realized he had to clear the air on the Brandy front, too. His life seemed filled with things he didn't want to talk about, but this could no longer be one of them. Not knowing was driving him crazy.

Brandy wasn't waiting for him when he pulled up to her house. Every morning she'd been either sitting on the porch or pacing the driveway, and now he had visions of her inside, hanging her head over a basin and moaning with morning sickness. He'd done a little research on the Internet, just so he could watch for signs. He knew that was one of the least charming.

Mrs. Wilburn called for him to come in after he rapped on the door. He found Brandy's mom at the kitchen table, a traditional Southern breakfast laid out in front of her, complete with grits, fried green tomatoes and sausage gravy on biscuits. He figured if Brandy had managed this, they had nothing to worry about.

"She's late getting off this morning. I had to wake her up twice." Mrs. Wilburn gestured to the seat across from him. "I'll get you a plate."

"No thank you. I helped with breakfast this morning. Mom and I made apple pancakes."

"I would love that job. I ought to run an inn, only I'd eat twice as much as I do already." She smiled, and he noted how much like

Brandy's her smile was. "I don't know why Brandy was so tired this morning. You haven't been keeping her up late this week."

Being tired in the mornings was another sign of pregnancy. Jared wished he hadn't consulted WebMD. As it was, he'd had to lock his door to make sure none of his brothers barged in on him in the middle of "Finding Out You're Pregnant."

"She's been staying up late reading," Mrs. Wilburn said. "I guess that's it."

"Reading?" He realized he sounded as surprised as if Brandy's mother had said she'd stayed up late conducting experiments in astrophysics. "I mean, I didn't know she was in the middle of a good book."

"She's reading up on child development."

He didn't know what to say.

"You know, what to expect from fourteen-year-olds. For camp." She gave a low laugh. "She's not much older than they are. She still seems like my little girl."

He imagined telling this woman that he might well have impregnated her little girl. He imagined phoning in the news from, say, China or the North Pole.

Brandy spoke from behind him. "Jared, I didn't know you were here."

He turned so fast he nearly upset his chair. "I didn't hear you coming. I just got here."

"Sorry I'm late. I just couldn't get going this morning." She seemed to be at the end of weaving her hair into one long braid. She went to her mother and asked her to put an elastic band around the end for her. Mrs. Wilburn fiddled with it a moment; then Brandy straightened.

"I'm all ready."

He thought she looked good. Not like somebody who had been

up all night fighting the effects of an invader in her trim body. She wasn't pale. She wasn't waving away the odors of Mrs. Wilburn's substantial breakfast. In fact, she reached over and grabbed a biscuit off a serving platter and a paper napkin to go with it.

"Want one for the road?" she asked him.

He didn't, but he was relieved she did.

"I always seem to be hungry these days," she said casually. "But I'm not going to overeat no matter how hungry I am." She looked pointedly at her mother.

Some women had morning sickness; some got increasingly hungrier. He was disheartened.

"You two have a good morning," Mrs. Wilburn told them, ignoring her daughter's barb. "Jared, you come for dinner one of these nights. I'll make fried chicken. It's a specialty of mine."

"Eating fried chicken is her specialty," Brandy said in a low voice as they left by the front door. "Mounds and mounds of it."

"Give her a break, why don't you? I like your mother."

"Don't start on me, Jared. I'm not in the mood."

He told himself she was not unusually irritable. And that when he got home he was going to block WebMD from his computer forever.

In the car, he started to turn the key in the ignition, then jerked the keys out and dropped them on his lap. He couldn't stand this another minute.

"Have you started your period?"

She looked up from spreading the napkin on her lap. "Well, it's so nice of you to ask. I didn't think you remembered."

"I haven't thought of anything else."

"You mean like an excited expectant father? Or like somebody who thinks his life has been ruined?"

"Like somebody who'd like an answer so he can start planning."

She bit her lip. "I had cramps day before yesterday. I thought for sure I was going to start. Then they went away."

"So what does that mean, do you think?"

"I don't know. I'm late sometimes, but not usually this late."

"Maybe you ought to take a pregnancy test."

"I'm waiting. Since I'm not regular, we have to figure differently. The test only works after about two weeks since, you know, you made love. It hasn't been that long yet. And maybe I got pregnant some time after that, which makes it even harder to tell."

"You did the math?"

"Yeah. Maybe after the weekend, if nothing's happened, we should buy a kit. We might be able to tell by then."

He rested his head against the back of the seat and closed his eyes.

"It's not the end of the world," she told him. "Maybe it was meant to happen. And if it was, we'll be fine. We could live at the inn, or here with Mom and Dad. Dad's always looking for people to sell cars for him. You could work your way up to manager before long. You'd be good at it."

Jared tried to imagine a life selling Buicks. Going on test drives, extolling the virtues of brake systems and entertainment packages, weren't on his list of career choices. Maybe he would change and someday that would be the dream he most wanted to fulfill. But right now, Mr. Wilburn's car dealership sounded like prison.

"We'll take it one step at a time," he said.

"But you're going to marry me if I am, right? You're not going to leave me to face this alone."

"I won't leave you alone."

"Good, then let's not worry about it. Whatever happens will happen."

Somehow, he didn't find that comforting.

* * *

Since it was Friday, archaeology camp was extended to include another campfire cookout. Eric had seen Noah and Gayle head out with the campers' lunch, return and leave again around five o'clock with dinner supplies. He'd spent most of the day destroying the interior of the old garden-shed apartment, and even though he was exhausted, he was exhilarated. His father was a talented carpenter, and together the two Fortman men had remodeled Eric's childhood home, his father's flagship store and the family's lakeside vacation cottage. His father might be something of an autocrat, but he had taught his son everything he knew.

Now it was time to knock off. About one o'clock, Gayle had brought him a plate of luncheon leftovers. Since lunch was usually something he scrounged on his own, this was a treat, warranted, he guessed, by his hard work. She had issued a casual invitation to the campfire to eat dinner and watch the second act of Dillon's play, and he had accepted.

He cleaned up what he could, then crossed to the inn to shower and change. Since he'd been up and out of his room too early to catch her morning call, he phoned Ariel for the usual Weather Woman update. By now he was pretty sure she was making up these incidents, but he didn't care.

"Weather Woman came in last night wearing a bright blue sari and a red dot on her forehead. She said she thought it would be fun to point out to the viewers that the weather had been as hot here yesterday as it was in Calcutta."

Eric laughed. "And somebody made her change?"

"Thing is, she didn't really know how to wrap it, or what to wear under it. One of the cameraman stepped on the hem, and she came apart in the studio. We saw a lot more of her than anybody wanted to, except maybe our anchor, who helped her wrap back up on the way to the dressing room. Slowly, from what I hear."

He perched on the edge of his bed and imagined what Ariel was wearing, and what she was doing as they talked.

"I missed hearing from you this morning," he told her.

"Eric, you sound better. How are you feeling?"

"I'm getting stronger. I've gained some weight."

"How about your head? In a better place yet?"

"Slow steps, I guess. I quit taking the sleeping pills."

"You're sleeping all right?"

"When I'm not dreaming."

She was silent for a moment, as if she was trying to figure out what to say to that. "I miss you. Why don't you come out here for a good visit? If you have bad dreams, I'll just wake you up. You'll be right beside me."

Expectation swept through him at the thought. Los Angeles, boiling over with places to explore, fascinating people. The city and the surrounding area could keep him occupied and stimulated for a lifetime. And Ariel thrown into the bargain. Temptations hard to resist.

"No?" she said when he didn't answer.

He stared up at the ceiling. "The boys expect me to be here for the rest of the summer. I can't let them down. That's one thing I'm good at that I shouldn't be."

"Oh well." She sounded disappointed.

"And Gayle's renovating one of the cottages on the property to accommodate guests. I took over today."

"You sound very at home."

The words had been said with polite goodwill, but he sensed an undertone. "I'm just working hard to make up to them for all the times I haven't been here."

"Them?"

He realized what she meant. "My sons, Ariel. Gayle and I are divorced. After the marriage ended, I wasn't *supposed* to be here for her anymore."

"Just keep me up to date, sweetie. If the ex and I are going to compete for your favors, at least give me a running start."

He was smiling when he hung up. Having Ariel want him was as much a boost to his mental health as a couple of years of therapy.

The campsite was bustling when he arrived. Dillon immediately dragged him over to a pegged-off rectangle where the kids had spent the week digging test pits to see if they were really over the trash pit or not. He explained that they had learned how to be careful, how to make measurements and take notes, and now they were finally getting to the neat stuff. He showed Eric the neck of a handblown bottle that had probably contained some variety of patent medicine and a Bakelite comb with half the teeth missing, the big artifacts of the day.

The kids were already filling their plates when Dillon finished the tour and took off. Eric waved to Gayle, who was dishing up baked beans and macaroni out of stainless-steel chafing dishes. He knew she had discovered that letting them get their own food for the first round meant a lot of waste. The heat had given her cheeks a rosy hue, and she was relaxed and smiling as she chatted with the kids.

He stood back and watched, enjoying the show and waiting for the campers and counselors to finish before he barged in. Travis, in cargo shorts and the same dark green T-shirt that all the kids seemed to be wearing tonight, came to join him.

"Nice shirt." Eric silently read the slogan. *Shenandoah Archaeology Camp. Dig it?* A boy and girl in Indiana Jones–style fedoras stomping on twin shovels filled the rest of the space.

"One of last year's campers designed it. I gave them out today."

"Clearly they're a hit." Eric folded his arms and leaned against a tree trunk, averting his gaze from his ex-wife.

"The kids have to survive the first week to get the shirt. So far nobody's dropped out." Travis called out something to one of the campers, a girl with a buzz cut and multiple hoops in both ears. She gave him a shy smile and shrugged in answer. Eric figured that as soon as Buzz Cut's parents turned their backs, tattoos and nose rings were next on the list.

"She worries me," Travis said quietly, turning back to Eric. "Very bright and hyper-aware of everything around her. If she can keep just one foot in the mainstream until we get her through high school, she'll have a fighting chance."

"You object to nonconformity?"

"Not a bit. I object to watching kids experiment with alternatives that are too dangerous for them to handle. As long as it's just hair and fashion choices, I'm easy."

"I was a straight arrow. Well, maybe I flew off target a time or two, but mostly I toed the line until I got to college. How about you?"

"I could hardly wait to get out of here, so I kept my nose clean and worked hard. I graduated early and took off. At the most, I figured I'd come home for Christmas and the occasional week in the summer."

"And here you are."

"Funny how things happen, isn't it?"

Unfortunately, Eric knew that the way things happened wasn't always funny, including his own reasons for being back in the Valley. "What brought you home?"

"I realized I could be happy anywhere, but here was easier for me than most places. I'm connected to my family's land, and I finally admitted it."

Eric wondered what *he* was connected to. The question was an interesting one. "Speaking of happiness…" he said, changing the subject, before he could delve any further. He'd been thinking about something all day as he'd pried cabinets from the wall and floor, and decided to bring it up. "Gayle's fortieth birthday is coming up."

"I know."

"I'm going to give her a surprise party. A big one. Probably at her church, if I can rent the social hall. With caterers and florists and a professional band. Everything in her life is about other people. I want something to be about her."

Travis gave a low whistle. "You've discussed this with her? No, I guess you haven't, if it's going to be a surprise."

"She wouldn't let me do it if she knew."

"I don't want to interfere…." Travis paused, and Eric knew he was choosing his words carefully. "But Gayle told me expressly that she wants to forget turning forty. I think she means it."

"I was married to her, so I know she hates to bother other people. But this is no bother. She's gone over and above for me this summer. I want to give something back, something nobody else would think of."

"She'll be the center of attention…."

"That's the point."

"Yes, I guess it is."

Eric grinned and slapped Travis on the back. "I'll need to know who to invite. Her minister can tell me who to ask from their church. Could you give me a list of people in the area who she's particular friends with? I don't want to leave out anybody, so be generous."

Travis gave a short nod. "The boys know?"

"Not yet, but I want them to help me plan it. I hope they can stay quiet."

"Oh, I don't think they'll tell her."

Somebody came up to ask Travis a question, and Eric saw that the food line had thinned. He went over to fill a plate so he could eat before he offered his services with cleanup. There were ribs and chicken to go with the side dishes, and a salad bar. Noah was manning the latter.

"I spent one semester working in the university cafeteria," Eric told his son as he dished up. "I can relate."

Either Noah had forgotten he despised his father or even Eric was better than the middle schoolers he'd been supervising. "At least you were serving college students."

"Don't kid yourself. That generation thinks blowing beer out their nostrils is high art."

"There have to be better summer jobs."

"Probably not around here. But I might be able to get you one in the graphics department of a television station once I settle down somewhere."

"Really?"

"Sure. Might not be glamorous, but it would give you a chance to see how things work. And maybe do some creative stuff once they see how good you are."

Noah managed not to smile, but just barely. Eric chalked up half a point in his favor.

After that he found plenty of people to talk to and did, learning firsthand from two of the campers what they thought of their activities, then listening to Brandy extol the virtues of her group of campers as opposed to all the others. Even after a day on the site, she looked pretty enough to pose for *Seventeen* or *CosmoGIRL*. Ariel had done a three-part series on teenage models and insisted he watch it, so he was something of an expert. Brandy might not be anorexic enough to win a contract, but she was certainly lovely enough. He wasn't surprised his oldest son seemed to be in over his head.

After dinner ended, he helped Gayle and Noah pile everything back in the truck. By the time they finished hauling food and dishes, marshmallow roasting had begun. By the time they'd scrubbed and folded tables, the kids had moved over to the ersatz theater for the second act of Dillon and Caleb's play.

Eric took a seat on the rear row of logs and patted the place next to him for Gayle.

Travis ambled out in front, and the kids quieted almost immediately. Eric knew what a feat that was. Travis made a few jokes, and the laughter was heartier than warranted. Clearly the kids liked and respected their camp director. Eric watched as he bantered with the campers.

"How many of you have decided after digging and screening all week that finding artifacts isn't worth the trouble? That there must be better ways to authenticate the past?"

"Every teacher should be this good," Gayle said.

"Quiet men like Travis have a different kind of charm. I can't tell you how many times I've seen it in the best statesmen and international leaders. You don't think much about them, then one day you realize they've set the world to rights while nobody was paying attention."

"You like him, don't you?"

"I don't know him that well. I'm not sure he likes me, but I'd say he's a good man to have as a friend."

"I've always thought so."

Something about her tone made him turn. "The two of you...?"

"Just two busy people with busy lives who find a minute now and then to share a little of them."

The kids had grown quiet. Dillon and Caleb came out the way they had last week, carrying their notebooks. Eric realized that Travis had given his son and his friend exactly what they would need to make it through middle school unscathed. Travis had given them a place where they could shine. Dillon, quirky and awkward, seemed neither here. He was unruffled, in command, and clearly a star in the making. This was the Dillon these kids would remember.

The gift was enormous. For a moment Eric felt a stab of jealousy that he hadn't been the one to offer it.

Chapter 17

1865

Blackjack slept soundly, never waking when my mother and I went together to check on him. He was feverish—she determined this by resting the back of her hand against his forehead—but never so hot that she chose to awaken him. She told me that sometimes sleep is the greatest healer, and that there would be time when he awoke to deal with whatever complaint had brought him to us.

Distrust was as widespread through our countryside as hunger or the freshly mounded dirt in our graveyards. I looked in on him twice to be certain all was as she said. He slept as if he were preparing for a deeper, more permanent, sleep. He didn't wake at the sound of my footsteps nor when I went through his leather bag to see if I could find out more about him. Uncle Eb had already removed a Colt Navy revolver before leaving us alone with him. He had taken it to his own cabin for safekeeping.

There was little else in the bag. A change of clothes, a few grooming items, but no military or personal papers. The bag could have belonged to anyone.

As the day progressed Uncle Eb and Ralph plowed fields in anticipation of planting. I thinned rows in Ma's vegetable garden, where thickly sown turnip and mustard were a solid carpet of green. She would cook what I pulled that night without the fat that had so often seasoned greens when I was younger. We would douse them with vinegar, instead, and be glad we had both.

An hour before supper, Ma came for me, taking the sack from my arms and instructing me to wash at the pump. Then, when I joined her, she told me her intention.

"Once I have to put supper on the table there'll be little time for nursing. I want you with me when I wake him."

This was no surprise. I was tall and strong enough to give the stranger pause, even with my thin arms and meager chest.

She brought a basin of water she had warmed, and clean cloths. I brought the basket with medical supplies.

"What if he dies here?" I asked. "Would we be blamed?"

"Who would know?"

I wondered how many men like this one were buried far from home, with no one to write their families and detail their fates.

"It's the chance he took when he rode off alone," Ma said, as if she were reading my mind.

She had tied a clean apron over her faded blue dress and taken a moment to pin back the loose tendrils of her pale hair, so that she looked as if her day had been less tiring than it was. I wondered if the stranger would still find her as pretty as I believed her to be.

From the bedroom doorway I saw that Blackjack continued to sleep. He hadn't moved since last I'd seen him. Even his forehead seemed creased with the same amount of intensity, as if he worked even in dreams to master his pain.

"They'll continue to come," Ma said. "For months they'll come. And then I fear even worse to follow."

"What do you mean?"

"With their president dead, who will remember and remind them what we've already suffered?"

"You think Abraham Lincoln would have been kind to us?"

"Kind? I don't know, but fairer than the men who'll replace him. And they'll send more men like themselves to bring us to heel. At least with the war we foolishly believed we might win. Now we can only watch as our losses are calculated."

I hadn't thought very far into the future, and Ma had rarely talked this way. The picture she painted was bleak, even frightening. And fear had been our companion for too long already.

She seemed to realize she'd gone too far. She drew back her shoulders. "But at least the war ended before you grew old enough that the army came for you. This is one day and one man. We'll do what we can with both."

I didn't tell her that I had wished every night that I was seventeen so I, too, could fight for freedom without her permission.

Blackjack didn't wake when Ma crossed the room or when she spoke to him.

"Wake up now, Mr. Brewer. It's time you opened your eyes." She spoke louder. "Mr. Brewer. Wake up now."

He slept on, although I saw him swallow.

"Mr. Brewer." She put her hand on his shoulder and shook him lightly. "Wake up now."

He sat up so quickly I was unprepared for what happened next. Blackjack grabbed my mother's hand and twisted her arm, pulling her down as he did until she was sitting half on top of him.

"Who are you?" he shouted.

I was between them in an instant, yanking his hand away from her and shoving hard against him. Ma scrambled back to her feet.

"Enough," she told me as I made ready to slam my fist into his shoulder. She grabbed my arm. "No. He doesn't know where he is."

"Who are you?" he shouted once more. His expression was wild, his face distorted. He made as if to try to grab her again, and I shoved him back against the pillows.

"You're in a bed in my house," Ma said more calmly than I would have expected. "You rode here this morning. You've slept all day. But it's time we had a look at your injuries."

He seemed to come to his senses a little at a time. First his eyes roved back and forth, as if he was taking in every detail. The room was not yet dark, and he seemed to find satisfaction by the end of his examination. Then he looked at me, studying me just as thoroughly. Finally he took my mother's measure.

"Where is your house?" he asked at last.

"On the banks of the North Fork of the Shenandoah River. Near Toms Brook, south of Strasburg."

He chewed his lip, his gaze wandering the room again.

"You don't remember coming here?" she asked.

He didn't answer, but I sensed he was preparing to bolt. I readied myself to stop him, and Ma did, too, but more directly. She drew the pistol my father had left with her and aimed it in his direction.

"I can and will use it," she said. "But only to protect myself and my son. You're safe unless you try to hurt us."

Oddly, this seemed to calm him. I suppose that even in his state of mind he realized that if she did wish him harm, she had the means to deliver it. The fact that she hadn't shot him seemed to allay his fears.

The fight went out of him. "I told you...I was on my way to Winchester?"

Ma handed the pistol to me. "You did. We stabled your horse and brought you to this room after you fainted. Now it's time to take stock of your injuries."

"I'm sorry for the trouble I've caused."

"So am I." She reached down and laid her hand against his forehead. "You're running a fever. Higher than you did earlier, I think, although that's not unusual in the evening. I've heard no coughing. Does your breathing give you trouble?"

He answered her questions until she seemed satisfied. She wrung out a cloth and sponged his flushed face. "Robby, get Eb and bring him up here. He'll get our guest into a nightshirt, so we can examine him."

I was hesitant to leave her alone with Blackjack, but she nodded, as if she understood. "Mr. Brewer and I have an understanding. He'll be the gentleman his speech indicates."

Blackjack's eyes caught mine, and he gave the slightest of nods.

Downstairs, I set Ma's pistol on the mantel. Outside, I ran to the cabin, calling for Uncle Eb even before I climbed the front steps. Both he and Aunt Cora hurried back to the house with me, Uncle Eb to help and Aunt Cora out of curiosity.

"Your poor mother's already got her hands full," Aunt Cora said after Uncle Eb outdistanced us. "We could keep him at the cabin."

The house had more room. And I couldn't imagine getting our guest down the stairs in his condition. When we arrived, Ma came out to the hallway and told us Uncle Eb was helping him undress. She had provided him with one of Pa's old nightshirts.

Perhaps I was just curious to learn more, because the interlude that followed seemed to take hours, although more likely it was only minutes. At last the door swung open and Uncle Eb came out. "Leg's broken," he confirmed. "Not much above the ankle, and he's been on it too much. Splint's bowed, plus it slipped. He'll need to stay quiet a while once we make sure the splint is right again."

Ma nodded. Uncle Eb had no training as a doctor, but he'd done his share of doctoring anyway. And Aunt Cora could walk the woods and climb into the mountains to find remedies for the digging or picking.

"Robby, you can help him bathe," Ma said. "While I look at his leg. He'll need a real bath soon, but washing will do the trick for now."

Blackjack was sitting up when we went into the room. He looked pale and listless, but he seemed aware of where he was and why. I wrung out the cloth in the basin and asked if he preferred to wash himself, but he gave a slight shake of his head. I told him I would do it, then, and began.

I doubt he was very aware of my attentions. He groaned a little as Ma investigated the leg, which seemed to be encased in something akin to barrel staves.

"Eb's right," she said at last. "It will never heal if you insist on using it. Riding, walking, and I suspect you've done more. You have to decide if you want to lose it, or if you want to be better than new."

"I'll take the latter."

"Ma..." I had progressed from Blackjack's neck to his arm, giving him the sort of bath I most preferred for myself, quick swipes that concentrated on my neck and palms, places Ma was sure to examine with the most interest. I unwrapped a ragged bandage from his left hand and whistled.

She looked up. "What is it?"

"Come look at this...." I pointed.

The stranger realized what I'd said and made to bury his hand in the covers, but Ma lifted it easily. "What sort of injury is this?"

He shrugged, as if it was nothing. "I fell from my horse.

Scraped my back and the back of my hand, but it's nothing to worry about."

The hand was deeply gouged, almost as if something had purposely set about tearing away the flesh. The edges of the wound were dark, as if dirt or something worse was embedded there. It wasn't as deep as some, but the bandage that had covered it was filthy, and the wound was angry and oozing.

Ma looked at it with distaste. "I'll apply a poultice, but that's the most likely cause of your fever."

"I heal quickly. I'll pay for your time and trouble."

"I'll be glad of it, thank you. I'm going to fix this splint. It won't be comfortable when I do."

"A soldier learns to ignore pain."

"Odd," she said, without looking up from the splint she was untying and readjusting. "I don't take you for a soldier."

"Why is that?"

"Your hands are too soft." Now she did look up. "As Robby most likely noted as he washed them."

"I am—was an officer, ma'am, and I had men who took care of my needs."

"Yes, so you said. And that's why you have such a fine horse."

"That's correct." He smiled, and despite his wan complexion, the smile brightened the room. I saw that Ma noticed, because she looked away.

"I'm so grateful to you for taking me in," he said. "You might have left me where I fell. I was lucky to meet up with good people."

"Gratitude is always welcome."

I watched as Ma manipulated the bandages and splint, and I saw him wince. At last she straightened. "That will do for now, until Eb can fashion something better. If you let the leg rest, I think the swelling will go down and it will heal straight. In a while I'll be back with that poultice and some supper. The food may not be what you're used to, but you'll find it sufficient."

"Again, my thanks."

Ma took the basin and rags I'd been using. She nodded and left, with the rest of us trailing behind. As Uncle Eb and Aunt Cora went downstairs, I took one last look at the stranger, whose eyes were now closed.

In the hallway, I found Ma staring at the only picture of my father we owned. All that was left of Lewis Duncan was a framed oval on a hall table. He had not been young when he'd married her, and certainly not young when I was born. His face had been square, and he'd had a bristly mustache that almost hid the shy smile that was usually in evidence. I wished that in this photograph the smile had been captured, too, because this stern, unsmiling face seemed a stranger's.

Ma was looking at my father with eyes that had just beheld a younger, more handsome man. Under those circumstances, any woman would find Lewis Duncan wanting.

"He was a good man," I said, my voice low. "There are none better."

"He left us to fight. At the time no one demanded he go." She sounded cold, and she isn't a cold woman.

"They would have made him serve anyway. He did what he thought he had to," I said.

"And now you and I are left to do the same." She lifted the photograph and raised it closer to her face. "I warned him that leaving us to fend for ourselves would end badly."

"How can you blame him for doing what was right?"

"Right? Are you like him, then?"

She set the photograph back on the table before she looked at me. "'If it be aught toward the general good, set honor in one eye and death in the other and I will look on both indifferently. For let the gods so speed me as I love the name of honor more than I fear death.'"

She quoted often and well, and I had been raised on my grandfather's collection of Shakespeare's plays. *Julius Caesar* was my favorite.

"My father was no Brutus," I said. "He served his country fairly and honestly."

"And like Brutus did what he thought he must in honor's name. Aren't such men the ones to fear most?"

"I will always be proud to be his son."

She turned away and left me there to stare at my father's face.

Chapter 18

Eric was exhilarated. Instead of nightmares, he'd spent most of the past night thinking of new and better ways to renovate the garden-shed cottage. Several times he'd gotten up to put his ideas on paper, making rough sketches and scribbling notes. When he'd finally fallen asleep it was simply to pass the time until morning.

Now breakfast was over, and he was enthusiastically taking measurements. He knew what Gayle planned to do here. She needed space for a family. Children could be disruptive in the main inn, where many guests had come for a quiet atmosphere. But families were a market she didn't want to ignore.

He did some calculations. There was a sizable living area where the kitchen had taken up one end until it had met with his crowbar, one medium-sized bedroom, and a bathroom that needed to be updated along with everything else. But if this wall was removed—and he was sure it wasn't load bearing—and the useless back porch was incorporated into living space? He got more and more excited as he saw that his ideas of the night before were sound and attainable.

Two hours later he stood back, flushed and proud and utterly exhausted.

"I brought you…"

He pivoted to see Gayle in the doorway.

"Some…coffee." She stepped into the room, or as far as she could go, anyway. She set a travel mug on the only surface that was left to hold it, a window ledge by the door. "Eric, what are you doing?"

"It was supposed to be a surprise. After I removed all the debris."

Her tone was oddly flat. "I can honestly say you achieved your goal. I *am* surprised. Exactly what are you doing?"

"I spent the whole night thinking about it. I know you planned to keep the space like it was more or less, with new wallboard, cabinetry and counters. But I have a better idea. You need space for families, right? And I'm guessing you were going to put a pull-out sofa in the living area for kids, but this way, by carving a little space from the living area, we can fit two bedrooms in here. See?"

He paced off what he could, stepping over chunks of Sheetrock and splintered timbers. "We'll extend the smaller bedroom into what's now that useless porch on the back. You can easily fit two twin beds in there, and a dresser. And the bathroom will connect them. It'll work for two sets of adults as well as children." He grinned at her and waited for praise. "So what do you think?"

"I think…" She looked away, her gaze roaming the room. Then she looked back at him. "I think you've forgotten this isn't *your* inn anymore. Your name isn't on the deed. It's not on any document that registers it for business with the Commonwealth of Virginia. The last time your name was connected with Daughter of the Stars was on our divorce papers, when you gave sole title to me."

For a moment he wasn't able to work his way through the mire of her words. "Wait, you're unhappy?"

She drew herself up, although until that moment she had seemed to be standing perfectly straight. "Unhappy? I'm trying to figure out exactly *when* you asked me if you could come in here and destroy my property?"

"You don't like my idea?"

"Idea be darned! I don't like your assumptions." She turned and left. One minute she was there; the next, the dust her departure stirred was a white cloud.

"Gayle!" He took off after her, which meant inching his way around piles studded with rusty nails and the occasional shard of broken glass. By the time he got outside he saw her heading up to the inn. He ran after her and was so winded by the time he caught up to her that all he could do was choke out her name again and grab her arm.

"I…thought you'd…be thrilled. I was doing it for you. You want more guests…don't you?"

She shook off his hand. "No! Our wells can't take it. The Valley hasn't had enough rain. I couldn't allow even four adults in there, much less extras on the pull-out. That would mean another bathroom, anyway. Adult guests don't want to share a bathroom if they don't have to. The Star Garden suite is supposed to be meant for a small family, pure and simple. Mom and Dad and two young children. Period. That's the absolute maximum we can handle."

"I hadn't thought of that."

"Because you don't run the inn anymore!"

She shook a finger at him, and he knew how the boys must feel when she was angry. "You can't just pick up where you left off, Eric! I am not your assistant, waiting to see what brilliant ideas you come up with for our future. You signed away your share of the inn because you knew you were leaving me with three children and more than half the renovations. And I remember, too, that you didn't expect me to make it here. Wasn't there some clause in the divorce papers about who got what if I sold the inn in the first five years? Well, I raised those children and renovated this place and made a success out of it. And guess what? I'm still here!"

Now *he* was angry, too. "Why? To spite me and show me you could?"

"Oh, that's just like you. It's all about you, isn't it? I can't even make a success of this place without you believing I did it to *prove* something to you. Do you want to know how often I thought longingly of you after you left? Wait here until I can think of a word that means not at all!"

She whirled and started back up toward the inn.

He caught her again and pulled her around to face him.

"Look, I know you didn't do anything to spite me. I didn't mean—"

"Of course you meant it. The world revolves around you. You probably think the grass grows just so you can walk on it."

He released her arm. "It surprises me, then, that you'd want me here, since you find me so lacking."

"I want you here because your sons need you. I do not want you here to pick up where we left off. I'm in charge of Daughter of the Stars. And I want the garden-shed renovations done my way."

"Fine! I'll put new walls where the old ones were."

"And you know what? In terms of you and me? Put some new walls up there, too, while you're at it."

This time, when she started back to the inn, he didn't stop her.

Eric was sorry he had planned another swimming lesson with Dillon. They had made substantial progress, but he knew the process couldn't be rushed. Dillon had spent most of his life afraid of the water. He wasn't going to learn to love it quickly or easily. At the most, by the time Eric left in August, he could be assured that, in an emergency, his son would be less likely to panic. That goal was small enough to be attainable.

After his fight with Gayle, however, he really didn't have the patience or positive attitude he needed for the task. He actually looked for Dillon to tell him that he was canceling for the afternoon, but he found his youngest son with his ex-wife, and he hadn't been willing to admit in front of her that he was reneging on their plans. So he'd sweetly reminded Dillon that they had a swimming lesson, raised one eyebrow ironically when Gayle glanced at him, and strutted off to put on his bathing suit.

He wondered if he really was the self-centered jackass that Gayle made him out to be.

On their way up to the swimming pool, Dillon chattered nonstop about the dig. Eric tried to listen, but for the most part all he heard was an internal monologue delivered in Gayle's angry voice.

"Do you think so?" Dillon asked.

Eric realized he had no idea what his son wanted to know, but clearly a yes or no answer was called for. "I'm not sure," he hedged. "This has to be up to you."

"Up to *me* to figure out if Jared and Brandy should get married?"

Eric realized he'd been caught. He tried for a save. "Up to you to have your own opinion about it. My opinion's a resounding no."

"I heard Jared tell Cray he wasn't ready to get married. And he said he's sure not ready to have kids."

Dillon had succeeded in getting Eric's attention. "Recently? You heard this recently?"

"That's what I just told you."

Eric thought about his talk with Jared. He'd been so sure it had gone well. But Jared was still talking about marriage when he clearly wasn't enthused? And having children?

The solution to the puzzle hit him squarely between the eyes. He actually winced. How could he have been so stupid? He'd thought one little talk with his son would put things right. And they *had* resolved a few things, but he had missed the whole point of the discussion about Brandy.

"God…"

"What?" Dillon sounded interested.

"I'm sorry. I just realized I…I left the sunscreen back at the inn."

"We haven't used sunscreen before."

"Right, well, that's irresponsible of me. We should have been using it. Next time."

He nearly missed the driveway. He backed up and turned in, parking where they always did. The house was still uninhabited. He checked to be sure things were still secured, as he had promised his former station manager he would, but the whole time he was walking the perimeter he was thinking about his oldest son. He hoped he was jumping to the wrong conclusion, but he was very afraid he knew why Jared had seemed so glum for the past week.

At the pool, Dillon shrugged out of his T-shirt, and took off his shoes and jeans. Eric did the same in slow motion. Between the fight and now this new worry, he yearned to be anywhere else. For a moment he almost wished he were back in a war-torn country dealing with hostile strangers.

"I'm not going to blow any more bubbles," Dillon said. "That's baby stuff and stupid."

"Oh, is that so?"

"Yeah."

Eric felt a twinge of anger, but he mastered it. He told himself that if he were Dillon, he'd be tired of blowing bubbles, too. "Then we'll move on to floating. It's the best part of enjoying the water. Once you learn to relax and float, you'll want to be in the water all the time."

"I can't float."

"You mean you haven't learned how. That's different."

"No," Dillon said with feigned patience. "I mean I can't. There's something wrong with me. I sink."

"That's because you haven't learned how to relax in the water, champ. Trust me, I know."

"How do you know? Maybe all my weight's in my head or something, or the bottom of my feet."

"You do have a unique way of thinking about things. That's why you're such a good actor."

Dillon relaxed his stance a little. "So did you like the play last night?"

Eric realized he hadn't told his son how much he'd enjoyed the second act. The girl with the buzz cut had read the part of Robby's mother, Miranda. The other readers had been fine, but when Dillon read, it was as if he actually became Robby. Eric had been so proud of his son. Dillon had clearly done a lot of work on his part.

And Eric hadn't even told him.

You probably think the grass grows just so you can walk on it.

"I'm sorry, champ." Eric clapped his hand on Dillon's shoulder. "I didn't see you afterwards. I was helping your mom get everything put away, and you guys were surrounded. It was great. I can't wait for the next act."

Dillon beamed.

"I think Robby will need swimming lessons, though," Eric said. "Living right on the river that way. So let's do a little research, shall we?"

"I can't float."

"We'll see about that." Eric sat on the edge and swung himself into the water. Reluctantly, Dillon did the same.

"Here's the thing about floating. We're in about oh, four feet of water here, right? Well, the water at the bottom, near our feet, is under a whole lot of pressure from the water at the top. Make sense?"

"So?"

"So, you understand about gravity, right?"

"Duh…"

"Okay, well, you'd expect gravity to just pull you straight down, no questions asked. And it would, except for all that pressure I mentioned. See, the water at the bottom is always pushing against the water at the top. When you displace that top water by trying to float on it, the water at the bottom counteracts gravity by pushing upwards and that's what keeps you from sinking." He stopped and hoped his grasp of the laws of physics was correct and, more important, helpful.

"So how come I sink? Like the water at the bottom doesn't like me?"

Eric had to smile. "How well you float has to do with density. The more body fat you have, the easier it is to float, because fat's not as dense as water. And how much air we have in our bodies matters for the same reason. In fact, that's what matters the most. So whether you relax and breathe deeply makes all the difference. The more air in your lungs, the better a floater you'll be."

"Or I could just eat a lot of candy bars."

Eric splashed him in response, and Dillon laughed.

"You've got plenty of body fat," Eric said. "And if you relax, you'll have plenty of air. Best yet, I'll be right here holding you up. And I'm a big strong guy."

"Let's see *you* float, then."

"Why?"

"Because in case you haven't noticed, I look just like you, and I'm going to be tall like you, so if you can float—"

"Then you can, too?" Eric doubted this was good science, but who cared? He swam out to the middle of the pool, flipped over on his back and relaxed, stretching his arms out beside him. He kicked up from the bottom and let the water take him.

After a minute he paddled his hands a little and kicked his feet until he was standing again.

"See? You're destined to be a floater, too."

"How do I keep the water off my face?"

"You might get a little. No big deal, right? You've been spending a lot of time submerged."

Dillon looked doubtful.

"But if you arch your neck, that will keep your face clear." Eric demonstrated quickly.

"Are you going to let go of me?"

"At some point. When you're floating all on your own."

"Then I'm not going to try."

Eric bit back a sharp reply. "Then I won't let go. Not until you tell me you're ready."

"You promise?"

"Didn't I just tell you I wouldn't?"

Dillon bit his lip, then nodded.

"Just remember, you won't be over your head, Dill. You'll be able to stand up any time you want. And when I feel you trying, I'll help you. So you don't have anything to worry about."

They went a little deeper, where Eric had done his demonstration. Then Eric rested his arm along Dillon's back. "Just lie back and kick up a bit. I'll get my other arm under your legs."

"I feel stupid."

"We always feel stupid when we're learning something new. Ignore it."

Dillon stood there for almost a full minute, as if he was debating whether to go along with this; then he sighed, closed his eyes and kicked his legs. Eric slipped his right arm under Dillon's knees, and in a moment, his son was floating. Stiff as a board, but floating.

"Okay, good start," Eric said. "Now, you have nothing to worry about. Just relax."

"I can't."

"Sure you can. Just try a little at a time. Start with your hands. Just let them go loose, then your arms...."

A dragonfly whizzed by. Bees buzzed in flowers along the edge. Birds sang from the small grove of trees. Eric couldn't sing worth a darn, but he could hum. Unfortunately, he couldn't think of a single song that fit the occasion. He settled for "Blowing in the Wind." From Dylan to Dillon.

He expected his son to call a halt to this new experiment, but little by little he thought he could feel Dillon relaxing. It felt strange to hold him this way and called up memories of all the times he *hadn't* held him as a baby. Gayle had never insisted, hoping, Eric supposed, that he would relent and learn to love this son on his own.

Now he was deeply ashamed. What kind of man couldn't love his own kid? The kind who had fathered Eric himself, he supposed. But then, his father had loved him, had nearly adored him, until the moment Eric had decided to live his own life. And wasn't that what came of giving a child everything? That one day he would take something he wanted, out of habit, and you would be left alone?

He felt a stab of pity for his father, one incompetent parent to another. They'd just erred on different ends of the scale. One giving everything and expecting everything in return. The other giving nothing and expecting…nothing.

"How'm I doing?" Dillon asked.

"I'm just so proud of you…son. You're doing fantastic."

"Don't let go."

Eric began to slowly rock him in the water. Back and forth, just a little, the way a father rocks a baby. "It's such a great day for this. The water feels so cool."

Out of the corner of his eye, he thought he saw the dragonfly gliding on air currents. He smiled.

One moment he was fine, thinking about how good the sun felt, how lovely the sounds were, the next his cheek felt as if it were on fire.

"Ouch!" Without thinking, he waved one hand at whatever had stung him and with the other slapped at his cheek. "Damn!"

Dillon flailed in front of him and began to kick in panic. Eric realized what he'd done and lunged forward, but by then it was too late. Dillon had gone under, then he'd flipped and emerged dripping in front of his father, his arms beating the water until he was standing firm on the bottom of the pool.

"You said you wouldn't let go!"

Eric could feel his cheek begin to swell. He suspected a

272

hornet, nothing as tame as a bee and certainly not a dragonfly. He was glad he had no allergies.

"Look." He pointed to his cheek. "I'm sorry, but something stung me. I just reacted, that's all. But I wasn't going to let you fall. I only had my hands off you for seconds. I—"

"You promised me! I almost drowned!"

"That's ridiculous! You didn't even come close. You can't drown in water you can stand up in. And I didn't mean to let go. It was a reflex."

"I don't care what it was! I was doing everything you told me to, and you couldn't do the one thing I asked for." Dillon's eyes were red, and Eric suspected it wasn't from the water.

He thought of a million things he shouldn't say and managed, somehow, not to say them. Instead he turned and swung himself up to the side of the pool. He didn't even stay to see if Dillon got out. He grabbed one of the towels he'd brought for them and dried off everything but his burning cheek.

He heard Dillon come up behind him. Eric was still working hard not to say something he shouldn't. Then he felt his son's arms circle his waist and Dillon's young body warm against his back for a moment.

"I'm…I'm sorry, Dad. Are you going to be all right?"

Eric turned and gathered his son in his arms. And suddenly he was sorry, too, overwhelmingly sorry for all the years when he hadn't had his arms around Dillon just like this.

When he could talk, he cleared his throat. "I bet the swelling's going down already. What say we try again? Second chances?"

"Okay. Only let's make sure there aren't any bees around."

Eric laughed and ruffled Dillon's hair. He didn't tell him that the second chance he wanted had nothing to do with swimming lessons.

Chapter 19

Travis's house was a two-story brick Colonial with black slatted shutters and forest-green trim. Two wings had been added by an Allen of an earlier generation, and to Gayle they always seemed like welcoming arms. Although the entryway porch was wide enough for several rockers, the seats were rarely occupied. One wing held a sunroom with fabulous views, and behind the house a terrace, created with bricks Travis had salvaged from various outbuildings, extended his living space.

The original living quarters were spacious and comfortable, but Gayle knew Travis spent most of his leisure time where he could look down on the river and out to the acres surrounding him. He rented his land to local farmers for pasture, corn and soybeans, and enjoyed the pleasures of farm life without the headaches.

Today she was delighted to be here. She rarely stayed angry. Her years of hosting the occasional irrational guest had taught her the value of facing annoyance, then letting go of it. The lessons had carried over into her relationship with her sons. She rarely lost her temper, and in response, they had learned to control their own.

But today she was still simmering from her encounter with Eric. No matter how many times she told herself that he'd only been trying to help, she couldn't put his high-handed destruction of the old garden shed behind her. She wanted him to feel at home this summer with his sons, but she didn't want him to take over. The lines were so clear that she couldn't imagine why he hadn't seen them. Or why he had so blatantly stepped across them.

She parked her car in a graveled area that was screened by spruce trees. The landscaping at Allen Farm was attractive but completely masculine. Healthy trimmed evergreens, old oaks and a few weeping willows closer to the river cast shade over the lawn. The grass was lush, but there wasn't a flower in sight. Old hydrangeas, most likely planted years ago when a woman was in residence, promised to bloom later in the summer. But even the ubiquitous day lilies, present in every farm and yard in the valley, seemed to have given up the fight here. Gayle had threatened more than once to sneak over in the dead of night and plant a perennial border.

She didn't even have to knock. Travis opened the door to welcome her. He took in the summery green tank top and lemon patterned floaty skirt and smiled, but the smile died when his gaze moved to her face.

"Uh-oh." He stepped back and opened the door wider. "Mint tea, extra strong."

She managed a laugh. "I'm fine. Not to worry."

"You could have fooled me."

She followed him to the kitchen. The room was large but not well designed, and definitely not updated. The appliances were harvest-gold, and the countertops were covered in a plastic laminate pattern so antiquated that he might find it at the bottom of an excavation someday. She doubted Travis cared, since his cooking skills were limited to thawing and reheating.

He did make a great glass of iced spearmint tea, however, and she leaned against a counter as he snapped ice out of trays and poured tea from a glass pitcher.

"So tell me," he said casually. "Is the extra work from camp getting to you?"

"Absolutely not. Noah and I have established a rhythm. It's getting easier."

He replaced the pitcher and dug out lemons. "There's going to be a lot more work with the kids camping here."

"I'm not worried. They'll be doing a lot of the prep work. I just wanted to go over menus this afternoon to make sure we're on the same page."

He finished the tea and handed her the finished product. "Sounds like you have it all covered. Let's do it in the sunroom."

The sunroom was Gayle's favorite. What walls there were showcased antique maps and Egyptian masks. Reproductions of papyrus columns peeked out from palm trees and flourishing schefflera. But her favorite piece was a coffee table with a glass top covering a display case. Travis had filled the case with artifacts that previous archaeology camps had uncovered. Buttons, pieces of a clay pipe, a set of dice, coins, shards of crockery. Looking at it was a trip into the past.

They settled on a sofa with glimpses of the river beyond them. Like the inn, Travis's house was no more than a stone's throw from the water.

"So…" Gayle pulled a folder out of her voluminous leather purse. The purse weighed a ton, but she needed all the space. She never left home without a calculator, a personal organizer, a cell phone, business cards and brochures for the inn, a perfectly balanced checkbook, one photograph of each of her children, including Leon, coupons in alphabetical order, a pack of tissues, extra car and house keys hidden in a secret pocket, and a notebook with lists for every conceivable shopping trip from wholesale groceries to tube socks.

"Maybe it's not as bad a day as I thought. At least you found your purse," Travis said.

She looked up. "You're looking at the most organized person you'll ever meet."

"Sorry, but Noah tells me the purse is a family joke. It's an office with a handle, but half the time you can't remember where you put it."

This time, when she laughed, it was completely natural. "Guilty. You know why?"

"I have my theory. One side of you knows you won't survive the life you've chosen if you aren't on top of every little thing. The other rejects having to be that way."

She was entranced. "Wow, you really know me well."

"I'd say so."

"Okay, then tell me how you knew something was wrong when you opened the door this afternoon?"

"You were rubbing the tip of your nose."

"What?"

He demonstrated. "Like this." He touched his nose with his index finger and slid it up and down a few times. "That's what you do when something's bothering you."

"Are you sure you're not an anthropologist?"

"I'm not studying you. We just spend enough time together that I notice things."

She felt suddenly vulnerable and oddly aware of him. "I'm impressed. And a little frightened. I thought I was better at hiding my feelings."

"You're actually very good. Not nearly as good as your mother, but somewhere in the ballpark."

She'd never really talked about her parents, but Travis had met them several times. She wasn't surprised he'd figured out her mom.

"Let's talk about menus." She opened the folder. "It's a lot more straightforward than my childhood. Here's what I came up with."

She handed him a copy and watched as he scanned it. The tea was delicious, and she'd sipped about half before he spoke.

"It's fabulous. Too fabulous. You don't have to work this hard."

She leaned back. "What can I cut?"

They discussed her suggestions, bandying ideas back and forth. She put down her glass to make notes. They laughed over some of it, argued a little and easily came up with a compromise. The menu debate was over in a few minutes.

"You're so easy to work with," she said, packing up her menu, now covered with notes.

"We didn't agree on everything."

"Well, we don't have to agree. It's just that when I work with you, I know you appreciate my ideas, even the ones we table, and we're coming from a mutual desire to make things easy for both of us."

"Why wouldn't we?"

She realized what she was really talking about. Not menus, but respect. Not Travis, but Eric.

"Are we getting to what's bothering you?" he asked.

"Get out your notepad."

He smiled. She basked in the unexpected warmth of it and felt herself relaxing. "Give," he said.

She told him about the fight with Eric that morning, about

Eric's idea for the old garden shed and his decision to work on it as a surprise. When she was finished, she felt better.

"I guess I overreacted," she said. "But, Travis, I haven't been that angry in a long, long time. I'm not even sure where it all came from."

"Maybe it's as simple as you said. You want things done your own way, and you don't have time to negotiate every little thing. Especially after the fact."

"Maybe." She wasn't convinced.

"Or maybe you're reminded of a time in your life when Eric was in charge and you were more or less along for the ride."

She wondered if she'd ever been that docile. Had she really just allowed Eric to run things according to his whims?

"You're rubbing your nose," he pointed out.

Her hand dropped to her lap. "I never let him walk all over me. He'll do that with anybody, given half a chance. That's probably why he's so good at his job. You have to be part steam-roller to flatten people and get the information you need. But when it didn't really matter, I did let him have his way."

"And at the end, you stood up for staying here? And he left?"

"There was more to it than that." She considered whether to go on. It wasn't like her to spill her guts, but so far the result was unexpectedly gratifying.

"I'd like to hear it if you'd like to tell me."

"He didn't want Dillon." She looked up. "You've probably gathered that?"

Travis didn't answer directly. "I think he's trying now."

"He is. But here's how badly he didn't want a third child. He had a vasectomy. Without consulting me. He had it overseas where they aren't as concerned with those sorts of niceties. He saw it as insurance. We were using birth control, but I couldn't take the pill. He was afraid something might slip up, but I wasn't ready to cancel our options, so to speak. So he went ahead and canceled them without me."

Travis didn't say anything, but she felt no condemnation. He was simply waiting for her to continue.

"Once he told me, I stopped using birth control, and I got pregnant. Eric assumed what most men in that situation assume."

"That you were having an affair? I can understand his concern. You're a beautiful woman."

She smiled at that. "Not so beautiful. The ragged, harried mom of two little boys. But thank you. And yes, that's what he thought."

"Clearly it wasn't true. You only have to look at Dillon to know that. Or you really only have to know what kind of woman Gayle Fortman is."

She looked out over the land easing down to the river. "Because Eric had the operation overseas, he didn't bother with the one-year follow-up. He thought the odds were so far in his favor there was no point. Only they weren't in his favor, as it turned out. Anyway, he was furious, more because we were having another baby, I think, than because he thought I'd slept with someone else."

Something flickered in his eyes, but his tone remained even. "How long did it take him to figure out the truth?"

"Longer than it should have. He left. Eventually he got himself to a doctor and discovered the operation hadn't been a success. But months went by. Things started to fall apart with his network. Finally he came back and told me he was sorry, but he had been so overwhelmed by the kids we already had, he just hadn't been able to face having another one."

"This sounds like the beginning of the end."

She got up and walked to the windows for a better view.

"Who knows when a marriage peaks and the rest of it's a fast slide on the downward slope? We reconciled. We found the inn and moved here. Dillon was born, and I knew right away Eric still resented him. But I was so happy, happier than I'd been anywhere I'd ever lived. Even with the tension with Eric. Even with the hard work and a baby I had little help with."

She turned around. "I don't want to make Eric sound heartless. He did try to make a go of things. Not everybody's cut out for family life, and he had the good sense to face the facts. But there he was with three sons and a country inn that was sucking us dry. When he got the offer to go to Bosnia, he saw it as a way out. He wasn't leaving us. He was just going back to the life he loved. The frequent breaks would make family life tolerable. Anyway, I think that's how he saw it. If he could just get away enough, he could be a decent father. He could return to wherever he'd stowed us and take up where he'd left off, as long as those visits weren't too long."

"And you said no."

"It wasn't easy, but it was easier than the alternative. And when he was finally gone, as painful as it was, I knew I'd done the right thing for everybody."

Travis got up and crossed the room. From behind her, he laid his hand on her shoulder. "So what's changed?"

His hand felt solid and real. She wanted to turn, put her arms around his waist and be held by his lean, strong arms, but of course she couldn't.

Instead she covered his hand for a moment in thanks. "Nothing's changed. Except that he's back for the summer. And I guess arguments come with the territory."

"I'm not sure they do, at least not arguments with this much emotion." His hand left her shoulder. "Not if you've really put Eric behind you."

"But I have."

"Gayle, you're the most married divorced woman I've ever met." This time she did face him. "What exactly does that mean?"

"I don't think you've ever really said goodbye to Eric. I don't mean that I think you've been holding out hopes you'll reconcile. It's more like you've taken a vow of fidelity. Your marriage ended, but as long as you don't move on to someone else, you haven't really failed. And for that matter, I'm not sure Eric hasn't done exactly the same thing. He never married again. I know there's a woman—"

"Ariel," she said without thinking.

"But he's here with *you*, not with her."

"Because of the boys."

"Because *you* offered him a home again," he said gently. "Gayle, you brought him back because you thought he needed you. But really, who needed who? Have you asked yourself? Because I think you have to. It's now or never."

Hours later she was still thinking of things she should have said to Travis. The boys were off with friends, and the guests were busy on their own. Without the sound of sneakers squeaking across the floor, the roar of video games, the carriage house seemed twice as large as usual. She'd made herself a salad and eaten only a few bites. Then, since no one was at home, she'd let herself into Noah and Dillon's room for another session with Buddy.

She had decided almost from Buddy's arrival that she wanted to use him to surprise Noah, who was obviously having a difficult summer. She had tried and failed to come up with a surefire way to retrieve the good-natured, happy kid Noah had been before Eric came back. There wasn't any easy way, she knew, but it had occurred to her almost immediately that teaching Buddy to talk would make Noah smile. After all, it shouldn't be hard. Eric and Dillon had been told that the little parakeet talked when they bought him. A refresher course was in order, that was all.

Buddy was chirping away when she walked into the boys' bedroom. She rolled Noah's desk chair over to the cage and put her nose against the bars.

"No place like home," she said clearly. "No place like home."

She'd chosen her phrase carefully. It was the punch line of a joke she and Noah shared. As a child, he had been entranced by *The Wizard of Oz*, watching the video so often that he had memorized large chunks of the dialogue. Now, as a teenager, whenever she asked him to do something he didn't want to do, he closed his eyes, clicked his heels and said…

"No place like home." Gayle wiggled her finger at the little bird, whose eyes were white with excitement. "No place like home."

Fifteen minutes later, Buddy was chattering away, but nothing resembling words emerged. She gave up and went back downstairs.

She was just pulling the salad out of the refrigerator again when someone knocked on the door. Before she could open it, Eric did.

"May I come in?"

She was in no mood for another confrontation, but during their marriage she and Eric had agreed on the value of sweeping problems under the rug. That which couldn't be solved was usually never mentioned again. So, hoping the rule was still in force, she nodded.

"I brought you something." He stepped inside and flashed the largest bouquet of flowers she had ever seen. "I'm not sure which are your favorites these days, so I sort of overdid it and bought everything I could find."

"Master of the grand gesture." She was afraid her voice betrayed her reaction. She was touched, surprised—and pleased. After the talk with Travis, the last frightened her.

"If you're going to make a gesture, go all out." He held the flowers out to her.

She met him halfway across the room. The flowers filled her arms. Lilies, stock and roses added a cool, sweet fragrance to the air. She buried her nose in the midst of them and tried to think of something to say.

Eric spoke before she could. "Gayle, I'm sorry. I really am. I had no business doing what I did. I really thought you'd be pleased, but it was stupid to make assumptions. We'll go over your plans, and I'll put everything back the way you wanted it."

She looked up at him. "Give me a few days to figure that out."

"Sure. It's going to take that long just to haul out the stuff I've already wrecked."

"Did it make you feel better?"

"What, making you angry?"

She had to smile. "No, wielding the sledgehammer and crowbar with such abandon."

He sent her his most winning smile, the one that had reduced the younger Gayle to mush. "You have no idea. A couple of weeks on a wrecking crew and I'd be in great mental shape."

"Then at least we can call it therapy."

"I'm forgiven?"

"You never used to apologize."

He raised a brow. "It would be a mistake to assume I've stayed exactly the same for twelve years."

She wondered how much he had changed. Since his arrival,

she'd seen both the Eric she remembered and hints of someone more mature and responsible. Certainly he was trying hard to make up to his sons for years of benign neglect.

"You're forgiven," she said. "And the flowers are beautiful. Thank you."

"Have you had dinner yet?"

"I tried. Salad just doesn't appeal tonight."

"Let me take you out. One of your guests was raving about an Italian restaurant in Edinburg."

A warning alarm sounded in her head. Yes, it was perfectly acceptable for them to go out to dinner together. No, after her talk with Travis, she wasn't inclined to do it. She felt confused in ways she hadn't for years, vulnerable and wary and altogether too open to suggestion. She didn't want to sit with Eric over a bottle of wine and reminisce.

"Another night," she said. "You'll like the restaurant. It reminds me of—" And then she realized she was reminiscing anyway.

He knew immediately. "Franco's? In Echo Park? I think of Franco's a lot. Nobody makes a better marinara sauce. Not even in Italy."

Old friends, old lovers, old husbands. No one else could finish sentences in quite the same way. No one else could stir up powerful memories with just a few words.

She turned toward the kitchen. "I need to put these in a vase. Or, more likely, in vases. Many vases."

"I'll help."

"Great. Then I'll make grilled-cheese sandwiches, if that sounds good."

"Much better than going out alone."

The flowers filled three vases, large ones, and Eric helped her set them in the living area and on the kitchen table. The third one she took into her bedroom. She'd put the most fragrant flowers in this one so she could enjoy them in the darkness, too.

Back in the kitchen, she found Eric pulling cheese and bread from the refrigerator.

"Cheddar or Swiss?" he asked.

"I like Swiss."

"Dijon or deli mustard?"

"Dijon for me."

"Whole wheat or rye?"

"Let's try rye."

She got out the frying pan and the butter. He made the sandwiches. Neither of them spoke until dinner was sizzling in the pan.

Eric leaned against the counter, arms folded. "I had a really good swimming lesson with Dillon. He's learning to float. By the time we finished he was floating on his own for half a minute. I think we turned a corner. He even did a couple of laps in the pool without fussing."

"It'll be such a relief to know he's not afraid of the water. I live in fear he'll end up in the river and panic."

"He's quite a kid. I've missed out on a lot."

He'd surprised her again. She decided to be generous. "The two of you got off to a bad start."

"My fault, of course. But I had myself pegged. I wasn't ready to be a father of three, and I knew it. What I didn't get was that I had to step up to the plate anyway."

She flipped the sandwiches, more for something to do than because they needed it.

She put down the spatula and faced him. "You've stepped up to it this summer, Eric. That's worth a lot."

"If I find my sons again, before they're lost to me completely, it's because you made it possible."

Before she realized what she was doing, she reached out and touched his cheek. She hadn't noticed the welt when he'd walked in, his face half-hidden by gladiolas and sunflowers. But now she realized he'd had an encounter with something even angrier than his ex-wife. "What happened here?"

"A hornet."

"Did you put something on it?"

He shrugged.

"Men," she said wryly. "Just like your sons. It's some weird rite of passage. One moment the boys wanted me to kiss every boo-boo, the next they didn't even want to tell me they'd broken their arms or sprained their ankles."

"They broke arms?"

"Jared, one arm and a dislocated shoulder. Noah?" She tried to remember. "A collarbone. And numerous sprains. Dillon? Oh, that list goes on and on. He's afraid of the water and not one bit afraid of anything else. He's fallen out of trees on his head, tripped over his own feet and broken his nose, suffered shin splints and a toe fracture, inflamed tendons. They greet him in the emergency room like some sort of mascot."

She flicked off the burner. "Let's get something on that sting."

"Why didn't I know about all those injuries?"

"You were a little far away to haul them to the hospital. I figured they would tell you if you called, but of course they didn't want to sound like babies."

"Don't worry about the sting. The swelling will go down."

"And now I know where they get their male stoicism."

She left and returned with the first-aid kit. "The sooner I do this, the sooner we'll eat."

"You sound like somebody's mother."

"That's what happens, I'm afraid. Find a chair."

He laughed, but he went over to the table and took a seat. Gayle followed, rummaging through the kit. "Did you remove the stinger?"

"I was a little busy keeping Dillon afloat."

"It's a good thing you didn't have an allergic reaction." She put her hand under his chin and tilted his face toward her. "Just a minute." She left to turn up the light to its brightest setting. Then she returned and tilted his chin again. "Nope, you didn't get it. Now that the area's so swollen, it's going to be harder."

"Let's call it a badge of honor and forget it."

"Let's not. It might continue to swell." She squeezed a little, and when he didn't wince, she squeezed harder. "I think I can scrape it out if you can hold still."

"I'm a model stoic, remember?"

She patted his cheek and went into the bedroom, returning with a credit card. "Okay. You're about to benefit from my American Express."

He laughed until she began to carefully scrape it along the site of the sting. "Ouch."

"Sorry. Give me another second. We're almost there."

She was able to free the stinger, and she wiped it away with a handy paper napkin. "I couldn't use tweezers. Sometimes the venom sac is still attached, and squeezing can release it."

He put his hand to his cheek. "How do you learn this stuff?"

"We have three sons who regularly find yellow-jacket nests the hard way." She straightened. "Okay, that's the worst of it. I'll get you some ice to put on it, which next time you should do immediately."

He stood, but she hadn't moved away quickly enough. They were chest to chest, her nose to his chin. She took a step backward and looked up at him. Eric touched her hair, pushing a strand off her cheek.

Neither said anything for a long moment; then he spoke, his voice soft. "After I moved out for good, it took years to get over the feeling I was coming back. I'd think, gosh, I have to remember to tell Gayle about this, or I'd see something at a market or in a shop that would suit you and find myself heading over to buy it."

For a moment she couldn't seem to remember how to breathe.

"And then...I'd remember," he said.

"And what came next? Relief? Sadness? Gratitude that we'd both moved on?"

"A mixture, I guess. But more sadness than I think you give me credit for." He dropped his hand.

"Sometimes it takes a while to realize something's ended."

"Relationships change, but they don't end unless somebody dies. And even then..."

"Being married ended. Putting each other first ended." She hesitated. "As it should have. Did you ever regret the divorce? Really and truly? Because I don't think I did. I was sad, too." Sadder, she supposed than she wanted to admit. At the time, *sad* would have been a poor choice of words.

"I was sorry it had come to that," he said.

She squared her shoulders a fraction. "Me, too, but I never really doubted we'd done what we had to."

"I regretted I couldn't be somebody I'm not."

She wondered how often and for how long. It wasn't in Eric's nature to spend time pondering past errors or the things that made him tick. His life zoomed by on fast-forward, and there had never been a pause button.

"I regretted I couldn't be the woman who sat at home and endlessly waited for you," she said. "But I'm enough like you that I needed to keep moving, too."

He laughed, but it sounded forced. "I wonder why we didn't figure all this out ahead of time?"

"Youth? Ignorance?"

He shook his head slowly. "No. I don't know why I asked the question, because I know the answer. We couldn't figure it out because we were blinded by love. And it colored everything we were and everything we did for all those years we were together. Say what you will about our differences, but that was one thing we always agreed on."

Chapter 20

Jared didn't want to pick up the pregnancy test for Brandy in Shenandoah County. He could just imagine how fast *that* news would get back to his mother. So on Sunday night, instead of going to the youth meeting at church, he drove Gayle's pickup to Front Royal, slinking in and out of CVS like a shoplifter.

He supposed that if he wasn't so embarrassed to admit he was "doing it" with Brandy they wouldn't be in this situation in the first place. He would have purchased condoms right off the shelf and not expected his girlfriend to provide expired ones via Cray's uncle's medicine cabinet. But he couldn't shake the feeling that the entire county wanted an insider's view of his personal life and was watching everything he did. For once he wished he lived in a bustling metropolis where nobody cared about his sex life or future.

Early on Monday morning, he packed his camping gear—and the test kit—in the car and had started around to the driver's side when his mother came out of the house.

He could see that Gayle was in high gear. He knew she'd already been up for hours. She waved him down before he could get in.

"Jared, do you mind taking Dillon with you? He usually walks over the bridge, but today he has all his camping stuff. I was going to take it over at noon with the lunch, but he wants to set up right away."

Jared had plans for the morning that didn't involve a little brother as witness.

He raked his fingers through his hair until he remembered that this was his mother watching, and her radar was ultrasensitive. He managed a smile.

"Do I have to? I mean, I have to get Brandy and all her stuff, and there's not going to be much room left in the car. Can't Dad take him over in his Mustang?"

"He's making trips to the landfill."

"Is Dillon ready now?"

"Probably not quite."

"Then I'll get Brandy first." Jared could just imagine the atmosphere in the car on the way to Mr. Allen's house. Either a positive or a negative answer would have its consequences. But one look at his mother's face and he knew taking Dillon with them couldn't be helped.

"That'll work," she said. "I'll make sure he gets everything together."

"Well, it's not like he can't walk home for whatever he forgets."

On the short drive to Brandy's house he had time to consider his options. If the test was positive, he had to keep his emotions in check. Otherwise Brandy would cause a scene that would still be building when they got back to his house. If the test was negative, and he appeared too relieved, the same thing would happen. She would insist he didn't love her.

There really was no reaction that would keep Brandy calm enough to fool his mother, no matter what the test kit revealed.

He wondered how he had gotten himself into this mess. But of course the answer to that was obvious.

He arrived at Brandy's just as Mrs. Wilburn was pulling out of the driveway in a Buick right off her husband's lot. Brandy was supposed to get her mother's older model, but not for a couple more weeks. She'd had a fender bender several months ago, and as punishment her parents had told her that she couldn't drive unless they were in the car. The restrictions would be lifted at the end of July.

He waved, and Mrs. Wilburn tooted her horn. After he parked, he let himself in through the front door, calling Brandy's name.

"Hey, I'm right here." She poked her head out of the kitchen. "Want anything before I start the dishwasher?"

He held up the bag he'd brought with him. "I bought a pregnancy test. I think we have to know where we stand."

She chewed her generous bottom lip. "What kind did you get?"

He opened the bag and shoved it at her. She wrinkled her nose as she read the back of the package. "We're kind of on the line here. But we can try."

"What do you mean, on the line? You said you should have had your period by now. And the package says—"

"Jar-Jar, I told you, it's not that simple. I don't always know. Look, we'll give it a try, okay? I'm willing. I'm just telling you it might not be that accurate yet."

"If it says you're pregnant, you're pregnant."

"And if it says I'm not?"

He wanted an answer. He really didn't think he could stand the suspense. "Just give it a try, okay?"

"No problem. I have to pee on a stick. Do you want to watch?"

There were few things he would rather not do. "You go ahead. Read the directions, though. You have to do it just right."

"Really? I thought I'd do it wrong, just to spite you." She swung the box in his direction, narrowly missing his arm; then she headed for the bathroom and slammed the door behind her.

It seemed like forever, but only a few minutes passed before she returned. She wasn't smiling, and for a moment, his heart sank.

"I thought *you* ought to be in on the fun part," she said. "I did the work, now we get to wait and see together."

"How long?"

"It says maybe as short as a minute, maybe as long as three."

"So what, we just stand here and stare at it?" The evidence was encased in plastic. He'd bought the kit that promised the answer would be clear. Now he wished there would still be room for guesswork.

"So what are you hoping for, a boy or a girl?"

He stared at her, and she shrugged. "Just kidding. Jeez!"

He looked down, and words were appearing. He could hardly stand to read them.

"See leaflet?" He looked up at her. "See leaflet? What does that mean?"

"Maybe I'm pregnant with a tree."

"Damn it, Brandy!"

"You don't have to swear at me!"

"Where did you put the instructions?"

"They're in the bathroom. Where do you think? On my mother's pillow next to a chocolate mint?"

He stormed into the bathroom and found the packaging. He read through it, his stomach knotting.

Back in the living room, he thrust it at her. "It says an error has occurred, and we have to start over with a new kit." He shoved his hands in his pockets after she took the paper from him. "We don't have a new kit!"

"What's the problem? You can get another one, and we can do it again tomorrow."

"We're going to be at camp! What, you want to do this in the Port-a-Potty with your campers watching?"

"You're being impossible!" She turned around and stomped toward her bedroom. When she came out, she had a backpack slung over one shoulder and a sleeping bag under her arm. "If we're *done* here, then let's get moving. Before I can pee on a stick to entertain my campers, we have to get there." Then she started to cry.

Jared grabbed her and pulled her close. She pummeled his chest, but only halfheartedly. "Look, I'm sorry," he said. "Stop hitting me."

"What's wrong with you, Jar-Jar? Getting upset about this isn't going to help. We'll know soon enough. Just get over it and get moving."

"It's not knowing. I'll feel better when I know."

She sniffed. "One way or the other?"

"Sure," he said. But of course it wasn't true.

Gayle could almost see the storm cloud hanging over Jared's and Brandy's heads when they arrived to pick up Dillon. She regretted asking Jared to come back for his brother, but it was too late now to change her mind. The ride was short, so she knew Dillon wasn't going to come to any harm refereeing what was clearly a fight. But she was sorry he had to be anywhere near the feuding couple.

"You have everything, honey?" she asked Dillon.

As only a young teen could, he made it clear without saying a word that his mother was rapidly losing IQ points.

"Okay, scoot," she said. "It's not like you won't have a million chances to get anything you forget."

"Yeah, and please don't make a big deal out of seeing me when you're there, okay?"

"I know the drill. No hugging, kissing or reminding you to wash between your toes."

He shook his head. She was glad he was learning forbearance and that her maternal stupidity was responsible.

She waved goodbye and hoped the three of them survived the trip.

Inside, Paula was chatting with guests, and the cleaning crew was tackling the kitchen. Gayle intercepted Noah before he reached the kitchen door.

"It looks like it's going to be another fifteen minutes, at least," she warned. "Maybe as long as a half hour before we can get in there to prep for camp. They're doing a top to bottom cleaning."

"I'm going to work with the quilters, then."

"You go ahead. I'll join you if I can."

"I think Ms. Henry has banned you from the room."

"Hallelujah."

Noah grinned. "She told me she's sorry she lived long enough to see the day she couldn't teach somebody to quilt a straight line."

"I hate being her dying regret."

"Not to worry. She says I make up for it."

"I don't know where your talent comes from, but hoard it. It's in short supply in this family. Oh, and, Noah, meet me in the kitchen in half an hour, no later. I don't know if we're going to be able to get everything ready as it is."

Gayle's tiny office had formerly been a mudroom at the inn's side entrance. Clutter wasn't an option, but somehow in the last week the office had gotten cluttered anyway. Glad for a little time to bring order, she started at the top of a pile marked To Do. She was printing out tourist information a guest had requested when Cissy poked her head in, her daughter riding one hip.

"I just wanted to say hi. I came to quilt, but there's no room. Reese, say hi to Ms. Fortman."

Gayle held out her arms, and Reese, an adorable plump-cheeked preschooler, launched herself into them. This morning she wore denim overalls and a bright pink T-shirt with ruffles around the neck and sleeves. Her baby-fine blond hair was gathered into a ponytail on top of her head and held in place by half a dozen plastic barrettes.

"I was supposed to have one of these," Gayle told Cissy.

Reese immediately fingered Gayle's necklace and began to count the wooden beads. "One, two, tree." She paused and started all over again. "One, two, tree."

"She gets up to six on a good day," Cissy said.

"Gween," Reese said, holding out the necklace and pointing to a bead.

"Very good," Gayle told her. "It certainly is green. Would you like a strawberry?"

"Strawberries are red. Two!"

Gayle gave her a quick hug; then, with Reese still on her hip, tiptoed into the kitchen and raided the berry bowl in the refrigerator.

Cissy was filing receipts when Gayle and Reese returned. They transferred Reese, who had a strawberry in each hand.

"I see she's all yours today," Gayle said.

"We've got big plans. We're going over to the camp a little later to see what Caleb's doing and take some more of his camping gear. Do you need help until it's time? I've got Reese, but I can still get some things accomplished."

"Boy, if you could do some of the filing and organizing in here, that would be a godsend. It's all in this pile and pretty clear. Noah and I are going to be in the kitchen as soon as the cleaning crew finishes. Maybe we could all go over together afterwards?"

"That'll work fine."

"Just make sure you add in the hours to your total."

"Whatever Reese doesn't subtract."

With Cissy and Paula both at work, Gayle was able to concentrate on the camp. Today she had extra supplies to haul and store in Travis's house. She worked around the cleaning crew and gathered boxes of food from the pantry, carrying them outside. Eric had been using the pickup for early morning trips to the landfill, but now she saw it was parked in its usual place. After the third box of supplies, she was leaning against it to catch her breath when Eric found her.

He was in jeans and a tattered gray T-shirt, which was tight enough to make the point he was gaining back the weight and muscle that had been missing when he'd first arrived.

He took a place beside her and stuck his feet out in front of him. "I'm available for carrying those boxes. I've been hauling worse all morning."

"How much debris is left?"

"Enough to keep me busy tomorrow, too. So why don't you let me help you get everything over to the camp?"

"Great."

"I don't mind doing anything you need, Gayle. It keeps me busy. I hate sitting around."

She thought of something she really needed. As close as they were, Jared had never been willing to discuss Brandy with her, and she doubted he was going to start now, when war had been declared. She wasn't just being nosy, though. She had a bad feeling she might need to prepare for almost anything.

"I do have a favor. I wasn't going to bother you with it, but…" She turned to face him and told him what she'd seen that morning.

Eric didn't look surprised. And he didn't smile, clap her on the back and tell her not to worry, as she'd half expected. In fact, he didn't say anything, but he looked concerned.

"What?" she demanded.

"I don't know. I'll talk to him again. But I think he's feeling trapped by their relationship. Maybe things have come to a head."

She had a feeling he wasn't telling her everything, but she was glad to leave it in his hands. "I'm glad I asked."

"So am I." Then he leaned over. She felt the brush of skin rougher than hers and smelled a spicy, masculine soap. He kissed her cheek, completely catching her off guard.

"What was that for?" she asked when he straightened. She was afraid her cheeks were turning pink.

"For remembering I'm Jared's father."

Eric couldn't get near his son until it was almost time for the evening campfire. Travis had divided the group so that one half of the campers spent the morning setting up tents and stowing their gear while the other half worked at the dig. Jared was much too busy pounding tent stakes and working out compromises on placement to have a conversation with anyone. At lunch he was busy helping the second group of counselors figure out what to do with their tents and gear, and after lunch he corralled his campers for the walk over to the site.

Eric knew that once Jared started supervising their excavation unit, he wouldn't be able to take a long enough break for a heart-to-heart. The counselors had been trained to watch the campers closely so no artifacts were destroyed by impatience or carelessness.

The air was beginning to cool when he drove back to the Allen farm and parked. His presence at the campfires was expected now, since his youngest son was one of the stars. He pitched in with the setup and cleanup, and although Noah resented his help, he knew Gayle was grateful.

When the meal was almost over, he finally saw his chance to talk to his son. Jared's campers had joined several other groups that were scraping plates and cleaning trash off the tables, and other counselors were supervising.

Eric made his way over and rested his hand on Jared's shoulder. "Looking forward to sleeping under the stars tonight?"

"Yeah, it'll be okay."

"They keep you moving, don't they?"

"I've had worse summer jobs."

Eric had paid attention during dinner, and he had noted that Jared and Brandy seemed to be trying hard not to look at each other. "Want to take a short walk before the campfire? Just down to the river to stretch our legs?"

"Sure." Jared checked his group to be sure everyone was busy; then he followed Eric.

The campsite was about an acre from the farmhouse, on the other side of a thin patch of woods. Travis had turned an old outbuilding into a primitive bath house, with a row of showers and a couple of toilets and sinks, divided down the middle by a concrete wall so there was a distinct his and hers. Portable toilets, one on each side, took up the slack during the week of camp. There was nothing fancy here. Travis wanted the kids to get the flavor of a real archaeology dig. There were lots of complaints about roughing it, but nobody really seemed to mind.

Both the camp and the waiting list were always full a year ahead of time.

As they made their way across a field to the river, they chatted about the camp. Eric waited until they were out of earshot of anyone else before he got to the real point of their stroll. He didn't know where to start, but he knew they weren't going to have a lot of time.

He was afraid he knew what Jared's problem was. He had been waiting for this opportunity since his conversation with Dillon on the way to their last swimming lesson, but he hadn't been waiting eagerly. Dreading what he might find out, he edged carefully into his selected topic.

"Do you remember last week, when I was more or less telling you what to do about Brandy? I want to apologize. I was giving advice without knowing all the facts. I ought to know better. I hope you aren't upset with me."

"I didn't think much about it."

"The thing is," Eric said, "I don't really know how you feel about her. Maybe you're so much in love, you just can't wait to get married."

Jared was silent.

"Or maybe you're feeling a lot of pressure."

"What do you mean?" Jared picked up a stone and threw it as far as he could into the river.

"Well, I don't know. From friends, maybe. Or maybe Brandy's pressuring you. You said she really wants to get married and have children."

"Yeah, she does." He threw another stone.

"Or maybe staying here just sounds easier and better than going away to school and being away from everybody you love. That can be hard."

"It's not that."

"Do you want to tell me what it *is?*"

Jared was silent. Eric wished he could take a crash course in raising sons. He felt completely at sea.

He realized their time alone was going to end in a few minutes. He got down to the point. "Or maybe she's pregnant," he said, "and you don't know what to do about it."

Jared had picked up a third stone. He'd lifted his hand to throw that one, too, but now it dropped to his side. "What makes you think that?"

"I was your age once. And if I'd had a girlfriend as pretty and willing as yours, I would have found it impossible to resist having sex with her. I think you're probably more responsible and mature than I was, but I'm not sure you've resisted, either."

Jared didn't look at him. "What did they do when you were my age? If that happened, I mean."

"Before my generation, girls went into hiding, had their babies and gave them up. Or they found some back-alley doctor and hoped they survived. With abortion being legal, my generation had more options. But that doesn't mean any of them were easy. I had friends whose lives were pretty shaken up by unplanned pregnancies. One girl had a baby and gave it up for adoption. She found her son a few years ago, and they became friends. But that's not always the case."

"Brandy wouldn't consider an abortion."

"That's her right. And I know you wouldn't push her." Eric hesitated. "Is she pregnant, Jared?"

"I don't know."

Eric's heart sank. "Okay. Do you know how to find out?"

"We tried a drugstore test today, but something went

wrong. We'll try again as soon as it makes sense. But we're here for the week."

Eric scrambled for a way to help. "No pressure, but I'll arrange a little time off for you both when you're ready. I can do that without revealing why."

"That would be good. In a few days, when it will be more accurate."

"How are you feeling?"

"Remember that time we went white-water rafting in North Carolina? Remember the hydraulic?"

Eric did. Jared had been a young teenager, ready for adventure. But when their raft had gotten stuck in a whirlpool, spinning madly in circles so that all they could do was grip the ropes lacing the sides and hope that eventually someone would get them out, Eric had questioned his own sanity. He had been terrified Jared would fall overboard and even more terrified that if he did, he wouldn't be able to find him in the water.

"The hydraulic spat us out," Eric said. "One moment I thought we were both going overboard, the next the raft was floating downstream."

"I don't think that's going to happen this time."

"You don't know. And remember what the guide told us? Even if you had fallen in, you would have been pulled down, but the hydraulic would have tossed you out in plenty of time. It happens a lot, and nobody's come close to drowning there." He paused. "If the worst is true and Brandy is pregnant, your mom and I will help you both figure out what's best for everybody. It won't be easy, but you'll have help."

"I don't want Mom to know. She has enough on her plate, and she's been worried about me and Brandy ever since we hooked up."

"Yeah, okay." Eric wondered how he was going to keep this

from Gayle. He hoped he could get the kids over to the house as soon as possible and get an answer. "But we'll have to tell her if it's true, okay?"

"It'll be pretty obvious."

"We'll have to tell her *way* before it gets to that point, and obviously Brandy's parents will have to know. But don't borrow trouble, okay? And don't forget I'm here to help."

Jared finally looked at him. "I'm glad you know."

Gayle hoped that Eric found a way to talk to Jared, but he deserved the chance to do this his own way, at his own speed. Still, even though she was trying not to pry, she had noticed that Brandy and Jared were carefully ignoring each other. She hoped Jared had just made it clear once and for all that he was leaving for New England in the fall. He had worked so hard for his scholarship, and she couldn't bear to think he might give it up.

"How about driving over to the site for a look? Before everyone descends for the campfire."

She turned to find Travis right behind her. "I didn't know you were there."

"You were a million miles away."

"Well, maybe not so many." She dried her hands on a dish towel. "I'd love to go over and see what you've done. Noah promised he'll take the leftovers to the camp fridge, so I'm done here."

"Great, but we'd better get going. They'll be on their way soon."

They chatted in the car. The campers were planning a Thursday morning hike up the trail behind the site to get a view from above. She planned to supply sandwich fixings so they could take their lunches, and now they discussed whether to add canned soft drinks to supplement bottled water. They settled on juice drinks instead.

"One of the reasons I chose to study archaeology is the surprise factor," Travis said, pulling up to the area they had designated for parking. "You never really know what's there when you dig. You can perform gradiometric surveys, research the historical record, dig shovel test pits, use metal detectors, but in the end, whatever's there is hidden until the moment you unearth it."

He parked and got out, and she did, too. "Have you found a surprise?" she asked.

"More of one than I wanted. Come on, I'll show you." He put out his hand to help her hop over a narrow ditch. "Watch where you step. All the units are covered with plastic, but the light's tricky this time of evening."

She walked beside him and felt herself relaxing for the first time all day. She liked catering the meals for the camp, mostly because she knew it was a help to Travis and it gave them some time together. But running the inn and dealing with family problems was a full load. She was looking forward to camp ending.

He stopped and pointed out what each group was doing. "You know we isolated this area as the place the trash pit had probably been located."

"And the metal detectors confirmed it."

"You've been listening and get an A. Okay, it looks like we were right. You've seen the things the campers are finding."

Every time she arrived at the site, Gayle was given an artifact tour. There was enough interesting material to keep the campers fascinated. Archaeology wasn't treasure hunting, but even though they were required to go slowly and document every part of the dig with notes, photographs and drawings, whenever someone found even the most insignificant item, everyone felt as if they'd struck gold.

"Enough to keep them busy," she said. "Nails, cartridge casings..." She tried to remember what else she'd been shown. "A shoe eyelet, an Indian-head penny..."

"Bones are a favorite. The Duncans must have had a serious flock of chickens."

"So what's the surprise?"

"Come over here." He motioned her to the pit closest to the river and pulled back the sheet of black plastic that covered it. He squatted on the ground and pointed. "See this?"

She came around and squatted beside him, peering down. "Rocks?"

"I think it's a stone wall. Or possibly the foundation of a fireplace."

"So this area was more than a hole where they dumped garbage."

"I shouldn't be surprised, I guess. No farmer with any sense digs a pit if he has something he can fill in already."

He got to his feet and pulled the plastic back over the top.

"So what do you think it was?"

"Something interesting, and now I'm not sure we should have gotten into this. I think the river has moved since Miranda Duncan and Robby lived here and we're closer to the site of the second cabin, where the Duncans' farmworkers lived, than I had estimated."

"Eb and Cora?"

"Probably. The Duncans never had slaves. But Eb, Cora and Ralph aren't just characters in a play. They're documented. In fact, Eb sued a local farmer in the 1870s, and I have a copy of the court case."

"What for?"

"He claims the man stole his cow. Apparently he was right. Eb got it back, and the neighbor paid a fine."

"You think this might be where their house was?"

"I've been able to talk to two great-granddaughters. I gather they were little more than babies when Miranda died, and their parents lived in or close to town, as did Robby and his wife. After Miranda's death there was no good reason to come out here. And by the time my father bought the land, the only thing standing was the larger of the two houses."

"It's amazing how fast we lose sight of the past."

"I had a rough sketch to go on, but it wasn't to scale. I'm going to guess this wall was one end of a cellar. And it's possible Eb and Cora's house was built directly over it." He gestured away from the other excavation units. "Extending that way."

"Why would they bury their trash this close to the house?"

"I doubt the house was standing by the time this was used as a trash pit. It had probably been gone for years. Robby or one of his children had the cabin or its ruins razed, the way my father had the farmhouse taken down later. And if I had to guess again, I'd say the root cellar extended out from the house this way and became the trash pit. That's what we're digging up now. It was a natural. Far enough away from the farmhouse not to be a problem, and the hole was already there. It's probably not the only trash pit on the property, of course, but one they started after this house was razed."

"When? Do you know?"

"No. After Miranda's death, a renter lived in the farmhouse until about 1945. Then it was abandoned, and my father had it torn down much later. By then nothing else had been standing for some time."

"You said you were sorry you got into this?"

"This isn't a significant site. No battles or encampments we know of, and between the river rising, floods and the plow, any prehistory's probably long gone. I don't think any agency will list it. But I still hate to disturb real historical evidence."

"So what are you going to do now? Fill in this pit?"

"No, now I'm curious. Besides, as close as it is to the water, there aren't any guarantees it'll be here after the next big flood. I'm just going to have to watch the kids even more carefully. We don't know what we'll find, and I don't want them flinging rocks around so they can get to the good stuff, like pieces of glass and buttons."

"You're a good teacher. You'll make sure they're careful."

"You should see them screen. I think some of them would miss a cannonball."

She had watched the kids at work. First they scraped dirt up with pointing trowels and poured it in a bucket. Once the bucket was filled, they took it over to one of the two screens Travis had provided, which were stretched across collapsible wooden frames. One camper set up the screen, which stood on two legs, and another dumped the dirt in the middle. Then the camper holding the frame shook the dirt through the mesh to a piece of plastic below. Whatever didn't go through on its own was broken up and pushed through by other campers, until only objects too large or solid to go through the mesh were left.

Some of the kids picked over every little thing, eternally hopeful. Some gave one careless glance and were ready to trash the contents, unless somebody stopped them and forced them to look harder.

"As a learning experience, it's great," she said. "As serious archaeology? Not so much."

"I have a friend who's agreed to help me supervise this particular unit. Just to be sure we get this right. She's training to be an archaeology technician, and she already has a lot of skills. In fact, it's Carin Webster, who wrote the play the kids are performing."

She was glad she was finally going to meet the mysterious Miss Webster, but she wondered why Travis had never mentioned her before. The two seemed to have a lot in common.

"You know, Eric might help you finish out the week if you ask him. He's not an archaeologist, but he covered a dig in Rome during their Jubilee. I know they gave him some training. He'd make sure they do things the way they're supposed to."

"He mentioned that to me the night of Jared's party."

"He's looking for things to do."

"What about the garden shed?"

"It's going to be a long summer."

He looked sympathetic. "I'll ask him. But I'm going to get Dillon's permission first. He may not want his dad on site. He's already coping with you."

"Everyone's coping with me this summer. I'm definitely not the fair-haired girl. Everybody has issues."

There was laughter from across the river, then the sound of feet running across the suspension bridge.

Travis glanced at his watch. "The invasion begins. You're staying for the campfire, I hope. Act Three of the play."

"I wouldn't miss it for the world."

"I wouldn't want you to."

She smiled at him. "You know, you seem to be the one person in my life who isn't after me about something."

He returned the smile, and his expression was warm. "Stick around, Gayle. Things could change."

Chapter 21

1865

As the days progressed, Blackjack grew stronger, and by week's end he was able to make his way downstairs. He spent the afternoon sitting by our well, surrounded and shaded by newly greening sycamores and oaks. A fine gold pollen had turned our grass the color of ripe pears, and when he came inside after this first day of freedom, his black hair looked as if it had been sprinkled by stars.

My days had been spent helping Ralph and Uncle Eb plow the fields in preparation for planting. Everyone knew a good crop was vital to begin recovery from the war, although years would pass before we produced what my father had coaxed from the land when he was alive. When Lewis Duncan scooped a handful of dirt and kneaded it with his fingers, it seemed like a living thing. I had believed that if my father held the soil long enough, vines would grow in his hands, or trees heavy with exotic fruits like those I read about in my grandfather's books.

My father said that along with books, my grandfather had passed down his imagination to me. I only know I find reading more pleasurable than farming, and no dirt I hold in my hand produces anything but the commonest yield.

That night Blackjack stayed downstairs for supper. The meal was plain and familiar. Beans and corn bread, greens with apple-cider vinegar, a taste of salted pork. We still had dried apples, which Ma cooked with honey Ralph had smoked from a bee tree. As always, I told myself there were many in the valley and beyond whose rations were plainer and thinner, and I tried not to think about our feasts during butchering season in the days when Pa was alive.

"It's kind of you to share your meal with me," Blackjack said. "These are hard times to be charitable."

"And hard times not to be," Ma answered. "The opportunity presents itself far too often to be ignored."

He laughed. "I'm told good deeds are their own reward."

"Full hearts and empty stomachs."

"At least you didn't suffer as badly as you might have under Sheridan. I'm reaping that reward tonight, for which I'm grateful."

"You won't be grateful if you stay much longer. This meal will wear on you. You'll dream of butter."

"A dream common to many in the South now, Mrs. Duncan, while the North eats cake."

We followed the meal with the brew that Uncle Eb now called "Not so Dandy" coffee. For so long I had not adjourned to the parlor after a meal that it felt strange and unpleasant when Ma asked me to take Blackjack there while she tended to the kitchen.

Dust floated in the last beams of a dying sun. Above our heads, on a frame my father had fashioned for my mother, a quilt hugged the ceiling. When Ma had time in the evenings, she would lower it in front of her and quilt a row or two. This quilt was one she called Virginia Star. She had never told me as much, but before the quilt was stretched out on the frame, I noticed cloth from shirts she had made for my father and some that was dyed the same butternut hue as his uniform. I thought the quilt might be a keepsake meant for me.

I often thought of the quilt my father had carried with him when he'd ridden away to war. The pattern had connecting *X*s, like the lattice at the side of our porch, climbing up and across the quilt surface. I remembered what Ma had called it, and I had asked Aunt Cora why Pa had chosen a quilt called Devil's Puzzle. Aunt Cora had replied that when lovers signed a letter, they added rows of *X*s to stand for kisses. She thought perhaps Pa just wanted to think fondly of my mother when he covered himself at night.

I had been up since before the sun made its first appearance, and now my eyes were heavy. Blackjack, dragging his injured leg a little as he walked, looked over the shelves of books that were my grandfather's legacy.

"These are a treasure," he said.

"My grandfather acted on the stage. My grandmother, too. Then he was the schoolmaster here."

Blackjack looked surprised. "Clearly an educated man."

"The youngest son of a clergyman, who was the youngest son of a nobleman in Essex." My mother had told me the story, but she had also cautioned me to be doubtful. In this one thing she had agreed with my father. My grandfather *had* been a man with a rich imagination.

"And you, Robby? Do you read often and well?"

"I've finished what school there is. I was supposed to go to the academy in Lexington. My mother planned for me to go."

"No plans now, I take it?"

"I read instead, and Ma tutors me. I've read all those books over and over."

He carefully removed one. "The collected plays of William Shakespeare."

"Only some. My mother keeps the other volumes beside her bed."

"Your mother is a woman of taste."

"She was named for Miranda, in *The Tempest*. My grandmother played the role at a theater in Delaware."

He smiled at me. When Blackjack wasn't smiling, it was possible to forget what a handsome man he was, but when he smiled, the reminder was direct.

"This is not an ordinary farm, and you aren't ordinary farmers. Tell me about your father."

I told him what I could. Pa had left not long after secession. Writing letters had been a chore for him, not because he couldn't write, but because he had taken on so many duties. Just before his death, his maturity and resolve had boosted his rank to sergeant-major. My mother believed that if he had contented himself with a lesser rank, he wouldn't have been such a prominent target. But I knew that thousands of men had died at the battle in Gettysburg. Had he remained a private, she would have blamed lack of rank for his death, instead.

"He was a courageous, loyal soldier," Blackjack said when I finished. "And you are surely proud."

I wondered how long any of us would be allowed our pride. The South had lost the war. My father's sacrifice was meaningless to my mother. I wondered how long it would be before I viewed it the same way.

I must have looked dejected. Blackjack tried to cheer me.

"Come, Robby, the war hasn't ended yet. Have faith. The Union's in turmoil. Our bravest soldiers are still fighting."

"No, it's done. Every man who dies now dies for nothing. And Ma says we'll suffer even more because Lincoln was killed. It will only enrage the Unionists."

"Lincoln's death was a triumph."

I heard the difference in Blackjack's voice. His concern and interest had changed to something colder.

"Why do you think so?" I was curious, since the only newspaper we'd seen had been old before it had fallen into our hands and hadn't been replaced by a newer one.

"He was a tyrant. He was a blight on the constitution of our forefathers. Had it not been for Abraham Lincoln, war would never have been necessary. You can blame him for your father's death. He was responsible."

My mother arrived with a pot to refresh our "Not so Dandy." I was glad for the interruption. The hard edge in Blackjack's voice softened when he thanked her.

My mother looked tired. Like mine, her day had been too long already.

"Your son showed me your books," Blackjack said. "You've done well to educate him."

"Nothing will come of nothing." She smiled a little. "You see? I take the books seriously and require Robby do the same."

"Ma, sit with us." I took the pot from her hands. "Just for a little while."

I could see her struggle. She had worked as hard indoors as I had out. She smoothed her skirts and sat. I left and returned with a cup and saucer, then poured her the last drops from the pot.

"Robby, play for us," she said.

On their wedding day, my father had given my mother a

piano. Of my parents, though, he had been the more musical, picking out songs with no music to guide him. He could hear a song once in the morning and play it for us that evening.

Ma was like me. Together we struggled over notes on sheet music, our fingers refusing the unfamiliar duty. I would sooner hoe a row of the tallest weeds. Now I shook my head, hoping she wouldn't insist.

"Mr. Brewer, do you play?" I asked, hoping he said yes.

"It's a fine instrument." Blackjack got up and touched the keys. Even with no ear for music, I could tell it was out of tune.

"It was," my mother said. "Before the war. Please, if you can play, will you entertain us now?"

Blackjack gave a little bow, then made himself at home on the bench, taking some time to position his injured leg.

He didn't play with the lively abandon of my father. Blackjack's playing was careful, with few mistakes and fewer reasons to listen. In the days he had been in our home, I had begun to believe he was a man who cared passionately about many things, but now I knew that the piano wasn't one of them.

My mother didn't seem to share my view. She watched him carefully, and I saw the sharp lines of her face soften and melt as he played. Then he began to sing. His voice was passably fair and filled our parlor.

"When the blackbird in the spring, on the willow tree,
Sat and rocked, I heard him sing
Singing Aura Lea.
Aura Lea, Aura Lea
Maid of golden hair
Sunshine came along with thee
And swallows in the air."

I suddenly understood why she seemed so pleased, and why she closed her eyes as if to hold on to the moment. In the past years there had been few like this, moments when we thought of anything except sorrow and hunger, or when fear wasn't our close companion. My mother was still young, meant for a life when music and gentle conversation were never such strangers. It was easy for me to forget this.

He sang all the verses, some I had never even heard. So many of our songs were about the war, plaintive or ferocious, but Blackjack had gauged my mother's mood and settled for a simpler theme.

She applauded when he finished. "It's been such a long time since anything more than a hymn has been sung in this room."

He turned and smiled at her. "I'm glad I could be the one to sing it."

"I would think you a gentleman, with a gentleman's education, except that new beard hides all signs."

His hand stroked his chin. "It's a change in appearance, and I feel in need of one now that my army service has ended."

"Very soon the summer heat may take care of that notion. Of course, you'll be on the road by then." She paused. "You'll be ready to ride again any day now."

He looked at me, as if to include me in the conversation. "I had hoped you would let me stay longer. I can pay for my board, help care for your animals and whatever else my recovery will allow."

I expected to see the sharpness return to her face, but she only tilted her head. "And is our company so intriguing that you can't leave us?"

"That intriguing and more. But just as important, in a week's time or two, more soldiers will be returning and the roads will be crowded. I'll have traveling companions, and there will be less chance of trouble."

Ma didn't say anything for a moment. I mulled over his words and tried to think why he might really want to stay with us. If he was one of Mosby's Rangers, as Uncle Eb had guessed, then he should be anxious to ride south to be with Johnston—if indeed Johnston had not yet surrendered. There might be some value in traveling with others, but only for a man who wished to lose himself in the human tide.

I wondered then if he was truly an officer, perhaps even someone whose name would be familiar to us. A man who wanted to evade capture by his conquering enemy, or perhaps a trial, now that the war had all but ended.

"We'll decide one day at a time," Ma said. "We may need your room for another who's more gravely injured."

"Then I would adjourn to your barn."

She gave a brief nod and stood. "Shall we tend to your hand? In the kitchen?" She looked at me. "Robby, will you pour a basin of warm water? Then perhaps you can bring in the tub and fill it so our guest can have a bath before he retires."

I knew I would be required to supervise the bath, since my mother obviously could not, so my steps were slow and reluctant. By the time I had readied the basin of warm water, she and Blackjack joined me. She sat him at the table and unwrapped the bandage covering his hand as I moved inside and out, pumping and pouring water in the hip bath.

"You've never mentioned how you got this," she said as she worked.

As I passed, I glanced at his hand. I could see that the wound was healing nicely. The swelling was gone and a scab was forming, although the area was so broad it would take time. But the edges were still dark, as if something was embedded there.

Blackjack watched her as she worked, with too much interest, I thought. "I took a bad fall on my horse, and she fell with me, which is how I broke my leg. As we went down together, my hand was ground into the surface of the road. Signs remain, I'm afraid, even after your poultices."

She lifted his hand and peered more closely at it. "Were there India ink letters here?"

I happened to be watching him. He looked surprised, but covered it quickly. "Youthful folly. Only a small tattoo, and now, joyfully, as invisible as the woman I memorialized. That would be the silver lining to a nasty accident."

"Better a scar than a memory?" Ma finished sponging the area. "There's no reason to bandage it tonight, not if you're going to bathe. You can wrap it yourself after the bath, and I'll do a better job for you in the morning."

"You've been extraordinarily kind."

She lit the lantern, since it was growing dark. "Kindness is one of the few indulgences left to us." She turned to me. "Robby, you'll help Mr. Brewer?"

I didn't relish the thought. But I knew that he would need my help getting in and out of the tub because of the awkwardly bound leg.

I nodded. She gave me the lantern, then started toward the door. But when she got there, she turned.

"What was her name?" she asked.

"Whose?"

"The woman you loved so well that you tattooed her name on your hand?"

"Daisy."

"Oh, I thought perhaps Josephine or Julia."

"No, her name was Daisy. All but a part of the *D* is gone."

Ma nodded, then gathered her skirts to slip through the door. She had been gone a moment before he spoke again.

"I don't suppose you understand how lucky you are to have a woman like that as your mother," Blackjack said.

I thought perhaps he was right, but I was sorry he had the good sense to see it.

Chapter 22

Gayle collapsed into the most comfortable armchair in the carriage house living room, slipped off her shoes and closed her eyes. The silence was a heavy cloak, and when the refrigerator thrummed to attention in the kitchen, she jumped.

While she knew she should consider solitude something of a luxury, the absence of sons felt strange. Jared, Leon and Dillon would be sleeping at camp all week, and Noah had elected to stay behind this evening and enjoy the remnants of the campfire with his friends. As she'd walked back to the Allen farm for her pickup, she had heard bits and pieces of a lively debate about Blackjack's true identity. With that question to puzzle over, she didn't expect Noah home much before midnight.

On arriving, she had done a last-minute check at the inn, turned off unnecessary lights, moved breakfast casseroles and raspberry coffeecakes from the freezer to the refrigerator, and made certain that Paula had remembered to fill both coffeepots and set the timer so there would be fresh coffee when the guests wandered down tomorrow morning. An older couple visiting from the Midwest had captured her and asked an endless list of questions. Clearly they hadn't paid attention at check-in or browsed through the folders in their room, which covered everything from the inn's history to calling long distance to Bora Bora.

She was so tired that she wasn't sure what she needed to do first. Take a nap so she would have the energy to run a bath and soak before bed? Take the nap *in* the bathtub? Fall asleep fully clothed on top of the vintage crocheted spread that graced her bed?

She was still considering the alternatives when someone rapped on the carriage-house door.

"There are extra towels and a hair dryer under the sink, just like it says on the sign in every single bathroom," she muttered, as she got up and trudged to the door. "Firmer pillows on the top shelf of your closet. Breakfast starts at eight-thirty."

She flipped on her innkeeper smile, opened the door and found Eric. He held out a bottle of red wine. "Zinfandel. A particularly good one, according to the guy at the Woodstock Café and Shoppes. And you need a glass. You look whipped."

She was too tired to refuse and risk a fight, and besides, a glass of wine sounded like the perfect prelude to a better night's sleep.

She opened the door wider, scanning the darkness after he joined her, just to make sure the inquisitive guests weren't planning a visit, too.

"I almost didn't make it," Eric said. "An older couple's staying in the room next to mine. When they saw this bottle, they had to know every single thing about where I bought it, why I'd chosen zinfandel, and if I thought Virginia wine was worth a try. I thought I'd never get away."

"Welcome to my world."

"You sit. I'll find the glasses."

"Top shelf in the cupboard beside the fridge."

She settled back into the armchair and closed her eyes. Some time later, when she opened them, he was standing in front of her with a glass and a plate of cheese and crackers.

"I bet you didn't eat tonight." He held out his wares, and she gratefully took both.

"I nibbled while I cooked."

Eric made himself comfortable on the end of the sofa closest to her and held up his own glass in toast. "The catering gig will be over soon."

"What are we drinking to?" she asked, mimicking the toast. "The end of a long day?"

"How about two people who've managed to stay pretty good friends, considering everything."

She lifted her glass higher in agreement, but she wondered if it was true. She supposed the end of the summer would tell the tale.

"Of course, we've hardly seen each other in twelve years." She took a sip, admired it, then took another. "There are advantages to having an ex-husband who jets from continent to continent."

"I'm pretty hard to fight with. Before you can warm up, I'm out of cell-phone range."

"I've wondered a time or two if that's what keeps you moving."

"That and the extraordinary number of sneakers these guys go through every year."

"It's just as well I can never find you. We might lose our title and trophy."

"We worked pretty well together today."

"How so?"

"You trusted me to find out what's up with Jared."

She'd been so tired, that conversation had slipped her mind. "And did you?"

"We took a walk together. We made some headway."

She waited for him to say more, but when he didn't, she didn't pry. She knew Eric would tell her what he could, when he could. In the meantime, Jared's problems were on his father's shoulders. And although she was worried, she also felt confident the matter was being well handled.

The novelty of that was delicious.

"So why are you smiling?" he asked.

"It's just nice, that's all."

"What is?"

"Having you involved. Not feeling like I have to do all this by myself." The moment she'd said it, she wished she could take it back. "I'm sorry. I didn't mean that as a criticism."

He waved her words away. "We both know it's true. You've done most of the worrying. While I'm here, you can let me have my turn."

"Then you'll earn your keep."

He sat back and propped his feet on the coffee table, as if he had been doing it for years. "Do we have that much to worry about? They're good kids."

"That's a generous thing to say, considering how Noah's treated you."

"It's pretty hard to tell him he's wrong. Although I'm feeling a strong need to work on his manners."

Gayle started on the crackers and cheese, silently offering the plate to Eric, who shook his head. "There's always something to worry about, even with good kids," she said.

"Like what?"

"The usual." From his expression, she realized he didn't really know what that meant. "Grades, nutrition, their friends, whether they're busy enough, whether they're too busy. Whether they'll make the third out in the ninth inning. Why they didn't get invited to the biggest party of the year. Why they feel obligated to announce in the middle of Sunday school that they're thinking of joining the Hare Krishnas."

"Who on earth did that?"

"Nobody yet, but I wouldn't put it past Dillon."

"Just remind him he'll be expected to shave his head and sell flowers in the airport."

"I'm afraid he'd be pretty good at both."

He laughed. "He reminds me of me at that age."

She doubted Eric could have said anything that would more clearly show he was finally beginning to bond with his son.

"So now will I start worrying about them after I leave?" he asked. "Does it come with the territory?"

"You never worried about them before?"

"Well, sure, when I knew they were sick, or when I figured out they were sitting on the bench too much during soccer games. But I guess little things like the food pyramid and Cs in geometry went straight over my head."

"They worried about you." She paused. "We all did."

"You mean after you heard what happened?"

"No, I mean whenever you walked out of our lives. When you and I were married and you were gone, I worried all the time. The boys took up the slack after the divorce."

"How much do they worry?"

"When they were little, I used to listen to their bedtime prayers, and you were always the top item."

"I guess telling them not to worry is an exercise in futility now."

"Now more than ever."

He worked on his wine a while, and she ate a couple of crackers. Sitting quietly with Eric didn't seem strange. Maybe it didn't feel quite natural, but it was comfortable enough. During their marriage, between his job and their rapidly growing family, they'd had very few quiet evenings. But they had often sat in silence when the opportunity occurred. Now she wondered if this was because they'd had such a small plot of common ground to nurture that they'd really had little to say to each other.

"I don't know if you'll ever have anything to worry about again," he said at last.

"No?"

"I spoke to my bureau chief this evening. He wants to know when I'm coming back."

"He doesn't have a lot of patience, does he?"

"What surprised me more was that he still wants me. After everything."

"You thought you were getting the pink slip?"

"More like green pastures. I thought they'd just want me out of sight somewhere."

"How did that make you feel?"

"Rushed."

She nodded over the top of her wineglass. The zinfandel was doing its work. She had been exhausted but not necessarily relaxed. Now the two shared a home.

"So what did you tell him?" she asked.

"I told him to start looking for a replacement."

She tried to read Eric's expression. She thought he seemed relieved, but there was something else she couldn't put her finger on.

"You don't look like a man who's sure he's made the right decision."

"I know I don't want to go back to the Mideast. Not now, and maybe not ever. The time may have come to find my own green pastures. Maybe get into production somewhere and stop putting my life on the line. Maybe I've just reached a saturation point."

"Burnout?"

"Maybe. Or a better sense of my own mortality."

She tried to imagine that, but somehow, a vision of Eric as someone who produced the news, not lived it from the world's hot spots, just wouldn't come. Despite what he'd been through. Despite his very real fears.

She probed a little. "You're still recovering. I bet the nightmares aren't gone yet, are they? Is this the right time to make a decision?"

"I know one thing I want."

She cocked her head in question.

"To give you a neck rub. It's been that kind of day. Come here."

Eric gave wonderful neck rubs. They were unforgettable, and no matter how exhausted Gayle had been when the children were young and he was still living with them, he'd been able to work miracles.

But they weren't married now, and this wasn't his home. She was wary.

"Hey, no strings." He grinned. "And no, I haven't forgotten this used to be the prelude to something else. But I'm not angling for anything except a chance to ease those knots out of your neck and shoulders."

She opened her mouth to say no and realized that was probably what he expected.

"You bet," she said. "I could really use one. Where do you want me?"

He looked surprised, then pleased. "Good for you. Right here on the floor in front of me."

She got up and settled herself between his knees, leaning back against the sofa. She schooled herself not to jump when he rested his hands on her shoulders. Then his thumbs began to work their magic, magic that was still surprisingly familiar.

He pressed and wiggled his thumbs for a while before he spoke. "I never really gave much thought to what I put you and the kids through when I gallivanted around the world."

"You were always so glad to go, I doubt you gave much of anything else a second thought."

He pressed harder, digging his thumbs into the muscles bordering her spine. "You make it sound like I couldn't wait to leave you. And that wasn't it."

"I think I knew that. There was just a certain sparkle in your eyes when you had an exciting assignment. Let's face it, you live for excitement."

"I did."

She bent her head farther forward to give him greater access. "When you came home, most of the time you still had some of that sparkle. Being with us was an adventure, too, at least for a little while. I could always tell when you would start thinking about leaving. Because the sparkle began to dim."

"Pretty predictable for somebody who prided himself on living on the edge."

"Funny, isn't it?" She leaned into the weight of his palms against her back. Eric had wide, strong hands. She remembered how, when he had first come back from Afghanistan, she had been appalled at how thin and old they had seemed, his fingers like talons. Now they felt capable, assured and strong. He was recovering, but what exactly did that mean?

"How does this feel?"

She laughed. The sound was shakier than she would have liked. "Like a neck rub twelve years in the making."

"Surely it hasn't been that long."

She knew he was fishing. *I'll tell you about my love life if you'll tell me about yours.*

"No one gives one quite like you," she said.

"What about Travis?"

"Travis and I aren't on the neck-rub circuit together."

"That surprises me. He seems like a man with excellent taste in everything."

She smiled at the compliment and was glad he couldn't see her. "We're good friends, and that's what we really value. We've both been married, both aren't presently. Both of us know what it means to see our lives take a turn we never expected."

"Then you're saying he doesn't turn you on?"

"Eric, where is this going?"

"I'm trying to figure this out. I don't want to step on toes."

"Since when?"

"Since at the moment no one's paying me to do it."

"Travis says…" She considered, then shrugged. "Travis says that I'm the most married divorced woman he's ever known."

"Travis thinks you're holding out for *me?* He doesn't know you very well, then."

"I don't know what he means exactly. Not that. Maybe just that after one marriage, I got stuck. Like a timid kid on a median strip. I crossed one lane safely enough, but it wasn't fun, and the traffic on the other side looks even scarier."

"I don't think that's it."

"So tell me your interpretation, Dr. Freud."

"If you don't fall in love again, then you won't fail again?"

She considered. "Well, my mother views all divorces as failures. I think that's why she's so nice to you. She's hoping she can persuade you to take me back, just so you'll have the same wonderful mother-in-law."

His laugh was deep, and it rumbled all the way to his finger-tips. "I like Phyllis, but I won't get married to *anybody* just because I like her mother."

"What about you, Eric?" She hung her head lower. She was trying not to purr with pleasure, and she was definitely trying not to think about how long it had been since a man had given her this much.

"You want to hear about my love life?"

She waited for a stab of jealousy and realized she would be waiting forever. "Why haven't you married again?"

"I figure if you're not good at something, you have two choices. You can repeat it over and over until you get good at it—"

"Which is what all those people with four or five marriages are trying to do?"

"Dr. Freud says yes. Or you can avoid it completely and take no chance you'll fail again."

"Which is what Eric is trying to do?"

He laughed. "Dr. Freud says that seems to be Eric's plan."

She wasn't sure if it was the wine, the caring hands or just having a laugh with a man who had once meant the world to her. But she felt warm inside, and yes, some of the warmth was sexual. She was aware of that, and wary. But some of it was even more complex. They'd once been friends, and now perhaps the embers of that friendship were slowly and carefully being fanned back into flame.

"What about Ariel?" she asked. "I like her, Eric."

"Every man's dream. His ex-wife and current lover as buddies." He squeezed harder. "Stay away from her. I don't want her to know my darkest secrets."

"That's the thing about you. You don't have any. What you see is what you get. And if Ariel loves you—"

"Who said anything about love?"

"Well, you said *lover.*"

"When has that ever meant the same thing?"

"I forgot I was talking to a man. Just for the record, I've tried to teach our sons a slightly different definition of those words."

"Then you think Jared *loves* Brandy? Or can you stretch far enough to see that their relationship is all about hormones and teenage lust?"

"I try to teach our sons that love is the big goal. Don't wink at them behind my back."

"I'm afraid Jared and Brandy's relationship has nothing to do with winking or anything I've ever said to him. Jared's turning into a man. And Brandy makes herself available."

Gayle closed her eyes. "There are some things I don't want to know."

"Not thinking about them won't change anything. But giving your opinion isn't going to change anything, either."

"All the boys were such cute babies. How did this happen?"

"You fed them and took them to the doctor, and they grew up. I tried to tell you we were in for trouble." He rested his hands on her shoulders. "Feel any better?"

She turned, resting her back against one of his legs. She smiled up at him. "That was perfect."

They sat like that for a moment; then he leaned down, lifted her chin and brushed a kiss across her lips. She had felt it coming and hadn't made any attempt to stop him. The kiss felt warm and affectionate. A kiss good friends might share, or perhaps a nostalgic kiss between old lovers.

The door slammed, and she jumped, turning so quickly that her head snapped around. The newly relaxed muscles in her neck felt like rubber bands snapping back into place.

Noah stood in the doorway, his expression furious. Leon was just behind him. "Great!"

Gayle did not make the mistake of appearing flustered or, worse, apologizing. She realized how this looked. In the blink of an eye she could see how the entire summer looked to Noah. No matter how good her intentions had been when she'd invited Eric here, she had confused her children and blurred the boundaries of a divorce that had been carved in stone twelve years ago.

And possibly not just for the boys.

"You're back early." She rose and put on a smile. "Your dad was giving me a neck rub. It's been a long day."

"I saw what my dad was giving you."

Eric was on his feet before Gayle could say a word. "I've had just about enough of this, Noah. I'm tired of being treated like a criminal, and I'm sure not going to let you treat your mother like one. If she needed a few minutes tonight when somebody took care of her for a change, then I think she can be forgiven."

"Great, you take care of her. I'm leaving." Noah turned and started back into the darkness.

Gayle looked at Eric. "I'd better go after him."

"No, I will. This is my battle, not yours."

"But I—"

"No *buts,* Gayle. You want me involved? I've got to be involved on my own terms."

He was right, but Noah was the child she understood best, the one she was in many ways closest to. Even as she thought it, she realized that was the sum and substance of the problem. The only way to solve it was to release her hold on him and let his father help.

"You're right." Tears welled in her eyes. "See what you can do, Eric."

He gave one quick nod, then strode to the door and closed it behind him.

Eric was halfway across the grass that separated the inn from the carriage house when somebody stepped out in front of him.

"Mr. Fortman."

He realized this was the teenager Gayle had taken in, Leon Somebody or Other.

He sidestepped and kept moving. "Look, another time. I need to find my son."

"You need to take a deep breath first."

Eric was so surprised he halted and turned to face Leon. "Look, I'm sure your motives are good, but—"

"You could screw up a lot if you go after him as angry as you are now."

"I'm not angry, I'm just…" *Angry.* The kid had nailed it, and Eric couldn't pretend otherwise.

"I think I know what he's feeling. Noah, I mean. He doesn't talk to me about it, but I know him pretty well."

"I know you're trying to help but—"

"I've been furious at my father, too. You met him, so you can understand. But somebody finally helped me see that being angry is just a way to keep him at a distance. It doesn't matter if I have a good reason or not. It's a way to keep from being hurt even more. And that's what Noah's going through. I don't know if you've given him a reason to be angry, and I don't want to know. But I can tell you that's what's happening."

Eric wanted to move on, but he recognized the courage this confrontation had taken. He took the deep breath Leon had recommended. "I can see why Gayle was so happy to bring you into the family."

Leon didn't smile. "Lots of people stepped forward to help me. Mrs. Fortman really stuck by me. She's as close to a mother as I'll ever have. So I'd like to help her. And Noah. He's like a brother."

"I'll think about what you said."

"Just one more thing. Like I said, Noah doesn't talk much about his feelings. But I think he, well, you know, believes you don't understand him and don't care if you do. He thinks you want him to be just like you."

For not saying anything to Leon, Noah seemed to have said a lot. Eric had to smile at Leon's attempts to cover up for his friend.

He stuck out his hand, and Leon took it. The teenager still looked worried.

"Thanks," Eric said. He shook the boy's hand; then he dropped it. "I don't know what's up with your father, but he's lucky to have you."

Leon seemed to relax. He almost smiled. "And I'm lucky to have a place to go when he forgets."

Eric clapped him on the back, then turned toward the inn.

"Mr. Fortman?"

"Uh-huh?"

"He's spending a lot of time working on that quilt. Noah, I mean."

Now Eric knew exactly where to look. "Thanks for that, too."

"I've got to get back to camp now. Good luck."

Eric watched him disappear into the darkness. In a moment he heard a car engine and saw lights disappearing in the direction of Travis Allen's house.

Eric started back toward the inn. He wondered what he should do. Talking hadn't helped. Noah really didn't want to hear anything he had to say. He'd tried bribery, in both the past and present. He'd tried to be a pal by bringing him Buddy, tried to be a stern father. He wasn't sure what else he could try.

He just knew one thing. He didn't want to lose his son. And he had to make sure he didn't.

The house was dimly lit, and the older couple with all the questions had apparently gone to bed at last. The banjo clock on the wall in the reception area struck eleven, but otherwise the inn was silent. Eric made his way to the morning room and stood in the doorway. Noah was at the quilt frame, a floor lamp poised over the quilt so he could see his stitches. He didn't look up.

Eric stayed where he was. "When I was your age and things weren't going right, I used to go out to my father's workshop. Once, after a fight with him, I stayed up all night building a bookcase for my bedroom."

Noah didn't answer. Eric waited and hoped.

"What did your father say?" Noah asked at last.

Eric tried to remember how the story had ended. "You know, the next morning I think he just came out and helped me carry it to my room. There wasn't any place to put it, so we set it in the middle of the floor and I walked around it for years."

"He sounds like he's not so bad."

"Not bad. Disappointed. I guess I've just stayed away from my family because somebody else's disappointment is pretty hard to face."

"Well, you're disappointed in Dillon. You make that pretty clear."

Eric moved across the room and took a seat kitty-corner to his son. "Noah, I've been disappointed in myself, not in your brother. Dillon came at a time when your mother and I were already having problems. I was restless, unhappy. I felt tied down."

"I don't need to hear this."

"Yeah, you do. Because you already know some of it, but not the part where I've been kicking myself from here to next Sunday for not knowing how to make things right. But Dillon and I? We're finally on our way. It just took really getting to know him. That sounds simple, I guess. But it wasn't. I've got a lot to make up for."

Noah glanced at him. His eyes were stormy. "And what about Mom?"

"What about her?"

"What's the deal? You leave for the hard part? When we're young and need a lot of attention? Then, when the worst is over, you come back to see what you've missed out on?"

Eric took his time answering. "I hope that's not what I'm doing."

His candor seemed to take Noah off guard. "If you don't know, then who does?"

"There are no easy answers. You know that. I can see it in everything you do. All your paintings, your sculpture, even the little clay figures you used to make when you were a kid, all of them say the same thing. Life's complicated. People are complicated. You knew it when you were little, when you were still scribbling and using fingerpaints."

Noah looked surprised. "You look at my stuff?"

"Of course I do. I've seen it all. You've showed me some of it yourself, and your mom's showed me the rest. And I've kept everything you ever made for me."

"Well, I didn't know you were paying attention."

Eric stared at him until he realized his eyes were in danger of filling with tears. "How could you think that?"

Noah looked away and shrugged.

Eric sat silently and watched his son quilt. Then he moved his chair a little closer. He cleared his throat. "You're not stitching a straight line."

"Anybody can do that."

"Not your mother."

Noah laughed a little. His eyes flicked to his father, then back down to the quilt. "I'm following my own design. Ms. Henry says that it's okay in these squares between the stars, that she'll follow my lead in the other ones if what I do's worthwhile."

"You really got into this, didn't you?" Eric adjusted the lamp so he could look closely at what Noah was quilting. Noah was stitching stars in the large blank spaces where the blocks met. They were free form, and spiraling in showers. "I feel like I'm looking into the heavens. It's the Milky Way, isn't it?"

"Maybe. I think I'm connecting all the stars in the sky."

"Maybe if you connect them all, everything will make sense." Eric put his hand on Noah's shoulder. "Everything will be revealed."

"I'd like that."

"Yeah, me too."

Noah didn't shrug off Eric's hand, and they sat that way for a long time as Noah quilted. Finally Eric moved his hand to his son's, threading his fingers through Noah's and stopping his progress. "Teach me to do that."

"What? Quilt?" Noah snorted. "You?"

"I'd like to learn. And it's one place where I'll definitely be better at something domestic than your mother."

Noah smiled. It came easily, and his eyes lit up in a way Eric hadn't seen since his arrival. "You mean it, don't you?"

"Oh yeah. I mean it."

"You said quilting was for sissies."

"Noah, haven't you figured out by now that I'm wrong a lot of the time?"

"Oh yeah."

Eric made a fist and punched his son's shoulder lightly. "So you'll teach me to quilt?"

Noah smiled again, then punched his father's shoulder in confirmation.

Chapter 23

The raspberry coffeecake was such a hit that Gayle passed out the recipe to each couple as they left the table. The egg casserole had one detractor, a twenty-something woman who had complained on arrival that the Shenandoah River wasn't as majestic as she'd expected. This morning she was upset that the breakfast casserole contained onion, to which she claimed to be allergic. Gayle presented her with that recipe, too, to convince her that no onion had passed her lips.

All in all, as mornings went, this was a normal one. In her first year as an innkeeper, Gayle had learned that taking negative comments personally led to burnout quicker than twelve-hour days and interrupted sleep. She practiced tolerance—and kept a short list of former guests who were invariably told the inn was full if they tried to reserve another room.

In the middle of breakfast one of the cleaning team called in with a sore throat but promised that her neat-freak sister was going to fill in for her. After breakfast the gardener arrived with several flats of annuals from an end-of-the-season sale and plumped out drought-inspired gaps in the front beds. The exterminator did his annual termite inspection; a mason showed up to give a quote on repairing a rock retaining wall.

Through it all, she wondered what it would feel like to share these burdens with someone else. For years she had told herself there were advantages to being a single mom and innkeeper. She could do things her own way, at her own speed. She could reserve disappointment for her own failures and never worry that someone she loved would fail her again.

Now, with Eric right here sharing the raising of their sons, the seductive pleasure of having help and support was eating away at her resolve. She was no fool. Eric's life was in flux, and she knew he was looking at the life he'd stepped away from with longing. They were becoming friends again, and the physical spark that had always flickered between them could easily be ignited if they allowed it.

She was surprised to realize she was tempted. She was more surprised that she had facilitated this by inviting him for the summer. Had she hoped in some deep, secret place that Eric had finally grown into a man with whom she could share a life, children and vocation? Or was she just so pathetically lonely that she had jumped at a chance for even this small degree of intimacy?

She didn't like either scenario. She hoped the one she'd announced at the beginning, that she wanted her sons to get to know their father, was the truth.

When the exterminator and mason left, Paula took one look at her face and pointed to the door.

"Go for a walk. I'll handle things here. You need a break."

"We've got three people checking out in a little while, and I haven't had time to go through the mail." Gayle held up a pile, with a letter addressed to Jared on the top.

Paula was already shuffling papers on the desk. "Go."

Gayle gratefully fled the scene.

She was standing in the middle of the former garden shed contemplating her life when she heard tuneless whistling punctuated by hiking boots on the gravel path. In a moment someone stepped across the threshold and halted. The whistling halted, too.

Eric spoke from behind her. "You know, it's not entirely a bad thing I removed that wall, Gayle. There was a lot of dry rot. When I build a new one, it'll be stronger and better. I'll even throw in new wiring."

She gestured him inside to let him know she wasn't fuming. Since she hadn't seen him since the scene with Noah last night, she wasn't quite sure what to say. So she ignored the neck rub, the kiss and the aftermath, and headed right for business.

"I've been thinking about your idea for adding a second bedroom."

He joined her, and together they stared at what was left of the old apartment. "What about draining the wells with too many guests?" he asked.

She didn't look at him. "Still a problem. But if I don't put a pull-out sofa in the living room and we put one set of bunk beds in the second bedroom with a play table and toy chest on the other side of the room, we'll still be limiting guests to a set of parents with two kids, only the accommodations will be nicer for everybody. The parents can put the kids to bed and still use the living room." She paused a second for effect. "And I can charge more."

"Good thinking."

Now she did look at him, because faceless apologies meant

nothing. "The idea had merit, and I'm sorry I went off on you about it."

"I hate to play 'trade the apologies,' but you had every right to go off on me. I guess I was playing 'what if' that day."

She was afraid to ask. Then she knew she couldn't let that go. "What if?"

"Yeah, what if I'd never walked away. What if I'd stayed here and been lord of the manor?"

For a moment that picture wouldn't even come. She supposed she had so thoroughly erased their past that she didn't know how to reload it into her personal computer. But a future? That seemed to be coming into focus, and it frightened her.

She glanced at her watch to hide her confusion. "Well, you can't be lord, but you can be chief carpenter. Want to put our heads together on how to make this work?"

Eric was chalking strange markings on the floor when she left. Gayle was almost satisfied that if he came up with any new ideas, he would run them past her first.

He had also filled her in on his conversation with Noah last night, and the progress they'd made. That and Paula's announcement that two guests had asked to stay another night, thereby filling the only vacancies the inn had left, led her to think it was going to be a good day after all.

Her opinion changed when she found the newly risen Noah sitting on the carriage-house sofa, head in hands.

Gayle opened curtains and turned on lights, hoping to make her point. "I thought you were going to get up about an hour ago. It's time to start cutting veggies to go along with the sandwich stuff."

"I'm not feeling too great."

She crossed the room and put her hand on his forehead. Since

Noah—unlike Dillon—never pretended to be sick, she expected to find he was feverish. He was. Just slightly, she guessed, but enough to notice.

"What hurts?"

"My head. My throat." He looked up. "Maybe I shouldn't be working around food."

"Let me take a look at your throat."

He groaned but opened up after she got the flashlight. His throat was red enough to be sore, but not enough to send him right to the doctor.

She flicked off the light. "Take some Tylenol and go back to bed."

"How are you going to get everything done by yourself?"

Gayle thought that Eric would probably help if she asked, but she hated to, since he was busy making a list of materials for the apartment. He'd agreed to help supervise at the dig this afternoon after lunch, so his day was already over-programmed, and she was afraid that special favors might incur special consequences.

"I'll call Cissy. Maybe she can."

Noah looked grateful.

Back at the inn, she made the call, and Cissy answered on the first ring.

"I can do it, but I have to bring Reese," she warned. "Marian's up in Maryland visiting her sister."

When she arrived thirty minutes later, Cissy was surprisingly efficient in the kitchen, even with Reese, in a green gingham sundress, who "helped" by rearranging saucepans and plastic containers in a bottom cabinet, and sifted and resifted half a cup of flour on the wooden table in the corner.

They assembled the ingredients for lunch and packed the car with all the other necessities, finishing in the nick of time. Cissy agreed to come along to the site, so she and Reese followed Gayle in her pickup.

Gayle was unloading supplies when Travis approached, along with a petite woman in jeans and a new camp T-shirt. Gayle looked up just in time to see the woman slip her arm through Travis's and squeeze his hand. The intimacy lasted only a moment, but it said volumes. On the intimacy scale, they were fairly well along. Even without an introduction, Gayle knew who this had to be.

Travis gestured to his attractive companion. "Gayle, I wanted you to meet Carin Webster. She's going to help me supervise for the rest of the week."

Gayle took Carin's hand and shook it with a firm, competent grip. "I know Travis must be delighted you agreed to come on board," Gayle said.

"I expected to be teaching summer school, or I would have volunteered from the get-go." Carin had a soft, feminine voice that went with a pixie face framed by short auburn curls.

"Carin's training to be an archaeology technician," Travis said. "We're going to be on a dig together at Monticello after camp ends."

"I never outgrew mud pies." Carin smiled at Gayle as if they had always been friends. "I understand your son is one of the narrators for my play."

They chatted about Dillon, the play, the high school, the camp. Gayle saw absolutely nothing to dislike about Carin, although she found herself searching. The vision of Carin and Travis squeezing hands wouldn't go away. She saw her best friend disappearing into the life of another woman. Even though she had expected this some day, she was sadder than she'd anticipated.

Travis drifted off, and Carin went to talk to some of the campers. Gayle and Cissy barely got lunch on the table before the horde descended. "Where's Reese?" she asked, stepping back to get out of the way of the first wave.

"One of the counselors took her." Cissy nodded to one side. Gayle saw Brandy with Reese on one hip. The girls she supervised were crowded around them.

"I've been keeping an eye on her," Cissy said. "Reese is as slippery as boiled okra."

"She's in good hands." No matter what Gayle thought of Brandy, she did know the girl was great with children and an experienced babysitter.

"Nobody worries like a mother," Cissy said.

"I think Brandy would like to be one."

"I'll take her aside and tell her what it's like to have a baby before she figures out who she is. Not that I wouldn't do it again if I knew I was going to get Reese out of the deal."

"Do you want to go and get her?"

"No, she's doing okay. I'm going to see if we got all the fruit. I thought we brought more, and this is going fast."

Gayle looked for Dillon but didn't spot him in the crowd. She wondered if he was over at the Allen farm. She knew some of the kids had been there sorting artifacts with Travis and would be the last group to eat. She went to talk to Jared instead.

"You have some mail from MIT," she told him, careful not to hug him in front of his campers. "I think the envelope's from the admissions office. Maybe it's something about orientation."

"I'll open it when I come home."

"If you think it's important, I could bring it out here for you tonight."

"Don't worry. Whatever it is, it's safer there."

She told him what his father was doing, and that Noah was fighting off some bug. He nodded and tried to look interested, but clearly his mind was elsewhere. The concerns she'd expressed to Eric came barreling back.

She couldn't bear being shut out any longer. "Jared, do you want to tell me what's wrong? Because something is."

"My mind's in a million places, Mom. It's nothing to worry about."

"I worry anyway."

"It's just stuff I have to deal with. Nobody else. Just a lot of changes coming up."

She waited and hoped, but he pointed out that his campers were now in line to eat and he had to go, too.

Gayle was on her way back to the tables when she heard a scream behind her. She spun around and saw Cissy racing toward the riverbank. And beyond Cissy, in the water, a blur of green.

Gayle understood immediately what was wrong. Somehow Reese had gotten away from whatever caretaker had been watching her and wandered down to the river. Now she was *in* the river, and the current was sweeping her downstream. Gayle, who was closer to the water than Cissy, began to run, but she was still so far that she knew by the time she got there, Reese could well be out of reach.

Seconds passed, precious seconds that could count for everything, but she ran anyway, angling in the direction of the current. From the corner of her eye she saw a splash downriver, near the low water bridge, and another blur of darker green hit the water and started swimming toward the little girl.

"Dillon!" Even from this distance, she recognized her son. The nightmare was suddenly worse. This was now too familiar, a deeply rooted terror that Dillon would somehow end up in the river and get swept away forever.

She realized she wasn't alone. In front of her, she saw Eric streaking toward the water. She hadn't seen him arrive, but clearly he'd gotten here in time. She wondered if he had been on his way to greet Dillon, who had probably been crossing the low water bridge. She had no time to figure out the logistics. She only knew that Eric, who was a stronger swimmer, was going to get to their son first.

She could hear shouts and the snap of sneakers against rock-strewn ground as others rushed to the bank. She continued in the direction of the current, trying to gauge where the water might take Reese and Dillon. She reached the riverbank and crashed through the brush beside it. Just beyond her in the water, she saw that Dillon had reached the little girl and grabbed her dress. As Gayle kicked off her shoes to go in after them, she saw Dillon lift Reese out of the water. Holding her against his chest, he was fighting with one arm and impressive kicks to get them both to the bank.

Before she could get in the water to help, Eric reached them and, lifting Reese from Dillon, urged his son toward the shore.

Gayle waded in to grab Reese when they got close enough. The little girl was gulping soundlessly, but she let out a screech once Gayle got her arms around her. Then she began to cough up water.

Gayle moved away from the riverbank and up into the field, where she could see a crowd descending. She held Reese at an angle so the water had a place to go. "Get a blanket!"

Against her, Reese coughed again and again, spitting up water, but in between she wailed and gulped. Gayle didn't have time to see if Eric and Dillon were okay. She stripped off Reese's wet dress and wrapped her in a windbreaker one of the campers had been wearing. Cissy arrived, and Gayle transferred Reese into her arms.

"She's breathing," Gayle said. "She's been spitting up water. But she's breathing on her own."

"I got wet!" Reese began to cry.

Somebody brought a knit afghan. Gayle recognized it as one that Cray kept in his truck. Gayle wrapped it around the little girl, tucking the corners between Reese and her mother.

Cissy was clearly struggling not to cry. "What'll I do?"

"We're going to take her in to the hospital right away, just to be sure she's okay. A doctor needs to look her over. But I think she's fine, Cissy. She wasn't in for as long as a minute before Dillon grabbed her and got her head above water."

"Where's Dillon?" Cissy turned to search for him. She was well aware that Dillon's swimming skills were skimpy.

"I think he can tell you," Gayle said, stepping aside as her son, dripping river water, pushed through the crowd around them.

"Is Reese okay?"

"She's going to be," Gayle said. She wanted to ask how her son could have been stupid enough to go into the river when he could hardly swim himself. She wanted to insist he explain why he had acted without thinking.

"Thanks to you," she said, because when it came right down to it, that was the only thought worth expressing.

Eric, dripping too, joined them. "Dillon, exactly what were you thinking when you jumped into the river instead of just yelling for help?"

Dillon turned and grinned at his father, a grin so much like Eric's it was almost like looking at twins. "I guess I was thinking it was a good thing you gave me swimming lessons this summer, Dad."

Little Reese Claiborne was okay. When word came from the hospital, Mr. Allen announced it to cheers, and Dillon was now the man of the hour. Jared still couldn't believe that his little brother, who didn't even like to take a bath, had jumped in and saved the little girl. Dillon hadn't been cocky about it. In fact, in a private moment, he'd told Jared he hoped nobody else fell in for a long time, at least not while he was around.

But whether he'd enjoyed the experience or not, Dillon had showed everybody what he was made of.

Unfortunately, Brandy had, too. She had disappeared immediately after Reese's rescue, and Lisa had taken over for her. Jared hadn't gone looking for her, because he didn't know what to say. From camp gossip, he knew that right before Reese had gone into the river, Brandy had been watching her. Nobody was quite sure how the accident had happened, but one thing was certain. As much as Brandy liked children, she sure wasn't ready to be anybody's mother.

Right before the campfire program was about to begin, Cray found Jared tossing a Frisbee with some campers.

"Hey, Jar, take a break for a minute."

Jared threw the Frisbee to Gary, the kid most likely to keep things going for a while, and joined his friend on the sidelines.

Cray didn't waste time. "Lisa says Brandy went home for a while, but she's probably coming back before we go back to the tents."

"Uh-huh." Jared watched his campers and made a mental note to make sure Gary didn't take this leadership thing too far and convince everybody to sneak out of their tents tonight.

"She feels really bad," Cray said. "She told Lisa she asked one of her campers to watch Reese while she ran to do something. The girl claims she didn't hear her. Brandy says that whether she did or not, it's her own fault."

"She's right about that. It *is* her fault."

"Yeah, well, she knows it. You shouldn't be a hard-ass. It would make her feel a lot better if you'd offer some sympathy."

Jared chewed the inside of his lip, but he didn't say anything.

"Fine, do it your way." Cray turned to leave.

"Do you think maybe this is a sign?" Jared asked. "She thinks she's all ready to be a mom, then she does something like this?"

"Yeah, well, maybe the way you're acting is a sign, too."

"What's that supposed to mean?"

Cray kept his back to his friend. "Maybe I was never the high-school hotshot, Jar, but even I know that when somebody you're supposed to be in love with screws up, you don't rub her mistakes in her face. Maybe you're not all that ready to be a husband or a dad, either."

"Yeah? Well, tell me something new."

Cray pivoted on one heel, as if he'd been practicing. "That's what this is all about? You're mad at her for maybe getting pregnant?"

"I was there when it happened. *If* it happened. I'm mad at both of us." A badly thrown Frisbee came his way, and Jared grabbed it. He threw it with such force that it sailed over everybody's heads and disappeared into the twilight. Nobody went after it.

Cray lowered his voice, since the campers were dispersing and some were ambling toward them. "Maybe she's not pregnant. Maybe everything's going to turn out okay."

"You think everybody's going to be better for whatever happens?"

"C'mon, Jar, I didn't say that."

"People have to live with their mistakes. You joined the marines. Don't you wonder if maybe you made a big one? Like what you did is going to change your life forever?"

"You know I looked at my options, and I did what I knew I had to."

"You closed a door."

"You close one, you open another. That's how things work." Cray slung his arm over his friend's shoulders. "No matter what happens with Brandy and, you know, the baby, you still have a million choices."

"I can't even seem to make a couple."

Cray shook him. "Come on, you'll work it out. Your life is great. How can you be so confused?"

Jared wasn't sure, but he did know that he and Robby, the kid who had grown up on the land where Jared was standing, had a lot in common. Robby's life had changed the moment the mysterious Blackjack Brewer rode up to his doorstep. And no matter how things turned out with Brandy, Jared's life was about to change, as well.

Even though he didn't know how the play was going to end, he was pretty sure that Robby was going to be called on to make some tough decisions. And whatever he decided would affect the people he loved the most.

Jared was afraid he could relate all too well.

Chapter 24

1895

Before the war, we knew as much about the world as we needed. News traveled with every person who passed or visited, and even though we were miles from any town, we never felt alone. But even though neighbors still stopped to tell us what they knew, now we hungered for every detail. We had always read the newspaper, but newspapers became rarer after the South marched into battle. Now they were like diamonds.

Two days after Blackjack asked permission to remain with us a while, Uncle Eb came back from town with the *Richmond Enquirer*. He had gotten a ride with a neighbor, an event that was rare these days. The roads were in disrepair, and so were wagons and buggies. Horses and mules had become nearly as exotic as elephants.

When Uncle Eb saw me sitting on the front step of the porch, he held up the paper proudly. I had wanted to go with him, but I didn't like leaving Ma alone at home with Blackjack. He seemed a gentleman, and he knew how to coax the most reluctant smiles from her. But Blackjack was still nothing more than a stranger about whom we knew little—and what we did know might well have been lies.

Uncle Eb's gap-toothed grin was unusual as he presented the newspaper to me. There was little any of us could be proud of these days.

"Almost didn't git it. Had to argue my way clear through the store. It was the last one they had."

With excitement, I took it from him. Eb and Cora could both read a little but rarely chose to, preferring to have me read to them.

"What does it say?" I asked, to be polite, but I was already scanning the front page.

This was the same newspaper that had once said about Lincoln: "What shall we call him? Coward, assassin, savage, murderer…? Or shall we consider them all as embodied in the word 'fiend' and call him Lincoln, The Fiend?"

I remembered this clearly, because I had read and reread every newspaper we could lay claim to so often that I had committed most of them to memory.

"It says here that bells tolled, and there were services in Lincoln's memory." I looked up. "In Richmond? The capital of the Confederacy?"

"Used to be our capital. Now it's got Union troops stationed on every blamed corner." Uncle Eb spat into the bushes. "There'll be more of that pretending, too, even if not one living soul in Richmond mourns the man. People trying to make friends with the enemy now."

I thought there was probably more to the mourning than Uncle Eb supposed. Ma had expressed the concerns of many Virginians. Maybe many of our citizens weren't truly saddened by Lincoln's death, but with the President gone and the North enraged by his murder, what would happen to us?

I read a little more, then raised my head again. "It says here that at the same time Mr. Lincoln was shot, somebody tried to kill Mr. Seward, the secretary of state, only they didn't get to finish the job."

I looked down and saw something even more interesting. With Uncle Eb standing over me, waiting for me to tell him what was there, I read quickly.

"They captured and killed the actor who shot the president," I told him, looking up. "John Wilkes Booth. In a barn right here in Virginia. And they've rounded up other people who conspired to help him. That means they plotted to kill him together." I looked down and then up again. "It says they'll surely hang, and anyone else who helped."

Uncle Eb wiped the sweat off his forehead with a sleeve. "Took 'em a while to get him, didn't it? Think of it. He shoots old Abe Lincoln in front of a whole theater full of people, including a bunch of army officers, then he runs across the stage in full view of God and the Union, and nobody stops him. I don't know how these strawfoots won the war."

I smiled and went back to reading.

"They're sure it was him?" Uncle Eb asked. "Because it would be just like them to get the wrong man."

I continued to scan. "It says here the cavalry caught him in a barn in Port Royal and set it on fire. Then they shot him through the neck. They got him out, but he died on the front porch of the farmer's house. Then they wrapped his body in a blanket and took it by ship to Washington. They arrested a man who was with him, too." I looked up. "They'll surely hang *him*, even if they can't prove anybody helped."

The door opened, and Blackjack came out. He still moved a

bit slowly, and the limp was noticeable if I watched for it. He used a cane he had fashioned from a gnarled tree limb, but all in all, he had recovered well. As long as he didn't overdo and kept the splint in place, Ma said he would be fine.

"Who are they going to hang, Robby?" he asked. "Not any more of our good sons of the South, I hope."

I waved the paper but held on tightly. "They killed Mr. Lincoln's assassin and captured a man who was with him."

For a moment he didn't speak. But his expression was blank, as if he was just trying to put the story together in his mind.

I suppose I'd made it clear I wasn't going to give up the paper easily. He dropped down on the step beside me but didn't try to take it. "Tell me what it says."

I told him what I'd told Uncle Eb. Then more. "They buried him on the grounds of the Washington Arsenal and covered the grave with a slab of stone."

The door opened again, and Ma appeared. She looked pointedly at me. "I didn't know work was finished for the day."

"Uncle Eb got a newspaper." I held it up as proof. "It's almost new. They caught and killed John Wilkes Booth, the actor."

"Not actor. Hero." Blackjack got to his feet, then added what he had said to me before. "Abraham Lincoln deserved to die."

"No one deserves to be shot down in cold blood," my mother said, before I could speak. "And from what I know of it, Mr. Booth shot Mr. Lincoln from behind. What kind of man kills another without any means of defense?"

"One who wanted him absolutely, utterly dead," Blackjack said. "One who thought death was too good for him, no matter how it was dispensed."

"One who thought he was God incarnate?" Anger seethed in my mother's voice. "As if one more death, one more powerful man removed from the scene, will change this mess we've made of our country?"

"Madam, your husband died for the South. Where are your sympathies?"

I listened with dismay. I knew my mother had not agreed with my father's decision to fight, nor had she been in favor of secession. But once the die was cast, she had done her part. Even before our food stores had been raided by both armies, we had gone without, providing whatever we could to our troops at our own peril. When the battles had come close to our home, she had tirelessly nursed the wounded and helped any passing traveler. Now I realized just how deep her resentments lay.

"I gave my husband to the Confederacy." She gazed down at Blackjack. "And now I have none. I gave a farm that was rich and fertile and now barely feeds us. Had this war continued, I might have had to give my only son, as well. Is that not enough for you, Mr. Brewer? Am I not *enough* of a patriot?"

"John Wilkes Booth killed a dictator, but now he's our enemy? How can one man's courage be greeted with such disdain in his own land, by his own people?"

"We reap what we sow. Sow violence and war, reap more violence. We will suffer for this. There will be no talk of conciliation in the North now, only revenge."

She turned her gaze to me. "Robby, there are chores to be done. The newspaper will still be waiting this evening." Before I could reply, she swept back inside, her head high.

Blackjack watched her go, but when she closed the door behind her, he didn't try to follow. Instead, without a word, he gestured to the newspaper. I gave it up reluctantly and watched him fold it under his arm. Then, with his cane tapping angrily, he limped off to read it beside our well.

* * *

Supper progressed in silence. My mother and Cora had made bread that afternoon, and it was a welcome change with beans. I knew the price of flour had risen to seven hundred dollars a barrel in Richmond in January. According to one of the newspapers we'd seen, there had been riots earlier in the war, and Jefferson Davis had been forced to threaten starving women with prison to make them disband.

Bread was a delicacy we would never have been able to serve had we not grown, then carefully protected and hidden, our own wheat. Tonight there was no salted pork and no stewed apples, but there was a dab of apple butter with the bread, and dried corn stewed with onions. With the war ending, I hoped the blockades and pillaging would also end quickly so we could eat well once more.

Ma stood to clear. Before she left the room, she addressed Blackjack without quite looking at him. "Eb bought milk and a little sugar in town with the money you've paid me, and I made pudding."

I couldn't remember the last time I had tasted pudding. "Pudding was my father's favorite," I told Blackjack as we waited.

He seemed to be thinking of something else and didn't reply.

"This is the way my mother makes her apologies," I said more forcefully.

He looked at me and frowned.

"I don't know what you've suffered, but we've suffered, too," I said. "And she's afraid we're going to suffer more. Still, I think she's sorry she was so forceful."

His expression softened. "Is that right?"

"There's no amount you could pay us that would entice her to bake pudding. She made it as a gift."

"You seem to understand her."

I understood no one better. Had my father been alive, I

wouldn't have needed to stay so close to my mother's side. I would have ranged farther, visiting friends and what was left of my father's family in Page County. Had the war not interfered, I would have been sent away to school next year. But the war *had* interfered, and Ma and I had been left to face it together. We were closer because of it.

"She has a mind of her own." He smiled, and even hidden inside his new beard, his teeth shone white.

Ma returned carrying a teacup of pudding for each of us. When she started to return to the kitchen, Blackjack rose. "I can't eat this unless you'll have some with us."

She looked surprised, then cautious. "I have dishes to tend to."

"Robby and I will help, won't we?" He looked pointedly at me.

"He's right, Ma. Come sit with us."

She considered, then gave a brief nod. She returned with a cup for herself and took her seat.

"Robby tells me that pudding is a rare treat. I thank you." Blackjack looked down at his. "I'm honored to share."

She didn't look at him, but she gave a faint nod.

"And I'm sorry if I was contentious earlier," he said. "I'm afraid I'm still adjusting to losing the war."

I looked up. He did indeed look like a man whose mind was filled with unpleasant thoughts. "Then you believe it's over?" I asked.

"Some still implore our soldiers to stand their colors, but with Johnston's surrender—"

"Johnston surrendered?"

"The day Booth was killed. You'll find it in your newspaper."

The date was nothing more than a coincidence, but I could see that he was grieved by both events.

Ma saw it, too. "There must be an ending before we can begin again."

He smiled a little, but his voice was sad. "'O, now, for ever farewell the tranquil mind. Farewell content. Farewell the plumed troop and the big wars that make ambition virtue. O, farewell. Farewell the neighing steed and the shrill trump, the spirit-stirring drum, the ear-piercing fife, the royal banner, and all quality, pride, pomp, and circumstance of glorious war.'"

Ma looked as surprised as I felt. He had spoken the words with great feeling. "You know *Othello?*"

"I am educated in the plays of Mr. Shakespeare, but not at all in the acceptance of defeat."

"We will all of us become better," she said.

We finished the pudding in silence; then Ma stood to clear the table. Blackjack got up to help and refused to listen when she told him it wasn't necessary. "Many hands make light work."

"A student of proverbs, too. What else will we learn about you?"

I noted a new lightness in her voice, and he must have noted it, too, because he smiled. "That I am uncommonly fond of pleasant evenings, of conversation and wit, and of a woman with a mind of her own."

I expected Ma to take offense, but she surprised me. Her pale cheeks turned rosy, and her eyes sparkled. "And of pumping water and washing dishes?"

"If with them comes companionship."

I must have frowned, because my mother looked at me and laughed. "Robby, shall I allow Mr. Brewer the pleasure of cleaning our kitchen?"

I wanted to see her at the quilt frame and not in the kitchen with Blackjack. "I'll help him. You must have quilting to do."

"I believe Mr. Brewer and I can finish without you," Ma said. "Perhaps you can help Uncle Eb put up the chickens for the evening."

I struggled for a reason not to leave the house, but one look at my mother's face and I knew there was no reason good enough to change her mind.

"I won't be long," I said.

"No need to hurry back," Blackjack said, as if he was reading my mind. "Your mother will be in good hands with me."

I looked at the smile that seemed to have permanently settled on her face and the way her hands fluttered upward to pin a stray lock of hair. I was very afraid that the last place my mother needed to be was in Blackjack's all too capable hands.

Chapter 25

"So last night Weather Woman comes in, lank hair, no makeup, and wearing the dreariest gray suit this side of the Midwest. Of course she's late, too, so there's no time to do anything more than powder her nose and tease the hair a little. Then, in the middle of telling viewers about a tornado in Iowa, she bursts into tears."

"Ariel, you're making this up."

"I swear, Eric, this really happened. She pulls out a huge red handkerchief, like a clown uses at the circus. You know, the kind that just keeps coming and coming, and she pulls and pulls and finally starts to blow her nose. This goes on so long I think the station manager is going to run on set, snatch her by her unfashionably wide lapels and drag her off camera.

"Before he can get to her, she looks up and says, 'I'm so sorry, but I've just been terribly upset ever since I heard about this tornado. Did you know two cows got caught up in the funnel? It was terrible, awful.' Then, she pauses, and we're all thinking she's really lost it. Finally she says, 'I'm afraid it was *udder* disaster.'"

Eric groaned. "Okay, that's it. Now I know you're lying."

"Of course I'm not lying. Last week she asked the viewers if they know what happens when the smog lifts in Los Angeles? Then she strips off her jacket, and she's wearing a local university T-shirt under it." She paused. "Care to make a guess which one?"

"No."

"UCLA. Get it? When the smog lifts, you see L.A."

He gave in to laughter. Not because of Weather Woman's puerile jokes, but because Ariel had taken the time to find them and work them into her cheerful morning gig on the telephone. Last week he had looked up Ariel's station on the Internet. A man named John Cravits was the staff meteorologist and always did his own weather reports.

"You're something else," he said fondly.

"Well, so are you, Ace. And I miss you. A lot."

He imagined Ariel's world. Late nights, later mornings, Napa Valley wine, traffic tie-ups and Bel-Air bashes. Hollywood's bony, tanned women, who at their worst looked like overcooked turkeys and at their best made a man feel as if he'd been on a monthlong fast. Air-kissing, back-patting, ass-kicking Los Angeles. For a moment he was so nostalgic for the taste and smell of Southern California that he was ready to hang up and call the airline.

"I miss you, too," he said, and meant it.

She sighed. "How's Gayle? How are the boys?"

He gave a perfunctory answer to the first, maybe too perfunctory, because he knew Ariel would wonder why he had glossed over his ex-wife so quickly. Before she could ask, he launched into the progress he was making with his sons.

"I guess it's working," she said when he'd finished. "You being there. Despite missing you, I'm really glad. Now maybe they'll come visit you all the time when you move out here with me."

He had been standing. Now he lowered himself to the edge of the bed. "It sounds like you have plans for my life."

"There's a good job opening up, Eric. And you're on great terms with every single person who's doing the looking." She named two men and a woman whom he knew and admired.

"What is it?"

"Associate professor of broadcast journalism at USC. And better yet, the teaching is only part-time. They're saying right up front that they expect whoever takes it to be gone for part of each year doing freelance or other work. In fact, they're encouraging it, because they're hoping whoever they choose will take his best students along for hands-on experience. And we know you'll be able to find plenty of freelance work, or you can start producing your own stuff. You'll have your choice once the word gets around."

"You mentioned my name?"

"Not really. I just said I didn't think you were planning to stay in Atlanta. That's all. Well, maybe a little about you considering some new directions."

He knew how Ariel worked. She was unrivaled for planting seeds that were guaranteed to grow into magical beanstalks.

"My kids are on the East Coast." It was the first thing he'd thought of as she spoke. Not that the job was perfect. Not that it meant he would be living close to Ariel for the first time in their relationship. Not even that it would give him the flexibility he needed to move back into reporting at his own speed.

Those things came a heartbeat later, when he also thought about Gayle and the life he had left behind a dozen years ago.

"Your kids can fly, Eric. They have airports in Virginia and direct flights to L.A. They're big boys, and the chance to spend time in a different part of the country will be good for them."

"When is the committee making their recommendation?"

"They've just started the process. You have plenty of time to get involved."

"Okay." He pictured her on the other end of the phone, the wide blue eyes and pointed chin. The black snaking curls. And the smile. He could hear Ariel smiling on the telephone. She knew she was reeling him in.

"Give Weather Woman my love," Eric said.

"Oh, I definitely will."

He was smiling as he hung up.

He was still smiling when somebody rapped on his door. Dillon pushed it open before Eric could get up to answer. His son was wearing gray sweatpants and a T-shirt that read Crime Scene In Progress in bold letters.

"Dad, you'd better come with me." Dillon motioned for him to follow.

"Wait a minute, aren't you supposed to be at camp?"

"I came home to see how Noah's feeling. I'm skipping breakfast."

Eric knew Noah was already feeling better, but apparently the word hadn't reached as far as the Allen farm.

He got up and followed Dillon into the hall. "What's the hurry?"

"Buddy's talking. You've got to hear this."

Eric smiled. All his sneaking into the carriage house and Noah's bedroom had paid off. "I figured he would eventually."

"Yeah, well. You were right, I guess. I've gotta get Mom, too. Noah wants you both to hear this."

This time Eric smiled to himself. He wanted Gayle to hear it, too.

They found her in the kitchen, running water into pans for the cleaning crew. "Hey, what are you doing here?" she asked Dillon.

"I came to see how Noah is. Mr. Allen said I could. But you gotta see what Buddy learned."

Gayle's eyes flicked to Eric's. "I bet he's talking, right?"

"You won't believe it," Dillon said. "Come on."

They watched him launch himself out of the inn's kitchen, grabbing a wedge of breakfast pizza—an inn specialty—as he ran out the door.

"You're going to love this." She dried her hands on a dish towel. "I know what he's going to say."

"You've heard Buddy talking, and you didn't tell anybody?"

"Not exactly."

Eric tried to piece that together. "Then how do you…" He realized what she was really saying. "Don't tell me you've been sneaking in to teach him to talk!"

"Sneak? I don't sneak, Eric. I live there." She narrowed her eyes. "Wait a minute. Have you…?"

He nodded.

She stared at him; then she burst out laughing. "I don't believe it."

"What have you been trying to teach him?"

"There's no place like home. And you?"

He wiggled his eyebrows, Groucho Marx style. "Up, up and away."

"That figures." She threw the dish towel at him, but he caught it and hung it up.

"Okay, we'll see who was better, you or me," he said.

"Better? Maybe it's just a question of which of us was smarter. I'm inculcating family values, and you're trying to send him into the stratosphere."

They were still laughing and arguing when they entered Noah's room. Noah, looking perkier than he had yesterday, was whispering to Dillon. Buddy was preening himself on his perch and looking very proud.

"I hear Buddy's talking," Gayle said. "Your dad and I have a bet about what he says."

"Umm… What do you think he's going to say?" Noah's eyes were fixed on his brother's.

They told him what they'd been doing.

Noah finally looked away from Dillon and straight at Eric. "So let me get this straight. You've been sneaking into my room, trying to teach *my* bird what *you* want him to say."

"Pretty much." Eric favored his son with his most disarming grin. "I thought you'd get a kick out of hearing him talk. I didn't look for love letters or bad test scores while I was here."

"Funny, Dad." He turned to Gayle. "And you're just as bad."

"My motives were pure."

"Well, let's end the suspense. See, it turns out, Buddy only talks if you take him out of the cage and put him on your finger and bring him up to your face. Here, I'll demonstrate. All ready?"

Gayle and Eric looked at each other and nodded.

Noah opened the cage door and slowly inserted his hand, index finger extended. Buddy hopped right on and only fluttered his wings a little as Noah took him out. Then, after Noah had spoken soothingly to him, he drew the little bird up toward his cheek.

"Hey, Buddy," he said. "How's it going?"

For a moment Gayle thought Buddy wasn't going to perform. He looked around, as if trying to decide.

"So what's new?" Noah asked patiently.

Buddy turned his head back to Noah, and his eyes grew round with excitement. He chirped and squawked, as if to warm up.

"Thataboy," Noah said. "Show us what you got."

Buddy ruffled his feathers and launched into the longest, most blatantly profane string of words Gayle had ever heard.

Finally, as if he had just sung at the Met, he nodded to unseen applause, stuck his head under his wing and began to groom himself.

Stunned, Gayle didn't know what to say, but Eric was never at a loss for words.

"Dillon, the next time you and I see a garage sale?" Eric said.

"Keep driving?"

"You got it."

Jared had lain awake most of the night wondering what he should do about Brandy. She hadn't come back last night, and Miss Webster had stayed over to supervise her campers. Lisa said Brandy wasn't feeling well, but Jared suspected there was more.

At breakfast, he managed to get Travis alone. "Mr. Allen, I'm sorry, but I need a little time off later this afternoon. Just an hour, maybe two. Do you mind?"

"Does this have something to do with Brandy?"

"Yes, sir."

"Bring her back if you can, Jared. Reese is fine, and from what I can tell, Brandy wasn't really at fault. If anything, she just trusted one of the campers to be more mature than she was."

"I'll tell her you said so."

"Then we'll see you both at the campfire."

Jared hoped that would be true.

He avoided his father, aware that if they ended up alone together, his dad was going to ask him whether he and Brandy had performed another pregnancy test. He wanted to handle this on his own, although he did appreciate Eric's offer to help. But it was definitely time for Brandy and him to face the music and make decisions.

This time he gathered his courage and went to the local Wal-Mart, hiding a test kit under a blue T-shirt off the rack, a package of three athletic socks and a plastic bag of chocolate-chip trail mix. He chose a checkout line with only one person, a stranger his mother's age who was buying sunglasses and sunscreen, and looked as if she'd driven to the Valley to snap quaint photos of log cabins and deer grazing on hillsides.

When it was his turn, he pulled out his wallet to make the transaction as quickly as possible. Only then did he realize the cashier was a familiar-looking woman from his church congregation. He'd been so busy choosing the shortest line of strangers, he hadn't even looked at the cashier.

It was too late to run. He hid the test kit under the socks and watched the little pile move toward her.

"You're Gayle Fortman's son, aren't you?" The cashier had a lopsided smile, but it seemed genuine. "I had your brother in my Sunday-school class last year."

Jared hoped she wouldn't pay attention to what she was scanning, and to make sure, he kept her talking. "Which brother was that?"

"Dillon. That's right, you have another one, too, don't you?"

He watched as she looked down and found the tag on the T-shirt and swiped it across the scanner. He was sweating so hard he was pretty sure he was going to melt into a puddle before she got to the test kit.

"Noah," he said. "He's my middle brother. Dark hair? He's an artist. He's the one who painted the new mural in the baby nursery. Have you seen it? It's a farmyard, with cows and sheep—"

He watched the test kit slide across the scanner, but the

cashier was paying attention to him, not to the package in her hand. The requisite beep sounded, and she started on the socks.

"And a haystack and barn," Jared finished. "Grass, you know, leaves. Here, let me bag those for you." He reached for a bag and threw the scanned items inside, adding the rest as she finished.

She smiled at him. "Not everyone's so helpful." She looked down at the receipt, then up at him again. "Your total is $33.45." She tore off the receipt and showed it to him.

Jared opened his wallet. He handed her two twenties and waited for change. The cash drawer opened, and she took out the bills and handed them over, then counted out two quarters and a nickel. Finally she placed the receipt in his outstretched hand.

"Next time look for the sales," she said sweetly. "The Clearblue Easy Pregnancy Test was discounted this week. You could have saved some money."

"I'll tell my sister…and her husband." He grabbed the bag and started toward the door in humiliation.

"I didn't know you had a sister, too," she called.

But he was so far away by then he figured she didn't expect him to shout a response.

The drive to Brandy's house was filled with a hundred silent questions and no answers. This time he planned to read the instructions himself. He doubted Brandy had messed up the last test on purpose, but it *was* possible. If this one didn't work, he would drive back and buy every single test on the shelves if he had to remove half his savings from the ATM to do it. They would have an answer tonight. He was going to make sure of it.

The only car at Brandy's house was her mother's old Buick, which would soon be Brandy's. Since the Wilburns usually worked late, he figured he and Brandy would be alone long enough to get this finished.

He was preparing to knock when the front door opened. Brandy stood back to let him inside. Her hair hung lifelessly over her shoulders, and her usually smooth complexion sported a zit in the middle of one cheek.

"Hey." He managed a smile. "Nobody blames you, you know. And Reese is fine. It turned out okay."

"I shouldn't have trusted anybody else. It was stupid. I guess I learned my lesson. I'll be a lot more careful if anybody ever trusts me again."

"They will. You're a great babysitter."

"After this, I'll be so careful I'll probably smother my own kids. I'll never let them out of my sight."

For a moment he couldn't move. Then he cleared his throat. "About that? I, well, I bought another pregnancy test. We have to know."

She waved away his words. "We don't need that test. I already know."

His stomach fell. She had run a test without him and discovered the worst.

She turned away and started toward the family room. "You got what you wanted, Jar-Jar. I'm not pregnant. I started my period."

He supposed that a month ago talking about a girl's period would have been way down on his list of stimulating topics. But he had never heard such welcome words.

He caught up with her and grabbed her arm. "You're sure?"

"What, you think I can't tell?"

"Well, sure you can, but I just need to know if you're being honest. You're not just saying it to make me feel better?"

"I don't care if you feel better." She sniffed. "I was hoping I was. I know we're too young and all that, but I just hoped, you know…?" She sniffed again. "I hoped you and I could maybe start our life together. I was going to finish high school at home and fix up a place for us really nice. You could have worked for my dad. It would have been cool."

"Brandy, that's like playing house. It's not real life. Babies cry, and they get sick and need things. We wouldn't have anything much to give one, and nothing to fix up a house. We'd have to live here or with my mom. I'd never make it to college. Don't you see this is good news?"

"You're just saying that because you don't love me. You don't want to marry me. You don't even want me in your life anymore. You think I'm stupid, but I can see what's what."

"Then you ought to see this is no life to bring a baby into."

She stared at him when he didn't say more. "You mean all that's really true? Everything I just said?"

"I don't think you're stupid, Brandy."

"That's it? The other stuff? Not loving me, not wanting me in your life?"

"I don't know what love is and neither do you. We're not old enough to figure out something like that. Not yet, anyway. I care about you, but I don't know anything else. I don't want to be tied down right now—"

He grabbed her when she tried to turn away, so he could get it all out. "Look, I don't want to tie *you* down, either," he said. "I'm not going to be here next year. If you tell guys I'm still your boyfriend, nobody's going to ask you out. You won't have a date for the prom, or for homecoming, or for anything important. And I'm not going to do that to you. We both need our freedom. Maybe later, when we're older and know who we are, we'll find each other again. I don't know. But for now, it's got to be over."

She began to cry. He tried to pull her close to hold her, but she pushed him away.

"Brandy, there's a whole world I need to see." He tried to make her understand. "A huge world just filled with things neither of us knows anything about."

"How are you going to see this huge world of yours tied to a chair in some lecture hall? You think you'll see much of it at MIT? You'll be going to classes and studying. It'll be like high school, only harder and farther away." Her eyes blazed. "That world of yours is just an excuse!"

He winced. He'd heard this argument before. One side of his brain duking it out with the other.

"I think you'd better go," she finished. "Go on. You've said what you came to say. Maybe you can get your money back on that pregnancy test. At least I did that much for you."

"Listen, you're important to me. We've had a good year together. I'm not going to forget you."

She pointed toward the front of the house. "Out."

"You're supposed to be at camp, too. I told Mr. Allen I'd bring you back with me."

She shook her head. "I'll drive myself over later, after the campfire. Or my parents will bring me. I'm not your responsibility anymore. Just leave. Get out. Now."

For a moment he wanted to retract it all. He felt as if he were teetering on a tightrope. He wanted to edge his way back to the platform and climb down to safety. But he had put one foot in front of the other too many times, and now going back was as dangerous and as far as going forward.

"I'll see you later, then." He turned and fled.

He took the long way to the site. The campfire had already begun when he took his place at the end of the log where his campers were seated. Mr. Allen was just finishing up talking about the differences between what we know and what we think we know.

Jared only half listened. At the moment, he wasn't sure if he knew anything, but he was beginning to believe that, like Robby Duncan's, his life was about to settle into a path that nobody had anticipated.

Chapter 26

1895

In the days that followed, I noted with dismay the many times Blackjack sought my mother and the many times he too easily found her. More than once, I found them chatting as if their friendship had begun in the cradle—although I was afraid there was more to it than that. She was softer when she was with him, and more attentive. The exhaustion that had been as much a part of her as bonnet and apron seemed to peel away when they were together.

Strange men, some in tattered butternut or gray uniforms, moved down our road, stopping for water or food. Some slept overnight in our barn, but the others pushed on, grateful for whatever we could give them.

In the evenings after supper I was still invited into the parlor. Sometimes Blackjack played our piano, and sometimes he read out loud while Ma worked on the Virginia Star quilt. Before he arrived, we had begun *Vanity Fair,* reading by smoky beeswax candles together. We had taken turns, although despite its moral lessons, neither of us had found the story improved our character.

Now Blackjack suggested we put the book away and read *The Tempest,* since Ma had been named for Miranda, the daughter of Prospero. *The Tempest* wasn't a play I enjoyed. There were not enough fierce battles, struggles with honor, impassioned soliloquies. But my objections were ignored, and I was made to read out loud, taking roles as needed. Both Ma and Blackjack coached me as I read, until I wondered if I was in school again.

I didn't like the way Blackjack smiled at my mother. I didn't like the way his head bent close to hers, the way he appeared to be reading along as she recited Shakespeare's words but was, in fact, gazing at her narrow wrists and long fingers.

I tried to stay nearby, but sometimes my mother sent me to do chores I couldn't escape.

On one afternoon I came back to the house after a morning away. Rain had fallen all through the night, and the soil had been too muddy to plow. Instead, I had helped Ralph repair a wagon wheel, although at the moment we had no mule or horse to pull it. The residents of our stable had disappeared with the Confederate Army. Blackjack's horse was the only one in residence, and the bay was not destined to be hitched to anything.

When I entered, I heard my mother and Blackjack talking in the parlor, so I stayed in the hallway and listened.

"You work so diligently on that quilt, although so many others are in evidence here," Blackjack said. "It's almost as if you need two dozen for each bed in your house."

"There'll come a time when my fingers will be stiff and my eyes poor. Then I'll still have quilts to keep me warm."

"You plan to stay here? With so little to gain and an entire world to explore?"

"Where would I go and how would I pay for it? Here, at least, we have land. Eb and Ralph can coax enough food from it to feed us until the leanest years are over. And the farm is Robby's legacy. What else do I have to give him?"

"A mother with stars in her eyes and wind in her hair? A mother who hopes for adventure?"

"Adventure is a man's hope. A woman hopes for a life that doesn't destroy her."

"Once you hoped for more. Sometimes I see it in your eyes. You hoped for love and the world at your fingertips."

"Every silly girl wishes for those things, but in the end we settle for less."

"Did you settle for less? Is that what marriage was to you?"

"That's an impertinent question." But she didn't sound as if she minded as much as she should have.

"Tell me," he insisted. "Your husband was a good man. On this we're clear. But was he a man you could love?"

"You forget yourself."

"I've learned to ask questions now, because tomorrow may destroy my chance to ask again."

I knew I shouldn't hear this, that whatever she answered wasn't meant for my ears. But I couldn't make myself move away.

"Mr. Duncan was much older than I. For all our days together he worked hard to be a fit husband, and I worked as hard to be a good wife."

"Words with no meaning."

"Words with all the meaning I care to give them."

"There's no love in them." His voice grew softer. "Did you ever know love?"

She was silent. I wished I could see what was happening, then was glad I couldn't. I turned to go, my pulse beating rapidly at the base of my throat when he spoke again, this time with words I recognized. The feeling behind them was easily recognized, as well.

"'Admired Miranda. Indeed, the top of admiration; worth what's dearest to the world. Full many a lady I have eyed with best regard, and many a time the harmony of their tongues hath into bondage brought my too diligent ear. For several virtues have I liked several women; never any with so full soul but some defect in her did quarrel with the noblest grace she owed, and put it to the foil. But you, oh, you! So perfect and so peerless, are created of every creature's best.'"

Blackjack had a musical voice. He said he had studied theater at school during a boyhood in New England and that it was his favorite subject. He also claimed to have been blessed with a nearly perfect memory, so he could read lines and easily remember them. When we read together, he was able to take any part and give it meaning.

The meaning was perfectly clear here. Blackjack Brewer was courting my mother with the play for which she had been named.

I left again, angry and confused about what I should do. I was now the man in our family, but nothing had prepared me for this. Blackjack Brewer was courting my mother in the house she had shared with my father. Yes, my father had been dead for almost two years, and deep mourning had ended. As required, she had worn what black crepe she could find at a time when too many needed it. Although my father was buried in Pennsylvania in an unmarked grave, she had promised to mark a grave here for him, as soon as we could afford a stone and stonecutter.

But even though many months had passed, I couldn't understand how Ma could so easily abandon all mourning and turn to a stranger. The only thing we really knew about Blackjack was that he kept secrets. Now the roads were filling with men. His leg had healed enough for travel; he and his horse had rested. But Winchester no longer seemed to call him, and I thought that Johnston's army had never been his intent.

I debated whether I should reenter the house, stomping my feet or calling for Ma. In the end, I went down to the cabin to visit Aunt Cora. I wasn't going to report what was happening, but I thought I might solicit a little advice.

As I approached, I saw she was on the porch shelling dried lima beans. When she heard me, she looked up and smiled. "What are you doing here, Robby? Eb was just looking for you down in the barn."

Earlier Uncle Eb had gone to bargain with a neighbor who had two mules. We were hopeful that we could come to some arrangement for one of them. At the moment we had to take turns hitching ourselves to the plow.

I perched on the step and gazed up at her. She was resting on the bench that ran between the two front windows, pressing her shoulders against the house for comfort. She owned shoes but rarely wore them. Now her toes stuck out under the hem of a much patched blue dress.

"Did Uncle Eb have more work for me?" I asked.

"Eb brought you something, but he didn't want to show it to you in front of that Blackjack fellow."

I heard the note of distaste in her voice and used it to my advantage. "You're not fond of Blackjack, are you?"

"What's he still doing here, anyway? Eb says he's well enough to move on, but he sure don't seem to be moving."

Aunt Cora's hair is almost completely gray now, although I can remember when it was as dark as mine. Like Ma, she pulls it back in a knot worn low on her head, but Aunt Cora's hair is thin and lank. Ma's is thick and glossy, and no matter what she does, it lies in waves against her head. Before the war, when she brushed it dry in front of the fireplace, my father would watch her as if this was all the gold a man really needed.

"I don't know what Blackjack's doing," I told Aunt Cora. "I don't feel comfortable leaving him alone with Ma."

I expected her to respond, but she was silent. I watched as she shelled the beans faster.

"What do you think of that?" I prompted at last.

"I think your ma's been without a man too long. She's sad and lonely, and he's a charmer. You're a good son, Robby, but you're a son, and sometimes a woman needs someone her own age she can talk to."

Blackjack had never said how old he was, but I guessed he wasn't as old as thirty, while Ma was already thirty-two.

"He's younger than she is," I said. "At least I think he is."

"That never stopped no world from turning."

I had hoped for reassurance, but instead I was rapidly growing more alarmed. "What should I do?"

She considered it awhile. This time I stayed quiet and waited.

"There's nothing *to* do," she said at last. "Your ma's all grown. She's a widow woman, and she ought to have some sense about men. You got to trust it, that's all." She paused. "Of course, it won't hurt to keep your eyes and ears open a little, maybe not pay as much attention as you should to their privacy. If you know what I mean…"

I was afraid I did, but I didn't want to sneak around and catch Ma and Blackjack together. Not only did it feel wrong, I wasn't sure what I might stumble on.

"You think he'll want to marry her? Maybe he wants our farm."

"I don't guess marriage is on his mind, and this farm, well, it ain't no prize anymore. Maybe we could use a man young enough to put it all back together. But I don't think Blackjack Brewer's the one for that job."

I didn't think so, either. But was that better than the other possibility? That Blackjack was only playing with my mother's affections while he waited for the exact moment to melt into the masses of men returning home?

Aunt Cora got to her feet. "Here's Eb."

Uncle Eb was just coming out of the barn. She waved, and he started toward the cabin. He looked tired, and I was glad there'd been no plowing today. Both he and Ralph needed a day without hard work.

When he saw me, he stopped, turned and went back to the barn. He came out a moment later carrying something under his arm. When he got to the porch, he held out another newspaper.

"Thought you'd like this."

I took it gladly. "When did you get it?"

"Just this morning. Henry Baggit offered it to me when I was there seeing about the mule. It's newer than the last one we got. I was holding on to it, on account of Blackjack made off with yours last time, and you had to wait till the next day to read it."

I grinned, glad for his thoughtfulness. "You want me to read it to you?"

"Got no time to listen right now," Uncle Eb said. "Last thing I heard, the old woman here needed some wood chopped for the cookstove. Else I don't think there's going to be any supper tonight."

"I hurt my back," Aunt Cora explained, since she usually split her own logs. "Eb's treating me kindly."

I was just as glad not to have to read out loud, because that was slower, and I was anxious to see what was happening in the world. Aunt Cora didn't much care for the news and would have found an excuse to go inside, anyway.

"Can I stay here a while?" I asked.

Uncle Eb frowned. "You mean rather than go up to your own house and have it snatched away? Durn right you can."

They left together, chatting about the visit to Henry Baggit's house. By the time they were out of earshot, I'd learned that Henry had stumbled over a nest of copperheads and nearly gotten bit, that the mule Uncle Eb hoped to trade for was as bowlegged as a horseshoe, and Mrs. Baggit was due to have another baby to add to the five Baggit children sometime in early summer. Uncle Eb wondered how the Baggits planned to feed the ones they had already. He thought a barrel of flour and any other food we could offer would get us the mule.

I opened the newspaper and started to read. Not surprisingly, the end of the war was still the main topic. The editorials were not as outspoken as once they'd been. Richmond was in disarray, and although the editors counseled courage and hard work, it was clear that a lot of both would be needed in the days ahead to return the city to anything like its former glory.

On the second page I found an article about the murder of the President. Details were available now, and I skimmed with interest a longer version of the capture of John Wilkes Booth in Port Royal.

The man who killed Lincoln had run for nearly two weeks. The doctor who had set his leg was in jail now and would be tried for treason, as would the man who'd been with him and others involved in the assassination. Some would surely hang.

Set his leg.

I frowned and started over. When the actor jumped to the stage below the box where he had shot the President, he had caught his spurs in bunting draped from the presidential box, landed hard and broken his leg above his ankle. Medical attention had been required, and although he'd managed to escape the city and ride to Maryland with the injury, once he arrived, he had to find help. The doctor who helped him, a man named Samuel Mudd, was someone he had known before.

Having recently seen how painful a broken leg could be if it wasn't attended to properly, I could just imagine what the assassin had endured.

I read on. In the end, the broken leg had helped to identify Lincoln's assassin, as had a tattoo on his hand, with the initials J.W.B.

The words blurred, and no matter how hard I stared at them, I couldn't read on. My mind was racing ahead. There was a drawing of the scene at Ford's Theater, where the murder had taken place. It showed the actor Booth fleeing across the stage. I held the newspaper closer, but the actor himself was little more than a dark suit holding a pistol aloft. He appeared to have a mustache and dark hair, appeared to be somewhat youthful. More than that I couldn't tell.

I forced myself to continue reading to the end. Most people believed the right man had been caught and killed. The dead man had carried Booth's diary and no fewer than five signed photographs of beautiful women, some of them actresses known to have worked with him.

But according to the newspaper, not everyone was so certain. The cavalry had caught Booth and nearly roasted him in a barn before they'd shot him through the neck and hauled him up to the farmhouse, where he'd died on the porch. The body had been identified by witnesses to the killing, although skeptics claimed the details were peculiar. Some sources said the body was so badly burned that a positive identification was unlikely, although others said that it wasn't burned at all. One witness said Booth's hair was the wrong color. Some wondered if the reward that had been offered might have inspired members of the cavalry to make the identification without enough proof. There were questions about whether Booth had conspired with others to kill Lincoln, perhaps those high up in either the Confederacy or even the Union government. Perhaps agents for these statesmen had helped him escape in the end, letting someone else die as scapegoat.

Questions, yes. But none as immediate as my own.

What was the real name of the man living in our house?

For a moment the possibility that we were harboring the murderer of Abraham Lincoln made my belly tighten in pain. I put down the newspaper and leaned against the post, sweat breaking out on my forehead even though the afternoon was pleasantly cool.

What was really tattooed on Blackjack Brewer's hand? Had he memorialized his love for a woman named Daisy by embedding a *D* with India ink? Or were the remains of his tattoo the remains of something more insidious, the initials of a man who had killed the President of the United States, then somehow escaped, leaving another to pay for his crime?

I tried to dismiss the injured leg and tattoo as nothing more than an accident of fate. But even though I tried, those details and others wouldn't be dismissed. Blackjack had stated repeatedly how much he despised Lincoln and how glad he was to see him dead. Of course, this was not an unusual stance. But Blackjack also had a vast knowledge of Shakespeare. Was it really possible for someone to have such an uncanny ability to memorize lines as he claimed he did? Or had he learned those lines years before, recited them onstage, bowed proudly to re-sounding applause?

John Wilkes Booth was said to have had a potent attraction for women. Even my cautious, reserved mother was falling for the blatant charms of the man who said his name was Black-jack Brewer.

I closed my eyes and wondered how it would feel to climb a scaffold, to feel a rope being placed around my neck, knowing all the while that the people I loved most in the world were sharing my fate. And at the same time I wondered how it would feel to report a man because he bore vague similarities to a murderer, a murderer who by all accounts was already dead and in the ground. To turn in Blackjack, knowing that he might be innocent of that crime but guilty of another for which he should be allowed to escape.

If Blackjack was—as we had suspected from the beginning—a Confederate officer or spy fleeing charges related to the war, then if we turned him in, we would no longer be patriots but traitors.

The two words chased each other through my head. I realized that with the difference of one letter each, all the other letters were the same.

I heard the front door of my own house close, and my eyelids flew open. Blackjack stood on the porch, gazing toward the cabin. As I watched, he started down the steps and toward me. He walked faster each day and now used the cane for little more than the occasional rut.

I did not want him to see the newspaper, with its exhaustive detail on the capture and killing of Booth. Blackjack would know I had read it and that I might have begun to make connections. For now, I wanted to keep that a secret.

I had only seconds to dispose of it before he was close enough to see what I was about. I folded the newspaper and slid it between two steps to the ground below, where I hoped it would be hidden from view. For the time being I had seen all I needed to. Now the end of the war and the rebuilding of the South seemed of minimal importance.

"I wondered if you might like a ride on my horse," Blackjack said, as he drew closer. "It'll do you both good, and I'm not yet ready to mount her. Your mother forbids me to get in and out of the saddle until my leg is a little stronger."

For days I had eyed the bay with longing. When my father was alive we were proud of his stable. He had the knack for breeding, and he had sold many a colt to strangers who arrived from as far away as Harrisonburg to buy from him. I had grown up on horseback and missed riding nearly as much as I missed meat for supper.

I was wary of Blackjack, though. I wondered why he made the offer. I was sorry when he sat down beside me, as if to discuss it.

"You've been good to share your home with me." His smile looked natural and genuine on his handsome face. "The war's been hard for you, Robby, and it's not easy to have a stranger in your home now, on top of everything else."

"We've had many."

"None so permanent."

I narrowed my eyes. "You intend to stay with us forever?"

He laughed. "No, I just meant none that had stayed so long."

"Why haven't you gone?" I asked boldly.

"Because I'm not certain where to go."

Having expected another smooth lie about Winchester and company on the road, I was taken aback. "What about your home in Winchester?"

"I think it's likely there's nothing left of it. I wonder, too, if it's sensible to stay this close to the scene of—" He looked at me and frowned. "Robby, are you ill?"

I shook my head. I suspected my cheeks had just drained of color. "The scene of *what?*"

"The war." He looked as if he still wondered about my health. "The *battles,* Robby. So much waste here, so much destruction. A lot of Confederates will try their hands out west, perhaps even Mexico. I've been considering it."

"What would you do there? What profession would you pursue?"

Of course he didn't reply "the stage." I had known he wouldn't. But so much would have been explained.

"I haven't thought that far," he said instead. "I have money to get me through for a while."

"Not Confederate money." I had noticed that he had given my mother Federal greenbacks and some silver. For such a devoted Confederate, this was surprising.

"I saw the necessity to abandon that some time ago, although it pained me to do so."

"Perhaps you have family who'll help you." I tried to sound nonchalant, but as I spoke, I thought of the Booth family, who, according to the newspaper, were well known in theatrical circles and surely capable of keeping their exiled brother in funds.

"I have prospects. But what of you and your mother? What will you do? Your mother deserves more than a life of hard work with little to show for it."

"What are you suggesting?"

He shrugged. "This damnable war."

He might be an actor and a good one, but I thought this sentiment came from his heart. I had dreams at night where I was walking down a road, carefree and happy. Then the road opened, and as I watched, a mountain grew in front of me. As I stood there, I knew the mountain was too high to climb and too wide to walk around. I could go back or stay where I was, but moving on would never be possible again.

We sat morosely. I wondered who he was. I don't know what *he* thought about, but at last he stood. "Let's saddle…Princess."

I noted the hesitation. He had never called his horse by name before. I wondered if he had made up this one on the spot.

I wanted to say no. I didn't want to share good moments with Blackjack Brewer. If I had to make a decision what to do about him, good moments would make that harder. I wished he would saddle Princess, or whatever the mare was really called, and ride away.

In the end, though, I went with him to the barn. And when I climbed on Princess's back, for those moments, at least, I could forget what might be true and just be a boy again.

Chapter 27

Every day that week, Eric waited until Gayle left for the dig; then he went off to make arrangements for her surprise party or firm up plans on the telephone. Luckily the church hall wasn't already rented for Saturday evening, and Sam's secretary had a list of local businesses to recommend. He had never pulled together a party this quickly, but considering, things went well.

He interviewed two caterers who were agreeable to work on such short notice and settled on the one with the less traditional menu. He hired a bluegrass band Jared said was a local favorite, a photographer whose wedding portraits showed promise, and a florist to provide table decorations and streamers. A local winery would provide two cases of their best vintages, and a baker was designing a birthday cake. He was lucky this was July and he wasn't competing for resources with a host of June brides. On such short notice, he wasn't able to do everything he wanted, but he was satisfied.

Today, since the campers were hiking up the mountain for lunch—and because he had no desire to go up the steep trail with them—he had made several appointments to finalize arrangements.

He was in a particularly good mood, since after last night's campfire Jared had taken him aside to tell him that he was not going to be a grandfather. Eric figured he'd had a big silly smile on his face all morning, and he hadn't cared who saw it.

Now he swung by the church to meet the florist for last-minute instructions.

Although his sons hadn't been as much help as he'd expected, with their feedback and a church directory he had put together a guest list of almost a hundred. With no time for formal invitations, he had asked some of Gayle's friends to form a phone tree. Additionally, he had spent every evening after Gayle went back to the carriage house making more calls. A lot of people were on vacation or otherwise committed, but about half had accepted the invitation, including Gayle's parents, who were flying in for the event. Some of the people he called made other recommendations for guests, and he'd increased the guest list accordingly. Now he was convinced enough were going to show up for a lively gathering.

He got to the church office before the florist and greeted Sam's secretary, Dovey Lanning, an elderly woman whom he recognized as one of the quilters who sometimes came to work on the Touching Stars quilt.

She peered at him over wire-rimmed glasses. "I hear you've been working on our quilt."

He flashed the famous Eric Fortman smile. "It's okay. I don't mind if you pull out my stitches."

"Don't know why we would. Not the best I ever saw, but surely not the worst. You show promise."

He was ridiculously pleased. He had asked Noah to teach him

to quilt simply as a way to understand his son better. It had worked, too. They'd quilted together several times since, and their conversations had brought them closer.

Of course he'd also quilted by himself a time or two for absolutely no good reason.

"It's a beautiful quilt," he said, and meant it.

"One of my favorite patterns. Like the Lone Star, only nothing lonesome about this one. A whole family of stars." She tilted her head in question. "But you didn't come to chat about our quilt."

"I'm here for the florist, but I'm early. Is the reverend in?"

"Reverend Sam's in the sanctuary. Probably rearranging the pews. We come in of a Sunday morning and nobody knows where to sit. We're all mixed up. He says that's the point." She shook her head, as if there was no way to account for their renegade minister.

"I'll see if I can find him."

"You find Reverend Sam, you tell him Mrs. Trident called again. He's dodging her calls. She's got a bone to pick with the sermon last Sunday."

"I gather it wasn't love thy neighbor?"

She snorted. "More like love thy enemy."

"That never goes over well."

She bent her head back to the work on her desk. "Tell me about it."

He found Sam, arms folded over his chest, staring at the simple altar at the front of the sanctuary.

"Looks like you're planning something," Eric said from the entryway.

Sam swung around to greet him. "Eric. Good to see you. And I'm always planning something. It generally gets me in trouble."

"Along those lines, there's a Mrs. Trident who wants you to phone."

"She'll have to take a number. Last Sunday I talked about the need for forgiveness. It hits people right where they live. Those who are happy holding grudges want to take them to the grave."

Eric wondered if he was one of those people. Every month he'd spent in Afghanistan was now colored by equal parts of fear and rage. He had dreams in which he picked off his captors one by one and watched them die, particularly Adib, who had pretended to be his friend.

Sam put his hand on Eric's arm. "After everything you've been through, anger's normal. It's part of the healing process. Just don't hold on to it longer than you have to. Don't nurture it." He paused. "That was more or less the sermon."

"You read minds?"

"In our prison ministry I work with men and women who've made anger their way of life. Some of them have a right to be angry, but as a lifestyle, it's the ultimate destroyer."

"What do you tell them?"

"Examine it, confront it, let it go. Give it to God, if they're willing to take that step."

"Sounds simple."

"Most difficult things do."

Eric decided he liked Sam. They were having a conversation. Sam wasn't preaching. And it sounded as if this lesson was personal and hard won.

As the two men started toward the doorway, Eric explained his reason for being there.

"I came to see if you'd be willing to say a few words about Gayle after dinner Saturday night. And the grace, of course."

"I'm amazed at how fast you've put this together."

"I'm surprised nobody else thought about giving her a party."

"She told everybody not to."

"She's going to love it." Eric realized he sounded a little unsure. "Gayle doesn't want people to fuss over her, but everybody needs a little fussing now and then."

"I'll be happy to help any way I can."

"I'm curious about something."

By now they were well on the way back to Sam's office, but he stopped, as if he thought this might be important. "What's that?"

"What keeps you here?"

"In this church?"

"In the church, the Valley, in rural Virginia. Don't you feel a little, well, overqualified for this gig?"

Sam smiled in a way that seemed to say he'd had this conversation before. "Some people paint on large canvases, some on small ones. The paintings seem equally valuable to me if the artist's talented and dedicated. It's a question of what's most appealing."

"And this appeals to you?"

"We aren't talking about me, are we?"

"You're pretty good at this counseling bit."

"It would have been a mistake to ask Monet to paint his water lilies in miniature."

"Or maybe it just takes a lot of ego to use that much canvas."

"No, it takes understanding of our abilities and inclinations."

"Sometimes people change."

"I hope so, or I'm wasting my life. But sometimes change isn't the point."

"Then what is?"

Sam clapped him on the back. "Figuring out how to use the talents you were born with."

* * *

Since the kids were going to be carrying lunch up the mountain today, Gayle laid out an array of sandwich fixings, fruit and cookies so they could pack their lunches. Noah was back at work helping, but when it came time to do cleanup after lunches were made, she realized he had disappeared.

"You look like you've lost somebody." Travis snitched a cookie before she could reprimand him. "Need help?"

"Noah took off somewhere."

"I saw him a minute ago. He was talking to Jared."

Gayle thought she knew what their conversation might be about. Brandy was back at work, but it was clear her son and his girlfriend were no longer an item. Brandy had been favoring every other male counselor except Cray with her infectious smile and long-lashed gaze. Her tank top was tighter, her shorts shorter, than in days past. And she had carefully avoided Gayle and Noah ever since they'd arrived.

Gayle was both relieved and worried. She didn't know who had instigated the breakup, but no matter who had taken that step, Jared was bound to feel hurt and confused. Young love was never easy.

"Are you busy this afternoon while the kids are hiking?" Travis asked.

She brought her thoughts back to him. "Do you need help supervising?" She looked around and spotted Carin at one of the excavation units with a camper. "Scratch that. You've got all the help you need."

"I thought we'd do our own field trip. They don't need me on the hike."

"You and me?"

"And Helen Henry."

She noticed, but didn't have time to examine, what was a palpable stab of disappointment at the addition. "Well, sure. Where are we going?"

"She's going to take us to look at Miranda Duncan's grave."

"Oh, that I'd like to see."

"I don't want the whole gang trooping through a little country graveyard, but I thought we'd take a camera so they can see the photos."

"When are we going?"

"I told Helen I'd call when you get back. We'll pick her up on the way."

"Let me just find Noah and we'll finish cleaning up."

"I'll be here waiting."

She didn't have to search for Noah. He arrived a minute later. "Sorry." He grabbed one of the dishpans holding leftovers and started toward the pickup. She took the other and followed him.

"Mr. Allen said you were talking to Jared?" She made a question out of it.

"Uh-huh. He's got something he wants to do this afternoon, and he asked if I'd take his place on the hike. He's going to check with Mr. Allen. Will that be okay with you? I'll come back and finish my share of cleanup."

"You feel well enough?"

"I feel great."

This time she didn't hint. "Where's Jared going?"

"He didn't say."

"I think he and Brandy broke up."

"You *think?*" He said it as only a teenager could.

"Did he say anything to you?" She stopped herself. "Forget I asked."

"Okay."

"It's fine with me if you take his place, but if he needs our car, I want to know why."

"He said he's borrowing Cray's pickup."

Now she had no excuse to question her oldest son. Whatever he did in somebody else's vehicle was his own business.

She and Noah finished carrying everything back to the pickup and dropped it off at home. Then she took a few minutes to freshen up and change out of her catering clothes. Wearing a vintage Laura Ashley sundress, she returned to the dig to find Travis.

"What happened to my food lady?" he asked.

She told herself she hadn't changed to impress anybody. "I thought the flowers on this dress were prettier than the mustard on my T-shirt."

"Good call. Let me tell Carin we're leaving. She promised to get everybody on the trail in a little while."

She watched as he crossed the site. He and Carin laughed about something. Carin pointed to the hole where three campers were working, and the two of them laughed again. Then he put his hand on Carin's shoulder and kept it there a moment as they finished their discussion.

She wondered exactly how far that relationship had progressed, and if it was ever possible for a married man to remain friends with another woman without damaging both relationships. She knew she should be happy for Travis, but she wasn't exactly there yet.

He returned. "Okay, let's go."

They started toward his Highlander. "Carin's a real asset, isn't she?" she asked.

"We're lucky to have her."

"She hasn't taught any of my sons. Maybe we'll be lucky next year."

"She's relatively new at the high school, but I've known her since we were kids. She grew up just outside Woodstock. Our parents were friends."

"I'm kind of surprised you haven't mentioned her before."

"Why?" He sounded genuinely puzzled.

"I guess I'm picking up vibes."

"Are you?"

"She'd be lucky to have you."

"I'll remember you said that. I'll send her your way if she ever needs a recommendation."

She decided he was as bad as her sons. Men possessed an innate ability not to deny or confirm anything.

"Y chromosomes," she said out loud.

"What?"

"Never mind."

As they drove to Helen's house, they chatted about camp. She told him she thought Jared had finally broken up with Brandy, and he agreed that he'd noticed the tension today.

Helen's farmhouse was standard issue Virginia. White frame, front porch with rockers, peonies blooming along the driveway. She was waiting on the walkway, and Travis got out to help her into the SUV. Gayle moved to the back seat, then leaned forward so Helen could hear her.

"We're lucky you have such a good memory."

"More than a few folks around Toms Brook wish I'd forget a thing or two."

Gayle bet that was true. "How's Reese doing today?"

"Played in the wading pool Cissy set up for her this morning like nothing ever happened. Course Cissy dumped out the water the minute Reese put one foot on the ground. She's been following her around all day like they were stitched at the hip."

"I'm glad you don't live right on the river. Cissy probably wouldn't sleep again until Reese gets married."

"The girl's got a good head. She'll move on."

Helen gave directions, and Travis wound his way along back roads. The Highlander was roomy and comfortable, a family car. She compared it to the sporty Mustang that Eric had rented for his stay. Of course Jared and Noah had been thoroughly delighted with their father's choice. Both of them had enjoyed a turn behind the wheel. But it was crowded when they were all together.

"Okay, there it is." Helen pointed up ahead. "Used to be a church there, an old one-room Methodist church with a tin roof and rickety bell tower. The congregation more or less died off. People who needed a fancier church moved on. The pastor got old but refused to retire. By the time he passed away, weren't hardly anybody left to find a new one. Now there's nothing here but the graveyard."

"Somebody will come along and build here," Travis said. "Maybe another church, maybe a housing development."

"Well, they'd have to leave the graves or move them, and Virginia don't make that easy."

Travis parked and went around the front to help Helen. Gayle could see where the church must once have been, but the site was now overgrown with trees and brambles. The cemetery wasn't even visible from the road. Only when they got closer could she see the outlines of headstones.

"This is a shame," she said. "Nobody's keeping up with it."

"Some of the families come out now and then and clear their own areas." Helen took her time picking her way across the ground, even though she was leaning on Travis's arm. "A neighbor of mine has family buried here."

"Maybe we could get the teenagers at our church to make it a project. I'll ask Sam if he thinks it's a good idea."

"A right smart idea. Teach them respect for those who've passed on."

Gayle figured that if Helen liked it, the idea was definitely a winner.

They walked in silence the rest of the distance until they reached a rusty wrought-iron gate, hanging from one hinge. It swung open with an awful squeal, and they stepped inside. What grass there was waved in a light breeze. Weeds crowded between headstones, along with the occasional wildflower. It was sad, but picturesque at the same time, a forgotten piece of history.

"The Duncan plot's over this way, best I can recall." Helen pointed to her left.

"I've been in close touch with the family, but nobody told me about this," Travis said.

"I reckon they're a bit embarrassed they haven't kept it up better."

They took their time picking their way between stones. Small white butterflies rose in a cloud at their approach. Golden black-eyed Susans nodded between long stalks of rye grass, and wild roses stretched toward the sun.

Helen stopped to get her bearings. "Okay, this is where I remember it."

This area had been tended better than some. Gayle guessed someone had been here in the past two or three months to pull weeds and trim the grass. But even so, it looked neglected and lonely.

"Here's the one belongs to Miranda and Lewis Duncan." Helen held out her hand.

Travis stooped and began to clear away the weeds in front of a large, irregularly shaped stone. Gayle could see it had eroded over time.

"When a stone is erected for somebody who's not buried

there, it's called a cenotaph." Ever the teacher, Travis finished pulling the weeds, then took out a handkerchief and wiped the stone clean.

"Can you make out the letters?" Gayle joined him, stooping beside him for a closer look.

"'In memory of Lewis Duncan, who died at Gettysburg, PA July 2, 1863.'"

"Carin's version of the story was right, then. Miranda did put up a stone for her husband."

"Miranda Duncan, beloved wife. December 8, 1833. July 9, 1928."

Gayle felt her throat tighten. "I wouldn't have expected Robby to add beloved wife after she died. Not if the play is accurate."

"Well, of course she *was* beloved to Duncan. We know he loved her."

"More likely it was just standard," Helen said. "The last nice thing you could say about somebody's marriage before it was forgotten."

That made Gayle even sadder.

Travis was rubbing the letters at the bottom. Then he looked up at Helen. "You were right about the quote being from Shakespeare."

Gayle was reading it as he spoke.

"What's it say?" Helen asked. "I don't remember the words."

Travis read them out loud. "'How many ages hence shall this our lofty scene be acted over in states unborn and accents yet unknown?'"

He got to his feet and looked down at it. "I think it's a quote from *Julius Caesar,* but Carin will know for certain."

"Was she talking about the war, do you think?" Helen asked.

"I guess we'll never know."

Gayle thought she could probably make an educated guess, and she knew she would be thinking of this when it came time for the campfire that evening. Miranda Duncan had been part of a vast stream of women throughout history whose lives had been altered by the decisions of men. And yet, Gayle thought, there was more carved into this stone than a comment on a heartbreaking war.

If Carin's play was in any way Miranda's real story, she had been a woman caught up in a curious and poignant love triangle. A husband and heroic soldier who, by Robby's account, she had never grown to love. A charismatic stranger who might well have been one of history's most notorious assassins. And Miranda herself, educated, beautiful, and yearning for something more than poverty and despair.

Hadn't women, throughout history, chosen to love men who did not deserve them?

And hadn't they refused far too often to love the ones who did?

Chapter 28

1865

I slept little that night. I ached from the unaccustomed hour on horseback, but that seemed trivial. After dark I had retrieved the newspaper, and it was folded under my pillow, waiting for me to read again at first light.

Unfortunately, I was afraid that reading the story of John Wilkes Booth a second time wasn't going to solve my problem. The similarities I'd already noted were enough that a court might demand to know why we had closed our eyes to them.

More kept me awake. Even when I tried to put aside the possible results of not reporting Blackjack, I was faced with other problems. Whoever he really was, whatever had brought him here, Blackjack was a Confederate sympathizer, and my father had laid down his life for the Confederacy. Something had brought Blackjack to us, and something had lengthened his stay.

In this time of unrest and upheaval, even an honorable man could end up enduring years of prison or swinging from a rope.

The coin had another side. Lincoln had sons, one nearly the same age I had been when my father died. As well as anybody, I knew what those boys must feel now that their father was gone. But more than that, having seen the result of the war, I wasn't certain killing was ever wise. Not because we had lost, but because of *everything* we had both lost, North and South, in the pursuit of an end that would better have been decided around a table by men with wise heads and willing hearts.

The man who had ruthlessly murdered the United States President had possessed neither.

But was it up to me to make certain that man was brought to justice? Blackjack Brewer might be many things, but he had never hurt us. The ride that afternoon had been solely for my benefit. He had done what work he could, paid generously for his care, and entertained us. How much of my concern centered on his effect on my mother? Had fear that she would be cruelly hurt spurred me to see what wasn't there?

Or, worse, how much was simply that I was jealous of the attention she showed him?

When dawn lit my room I bathed quickly at the washstand, slipped on my clothes and took the newspaper to the window. As I had feared, a quick glance through the rest of the pages showed there was nothing else to be learned.

I had never missed my father more. I tried to imagine what he would tell me, but he had been gone for so long that his voice no longer sounded in my head.

I needed someone I could talk to. I considered confiding in my mother, but if I was too involved in the situation to see it clearly, she would be even more so. I considered Aunt Cora, but although she was wise in her own ways, I didn't think she would understand all she needed to. Ralph lived entirely in the moment and liked to say that whatever wasn't biting him wasn't worth swatting.

That left Uncle Eb, who lacked education but not logic. If I was going to convince him, however, I needed more evidence. In the night it had occurred to me that if I could see what was left of Blackjack's tattoo, I might have what I needed. I suspected there had been no accident on the road, that he had scraped away what damning evidence he could, a painful and, as it turned out, fateful decision. The festering wound had brought him to us.

I devised a plan, and although it was weak, I was hopeful. I would wait until that evening, then I would offer to fill another bath. I would stay to help him in and out, since his leg was still in the splint and maneuvering was difficult. I thought he would remove the bandage so that the hand could be bathed, as well. Then, when I was helping, I would take a closer look, as if I were interested in how well it had healed. If I could arrange it, the plan was simple enough. I just hoped I could see what I needed to.

I hid the newspaper once more, then went downstairs. Ma was already working in the kitchen. Not so Dandy simmered on the stove, and I could smell johnny cake baking in the oven. Ma turned when I came in.

"Robby, we've gone long enough without meat, and it rained again last night. It's still too wet to plow. I'd like you to go down to the river and see if you can catch some fish. Go right after breakfast. I'll pack you something for your dinner."

I wondered if she just wanted me out of the house so that she and Blackjack could be alone together. But she quashed that notion. "If he will, Mr. Brewer can go with you. Two poles catch more than one."

Before the war, I had never been fond of fish, but now the

thought made my mouth water. I knew a promising spot within easy walking distance where Blackjack and I could throw our lines from the bank. Stationed in one place and anchored by his injured leg, we wouldn't fill a creel, but with luck there might be enough for our supper.

By the time he arrived for breakfast I had gathered equipment, dug for worms in the chicken yard and planned our morning. My mother greeted him formally and served us both, treating us to eggs with the johnny cake. I explained the plan to Blackjack, who seemed receptive.

"We'll have a way to walk, but we'll go slow," I told him, my gaze flicking to his hand. Unfortunately, his shirt fell below his wrist, as it always did, and farther below, a strip of cloth wove between his thumb and the side of his hand. I had no view of the tattoo.

"It would be good to remove the bandage on your hand and let the air and sunshine do their work," my mother told him. "I'll do it after breakfast, and we'll see how you've fared."

I tried not to let my excitement show. If his hand had healed enough, my mother might leave it uncovered. That would save me drawing him a bath.

I wanted to stay for the unveiling, but Ma sent me out with scraps for the chickens. When I returned for him, I found Blackjack waiting. Both hands were covered by cotton gloves.

Once the path to the river had been much trampled, my father and I often riding down to fish, with Eb and Ralph doing the same. But now it had grown up, and we moved slowly. I carried our equipment, and Blackjack carried his cane and pole. I worried as we went, wondering if I would ever get a look at his hand, and if it would help me make the biggest decision of my life.

At last we stopped where my father and I had often started.

I could leave Blackjack there, moving down the riverbank on my own, although that was not what I intended. Most days I would have looked for a place in the shade, but this morning I chose the sunniest spot and set down my bucket of worms, the dinner basket and my pole.

"Have you done much fishing in these parts?" I asked. "Is it different up near Winchester?"

He winked. "There's water and fish in both places. Some days you can lure them to take the bait, and some you can't."

A rock outcropping hung over the river in a clearing not far away, and I suggested he settle himself there. I turned to get supplies, and when I turned back I was disappointed to see that he had already baited his hook and dangled his pole in the water. If he had removed his gloves to do so, he had slipped them on again.

I often waded as I fished, but this morning the water was too chilly and the sun not high enough. Besides, I wanted to stay close by in case Blackjack rolled back his sleeves and removed his gloves. I climbed down a few feet until the river was lapping at my toes, baited my hook and flung my line into the water.

We fished in silence for a long time. Out of the corner of my eye I watched to see if he showed any signs of having fished before. He seemed perfectly comfortable with the process, if not eager to be there. I caught a small sunfish and tossed it back. He hooked a floating branch.

The sun was rising above the trees and would soon beat down mercilessly on Blackjack's rock. Yesterday had been cool, but last night's rain was already turning to steam, and the day was going to be unseasonably warm. I dipped my toes in the water, then rolled up my pants legs and waded in almost to my knees. The water nearly froze my flesh, but I got used to it quickly.

As the sun rose higher, I kept an eye on Blackjack. After a

while he took off his vest and set his slouch-brimmed hat lower on his forehead to shade his eyes. I edged closer.

"Do you usually have better luck in the morning?" he asked.

This time *I* winked. "There's water and fish all times of day. Some mornings you can lure them to take the bait, and some mornings you can't."

He laughed at his own words twisted and tossed back to him. "I fished often as a boy. With my brothers and sisters. I was never the best of the lot. I was easily bored."

Brothers and sisters. I longed to know more about the Booth family, although how would I know if anything Blackjack said was true?

"Are you bored now?" I asked.

"Uncommonly. And you?"

"Not bored. Growing hotter, though. It must be even hotter up there on the rock. At least the river cools my feet."

"I like being outside for a change. The sun feels good."

I was sorry it did.

I moved downstream and out a bit, casting my line once more. This time I was successful. After a few minutes I pulled out a bullhead nearly the length of my forearm.

"We catch a few more of these, Ma won't be too disappointed." I strung the fish on a line, baited my hook and cast again.

"I doubt your mother is often disappointed in you," Blackjack said.

"I do my best." I hoped it was true.

"What plans do you have for your life, Robby?"

"To do whatever I have to."

"To bring this farm back into production?"

"To take care of Ma. To keep the land safe. To honor my father's memory."

"All important goals."

I glanced at him. He was swiping at his forehead with a sleeve. Hope blossomed inside me.

We grew silent again. I caught another bullhead, smaller but still large enough to eat. It joined the first. I stretched and watched Blackjack, as if cheering him on.

"More worms?" I asked, hoping he would remove his gloves to bait his hook.

"I haven't had your luck. It's possible I may only need this one for the day."

I walked out on the rock to join him. "I'll take your line if you'd like to get up and move around a bit. It'll cool you off."

He handed me the pole; then, as if he had somehow heard my wish, or at the least had begun to believe it was as hot as I said, he stripped off his gloves.

As I'd guessed, the wound on his hand was no longer bandaged. A thick scab covered the middle of it, where the wound was the deepest, but the remainder was red, the skin puckered. Whoever had painstakingly adorned his hand with India ink had done their job well. I could make out the *J* that Blackjack claimed was the remnant of a *D* for Daisy to the left of the scab. But just to the right, I clearly saw the remains of another letter.

A *W*.

"Not a pretty picture, is it?" Blackjack asked, getting to his feet as I'd suggested.

I'd been caught. I looked up and hoped I was at least something of an actor. "It looks like it's healing well," I said, struggling to sound collected.

"Thanks to your mother's excellent nursing skills."

"There are still traces of the tattoo."

"I'm afraid so."

"More than just a *D*," I said.

"*D* and *B*, he agreed, casually tracing the latter with his fingertip, although it was hard to see. "Daisy and Blackjack, connected by two hearts. See, here's what left of them." He traced what I'd taken as a *W*, moving his finger as if to trace the supposed remainders of two connected hearts that were invisible to me.

"Faint hearts, I suppose," he said. "Well, I can only be glad *I* was too faint of heart to have our entire names spelled out and entwined with vines and love birds."

"You would have needed your whole arm for that," I agreed. But I'd seen what I'd hoped to. Now I was almost sure there had never been a *D* on Blackjack's hand. There was a *J* and apparently a faint *B*. And in between, no longer quite hidden, the remains of a *W*.

I had everything I needed to go to Uncle Eb.

Unconcerned, Blackjack stretched his arms over his head. "Let this be a lesson. If you ever fall in love—and you will, I'm afraid—don't convince yourself she's the only woman you'll ever want. Don't ink her name or initials on your hand so that every woman who sees it from that day forward will know."

I thought of the man killed in Port Royal, a man who had died carrying *five* photographs of beautiful women.

I looked at the sky above me. The sun was moving slowly. We had at least another hour before it was overhead. Then we would eat, perhaps fish a little more. The only way we could go back to the house earlier would be if we quickly caught enough to satisfy Ma.

I got to my feet and pulled in his line. Blackjack's worm had slipped off. "I'll put a new worm on for you. We shouldn't stop now, not when they're finally biting."

He looked surprised at my sudden burst of enthusiasm. I took his pole with me to bait his hook.

* * *

The fish didn't cooperate. After a good start, my bullheads had little company. Blackjack caught several sunfish just large enough to clean, and I caught a small suckerfish. The sun was sinking toward the horizon when we packed up for home. We would have enough fish for supper, sharing some of the catch with Uncle Eb's family, but no one would eat their fill.

I cleaned and prepared the fish by the riverside and gave what I had to Ma once we arrived. I could tell she had hoped for more, but she praised us anyway.

After I washed the smell of fish from my hands, I followed her into the kitchen. "I'll take what you don't want to Aunt Cora."

"I told Eb to expect it." She was looking out the window, where both of us could see Blackjack washing at the pump.

I didn't like the way her gaze followed him or the slight smile on her lips. I hadn't liked that smile before, but now, knowing what I thought I did, watching it was like cleaning a cut with vinegar. I spoke before I could stop myself.

"No matter what you're thinking, he's not the man Pa was. Maybe he's younger and maybe he's handsome. But Pa would never hide out with strangers the way Blackjack's doing. He would take care of his own problems. He wouldn't involve anybody else."

She was looking at me now, her gaze strong and steady. "What are you talking about?"

"Can't you see something's wrong about Blackjack? He could have moved on days ago, but he wants to stay here for some reason. Maybe it's the company, and maybe it's not."

"What do you mean, the company?" Her eyes were angry now, although her voice remained soft.

"I mean maybe he likes knowing you're so happy, him being

here. You smiling and laughing like a girl. You think the rest of us can't see it?"

She didn't move. "There are some things you can't understand."

"I understand more than you think. I understand more than *you* do."

Blackjack had finished at the pump, and in a moment I heard footsteps on the side porch, then heard him wiping his boots before entering the house.

"Take half the fish to Eb," my mother said, her voice trembling. "And stay there for supper, unless you can remember what it means to respect your elders."

"What'll be *left* for me to respect if I don't come home and watch out for you?"

She slapped me then, something she had never done before. "Get out, Robby! I'm ashamed to be your mother."

"Well, I'm ashamed to be your son!" I grabbed the plate of fish, tossing half of it on the bare table for her, whirled and left.

I took the long way to Uncle Eb's, walking through the field beside our house, then around to their back door. Aunt Cora was at the fence post pounding a piece of salted beef when I arrived. She looked up and grinned.

"Look what Eb got today." She held up the meat for me to see. "He traded some dried corn to Walter Henderson, and there's enough for all of us."

"I brought you some fish." I held out the tin plate.

"Now look what *you* got. Who did most the work, you or that Blackjack fellow?"

I forgot to answer. I felt sick. Ma and I rarely argued. She guided with gentle words, and if she needed more, a stern look usually did the job. I felt betrayed and, worse, I felt as if soon I would be betraying her.

"Cat got your tongue, boy?"

I stepped forward and offered the plate. "Aunt Cora, where's Uncle Eb?"

The wrinkles in her forehead deepened. As she took the plate, she peered at me through narrowed eyes. "He's out checking to see if the north field can be plowed tomorrow."

"I'm going to see if I can find him."

"You want to tell me what's wrong?"

I shook my head.

"Reckon I'll know soon enough anyway," she said.

I left the cabin and walked along the road away from the house. I hoped Uncle Eb wouldn't start back by the river path, which was longer but prettier at this time of afternoon. I kept my eyes open, practicing how to explain my suspicions.

Once I passed the woods that separated the homestead from the field, I spied him coming toward me. He was walking slowly, hands shoved in the pockets of patched overalls. He lifted one in a wave when he saw me, but neither of us walked faster. I was afraid to tell him what I knew, and he was simply growing too old to hurry.

"You looking for me?" he asked, when I drew close enough for conversation.

Every sentence I had rehearsed went out of my head. "Uncle Eb, I think Blackjack might be the fellow who killed Abraham Lincoln."

He cocked his head and frowned. But he didn't tell me I was fanciful or foolish. I had known he wouldn't, and he didn't disappoint me.

"Let's sit and talk about it." He tilted his head toward a fallen tree at the edge of the woods. We sat beside each other, legs straight, heels resting on the ground. I could feel the forest darkness spreading toward us. Soon it would be evening and too late to go into town to alert anyone.

"Start at the beginning," he said.

Uncle Eb listened as I told him everything I knew. When I finished, he just sat there for a moment. Then he gnawed at his lip.

"Tell me, if your boarder is Lincoln's assassin, why did that man they caught in Port Royal have Booth's diary with him?"

This had puzzled me, too. The five women's photographs had been found inserted in Booth's diary, which had been removed from the body of the man shot in the barn.

I told him what I had figured out. "Maybe that man was a decoy. In a war, when a general wants to sneak up on his enemy, he sends some of his men to attack from a different direction, so the enemy forgets to pay attention to what's going on at the side or the back. Maybe the man they shot was supposed to lead them away from Booth, only they killed him before the truth could come out. Then those soldiers said it was Booth so they could get that reward money."

He'd been working on a plug of tobacco. Now he spat into the bushes and wiped his mouth on his sleeve.

"There are some similarities, that's sure as the sun come up this morning. There's a word for that, though. Coinc'dence. Not that I'm saying that's it, mind you. But it could be."

"If he is Booth, and if somebody figures it out and comes looking for him, and if they find him here, or find out we took him in…"

He spat again, performing the same ritual. "I reckon we could just ask him to move on down the road."

"And if he does, and they capture him? And he tells them where he's been hiding out?"

This thought didn't take Uncle Eb by surprise. I could see he'd already considered it. "True, it's taking a chance."

"Uncle Eb, I think we have to report this to somebody in town, maybe the army if you can get to them." I wasn't even sure who we should tell, only that we needed to tell somebody in authority so that no one thought we had purposely harbored a fugitive.

"And you're willing, are you, to turn him in like that? Not knowing for sure who he is?"

Even as I'd made my case, the unknowns had swirled in my head until I was no longer sure of anything. "If he's not John Wilkes Booth, then maybe they'll just let him go."

"No, he's somebody," Uncle Eb said. "You know it. I know it."

"They're letting men out of prison. They'll be letting more out. All he'll have to do is swear he supports the Union."

"Unless he's wanted for more than fighting on the losing side."

I put my head in my hands. I felt physically ill. The fight with my mother. The knowledge that I might be condemning a man who didn't deserve it.

The fear that we might be harboring the man whose name would go down in history as the assassin of a United States President.

"I'll make my way over to the Hendersons' place again," Uncle Eb said at last.

"When?"

"Now. You tell your aunt Cora I won't be home for supper. Walter's got a horse he'll let me use. I'll ride into town tonight, and in the morning I'll see about telling somebody what you've told me. I'll stay in town and be back when I'm done."

"Somebody?"

"Somebody in charge. I'll find the right person."

I listened and nodded, but inside I only felt worse.

Uncle Eb patted my shoulder. "You grew up too fast, Robby. No way to keep you young, but it's sure not fair."

Until then, I hadn't known how old I could feel.

I stayed there a long time after Uncle Eb left for the Henderson farm. Then, as darkness fell, I went back to the homestead to tell Aunt Cora and Ralph that Uncle Eb wouldn't be back that night. I told them that when he'd seen Walter Henderson earlier that day, Mr. Henderson had offered him a ride into town early tomorrow morning, and now he'd decided to take him up on it.

I didn't want to go home, but when Aunt Cora offered me supper, I refused. Instead, I went to my favorite spot by the river and watched the stars come out.

Chapter 29

Friday at dawn Gayle stood on the terrace and told herself it didn't matter that this would be the last dawn she would see in her thirties. Twenty had been a birthday to celebrate, and thirty had been so busy it had passed without a squawk. But forty seemed momentous. The inn was still hard work, but she had excellent help and few long-range challenges. The boys were growing up and would soon be leaving home. She wondered how she would feel for the rest of her working life, making pancakes and polite conversation without them.

She hugged a coffee mug against her midriff and stared across the water. A gray mist filled the air, and although she was sure the sun had risen, all actual signs were blocked by heavy clouds behind the mountains. The weatherman had said that the remnants of a tropical storm were on their way to bring much needed rain for the weekend, but the onset seemed more immediate.

On the other side of the river there were only trees where a farmhouse had once stood. She wondered if Miranda Duncan had ever come out at dawn to gaze at the river like this. Had she looked back on decisions she had made, relationships she had engaged in, with doubt or satisfaction? Had she asked herself on the eve of an important birthday what the rest of her days would hold?

"I thought I'd find you out here."

At the sound of Eric's voice, Gayle did an about-face. She'd heard the inn door open, but she had expected to be joined by one of her sons.

"Did you even go to sleep?" she asked. "I've never seen you get up for a sunrise if you didn't have to."

He toasted her with a coffee mug, twin to her own. "I'm not sure why I'm up. Do you mind if I join you?"

"I'd welcome it. I was getting a little maudlin."

"That usually works best after a minimum of four stiff drinks."

"Well, sometimes it's easy enough without booze."

"Don't tell me this is about your birthday."

She put a finger to her lips. "Bad word. I'm surprised it's not tucked away in Buddy's repertoire."

"I swear, Gayle. The woman we bought that bird from told us he talked. She just forgot to tell us what he said."

"If Noah can sneak him in, Buddy will be the hit of his college dorm."

His laugh was low and sleepy. "At least now we know why she was in such a hurry to get rid of him."

Gayle turned back to her view and wished the landscape would brighten. "I come out here every morning. It's my quiet time."

"I remember. I know I'm interrupting."

"Company's nice for a change."

He came to stand beside her. She could feel the pleasant, almost protective, warmth of his tall body. "How nice?"

She turned just a little so she could see him better. "What do you mean?"

"You've been alone a long time—"

"Three sons is hardly alone."

"You know what I mean. Then here I come again. I invade your space, take up your private moments." He nudged her hip with his seductively. "Give way cool neck rubs."

She had been aware of him towering over her, and of the sliver of excitement that came from it. She could pretend to misunderstand, but Eric would eventually pin her down. She was up against a pro.

Instead, she countered. "What's it been like for *you?* Being here? Being with the boys…?"

"Being with you?"

"I was edging into that."

He smiled down at her. "It's the road not taken, isn't it? Don't we always wonder if we made the wrong turn? That's what Dillon's play's all about. Decisions."

"It certainly seems to be."

"I still ask myself if I should have stayed. When I left for good, didn't you wonder if you should come with me? You were invited."

"You didn't want me."

He swirled his coffee and turned his gaze to the horizon. "I never said that."

"Eric, you were beleaguered. You'd just had an affair to prove it. You had a new baby after taking steps to prevent one."

"Immaturity warring with selfishness. The jury's still out on which side won."

"I'm not angling for an apology."

"Maybe it's too long ago to remember everything I felt, but

after I left, I missed you. I kicked myself for everything. I even considered not signing the divorce papers."

Despite not wanting to, she could believe him.

"And you?" he asked.

Like him, she turned back to the horizon. This was a conversation best carried on without eye contact. "You're right, it *was* a long time ago. I know I shed my quota of tears. I wanted things to work out. I remember looking up airplane schedules and rentals in London so we could be closer to you and at least try to put the pieces back together."

"But you didn't buy tickets."

"The road not taken."

"Maybe at the time we did what we had to. But these times are different."

There it was, in the open at last, the possibility of reconciliation. And now there was no place to hide.

She still didn't look at him. "Aren't we the same people? After the boys leave home, I'm not sure what I want for my future, but I don't want to trek all over the globe with a man who's happiest in the thick of battle."

"Maybe we wouldn't have to go anywhere. Maybe I could get a job in D.C., like we talked about all those years ago. You could keep the inn."

"Why should you stay around?"

He set his mug on a ledge; then he put his hands on her shoulders and turned her toward him. "Because maybe this is where I need to be, with you and the kids, like a real family again."

She searched his eyes. "*Like* one?"

He winced. "Be one. Maybe vows, rings. The whole nine yards."

She fell back on numbers, because what else did she know for sure? "Sixty percent of second marriages end in divorce, and that's simple second marriages. Not remarriage to the person you divorced."

"You're certainly up on the statistics. Does that come up in conversation a lot?"

She had to smile a little. "I'm conversant with the Internet."

"And you were busy *conversing* with the Internet on this topic?"

"We divorced for a reason. Is there any *good* reason to think we wouldn't have the same problems if we tried again?"

"We're older, smarter, calmer, and maybe both of us are ready to find solutions."

She listened to his words but even more to his voice. Eric was the most persuasive person she knew. His job was to sell the news, to make viewers believe every word he said, to inspire trust and faith so they would never willingly choose another correspondent.

He didn't sound persuasive now. He sounded as if he were asking questions. He sounded as if he were putting together a story on divorce and remarriage, all the pros and cons. He *looked* like a man flying blind.

She searched his eyes for more clues. "Is this just about being a better father? About making up to the kids for being gone so much? Finishing up their childhood on-site?"

"I think it's about a lot of things. I guess that's one of the big ones."

"The worst possible reason to reconsider our relationship would be the boys. They need us both, but they don't need us together. Right now you're forging new bonds, and no matter what happens between *us,* that's what really matters."

He dropped his hands. "I don't know how much of this is about them and how much about…"

She waited for his answer to stir her emotions, but from the start the conversation had been more academic than emotional, and that seemed wrong and, in its own way, telling.

"What *is* it about, then? Were we such soul mates that we can't live without each other?"

He smiled, not the famous Fortman grin but something more genuine and sweeter. "I don't believe in soul mates, but I loved you."

She felt herself softening. "Maybe that's why neither of us moved on to somebody else."

"Because we were still in love?"

"No, because it's hard to reconcile loving somebody with failure."

"What if we've finally learned what we need to know?"

Or what if they were both just better at pretending? That thought wouldn't leave her. Nor would another, that here they were, talking about love, divorce and marriage, and her hands were still steady. Her heart wasn't pounding so hard that her chest could hardly contain it.

The first time they had fallen in love, their feelings had been white hot, like stars blazing across the sky. She had lived for the sight of him. And now, what did she feel? A yearning to set the past right? To at long last turn failure into success? But what had happened to the heat, the rush of blood and the desire to free fall through space in each other's arms?

Was the same maturity that might help them work out their problems the reason that no stars blazed in their private heavens?

As if he'd read her thoughts, he leaned over and kissed her forehead, then her lips. "Don't make a decision on the spot, okay?"

He smelled like coffee and soap and Eric, but she felt herself backing away. "This will confuse the boys. This isn't something we can talk to them about."

He held up his hands. "It's the first of many conversations just between us. We'll take it slowly, backtrack as often as we need to. No pushing or shoving. No tug-of-war. No mistakes this time."

"As if our lives aren't complicated enough."

His expression was grave. "If this is only a complication, then that's an answer, isn't it? Can you say that's all it is?"

She couldn't and didn't. But later, when she was hard at work in the kitchen finishing breakfast preparations for the morning's guests, she wondered what she should have replied. And she knew that, for now, no answer would have been good enough.

Gayle's birthday party was planned. The meal was an informal buffet, so an exact head count wasn't necessary. Sam had asked a few members of the women's auxiliary to step in and help the caterer and florist with the setup and cleanup. Several people had agreed to greet guests while Eric fetched Gayle.

With most of the work finished, Eric felt let down. He had enjoyed the phone calls, the sense of moving a project along and doing something important. If he was truthful, he had enjoyed being recognized and having a chance to talk about his work. As pathetic as it was, he had basked in those brief moments in the spotlight again.

As he drove to the dig after breakfast, he thought about his talk with Gayle. Unlike some women, she was most desirable when she wasn't fully awake, softer, easier to reach, less capable of hiding her emotions. Watching her, talking about the birthday to come, he had felt a wave of affection, and he supposed that was why he had impulsively broached the idea of reconciliation.

But the idea hadn't appeared out of the blue. Since arriving, he had considered and reconsidered the idea of staying in the Valley and taking back the life he had abandoned. Could he make up for past failures to Gayle and the boys by spending the rest of his days being a good father and husband? Or was this just another train wreck waiting to happen?

He thought about his friend and cameraman who would never have the opportunity to see his daughter grow up or be a real father to her. Howard had died doing what he loved most, but to what purpose? To produce a few minutes of film that no one would remember a week later? To ask murderers to share their world view on international television? Was that the way Eric wanted to die? In the middle of a war, scrambling for an interview?

When he'd considered moving back for good, he had cautioned himself to wait to make decisions. He owed Gayle a lot, but he didn't owe her more heartache and rejection. He'd provided plenty of that already.

Now he wondered how he would have felt if Gayle's eyes had sparkled with anticipation at the possibility of marrying again. Then there would have been no room for retreat. Imagining it, he felt trapped in some of the same ways he'd felt twelve years ago.

But Gayle's eyes *hadn't* sparkled. She had been wary and armed with all the right questions. Unfortunately, he didn't have many answers. Yes, he loved their sons and wanted to be the best possible father he could manage. Yes, maybe he still loved her. He just wasn't sure how, and he thought her feelings for him were every bit as cloudy.

Finally, despite wanting to leave Ariel out of the equation entirely, he couldn't help but think of her. Self-centered, driven, single-minded, take-charge Ariel.

Beautiful, funny, intelligent, compassionate Ariel.

He was fresh out of adjectives, insight and energy, and he was glad the dig was so close. His head was spinning with what-ifs, and he didn't want to think about this anymore.

When he drove across the low water bridge, the haze still

hadn't lifted. Since this was the last full day of digging, he had expected to find the campers goofing off. Tonight was the final campfire, when they would find out the end of Robby's story, and tomorrow after breakfast they would break camp and go home. But by the time he drove up, the kids were already hard at work.

He parked and found Travis screening dirt with two of the campers. "I thought I'd find everybody sitting around," he said.

Travis shredded a lump of clay over the screen as one of the campers shook the frame. "No, they've all been so involved, they're not ready to let go yet. They still might find something exciting."

"Where do you want me today?"

"With me." Travis reminded the boy to put on a glove before he started breaking up lumps of dirt; then he stripped off his own and dropped it in a bucket. At his signal, Cray left a conversation he was having with Jared about twenty yards away and came over to supervise.

Eric raised his hand to his son. Jared did the same and sent Eric a perfunctory smile before he strode quickly to the other side of the site. Eric suspected he had just gotten the brush-off. Ever since he had told Eric that Brandy wasn't pregnant after all, Jared had made a point of avoiding his father. Eric figured he was embarrassed by the whole episode.

"Here's the thing," Travis said, as they walked to the excavation unit that was closest to the river. "We may have a difficult situation developing here, a combination of unfortunate factors."

Eric felt a stab of excitement. "I'm all ears."

"You know we've stumbled on the foundation of the farm workers' house."

"Eb and Cora."

"Among others over time, I'm sure. We've been digging in what was probably originally their fruit cellar, but I didn't realize that until we found the foundation of a chimney. Since then, it's become clear there was a cellar on the other side, which would have been directly under their house."

"The river must have really moved in this direction since then. They wouldn't have built so close to it, would they?"

"Rivers are living creatures. Floods erode the riverbank, the river settles into the new channels and causes more erosion as it rises and falls."

"So what's the problem today?"

"The problem is that we've opened a can of worms. I thought we were going to be sifting through a trash pit. Instead, we've uncovered a foundation." He paused. "And not just any foundation."

"Something you didn't expect in terms of building materials?"

"With small houses of this era, you expect to see almost anything. It wasn't uncommon for a cabin to perch on four piles of rocks, one at each corner. I've seen some so rickety the Three Little Pigs probably did a better job with straw and mud. But this one's not that way. The cellar wall's two feet thick, and I don't know how deep it goes. Stacked stone—and expertly done, by the look of it. If Eb and Ralph built it, they were real artisans. But I'm guessing it was built earlier, that maybe this was even the original farmhouse."

Eric waited for Travis to get to the point. So far, he couldn't see the problem.

"No matter how good somebody is at stacking stone, there are always nooks and crannies," Travis said. "Little pockets between them."

"Of course."

"Good hiding places."

Now Eric was paying closer attention.

"You know Carin and I put together the Duncan story from

flimsy evidence. The tale that a man who might have been John Wilkes Booth was on this farm right after the assassination is strictly anecdotal, passed down through the family and some of their acquaintances. I've been talking to the kids about scientific method, historical record, pure fiction. We've made sure they understand the play is fiction."

Travis seemed to realize he'd been lecturing. He smiled a little. "Anyway, you've been to the campfires."

"I've been impressed."

"Glad to hear it. While we were doing the research, we found out something else about Miranda Duncan. As you know, she lived a long life. Toward the end, things began to disappear from her house. One of her great-granddaughters told me that after the funeral, her mother looked for some family mementos and never found them. She mentioned a set of Shakespeare's plays and some silver."

"Thoughts on what happened to them?"

"The family just assumed visitors or some of the locals they'd hired to look in on her had taken things, or Miranda had thrown them away by mistake. She was old, her eyesight and hearing had suffered. Some people thought her mind was going at the end."

"So what have you found?"

"I'll show you." Travis retrieved a bucket that was sitting under a nearby tree and returned with it. He lifted out a plastic bag. "Isn't this a beauty?"

Eric took the bag and held it up to what passed for the sun that morning. Inside was a small fork. He whistled. "Real silver, do you think?"

"If it is, it was made before 1860, because the word *sterling* isn't stamped on it. I'll be able to tell more once we clean it up and check the reference books."

"Do you think Miranda put it here?"

"Maybe when she got old, or maybe it was simply overlooked when she retrieved the silver she'd hidden during the war."

"That's got to be the find of the week."

"You can imagine every kid wants to dig for treasure right here. And I can't let them."

Eric understood why. No matter how well trained they were, the kids weren't going to be patient enough to do this the right way. He understood their feelings. Even he was itching to get in and dig to see what else Miranda had hidden.

Travis put the fork back in the bucket. "I'm tempted to fill in this hole until I can round up some experienced adults, but that's going to create problems, too. We could destroy valuable artifacts or, at the least, move them out of position. And there's the question of time. We'll lose more of what's here every time the river tops its banks."

"What are you going to do?"

"I thought you and I could work with a couple of the most patient kids."

"I'm assuming you don't mean Dillon."

Travis laughed. "Afraid not. But Caleb can do it, and maybe a couple of others. I want to see what we can find today and tomorrow morning, so we need to move the dirt quickly but carefully. Then we'll decide what to do. If I think it's safe to fill the unit back in, we will. Or maybe I can get some archaeologist wannabes out here to do a proper job of finishing it next week."

"I've got the whole day. I'm waiting for supplies for the garden shed."

"Terrific. Thanks. There's just one more thing."

Eric was already looking for equipment. "What's that?"

Travis lowered his voice. "Just so you know. Miranda may not have been the only one to hide things on the property. You'll hear more about that tonight, and I don't want to spoil Dillon's final speech. I'm just telling you now, so you'll know what could be at stake."

Eric whistled softly. "You think something to do with Booth might have been hidden here?"

"Apparently Miranda liked this spot. Maybe Robby did, too."

"Come on, you don't really think Blackjack was John Wilkes Booth, do you? It's great entertainment, but there must be stories just like it all over the country. The Elvis sightings of that generation."

"I'll be talking about this tonight, but in a nutshell, some people are still convinced Booth escaped. The most popular tale says he made his way to Enid, Oklahoma, took the name of David E. George and committed suicide some years later. Before he died, he told at least two people he was really Booth."

"How did he explain that? The army shot and killed somebody they thought was Booth and buried him. And wasn't the man they killed carrying Booth's identification?"

"This George fellow said the man who died in Port Royal was somebody who'd gone to retrieve his effects from a marsh. That's why the guy they shot had all Booth's identification with him. Some people in Oklahoma were so convinced by the story, they refused to bury George's body. They embalmed it and presented the mummy as a sideshow attraction until it disappeared. Nobody's sure what happened to it."

"Are you saying you think Booth really *was* here before he ended up in Enid?"

"Me? I think John Wilkes Booth died after he was shot in a barn in Port Royal. Just the way history tells us. But there's nothing like a good mystery to give kids a lifelong interest in the past."

Eric heard more in Travis's tone. "And?"

"And I guess I'm not above enjoying one myself."

Because it was the last campfire, Gayle and Travis had decided to splurge on barbecued chicken with all the traditional trimmings. She spent the day pre-roasting chicken quarters so they could cut the cooking time at the site. Travis had promised to ask the kids to dig two long trenches near the campfire, and by the time she arrived, hickory logs were burning down to coals. She had borrowed five-foot grills from the church, and she flagged down two sturdy-looking boys to help Noah take them to the pit.

She was just loading her arms with grocery bags when Travis appeared to help.

"Looks like a feast."

She twirled and piled the bags in his arms. "You order a feast, you get a feast. Nobody goes hungry tonight. And I've got a surprise. Homemade ice cream. I borrowed hand-cranked churns from my church. But we'll need to get a start right away so it can set up once it's thick."

"You're hired for the rest of your life. "

"Uh-uh, we take this one year at a time, buster. I'm going to sleep for a week starting tomorrow."

He didn't look worried. "We've worked the campers hard today. Maybe cranking the ice cream will finish them off. Which would be a good thing, since it looks like serious rain later tonight, and I don't want kids wandering around outside their tents in the mud. Wandering's more or less a last-night ritual. I never get any sleep."

"I hope the tents are waterproof."

"I thought about sending the whole kit and caboodle home

after the campfire, but a change in schedule's too complicated. Some of the parents have probably made other plans. I guess the little darlings will just have to get wet."

"It's gone well this summer?"

"The usual problems. But yes, if we end with the head count we started with, I'll be happy."

She laughed and grabbed two more bags for herself. "Let's get this stuff over to the tables."

On the second trip to the truck, Travis and Gayle corralled a couple of girls to help carry the ice-cream makers to the eating area. Among them, they also carted sacks of ice, the ice-cream mixture Gayle had prepared and rock salt. Gayle showed the girls how to layer the ice and salt, and fill the canisters with ice-cream mix.

Satisfied, she stepped back. "I made chocolate chip and fresh peach. Two of each. That ought to do it. When you get tired, just mention to somebody how much fun it is, and they'll take over. It worked for Tom Sawyer."

She went back to the car for a stockpot filled with baked beans to set beside the chicken but was delighted to find it had already been carried to the grill.

Travis was pulling out the last of the supplies. "Fresh corn?"

"Lots of it. I'm going to show the kids how to roast it over the coals." She peered inside the truck. "You already got the rolls? The macaroni salad?"

"Everything's all set but the corn." He gave a sharp whistle to summon two more kids and handed them grocery bags filled to the top with bright green husks.

Gayle stretched, then she put her hands in the small of her back and leaned away from the pickup. Travis lounged against it and watched her. The kids were carefully avoiding them now, as if they'd seen that getting close meant more work.

"Tough day?" he asked.

"Just a complicated one."

"I don't think it's camp that's wearing you out."

She started to rub her nose, then laughed at herself. "Whoops."

"Need a listening ear?"

"I wouldn't do that to you."

"Eric?"

She wondered how Travis knew, and he smiled a little, as if he understood. "I'm not a mind reader. He keeps staring into space."

"Let's just say it's the last day of my thirties, which calls for some navel-gazing. And Eric and I are rethinking our lives. And I'm not sure I understand why."

"Maybe it's just been a long time coming."

"What do you mean?"

"Did you want to go on the way you were? For the rest of your life?"

"What way was I going?"

"I guess you have to figure that out."

Impulsively, she put her hand on his arm. "Am I nuts to be considering getting back together?"

"*Are* you considering it?"

She wasn't sure her thoughts were that well formed. The idea had been broached, but she thought she and Eric had both backed away at more or less the same speed. Still, now that the possibility had been put out there, she knew it could no longer be ignored. And whatever they decided was an ending of sorts— as well as a beginning.

"I don't know how seriously." It was as much of an answer as she had.

"When Chloe died, I thought the world had ended. But once the worst of the grief passed, I could move on. She was gone, and it was irrevocable. It's different for you. Eric's always there in the background. You share your sons. You'll always have a part in each other's lives."

"But *have* you moved on? It's been a long time, Travis." Her tone softened. "Have you finally fallen in love again?"

He didn't smile. "A while ago."

She wanted to be happy for him. She struggled to attain it. "I'm glad for you…."

"There's a *but* somewhere."

"But I guess I feel like I'm losing my best friend. I know that's selfish. I really want you to be happy. I just see things changing. For the better for you, of course, and maybe for me. But I'm going to miss…" She stopped herself. "Miss having your ear any time I want it."

"There's no doubt things will change." He pushed away from the pickup. "Decisions to make, huh?"

"Why don't you just tell me what I should do about Eric? It will make my life easier."

"Because then you would still feel stuck. You don't want that. You have to find your own way on this."

"I guess, if the play's at all accurate, Miranda Duncan had to deal with all these feelings too. And she lived to be…what? Ninety-five? I guess I'm destined to be a very old lady."

"I hope I'm around to see it." He slung his arm over her shoulders and gave her a brief hug. "You'll stay for the last campfire? Tired or not? I don't want you to miss the ending of the play."

She leaned against him and wondered how long they would be able to do this. He felt solid and warm, and she didn't want him to move. "Wild horses couldn't drag me away. Not even a feather bed."

He squeezed her shoulder before he moved away. "Come see

what we're doing at the unit near the river when you have time. It's been a productive day."

She watched him go. And despite all the work, she was sorry archaeology camp was ending.

Chapter 30

1865

The hour was late when I finally started home. I expected to find a quiet house, but instead I found my mother in her nightdress and wrapper standing outside, looking up at our roof. Her hair hung in one bright braid over her shoulder, and her arms were folded tightly over her chest.

She turned when I approached. Her tone was carefully neutral, so I couldn't tell what she was feeling.

"Where have you been?"

"Down by the river."

"I've been worried."

"You told me to go. I went."

She looked back up at the roof. "I just went down to the cabin to look for Eb. Cora says he's gone over to the Hendersons'. You saw him?"

"Yes, ma'am. He's got a ride into town first thing in the

morning." Lying didn't come easily, and I felt ashamed, although I was still angry with her.

"I shouldn't have hit you."

I shrugged, although she wasn't looking at me. "Why are you standing out here?" I thought about what she'd said. "And why were you looking for Uncle Eb?"

"Robby, I apologized. Now your part is to accept it or not, but not to ignore it."

"Yes, ma'am." I paused. "I guess I don't have the right to question what you do." I couldn't say more. Now there was no point in arguing about Blackjack's presence. I had made an irrevocable decision.

"We'll put it behind us, then. And I went looking for Eb because a coon's stuck in our chimney. It's probably a female looking for a place to have her young. Only she's crashing around and squeaking like she can't get out. Eb plastered some cracks last month, and I think the inside's too smooth and she can't get a grip. I looked up with the lantern, and I could see her thrashing around."

"What about Ralph?"

"It appears Eb brought back more than beef today. Seems he brought some joy juice, too. Ralph's been sampling it. He's no good for something like this."

I heard the front door close, and Blackjack came down the steps. He wore no hat or vest, and looked as if he might have been getting ready for bed. He joined us on the lawn and turned back to look at the house.

"I imagine this has something to do with the noise in your chimney?"

"A raccoon." My mother repeated what she had told me.

I wondered what Uncle Eb would do if he were here. He

wasn't a cruel man, but he was a practical one. I doubted the raccoon would be better for it.

"Poor thing," Blackjack said. "That'll be a horrible way to die."

"Horrible for all of us," Ma agreed.

"And you're certain she's stuck?"

"I'm sure she would have escaped if she could."

"Then there's only one thing to do."

I expected Blackjack to say we needed to shoot her, then net or hook the body tomorrow and heave it up. Instead, he walked around to the side of the house and stared up at the roof. My mother glanced at me, and I shrugged. We followed him.

He was inspecting things from this new angle. "Robby, will you find me a brick or a small rock? And I'll need either a good thick rope or some old sheets I can tie together."

"What are you going to do?" Ma asked.

"Climb up that tree, get on your roof and lower the rope so she'll be able to find her way out. We'll tie something to the end to be sure the rope goes down, and we'll have to anchor it on the other end, maybe by tying it to the tree."

"There's a rope hanging in the barn that should work," I said. Every old sheet we'd ever possessed had gone to making bandages during the war.

"Get it, and we'll tie some knots for Milady Raccoon to use as steps."

"I'll get it," Ma said. "But you're not going up on that roof. Not with your leg the way it is."

"On the contrary. I was the tree-climbing champion in my family, and I'll be extra careful of the leg. But it's my idea, and my job to carry it out."

"I can do it." I stepped forward. "And we have a ladder."

He grinned at me, looking for a moment as he must have as

a boy. "Don't spoil my fun. And it's my pleasure to do something in exchange for all you've done. Now, go see about a weight." He paused. "And, Robby, I'd like my revolver. I don't know what you did with it when I was ill, but it would serve me well on the roof. Just in case."

I could tell my mother was silently debating whether to let me obey, but in the end she left for the barn, and I left to get the revolver from Aunt Cora and to find a suitable weight.

I returned first. Blackjack casually pocketed his gun; then he examined my rock. He agreed it was the perfect size to send down the chimney.

"I'll have to do it carefully or I'll knock Milady unconscious." He looked up at me and lowered his voice. "I know you and your mother are fighting, and I have a good enough idea what it's about."

"It's not your concern."

He lowered his voice further. "I can't stay much longer. Just give me a few more days. It's good for your mother to have a friend. It's good for me, as well."

I couldn't say anything without lying, so I said nothing.

He shook his head. "It's so easy to pass judgment at fourteen. I remember too well."

How I wished it *were* easy, that I was just a boy reacting to the sudden addition of a man in my mother's life. And at heart, was that my real concern? Had I exaggerated everything else as an excuse to remove Blackjack from our lives, the way we were about to remove the poor raccoon? Only most likely with much more cruelty and, ultimately, destruction.

My mother returned before either the conversation or my thoughts could go deeper. "I've brought two. The thicker one might be best inside the chimney, the thinner tied to it. Together they should stretch to the tree."

"I'll do it." I held out my hand for the rope. I didn't like climbing on the roof and knew that climbing around at night would make that worse. But I didn't want Blackjack to be a hero. Not for my mother and not for me.

Blackjack took the rope before Ma could hand it to me. "There's always a danger of hydrophobia with these coons. And I'm not going to let you take the chance of her getting out and attacking before you can get away. Your mother needs you too much." He smiled at Ma. "Don't you?"

Ma just looked worried. "I've no desire to see either of you tumble off the edge. Perhaps we should wait until morning."

"No, coons are active at night. This is the best way." He cupped my shoulder and shook me playfully. "But I'll need you down on the ground to tie the rock to the rope when I lower it, so I don't have to carry it with me."

Despite myself, I was grateful.

"How will you get up the tree without putting weight on your leg?" Ma asked.

"Carefully." He smiled tenderly at her as he tied four knots in the thickest rope. "I'll use my arms. Don't worry. If I can't, I'll come down. I've no desire to reinjure myself."

There was nothing more to be said. No one would sleep with the coon thrashing around in the chimney all night, and Blackjack was determined to do this the kindest way. Grudgingly, I had to admire him both for that and for his willingness to risk his safety.

The rescue only took minutes. He was surprisingly agile for a man with a leg that hadn't completely mended. He went up the tree faster than I'd expected and carefully made his way to the chimney across the wood shingles my father and Uncle Eb had hewed by hand. Below on the ground, Ma and I watched and listened. I'd expected him to be quiet, but he surprised us both. He began to sing, as if to prove that music did soothe the savage beast.

"When the blackbird in the spring, on the willow tree,
Sat and rocked, I heard him sing
Singing Aura Lea."

"I'll never hear that song again without thinking of him," Ma said, as if to herself.

I was afraid I wouldn't, either.

He lowered the rope over the side, and I carefully tied the rock, circling it in several directions so it wouldn't fall out when he hauled it up. He continued to sing until he had lowered the rock slowly into the chimney. As he made his way back to the tree, he stretched the rope behind him; then he secured it to a branch.

In a few minutes he was beside us again. "Now we wait."

I couldn't keep my thoughts to myself. "You could have shot her. What difference does it make to you? You risked your life up there just to save a raccoon."

"Despite what you might think, I have no desire to make any living creature suffer. In war, sometimes we kill to save lives. But that distinction's never an easy one to draw."

"You thought it was perfectly fine that John Wilkes Booth killed the President. Isn't a human life worth more than a raccoon?"

"I think the man who killed Abraham Lincoln believed he could change the world for the better." He sounded sad. "Perhaps his greatest sin was thinking himself capable of such a decision. Because now it appears he was wrong, and more men are dead because of it."

I felt as if an icy wind had blown over me, and I shuddered.

Blackjack looked at me, his gaze steady and unwavering. "It's a subject you keep coming back to."

My mother pointed to the chimney. "I think it worked. Look."

We gazed up at the roof, and as we watched, a small shadow crept along the ridge, then disappeared into the foliage of the tree.

"Let's go inside and see for certain," Blackjack said.

I made an excuse about checking the chicken yard and the barn, since Ralph might not have done it in Uncle Eb's place. "I'll be in after a while."

"Don't dawdle," Ma said. "Tomorrow you and Ralph will have to plow without Eb, and you'll need to be up early."

I watched them go inside together, then I did what I'd said I would. But I moved as if in a dream.

My life had been straightforward until now. There had been few decisions to make. I wore what clothes I had, ate the food in front of me, did the chores that needed to be done. No one had prepared me to decide another's future. I wondered if this was what it meant to be a man.

Blackjack Brewer had a tender heart. He had risked his own safety to save a raccoon. He had never been less than kind to me. And whatever his link to my mother, he had made her smile again. There was as much evidence *for* him as the tattoo, broken leg and knowledge of Shakespeare were evidence against.

I ended a long ramble around the farmyard in the barn. Mice rustled in the hayloft, and Blackjack's mare stood quietly in her stall. I leaned against a post and watched her.

"I thought I might find you here."

I jerked my head and saw Blackjack behind me.

"I'm sorry. I didn't mean to startle you." He came to stand beside me. "I thought you heard my footsteps. The coon's gone. Remember that trick if it ever happens again."

We stood that way without saying anything, until I thought the silence would choke me.

"You seem to be deep in thought," he said at last. "Is there something I can help with, Robby?"

I realized that for years to come, I would ask myself exactly what he meant by this question. Did he know I suspected him of being Lincoln's assassin? Or was he simply asking out of kindness if I had a problem he could help with? I didn't want to know the answer, because my problem had finally been resolved, my decision made once and for all. Blackjack's arrival in the barn was the only piece of help I had needed.

I faced him squarely. "You need to pack and go. Tonight. I know who you are, or at least I think I do. But I don't want to say it out loud, and I don't want you to admit or deny it, in case I'm ever asked. I just want you out of here. Uncle Eb's riding into town tonight, and it's likely he'll be back in the morning with soldiers."

He didn't seem surprised. "You sent him?"

I nodded.

"But now you're telling me to go?" He smiled sadly.

"God speed you on your way."

He watched me for a moment; then he sighed. "This has been hard for you."

That wasn't what I'd expected to hear. "Once she finds you're gone, it's going to be harder for my mother."

"You wouldn't have sent Eb to report me unless you meant me to be caught. What changed your mind?"

"Something you said tonight."

"And what was that?"

"That Booth's greatest sin wasn't the assassination, it was thinking he was capable of deciding who should die. I'm not ready to commit the same sin. Whoever you really are, *whatever* you've done, you won't get a fair hearing. Not for a long time, and surely not tomorrow, when they come for you."

"I see."

"Then you'll leave?"

"Immediately."

There was nothing left to say. We walked back up to the house in silence, and I waited on the porch while he got his things. He came back so soon that I knew he hadn't awakened my mother to say goodbye. I was grateful for that.

I had no reason to accompany him back to the barn. He would saddle Princess and leave, and my decisions would be over. Tomorrow, if soldiers came looking for him, I could tell them the truth. A man with some astonishing similarities to the one who had shot Lincoln had recovered here, but when we woke up in the morning, he was gone.

I would tell the soldiers what I knew, which was no more than Uncle Eb would probably already have recounted. I would guess out loud that the man realized he had aroused suspicion. With only my observations and no Blackjack to question, I doubted they would pursue him. Everyone believed the real John Wilkes Booth had died in Port Royal. Why would they waste time looking for a man who was already in the ground?

I walked down the steps with him. He stuck out his hand, and we shook. Then he drew out something from his sack and handed it to me. "I'd like you to give this to your mother."

I took it before I looked down. In the moonlight, I could see I was holding a small leatherbound book.

"Shakespeare's sonnets," he said. "She has the plays, but not the poems. I've marked one for her. Will you see that she gets it?"

"I went through your things when you came. I never saw this."

"The sack has a false bottom. Something for you to remember the next time you suspect you're harboring a fugitive."

I didn't laugh, and neither did he. There was nothing more to say.

He gave a short salute, which was as much a wave goodbye as anything. Then he turned, and in a minute he had disappeared into the darkness. I waited there until I heard the sound of hoofbeats. I saw a shadow along the side of the barn; then the hoofbeats grew fainter until they could no longer be heard.

I stuck the book in the waistband of my trousers under my shirt and turned to go inside. I hadn't heard the door open, and I hadn't heard my mother come out. But when I looked up, she was standing on the porch.

"He's gone, then." She came down the steps and stood beside me, gazing off into the distance where Blackjack had ridden away.

"I'm sorry."

She began to cry.

I didn't know what to do. Ma's tears were as unexpected and alien as the decision I'd been forced to make. I couldn't remember seeing my mother cry. She hadn't even cried when the word had come about my father, although she had held me as I'd cried hard enough for both of us.

My sadness turned to something else. She was crying for a man she'd hardly known, young, handsome and charming, yes, but in the end, still a stranger. They had never been wed. He had not adored her, provided for her, given his life for a cause because he believed winning would keep her safe. Blackjack had ridden into our lives, put us in danger, taken what he could, then simply ridden away.

Despite myself, anger filled me, as it had earlier that afternoon. "You never cried for my father!"

She reached for me, pulling me close. Her arms went around me.

"It's like that morning. Just like it. Just…the same. Oh, I remember everything about the morning your father rode away, Robby. I don't…want to remember."

I couldn't pull away. I loved her too much to hurt her more, but I didn't understand. "It's *not* the same," I said. "Blackjack isn't your husband. How can you cry for him when you never cried for Pa?"

"That morning…that awful morning when he rode away…I knew things would never be right again. I knew…I…we would lose your pa. He was such a good man. I knew he would…sacrifice himself for others…if he was called to. And I'd never been able to tell him how much I loved him—I'd never even known how much until that moment. I stood right here, just like tonight…and I heard the hoofbeats of his horse fading into…the distance."

My arms tightened around her then, and I was crying, too. "He knew," I told her, and for the first time in my life, I realized it was true. "Oh, Ma, that's why he chose that quilt, don't you see? *X*s. Like kisses. He knew…you loved him. He took your love with him."

Maybe I was a man then, and maybe men aren't supposed to cry, but although the tears scalded my cheeks, they cleansed us both.

Much later, I made sure Ma got to her room. She took my father's photograph when we passed through the hall and set it beside her bed. I went to my own room to undress, and it was only then that I realized I still had the book Blackjack had asked me to give my mother.

I wondered what she had felt for our temporary boarder. Nothing like what she'd felt for my father. Of this I was now sure. But had she loved Blackjack, too? I didn't think so. I thought he had been a diversion, something to think about instead of a difficult life. He had brought light into her darkness, enough that the heart she had so carefully sealed had been opened, and she had been forced to feel again and acknowledge what she had lost.

I stared at the book. I could see that a page was marked with a leather lace, but I didn't open it. I didn't want to see what Blackjack's final message to Ma might be. Even more, I didn't want to see if a certain name graced the inside of the cover.

Some questions are better left unanswered.

I placed the book under my pillow. Early in the morning, I would hide it where no one would ever find it. I knew exactly where and how. If someday I changed my mind, it would still be waiting, intact. But I doubted I would ever want to look at it again.

I got into bed and closed my eyes, but the image I saw was a man riding away. Whether the sun shone too brightly or night was dark around him, I couldn't tell. I heard hoofbeats moving farther and farther into the distance.

I fell asleep to the sound and knew it would haunt me for the rest of my days.

Chapter 31

The rain began during the night, for a short interval just a gentle shower, then a steadily accelerating, crescendoing downpour that shrouded landmarks and slid in silver sheets off the terrace. Most rain was a natural lullaby, but this was accompanied by wind that rattled shutters and lashed against windows. When a strong gust sent something crashing into a wall of the carriage house, Gayle knew she wasn't going to sleep another minute.

Belting a robe around her waist, she padded into the family room to turn on the outside light. A heavy Adirondack chair that had been sitting at the edge of the carriage-house deck was now on its side, just a few feet from the French doors.

"Wow." She flipped off the light, afraid it might wake Noah, but she was too late. He came down the stairs, clad in flannel boxers and a Vampire Hunter T-shirt.

"What was that?" He said it so quickly it sounded like one word. "Even Buddy's cowering and cussing."

"A chair. This must be the remnant of that tropical storm that hit Florida. I knew we were going to get some rain, but it must have come right up the valley between the mountains. It's hitting us just right."

"We could turn on the TV—"

The lights went out.

"Or not," Noah finished.

Gayle's eyes adjusted slowly, but moments later she could see the dimmest outlines. "I'm worried about the campers. Do you think we ought to drive over and get our crew?"

"Yeah, we could do that—if you don't mind them not speaking to you for the next hundred years."

"I've seen those tents. They look like something from a Civil War reenactment. They aren't exactly state of the art."

"Mom, they're camping next door. Mr. Allen will make everybody get inside his house if there are problems."

He was probably right. Dillon would be the most embarrassed if she showed up to fetch him, but neither Jared nor Leon would be pleased with her. And besides, the older boys wouldn't leave unless all their campers left first.

Noah whistled. "Wow, it's really dark in here. It's, like, black."

"I've got flashlights in the kitchen drawer."

"I know where you keep the candles."

"Me, flashlights. You, candles."

A few minutes later the room was softly lit. Noah didn't show any signs of going back to bed as Gayle took one of the flashlights.

"I'm going to throw on some clothes and go over to the inn just to make sure everybody's okay."

There were emergency lights in every room of the inn, but some guests might still be edgy. Gayle suspected that Miss Onion Allergy, who prided herself on quality control, would be up and complaining. There was a backup generator, but she was in no hurry to turn it on. The storm was loud, but the generator was louder.

Noah didn't stir. "You're going to get soaked."

"You're such a nice son. You could do this for me."

"I sure could." He didn't offer.

Gayle was already on her way to her room anyway. Both of them knew who really had to go and deal with consequences.

Minutes later she was dressed, and her jeans and shirt were covered by a bright yellow slicker and hat that the boys had given her for Christmas. She owned matching boots, too, but she was depending on slip-on sneakers to do the job tonight.

In the family room, a bleary-eyed Noah was still staring at candlelight flickering on the wall. "Maybe you ought to tie a rope around your waist and anchor yourself to a tree."

"Feel free to go back to bed, dear."

"You might need me."

"I can probably think of ideas like tying myself to a tree without you."

"I'm a creative thinker. What can I say?"

"Not another thing."

She let herself out the door closest to the inn and waited for a lull. When it seemed like Mom Nature might be taking a breath, she streaked across the yard, sneakers squishing in the soggy grass. Lightning wasn't a problem yet, and she was grateful.

Entering through the kitchen, she peeled off slicker and hat, and kicked off sneakers. There were two emergency lights, both giving off just enough of a glow that she could move around islands and counters without stumbling. She shoved the swinging doors and went through to the reception area at the same moment the telephone rang.

A tall figure materialized on the stairs, and her hand flew up to cover her mouth.

"Gayle?"

Her heart was beating double-time. "Eric! You scared me witless."

"I'm sorry. A couple of guests were up. I was making sure people were okay."

She grabbed the receiver before the answering machine could pick up, then remembered the answering machine depended on electricity. She was glad that this phone was more or less a dinosaur.

"Daughter of the Stars," she said.

"Gayle? Travis. Are you all right over there?"

"Fine. What about you?"

"I've got a dark house full of soaking wet campers."

"You need us?" The *us* came out without thinking, but of course she knew Eric would help.

"The kids are calling their parents. If we can't reach their folks, I'll keep them here."

"We can take some if you need us to."

"Let's see how it goes. But the Johnson kids live across the river, and their dad's car is in the shop. Before they get rivered in, I need someone to drive them home. You've got the truck, and you know the roads."

"I'll be there in a few minutes. Then I'll come back and get Dillon and anyone else willing to come here. Tell Caleb not to wake the Claibornes. He can come home with us."

"If he hasn't talked to them already. A lot of the parents have been calling."

She hung up and told Eric what was happening. "One of us had better stay here. I need to go, since I know the roads better. The Johnson kids live several miles down."

"I hate to see you go out in this."

"I'm just glad you can stay here in case something comes up."

"It makes sense to have a team in place, doesn't it?"

She didn't know what to say to that. It felt like such a luxury to have a man helping her. She couldn't deny it.

"You know what else?" he asked.

"No."

"Happy birthday."

She closed her eyes. "I hope this isn't an omen."

"Just because you've started your forties with an emergency doesn't mean it's a trend."

"I'll be back with the kids."

He smiled. "I'll be waiting with lots of towels."

By dawn the rain had stopped, but Gayle didn't bother to greet what passed for sun. She had spent too much of the night ferrying other people's teenagers home and packing up her own water-logged brood. The low water bridge had remained above the water line when she'd crossed back to Travis's house, and now she thought that if the rain was finished, nobody would be cut off. Crisis averted.

She was just drifting back to sleep for a few precious minutes when her bedroom door flew open. She tried to put the pillow over her head, but Noah tugged it away. She lay in place and listened to a chorus of "Happy Birthday" and tried not to cry like a sentimental sop.

"Not everybody gets raspberry coffeecake with candles," Jared said. "Sit up, Mom."

She groaned, but managed somehow. Through bleary eyes she saw that the room was filled with the male of the species. Eric, her sons, Caleb and Leon. "Why aren't there any girls in this family?" she asked.

"If my understanding of genetics is correct, it was my fault." Eric put a tray with an insulated carafe of coffee beside her. "You are not to get up this morning. Stay in bed. The boys have breakfast under control, and Paula's here to make sure everything else goes okay."

She almost couldn't remember a morning off. Not a whole morning off with nothing to do. "Thank you. All of you."

"Here's the paper." Jared held out the *New York Times*. "Last Wednesday's, but who cares?"

"Wait a minute, is the electricity on?"

"Came on about five," Eric said. "All is well, and you can relax."

"We've got presents and stuff, but we'll give them to you—" Dillon glanced at his father "—later."

Noah set a tray with eggs and bacon beside her. Leon added a bowl of fresh fruit. They left enough coffeecake to vault her up to the next dress size. Then, pushing and shoving and oozing testosterone, they left her alone to enjoy herself.

All she could think about was that someday soon, all these guys wouldn't be in residence anymore. That this moment had passed too quickly. That four decades had passed too quickly.

Then, resolutely, she put that revelation aside, flipped on the CD player beside her bed, and determined to enjoy her leisurely and well-deserved treat.

An hour later, Jared came in for the tray. He looked tired and preoccupied, but he smiled. "How was it?"

"Fabulous. Whose idea was this?"

"We thought of it together."

She patted the bed, and although he seemed reluctant, he sat.

"This was exactly the kind of celebration I like," she said. "I'm so glad you did this and not something big and splashy."

He bent over to tie his shoe, which seemed to take a while.

"Well, you said you wanted a simple family party," he said while he was still upside down.

"You've had a hard week, haven't you?" she asked.

"You're going to pry, aren't you?"

"I'm trying hard not to, but it's my birthday, so humor me."

"That's going to go on all day, isn't it?"

"As long as I can make it work."

He sat up. "Brandy and I broke up."

She felt an absurd stab of relief. Jared's life was back on track. He was going to MIT as planned, and now all was explained. His long face. The obvious tension. The way he had avoided talking to his mother.

"I can just imagine how hard that was and is." She touched his hand. "You're okay?"

"Uh-huh. With me going away and all, it didn't make sense to stay a couple."

"Sometimes things make sense but they still hurt."

"Like when you and Dad got divorced?"

"Like that."

"Since he's been back, I understand better."

She was surprised. "I'm not sure what you mean."

"Dad's great, don't get me wrong. But how did you ever get together? Could the two of you *be* more different?"

She didn't know what to say. Vindication wasn't exactly the result she'd expected when she'd invited Eric to stay for the summer.

She turned the conversation back to her son. "You and Brandy were pretty different. That should help you understand. We're not always attracted to people just like us."

"I don't want to be like Dad, not in every way, anyhow. But maybe I am. I'm not a homebody like you are. I want to see the world."

"Of course you do. You're supposed to. Has that been worrying

450

you? That you were abandoning Brandy? You're eighteen, Jared. Both of you need to see the world and figure out who you are. Then you can make better decisions about your future."

"Well, that's what I'm doing. I'm…" He looked away. "I'm going to do everything I can to figure out who I am."

She patted his leg. "Good for you, and I know Brandy's going to be okay. By the time her senior year is over, she'll be a lot more grown up, and by then she'll probably be ready to fly the nest, too."

He got to his feet. "Dad said to tell you he's over at the dig with Mr. Allen. They're checking to see what's up after last night. And I think they're working on one of the units, trying to see what's there before they cover it up."

Gayle was relieved. Eric would probably spend a good part of the day at the dig. She wouldn't have to talk to him about their future or even try to figure out what he was thinking today. And if she was really lucky, she could put her own thoughts and feelings on hold as a birthday present to herself.

"I bet I'm going to get a good dinner out of this birthday, aren't I?" she asked.

"You'll think a professional cooked it." He leaned over and kissed her head. "I love you, Mom. Don't ever forget it."

Eric got out of his car to greet Travis, who had pulled up right after him. The ground where they parked was wet, but, at least for now, the sun was out.

"For a man who probably didn't get a wink of sleep last night, you look almost rested," Eric said.

"I'm basking in the knowledge that camp is over, no matter how it happened to end."

"You did a great job. I'm glad Dillon could take advantage."

Travis opened the rear door of his Highlander and started

setting tools on the ground. "I like your boys. They're smart, well mannered and funny. I'm always glad to have them around."

"They like you, too. I get the impression you've been a stand-in father when I've been out of the picture."

"You're one of a kind in their lives."

"I guess I'm trying to say that I appreciate you being there when I haven't been. For the boys…and for Gayle."

Travis slammed the door; then he leaned against it, his arms folded. "It's no hardship being there for Gayle, Eric."

"I didn't think it was."

"I don't have to tell you how special she is."

"I'm the guy who divorced her, remember?"

"Something she's never forgotten."

"This was meant to be a simple conversation." But even as he said it, Eric realized he'd probably been pushing for more.

"We'll keep it simple, then. For years Gayle's made the best of a difficult situation. I don't know another woman who could have raised three sons alone and run an inn while she was doing it. Somehow she managed to stay active in the community, the schools and her church, and make friends while she was at it. And all the while, she put her personal life on hold."

"You're saying that last part is my fault?"

"No. I'm saying that's what she did."

"But I hear an indictment."

"Then maybe you're hearing it through a load of your own guilt, I don't know. But it's not my role to point a finger or even to figure out where to point it. What I am getting to is this. She was hurt. Badly, although she'd never admit it out loud. She could be hurt again."

"Are you in love with her?"

"Does it matter?"

Eric didn't know.

Travis pushed away from the car and picked up a bucket. "She didn't know what she was getting into when she invited you for the summer. But maybe it's for the best. Because if you walk away again, this time it really will be over."

Eric heard himself protesting, even though, considering the last real conversation he'd had with Gayle, it was stupid. "Look, we've been divorced for twelve years. That's about as over as it gets."

"Tell me how long you had to think about coming back when Gayle invited you. Did you sweat over it? Or did you feel like you were coming home?"

"You ask a lot of questions."

"You have no idea how many more I'd like to ask."

Eric lifted the second bucket and tucked a shovel under his arm. Travis hadn't confirmed that he was in love with Gayle. It was possible his feelings were those of one loyal friend for another. But Eric still felt he ought to be straight about one thing.

"I don't know what's going to happen next. Maybe I need to warn you."

"You don't. For the record, I think this whole thing may have been inevitable."

They walked to the excavation unit in silence. Eric knew the river had risen higher from the rain, but he was surprised to see that water had sloshed into the site and crept toward the area where they had been working.

Eric glanced at his watch. It wasn't even ten. "I have to be at the church by four to help oversee the party preparations. You'll be there tonight?"

"Carin and I are coming together." Travis was squatting on the ground to pull off the plastic sheeting that protected the unit, but he glanced up. "Does Gayle suspect?"

"I don't think so."

For a moment Travis looked as if he pitied Eric. "You've worked a miracle, putting it together so fast. She'll see that."

For the first time since he'd decided to make a real celebration out of Gayle's fortieth, Eric had a moment of doubt. "I know she says she doesn't like big parties, but she'll like this one. It's all about her."

Travis peeled off the plastic and threw it to one side. "Let's see what we can uncover. Then you can help me figure out what we should do. There's more rain on the way, maybe even by late afternoon."

"Do you think it's going to flood?"

"The meteorologists tell us we're going to get rain about ten times more often than we actually get it. They're a local joke. So my fingers are crossed."

Eric thought of Weather Woman and Ariel. He wondered if he would ever see a weather segment again without thinking of both of them.

Chapter 32

Beginning at noon, Gayle was banned from the kitchen. She saw the boys coming and going, but whatever they were preparing for her birthday dinner wasn't simmering on the stove or the aroma would have filled the inn. There'd been plenty of banging around, though.

On a day like this one, she was particularly glad she had taught them to cook. She spent so much time in the kitchen, it had been natural for them to keep her company there and eventually to slide into assisting. Jared made a delicious spaghetti sauce, and Noah had a special recipe for stuffing a roasting hen with lemons and garlic cloves that was a family favorite. Dillon was their pastry chef, and she suspected today he would be in charge of her cake.

In the late afternoon she put on her favorite black lace skirt and a black scoop neck T-shirt to show their meal the respect it deserved. She slipped on gold sandals and a gold chain with charms of each of her son's astrological signs, and rummaged for a gold barrette to clip in her hair.

At the bottom of her jewelry box she saw a familiar velveteen pouch. She stopped rummaging, and against her will she lifted the pouch, shook it open and gazed at the objects in her palm.

The two gold rings hadn't graced her left hand for a dozen years. She and Eric had been young and anything but wealthy. But before proposing, he had scraped together the money to buy a lovely round diamond. A few months later, when they'd repeated their wedding vows, he had added a matching gold wedding band encrusted with six tiny stones.

When the marriage ended, Gayle hadn't thrown the rings in the river, as a local friend had on the day her divorce was final. She hadn't sold or pawned them, or returned the rings to Eric. She had removed them and stored the velveteen pouch at the bottom of her jewelry box.

Now she wondered why. Even if she'd had a daughter, the rings were not heirlooms, and her sons would never want to start their own marriages with mementos of their parents' failure. She supposed she simply hadn't known what to do. She hadn't felt vindictive, just terribly sad. And the thought of the rings ending up in a pawn shop? She hadn't been able to stomach it.

Now she wondered if she had simply waited all these years to restore the rings to their rightful place. Somewhere deep inside, had she hoped the day would come when Eric recovered from his addiction to excitement and came home at last?

She slipped the rings into the pouch and tucked them back where they had waited all these years. She didn't know what the future held, but if she and Eric worked out their relationship, she would wear these rings again and be glad she had kept them. If they didn't, she would give them back. Eric could decide what to do with them, but she no longer wanted reminders in her jewelry box.

In the bathroom, she put on a little makeup and combed her hair. Gazing in the mirror, she decided she didn't look a day over thirty-nine. She was more worried about where all the years had gone than the ones that were coming. But this birthday would soon be over, and with it, all the anxiety of entry into a new decade. She would slip back into her routine....

Or begin a new one with Eric.

Just as her stomach knotted, someone knocked. Glad for the interruption, she crossed the room and flung open the door. She hadn't seen Eric since breakfast. Now she saw that in honor of the occasion he had dressed up, too. He wore a navy shirt unbuttoned at the throat and a tan blazer, and when he saw her, he gave a wolf whistle.

"You look great," he said.

"It still happens occasionally."

"A lot more than that."

It was a good day for compliments. She smiled to let him know this one had been appreciated.

"The boys will be happy you got dressed up for their dinner."

"How are things coming?"

"Terrific, only they want to eat here at the house. They're afraid guests will wander through if we eat in the dining room at the inn."

"They're right about that."

"So they asked me to take you for a drive while they set up. They want you out of here."

Knowing her sons, she suspected the setup would be done at the speed of light. "We can't just go for a walk?"

"Well, we can if you want, but you haven't been out in my Mustang. We can put the top down, unless it starts to rain. It's da bomb."

"What?"

"Da bomb. That's what one of the campers told me. Apparently that's good."

"I suddenly feel even older."

"I had the same reaction."

They headed outside, and Eric opened her car door, then put the top down. There was still no sign of the boys, but she supposed they were in the inn's kitchen, using every pot and pan she owned. She wished she could watch.

The sky was the color of pewter, but no rain had fallen since morning. For now, they could enjoy the convertible.

"How did the dig go?" she asked once they were on the road.

"Exciting. At least an acre of mud, the river rushing by carrying branches and debris, kids popping over to show their parents where they'd been digging."

"The campers were supposed to provide tours this morning when their parents picked them up. Too bad the rain changed that."

"Those who still wanted one got one. But the most exciting part was what Travis and I may have found."

"More artifacts?"

"It looks like the Duncans, one or both of them, used the foundation of the old cabin as a place to hide things. They entered from what was then the root cellar, then either removed loose stones and hid whatever they needed to behind them, or just edged things into openings and covered the evidence with smaller stones. You know Travis found a fork?"

"Has he been able to figure out how old it is?"

"I don't think he's had time. But today we found a serving spoon."

"This sounds like a treasure hunt." Silverware was a significant find, but hardly worth the sparkle in Eric's eyes. The fact that the spoon had probably been hidden during the Civil War made it more interesting, but she suspected there was more to his excitement.

"It's what we haven't found, or at least haven't unearthed, that's particularly interesting."

She noticed that they were driving in the direction of the Shenandoah Community Church. "Eric, you're headed toward our church. Would you like to drive by and at least see it from the road before we turn around?"

"Good idea. Where do I go?"

She gave directions, then settled back to hear the rest of the story. "So what haven't you found but want to?"

"We got to the edge of the unit, and toward the bottom of the area we'd excavated, it looked like some of the stones were out of line. That's not really that odd, since the foundation is centuries old. But Travis shined a light into the corner, and we saw metal. There's something behind those stones, and he thinks, from our limited view, that it resembles a lockbox of some sort."

"Wow, I'm surprised you could tear yourselves away."

"It was already late by then. We had to leave, but there's always tomorrow."

"So you're going to continue? You're not going to leave it for next summer's camp?"

"Travis says that unit is so close to the river that if it floods, we could lose whatever's there. He says under the circumstances, and with evidence from family stories, we probably ought to at least see what we can find."

"You don't really think this is something Robby put there, do you?"

"What are the chances? We'll probably find Confederate money or moldy family photographs. Whatever Miranda's family noted was missing before she died. And the Blackjack story is a huge leap, anyway. Who knows if any of it is true?"

"I don't know how much Carin made up, but I'm glad I heard

it. What if some—or even most—of it really happened? Can you imagine what it was like to live here during the war? The incredible waste? The horror of having troops from both sides moving through, helping themselves to everything they could, then Sheridan burning crops and barns and mills? I don't think we can understand how that feels."

"I can understand."

She was instantly contrite. "You've seen too many wars up close, haven't you? The story probably sounded too familiar."

"It's one thing to report a war, then come home and leave the worst of it behind. But a lot of families are having Iraq and Afghanistan brought right to their doorstep. They're burying the people they love and grieving the way Miranda did."

"I feel sorry for Cray's mother now that he's going to be a marine. If we lose a son or a daughter, politics fade into the background. Our children still aren't coming home."

"We've lost a lot of journalists in the Mideast. More than people realize. But we choose to go and do our jobs, and we can leave when we know we're in over our heads."

"You almost didn't get out."

"I'd still rather do what I was doing than man traffic stops or search buildings."

She wondered how they had gotten on this subject, and she wanted to leave it behind. They were coming up on the church now, and she pointed it out. It looked like many throughout the South, white with a tin roof and graceful steeple. "That's Shenandoah Community over there."

"It looks busy tonight."

She was surprised, because she kept up with activities and didn't remember anything going on. But he was right; there were a number of cars parked outside.

"It must be a rental group. There's nothing on the church calendar."

Eric put on his turn signal and made a right into the lot. He parked at the end of a row and removed his keys from the ignition. "Can we take a tour anyway?"

She put her hand on his arm. "I just wanted to drive by so you could see it. The boys must be all set up by now. I think we ought to go home and leave these folks in peace."

"Really? I'd like to see the chapel."

"Then come to church with us sometime."

"This is more my speed. In and out?"

"I don't know…. That's Sam's SUV in the minister's parking spot. I don't want to intrude."

"You won't be."

As everything fell into place, she suddenly understood. The reason no tantalizing smells had wafted from the kitchen. The trumped-up excuse to get her out of the house. The reason that Eric, who'd had no real need to, had dressed up.

"You didn't."

He turned on the Fortman grin. "Nobody should celebrate a fortieth birthday alone, Gayle. Your friends are here to celebrate with you."

She closed her eyes. For a moment she imagined wrenching the keys from his hand and driving home to barricade herself in the carriage house. The joy she'd felt at a simple family party was gone. She felt like a captive running the gauntlet.

"Gayle?"

She opened her eyes and managed a smile. "Well, it's really a surprise, that's for sure. I don't know how you pulled it all together."

"I had a ball. And it was meant to be. Everything just fell into place." He put the top up and opened his door. She had only seconds to lecture herself about how hard he had worked and how happy this had made him.

She squared her shoulders. She would go inside, make sure everyone knew how glad she was to see them, thank them for turning out in her honor, pretend she enjoyed being the center of attention, then go home when it was over, exhausted and drained and sorrier than ever that she'd been forced to turn forty today. But somehow she would pull it off.

He helped her out of the car; then, impulsively, he pulled her close and kissed her. "Happy birthday, Gayle. You're still a beautiful, desirable woman. I'm glad you're in my life."

Although their bodies were nestled together and his arms held her tight, she felt a chasm between them. When the kiss ended, she forced another smile, but at the moment, she couldn't say she was glad Eric was in hers. This evening, Afghanistan was not far enough away for her ex-husband. Even Mars wouldn't suffice.

Then, as if it were a new thought and not one she'd toyed with many years ago, she wondered if the only reason their marriage had lasted as long as it had was that Eric had been away so much. Just how long would it have lasted if they hadn't had constant vacations from each other?

"Are you ready to go inside?" he asked.

She wanted to stay in the parking lot and finish the conversation with herself. She wanted to flee. But with a smile locked in place, she nodded and went to greet her friends.

Eric was delighted at the turnout. In fact, he was delighted with everything about the party. The rain had held off until almost everyone arrived. The food—New Orleans–style jambalaya served with a variety of salads—was surprisingly authentic. The bluegrass band was better than he'd expected. The birthday cake was sinfully rich, and the local vintners had done themselves proud.

Virginia might not be the Napa Valley, but its white wines were good. He wondered if he ought to look into land near the inn, where he could put in a few acres of grapes. Even as he considered it, the thought of doing the same things, pruning, fertilizing, harvesting, for seasons on end, depressed him.

"Eric?"

He looked up from his second helping of jambalaya to see a young woman with curly brown hair who looked vaguely familiar. As she held out her hand, he struggled to place her.

"Kendra Taylor," she said. "I'm a reporter at the *Post*. I met you a few years ago."

The name clicked into place. They had been introduced at a conference or meeting of some kind, although he didn't think much of a conversation had taken place.

"Kendra." He shook hands and admired her. She was thin, and despite an array of freckles, she had the healthy glow and elegantly insouciant posture of a Ralph Lauren model. The dress, however, was definitely not off the rack. The paisley shawl draped around her shoulders was the best pashmina.

"I've thought about calling you," she said, "but I knew you'd probably want time just to put things together on your own. We have something in common."

"Besides the news?"

"I nearly died last year during a carjacking, and it took months to put myself and my personal life back together. Gayle knows the story."

Now he thought he remembered Gayle mentioning Kendra. And somewhere in his mind he could picture her byline. "You live here? You cover the local news for the *Post?*"

"No, I live in Northern Virginia, but my husband and I own land nearby on a different part of the North Fork. And I'm an investigative reporter. Isaac runs a grassroots environmental organization that focuses on the health of our rivers."

"How do you know Gayle?"

"Our land used to have an old cabin on it, but it burned down last summer. After the carjacking, I lived there by myself and attended this church. Now Isaac and I come back and stay at Daughter of the Stars whenever we can get away. We're about to build a new house where the cabin stood, so we'll be in and out a lot."

Eric thought this was all very interesting, but he also thought there was more to Kendra's seeking him out than a shared interest in journalism and Shenandoah County.

She read his expression correctly. "I went through a really tough time after the shooting. I know what it's like to be certain you're going to die and end up living instead. And I know how long it takes to recover."

Now he understood. "PTSD."

"Yeah. Bad dreams, flashbacks, irrational fears, the whole nine yards. It's possible I'll have some of the symptoms forever."

"It was a little rough, but I'm doing fine."

She didn't smile. "I doubt it."

He didn't know what to say to that. Because although the nightmares had diminished in intensity, he still had them. And he still felt as if his heart would stop beating when he even thought about climbing up a mountain trail or a ladder.

And he still couldn't face thoughts of going back to the work he had loved so much.

"Sometimes it's good to talk to somebody who really understands," she said.

He wasn't going to admit his fears to a stranger, but he was curious. "What was the hardest part for you?"

"That's really a tough question, because so much was hard." She paused to consider. "The future," she said at last.

"What part of it?"

"Facing it. Believing I'd ever be able to move smoothly from one day to the next again. And I guess, most of all, making good decisions. Because once you're sure your life's about to end, it's hard to think about the future. For a long time I felt like it was silly to plan for something that could end so abruptly. When problems in my marriage seemed overwhelming, I simply abandoned ship and came out here. Because why use energy to confront problems when everything could end like that?" She snapped her fingers.

He winced.

She looked sympathetic and lowered her voice. "There's good news. I came out here and I started feeling better. You'll probably meet Isaac tonight. Things are good for us again. That's the upside of what we've been through. I stopped hiding, because I didn't see anything to protect. And for whatever reason, that can be a real plus."

He tried to put all this together. Just from looking at her, he didn't think this was a woman who talked easily about her insights or her life. He suspected coming up to a near stranger and revealing so much had been difficult. But they were talking not as stranger to stranger but survivor to survivor. And he thought she felt duty-bound by that odd common bond to offer what she could.

"Making decisions about the future is the hardest." The words came out of his throat, stronger than his attempt to silence them.

She didn't look surprised. "Yes, of course. So a piece of advice? Don't. Not until you're ready."

"Can you say that? After you were shot, you left your husband and came out here. That was a pretty big decision, wasn't it?"

"But I put everything else on hold. You and I have the best excuse in the world for that. Most people will understand."

"My bureau chief isn't what I'd call patient. I had to tell him to take a flying…leap."

"He's heard it before. He'll be back. Nobody will want to lose you."

His next words were out before he could think them through. "I don't know why. It's my fault a man died."

She clearly knew every detail, just like everyone in the business would.

"Eric, Howard Short was a big guy. I met him. He was aggressive and driven, and I'd be surprised if he let you drag him along against his better judgment."

"You knew Howard?"

"We sat next to each other one night at an awards ceremony."

He imagined that scene. "He propositioned you, didn't he?"

She smiled a little. "He propositioned me."

"That was definitely Howard."

"I liked him anyway. He was a man who did what he wanted. If you could ask him now if risking his life was worth it? What do you think he'd say?"

"I don't know."

"Okay, then what would *you* say?"

That it *had* been. Every story, every hardship, leaving his family. Even a night on a ledge when he had faced imminent death. The answer was so clear it was almost as if he heard a voice speaking in his head.

Kendra was nodding, as if she knew his thoughts. "Some jobs own you, Eric. Yours is one of them."

He didn't like that revelation. "Does yours own you?"

"Probably not as much as it should."

"Be glad."

"We are who we are." She rested her hand on his arm. "Take it easy on yourself. And call me if you ever need to talk to somebody who stood where you're standing. Okay?"

"I appreciate the offer."

He watched her walk back through the crowd. A path cleared, and he saw Gayle surrounded by her friends and family. For a moment he felt as if they were all a million miles away. The question was whether he wanted to keep them there.

And the answer was that he really didn't know.

"A birthday's just a birthday," Gayle's mother said. "I've given up celebrating mine. I'm not sure what all this fuss is about."

"That's something we agree on." Gayle sipped her second glass of chardonnay. "But it was thoughtful of you and Dad to fly in for the party."

"Well, Eric does know how to ask nicely." Phyllis Metzger looked fondly across the room at her ex-son-in-law. "And the fact that he did this for you says a lot, I think."

"Don't read anything into it. He's doing everything he can to thank me for having him with us this summer."

"You're determined to make less of it than it is, aren't you?"

Gayle was too tired to be tactful. "I'm determined to say what I think, for a change. There have to be compensations for all those years behind me."

"Then what do you think of Eric?"

"That he doesn't have a clue who I am."

"Well, with that attitude—"

Gayle put her hand on her mother's arm. "Please don't go

there. Okay? This is *my* life, and I have feelings about it. If you haven't talked me out of them by now, it's probably never going to happen."

Phyllis's eyes widened. Gayle saw confusion, then just a touch of hurt. But she didn't apologize. It was time, past time, to level with her mother.

Instead, she squeezed her arm. "I love you, and I have only the greatest respect for you. But in this way, we're different. I hope you'll let us be."

"How long have you felt like this?"

"Longer than I should have without saying something."

Phyllis's eyes softened. "I've just tried to protect you."

Gayle supposed in a way it was true, but bulletproofing a heart had too many side effects. She was tired of them.

"I'm going to have to find my own ways to do that," she said. "After all, you taught me to be independent."

"You were always independent, Gayle. But too starry-eyed. I just worried you'd be hurt."

Gayle leaned over and kissed her cheek. "Thank you for that."

The band had been playing something lyrical and relatively soft. That ended, and suddenly they swung into "Happy Birthday."

The crowd began to sing, and Gayle glued on a smile and nodded her thanks.

When the band fell silent, somebody rapped a spoon against a glass to quiet the crowd. Gayle steeled herself for what was about to happen.

Sam stepped up in front of the band. Elisa, who was standing beside him, caught Gayle's eye and winked.

"Thank you for coming tonight," Sam said when it was quiet enough. "Eric Fortman and the Fortman boys asked me to say a few words. Now, I know Gayle rather well. She more or less runs the church, and we all do what she says. But not because we're afraid of her. Because she has the best judgment and ability to help us see reason of any deacon I've come across in my ministry."

Everybody laughed. Gayle wanted to sink through the floor.

"So I know Gayle, and I can tell you without having asked her that she finds being in the limelight excruciating. Gayle's one of those people who works behind the scenes and prefers to stay there. So let's have one round of applause for the woman with the birthday, then we'll take her off the hot seat and let her enjoy the party. Gayle, we're all so glad we know you."

Everyone began to clap. Gayle gave an embarrassed wave, then ducked her head. But as she did, she said a prayer of thanksgiving that Sam understood her so well, and that he, not Eric or anyone else, had been elected to pay tribute.

The band struck up a bluegrass selection Gayle had heard before, and despite herself, she had to smile.

"I Just Don't Look Good Naked Anymore." She hoped the song was a little premature.

"Darling, I don't want to know if that song's true or not, but I'm betting you're not quite old enough to worry," Phyllis said. "At least you still look great with your clothes on."

They were laughing when Travis and Carin approached. Until now, Gayle had only seen them from a distance, but they looked contented in each other's company. She shook Carin's hand and kissed Travis's cheek. Then she introduced Carin to her mother.

Phyllis made polite conversation with Carin, and while she did, Travis pulled Gayle to one side and gave her a colorful envelope. "Happy birthday."

"Shall I open it now?"

"Go ahead."

She took out the card, which was gently humorous, and smiled at the message. Then she saw what was folded inside.

"Travis. What a perfect gift." She kissed his cheek again. "But I wasn't expecting anything. You know that."

"Then think of these as a thank-you for all your hard work this summer."

The gift was five tickets to a concert at the summer music festival in nearby Orkney Springs. Travis knew how much she loved music. The gift was perfect. They could take a picnic, make a night of it.

"You'll come?" she asked.

"No, it's for you and your family."

He had automatically included Eric. She laughed a little. "Oh no, please come. Eric is bored silly at concerts. We'll both be grateful."

Phyllis interrupted. "Gayle, did you know this young lady is newly engaged?"

For a moment Gayle couldn't think what to say. She was surprised Travis hadn't told her his plans, but then, why should he? He had a life. They were friends, but with that designation came a measure of privacy. And hadn't she been warned? They'd talked about the way their lives were changing and, with that, their friendship.

Now she was embarrassed that she'd insisted he come to the concert with her family. To make up for it, she took Carin's left hand, which sported a small ruby. "Carin, what a lovely ring."

"Ray knows I'm not much for diamonds. It *is* pretty, isn't it?"

She had been about to offer her congratulations to Carin and Travis. Now, for the second time in less than a minute, Gayle didn't know what to say. Seconds passed.

"Ray?" she asked after she'd recovered a little.

"Ray Jorgenson, my fiancé. Gayle, haven't you met Ray? Hasn't Travis mentioned we're a couple? He and Travis are cohorts."

"Ray's an archaeologist with the Virginia Department of Historic Resources," Travis explained. "I introduced him to Carin at a meeting of the Archaeological Society of Virginia. I think you met him at my house last year."

Carin bubbled over. "He's going to move to the Stephens City office, and we'll live somewhere between our jobs. Probably Middletown. We're house hunting."

"I'm delighted for you." Gayle squeezed Carin's hand. "And I'm glad the school won't be losing you."

She glanced up at Travis, who just smiled. She narrowed her eyes. He hadn't done one thing to correct her impression that he was in love with Carin.

There was no time to confront him, though. He took Carin's arm, and they moved on. A stream of well-wishers approached. Gayle's mother moved away, and Eric took Phyllis's place.

"You doing okay?" he asked.

"It's a wonderful party." And it was, only she would have enjoyed it a lot more on another day and in another person's honor. Still, her annoyance with Eric had melted. He had arranged this for her. He might not understand what made her tick, but he did care.

"I'm glad you think so," he said. "Putting it together on short notice was a challenge."

"You like challenges."

"Particularly when they turn out so well."

The guests moved in, and Gayle thanked them for coming. Her sons had skirted the edges since the party had begun, but now Dillon tackled her for a hug.

"You're not mad?" he whispered, glancing at his father, who was talking to Sam and Elisa.

She hugged him again, then released him. "No. It's a lovely party."

Dillon didn't look convinced. "We tried to tell him. He doesn't *tell* very well."

She laughed. "He definitely has a mind of his own."

"Yeah, kind of like me."

That might be true, Gayle thought, but even thirteen-year-old Dillon had realized this event wouldn't make his mother happy.

As if to prove her point, he added, "Jared's going to make your favorite spaghetti next week, and I'm going to bake you a cake, and Noah's going to make that salad with the marinated vegetables. Just for us."

"I can't wait."

Noah was the next son to approach. "You're holding up?"

"Uh-huh. Wasn't the jambalaya great?"

"I'm going to try making it. The caterer said it wasn't that hard." He glanced at his father. "He really wanted to do this, Mom."

She was glad to see Noah acting protective of Eric for a change. "And he did a walloping good job of it, too."

Noah looked relieved. He left to talk to Helen Henry about the Touching Stars quilt. She had come with Cissy and her family.

And finally Jared arrived. She thought he looked wonderful and grown up in a black T-shirt and khaki blazer. He had Lisa and Cray with him, but Brandy was noticeably absent. Gayle was glad his friends had come to keep him company.

Eric finished talking to the Kinkades and joined them. The others wandered away, and the family, along with Jared's two friends, formed a tight knot to one side. "Great party, huh kids?"

Jared's gaze flicked to his mother's. He looked sympathetic. "I don't know how you did it, Dad."

Eric turned his attention to Cray. "So I hear you're heading off to the marines?"

"Yes, sir."

"That's a big step."

"I thought about it a lot."

"I know you must have. You and Jared have been best friends forever, haven't you? I bet it's going to feel strange not to be together next year."

"Well, they've promised us we will be, once his enlistment is—" Cray came to an abrupt halt.

Gayle had been half listening, but now the silence was louder than the conversation had been.

She leaned forward. "I missed something. What's this about enlisting?"

Jared's eyes were blazing. "You're an idiot," he said fiercely, directing the insult at Cray.

Cray looked as if he wanted to crawl into a hole.

"No, Jared, it's my fault. I just wasn't listening very closely," Gayle said. "I must have misunderstood."

Eric put his hand on his son's shoulder. And not gently. "Exactly what did Cray mean, Jared?"

Jared shrugged off his father's hand, although it couldn't have been easy. "This isn't the right place to discuss it."

"I think the discussion has already begun," Eric said.

"We'd better go." Cray took Lisa by the elbow, and steered her away and into the crowd. In a moment only Jared, Gayle and Eric were left.

Jared chewed his lip, then turned up his hands in disgust. "Okay. I was going to tell you once Mom's birthday was all over. I didn't want to spoil it, but Cray's never been able to keep a secret. I should have known."

"Tell us what?" Gayle's hands were suddenly cold, although the room was warm. She rubbed them together, but that didn't seem to help.

"I'm joining the Marines, Mom. I've already finished the preliminaries, and I'm signed up to go to Richmond on Wednesday for my physical and enlistment. They have a buddy system. Cray and I will be going to Parris Island together in the fall."

The party continued around them, but Gayle only heard the silence that followed Jared's announcement. She remembered afternoons after Eric's arrival when Jared had disappeared for long periods, as well as the day last week when he had asked Noah to cover for him. She had just assumed he was with Brandy, but now she knew better. She couldn't believe she had been so easily fooled. They had always been close. She couldn't believe he'd made this decision without her.

"You're joking," Eric said at last.

Jared stood a little taller. "Why? Would it be worth a laugh? I've thought about it a lot. All the time, since back in the spring when Cray told me that's what he was planning to do."

"But what about your scholarship?" Gayle asked. "Jared, you worked so hard to get into MIT."

"I've talked to the admissions office. There's a good chance the scholarship will be waiting when I get out. And the school promised to defer my admission. I have it in writing. But who knows what I'll want by then? I mean, there's a whole world out there I've never seen. Every time I thought about sitting in a classroom for four more years, I felt awful. I *have* worked hard, you're right, but school's not real life."

Eric waved away the rest of Jared's speech. "You can't do this. We're not going to let you."

474

"I don't need your permission." Jared was polite enough, but there was a note of defiance in his voice. "And my decision is made."

"Jared! How could you get this far without even talking to us?" Gayle demanded. "Why?"

"Why? To avoid this kind of scene. This was my decision, not yours or Dad's. And I already knew what you'd say."

"Yet you went ahead?" Eric was furious. Gayle put her hand on his arm, but he shook it off, the way Jared had shaken off his. "You think being a marine is just hanging out with a bunch of guys, drinking beer and seeing the world? Do you know how many are dying in the Mideast every single day?"

Jared stepped forward so he and Eric were face-to-face. "Yeah? Well, do you know that while you were in Afghanistan reporting the news, you were almost killed? I realized then that a lot of soldiers have to go over there and put their lives on the line so we can make peace and stop trying to kill each other. I might as well be one of them."

"It's a lot more complicated than that!"

"It wasn't so complicated when you were out on that ledge, was it, Dad? And where would *you* be right now if soldiers hadn't been there to rescue you? I know you and Mom don't like this war. I'm not stupid, I know it's a difficult situation. But I also know there are people living in Iraq and Afghanistan who need good soldiers trying to protect them. And I'm going to be a damn fine marine!"

"Jared, you're not going! I don't care what arrangements you've made. It's not too late to back out."

"My mind is made up."

"Do you have any idea what this will do to your family?"

Jared just stared at him. Then he smiled, although the smile never reached his eyes.

"Better than most people, Dad. Because I spent my whole childhood wondering what was happening to *you*. Don't get me wrong. I'm not joining up to get back at you, but for once it looks like you're going to understand what you put us through. And I guess that's the only thing I'm sorry about. Because I know from experience, you're not going to like it."

Chapter 33

By midnight another storm howled outside the windows of the carriage house. Unable to sleep, Gayle sat alone on the sofa, sipping herbal tea. She was alone in the house. To avoid further recriminations, Jared had gone home from the party with Cray, and as they sometimes did when Jared and Leon were away, Dillon and Noah were sleeping in the room above the garage.

Usually the younger boys slept in Jared's room because he had a television and VCR, and no mother just yards away to police bedtime. Tonight, Gayle thought that her younger sons wanted to ground themselves in Jared's personal space. Neither seemed to know how he felt about Jared's plan to enlist in the marines. Sleeping in his room was a form of mourning.

Despite the storm, the guests seemed contented. Nobody had been up when she'd done her final sweep of the inn. Now that there was no surprise to spoil, her parents were comfortably settled in the Seven Sisters room, although when Gayle looked in on them, her mother had provided a page of notes suggesting improvements in lighting and the better placement of towel racks.

Eric's light had been off.

Eric had improved so steadily since arriving in Toms Brook that Gayle took his better health for granted. But after Jared's announcement, he had looked tired and pale again, hearkening back to the man who had first returned from Afghanistan. This, she thought, would be another night filled with bad dreams.

Tonight had been filled with so many surprises. The party itself. Carin's engagement to someone other than Travis.

And, most of all, Jared.

Her eyes filled with tears. She had never felt like such a failure as a mother. *Not* because her son was entering military service, but because he hadn't discussed his decision with her.

She understood why. Almost since the Iraq war's beginning, she had been concerned, and she'd grown more outspoken as months had passed. But the boys knew they could disagree with her stands on national issues, and Jared's decision to join the marines was not about politics but about a need to serve and protect, as well as a need to prove himself.

She understood the latter perfectly. Although she had coached their soccer teams, and made sure they were active in Boy Scouts and Little League, she hadn't been able to teach them what it meant to be men. There had been men in their lives, and Eric had been on and off the scene, but they had missed a father in residence. Now Jared needed to prove his masculinity in an institution that prided itself on machismo, courage and honor.

Even though she understood these things, she was still brokenhearted. Her son was about to place himself in harm's way. Willingly, even enthusiastically. She knew only too well what that could mean. Someday she might find a notification officer and a chaplain standing on the other side of her front door with the worst news a mother could hear.

Almost as if she had conjured the image, someone knocked. Before she could answer, the door opened and Eric stepped into the entryway, shaking one of the inn's umbrellas behind him.

"I saw your light. I'll go if you want me to," he said.

She motioned him all the way inside, then got up to head for the bathroom. "There's not a lot of sleeping going on in here anyway."

"The boys in bed?"

Back, she tossed him one of the inn's many guest towels and watched him bury his face inside it. "I don't know. They're staying in Jared's room tonight."

She went back to the sofa, and when he was more or less dry, he stopped in the kitchen. She heard the refrigerator open. "What can I get you?" he called.

"Not a thing." She didn't tell him to help himself. Clearly that was already in progress.

Empty-handed, he crossed the room and plopped down beside her, propping his feet on the coffee table as if he did it every night.

She abandoned her empty tea cup. "I'm sorry there's no beer. I don't see any point in tempting the boys and their friends."

"You don't think Jared drinks?"

"Silly you. He's an eighteen-year-old boy—" Her eyes filled with tears again. "Man," she said softly.

"Gayle, what are we going to do about him?"

She closed her eyes and rested her head against the back of the sofa. "What did your father do when you told him you had plans for your life that weren't the ones *he* had for you?"

"He told me I would do what he said or be damned. When

I refused, he told me I wasn't welcome in my own house. And he meant it."

"So you see how much good it does to make decisions for a grown son?"

"Jared is not grown! He just graduated from high school."

"He's grown enough to sign his name on enlistment papers without our permission. He's grown enough to put his life on the line for his country, like a lot of young men and women whose parents had other plans for them."

She opened her eyes. He had turned and was looking straight at her. "Don't tell me you agree with this?" he asked.

"With what? His decision—or his right to make it?"

"Maybe you don't understand what could happen."

She was amazed he could even form those words. Anger flared.

"I understand perfectly, but let me introduce you to your son. This is the young man who always wanted to be in the color guard in Boy Scouts. He didn't want the troop flag or the state flag. Jared was only happy when he was carrying the American flag. If he hadn't had so many other leadership responsibilities, he would have made it all the way to Eagle Scout. Your son believes in God, country and honor, and he's exactly the kind of recruit the marines are looking for."

"I should have provided some balance."

She searched his face. "Which of those things would you prefer he not believe in?"

His shoulders drooped. "It's what he's doing with them."

The drooping shoulders pricked a hole in her defenses. She lowered her voice.

"I don't want him to enlist, either. What mother does? But when you sat down, you asked a question, so here's what I think. Tomorrow we're going to talk to Jared calmly and sensibly, tell him we want to be sure he's not making a mistake. Then we're going to drive to Richmond on Wednesday and watch his enlistment ceremony."

"You can go, but I won't be there."

She tried to absorb this. Eric's response sounded all too familiar, although this time it was out in the open instead of hidden under an excuse. He was going to let her make that difficult trip alone, just as he had left her to do so many unpleasant parenting tasks by herself.

"Do you think that's fair?" she asked. "To me or to him?"

"How can I go to Richmond feeling the way I do?"

She remembered all the times in the lives of their children when *she* had wanted to be elsewhere. When she'd been tired, sick, overwhelmed. When the boys had needed stitches or booster shots. When she'd had to give them bad news or confront them about bad behavior. But she had never been able to leave, because no one had been there to fill in. Eric had never been home for the dirty work.

Of course she'd had resentments. Of course she'd gone to bed angry at her ex-husband, who was off pursuing his career while she raised his children. But now, as if those days had been lived in black and white and *this* moment was in Technicolor, she saw how unfair Eric's behavior had always been and how, by silence and forbearance, she had allowed it to go on.

She had followed behind Eric, making excuses, cleaning up and filling in for him, and why? Because that had been easier than demanding he do his job.

She sat up straighter and jabbed a finger at his chest. "Running away would be just like you. You don't like something, so you just don't show up. Wet diapers, high fevers, angry teachers who want conferences? It was always too much trouble for you. Now this. Exactly why am I such a fool? I was beginning to believe you'd changed."

"Well, one of us had to be less than perfect."

When she could speak, her voice was shaking. "If I tried to be perfect, it was to make up for your lack of interest. I figured our sons needed one parent they could count on."

"Is that it? Or maybe you liked casting me as the bad parent so you could be the good one, Gayle. How many times did you let me know I was needed?"

"Why weren't you on the telephone asking questions? Why weren't you flying here between assignments to see what your sons needed?"

"Maybe because you made it clear you had everything covered! Who needed *me?* And how was *I* going to compete?"

She started to get up, but he grabbed her hand and pulled her back to the sofa. "Gayle…" He shook his head; then his expression crumpled. "Don't you get it? I…can't watch. I just can't go to Richmond and watch. Do you know the statistics?"

"Do you know your son?"

He squeezed his eyes shut. "I want to. I don't want him dead in a roadside bombing."

"You owe him your support and loyalty. We both do. And the way you show it is to drive down to Richmond with me."

"This is our blond-haired baby boy. How can you be so strong?"

Strong? That word was the last straw. Fury turned to sorrow, and she began to cry. The tears had threatened since Jared's announcement. Now they came in choking, uncontrollable waves.

"Gayle, I'm sorry…." Eric put his arms around her and pulled her resisting body to his chest.

"Let go…of me."

He didn't. He let her cry as he held her, slowly stroking her back. When the crying tapered off a little, he spoke softly.

"I'm so sorry. I really am. Of course I'll go. I'm just so sick about this. I was spouting off, but I didn't mean it. I'm not going to leave you alone."

She tried to pull away, but he wouldn't let her. "Shhh…I'm sorry, and I mean *that*. For everything. For tonight, for ever thinking I had what it took to be a husband and father." His voice broke. "And I thought things were tough when the kids were little…"

She cried harder again, and he pulled her closer and rested his cheek against her hair. His arms were strong and comforting. Having them around her made her realize how much she had missed being held like this and how much she had missed being able to let someone else take charge, if only for moments.

The storm had nearly passed when he fished around on the end table, then handed her a tissue. "Jared wouldn't be doing this if I'd been around."

She sniffed and wiped her nose. "It's not…that simple."

"Maybe not, but it's a big part of the equation. I wasn't here to teach him what it means to be a man, so he's going to figure out the final pieces in the marines."

It was so close to what she'd been thinking before he'd come in that she didn't know what to say. Then she realized that she did know, after all.

"Maybe that is a part of it." She wiped her cheek with the back of her hand. "But the bigger part? He wants to fix what happened to you."

"I know that, too."

"He's always been the son who…fixes things. The mender. The one who tries the hardest to put things right."

"Will talking to him help? If we explain all that?"

"No. This isn't out of the blue. The signs were already there. After 9/11, he even considered applying for a scholarship to Massanutten."

"The military academy in Woodstock?"

She forced a laugh, but it was only a gulp. "Not the ski resort."

"You never told me."

"You were busy at the time. There…was a lot of news to report."

She pushed away from him and tried to brush her hair off her wet cheeks, but he put his hands on her arms.

"It's been too hard for you. I'm going to need tutoring, Gayle. This doesn't come naturally to me."

She wanted to stay angry. Being angry was so much easier than facing everything else tonight. But how could she stay angry when it was love for Jared that had motivated Eric's outburst? This man loved their son as much as she did, perhaps differently, perhaps somewhat erratically, but Eric did love Jared. And his dreams for his son had been radically altered tonight.

His expression softened. "You're a hard act to follow, but it's my own fault I haven't tried harder. You took care of things, and I just let you."

She liked being held in place. She liked having him searching her face to see what she was feeling. So many times after Eric had left she had yearned for someone to share her life and burdens with. Someone to be with her when hard decisions had to be made. Someone to make them when she was overwhelmed. And tonight she was overwhelmed again.

But even as she realized how seductive it was to have Eric with her, to feel what strength he had to give her and absorb the companionship of another lonely soul, a warning voice sounded in her head.

"I loved you." He stroked his thumbs up and down her arms

as he held her there. "But I never, never appreciated you the way I should have."

She knew how vulnerable she was. "This isn't the right time for this."

His smile was unsteady. "When would be a better one?"

He seemed so familiar, so much a part of who she once had been. It was too tempting to fall back into that place and time. Even as she said the next words, she didn't know if she meant them.

"Maybe you'd better go."

"Is that what you really want?"

She couldn't lie. She *did* want to be with the only person in the world who felt what she did tonight. And yes, memories of making love with Eric were surfacing so rapidly that she knew they couldn't have been deeply buried. She had loved him once. She had loved having him touch her. She had found comfort and delight in his body, and she needed both tonight.

She looked away and tried to steel her defenses. "This isn't a good idea."

He turned her face back to his. "It's not an idea. It's a feeling. I want you. You want me. We're adults."

"With a complicated…past."

"Gayle, there's nothing all that complicated about what we're feeling."

Tears filled her eyes again, but she touched his lips as if to silence them. "Oh, Eric, I just can't bear any more pain."

He kissed her fingers, and when she withdrew them, he spoke. "Then let me give you pleasure."

"We're going to regret this."

He leaned forward and brushed a kiss across her lips. "I don't want to be alone tonight, and neither do you. Haven't we both been alone too long, Gayle?"

This time, when he kissed her, it wasn't casual, and it wasn't affectionate. She silenced the warning voice that had insisted she send him away. She let him persuade her to forget the problems that were still between them and the ways they would now be harder to solve.

She forgot everything except the need to bury her sorrows in the same act that had given her three precious sons. And she hoped that when logic and sanity returned, she would not be more sorrowful still.

Chapter 34

Gayle was still sleeping when Eric left the carriage house. They had fallen asleep together in her flower bower of a bedroom. Yesterday morning, when he and the boys had delivered her birthday breakfast tray, he had been surprised to see how unrelentingly female the bedroom was, how devoted to preserving her essential femininity. Strip away the efficient innkeeper, the devoted and patient mother, the logical church deacon, and there dwelled a woman whose soul was clothed in lace and draped in pearls.

He and Gayle had never shared that room. He had left her before the renovations to the carriage house were finished, left her when only four bedrooms in the inn were completed and the kitchen stove was still on back order.

He remembered now that while they had struggled to get the plumbing updated and the cabinets hung, she had washed dishes in a bathtub and stored them in boxes in the dining room. Flinching, he remembered that Gayle had almost never complained, because seeing the inn come alive had meant so much to her.

Every paint chip, every fabric and carpet sample, had been lovingly examined, and the potential had vibrated in her imagination. The long hours of physical labor, the mess, the constant demands of small children…none of it had been too much for her.

All of it had been too much for him.

And, sadly, all of it was too much for him again.

Dawn hadn't even arrived, yet the reality of coming back to the Valley, of resuming a marriage he had abandoned and fitting himself into a small-scale life with simpler pleasures, was clawing its way to the surface. Since he had awakened beside her with all the pressures and possibilities, he had felt bloody and raw, as if with his last ounce of strength he had tried to squeeze himself into a space in which he didn't belong. And he had not been successful.

The revelation had begun last night as he and Gayle, in sorrow, regret and loneliness, had given in to temptation and made love. As he had fallen deeper under the spell of his physical and emotional needs, he had shoved away his fears, telling himself they were simply reconsummating vows they had taken so long ago.

They were renewing commitments.

But even then, he hadn't been fooled. Now he wondered if he had fooled her.

He had wanted their lovemaking to be the final evidence. He had tried to prove to both of them that he was finally capable of becoming the man and husband she needed. He had hoped that afterward, when they fell asleep in each other's arms, he would be sure he loved her so much and in so many ways that whatever problems remained could be resolved.

Instead, this morning he knew for certain that the problems were larger than either of them, a separate presence in their relationship that was a shadow they could only escape if they moved in different directions.

Love, its quantity and quality, had little to do with this. And now, as before, the problems had nothing to do with sex. Their bodies were happy together. But their hearts and souls were another matter.

If two people could create a good marriage purely by wishing, then he and Gayle should have the best marriage in the world. But wishes and regrets were not the foundations of a relationship that would see them through the ends of their lives. Their sons would not be better off if he and Gayle chose to try marriage again, and neither of *them* would be happier, either.

Their marriage had ended when the divorce papers were signed, only neither of them had really let go, neither had really said goodbye. It was time to do both so they could move on, unfettered by hopes of resurrecting a marriage that should never have taken place.

But what if she saw things differently?

In the rush of feelings he'd experienced since waking, that was the one that haunted him most. What if Gayle awoke this morning convinced they had made a fresh start? Since coming back to Toms Brook, he had faced and tried to deal with his neglect of his sons. Last night he had tried to face and deal with his failed marriage. But what had he really accomplished? Hurt Gayle more? Hurt Gayle again?

If she wanted to give their marriage another try, could he be man enough not to back away?

Thunder clattered in the distance, and the dark skies matched his mood. Rain spattered against his umbrella, and through a deep mist he thought the river was rising below them. In the earliest light of morning, trees along the bank that were normally well above the water line seemed to grow straight out of the currents. And even from this distance, he could see that the Shenandoah was rushing swiftly northward.

He left the umbrella by the door and made it to the Lone Star room without encountering anyone. He stripped and got into the shower, turning himself over to the fine, hot spray for a recess from regrets. He and Gayle would have to talk, but he hoped he would have time to think of what to say and how to say it. In the meantime, he hoped the shower, and perhaps another hour of sleep, would prepare him to face whatever was to come.

Ten minutes later, he walked back into his room wearing nothing but a towel draped around his neck. Dillon was sitting on his bed.

"Dillon, what in the name of everything holy are you doing in here?" Eric whipped the towel around his waist and tucked it in at the side. His gaze flicked to the bed, and he remembered that before visiting Gayle last night, he had first tried to go to sleep here. The bed looked slept in.

"The river's rising." Clearly Dillon thought his father's state of undress was of no particular interest.

Eric was relieved. Dillon seemed to have no idea that his mother had not been alone last night. Even in the midst of seduction, Gayle had probably realized that the boys would never find out, but Eric had hardly given it a thought. Now he was glad that, despite his carelessness, that particular secret was safe.

"I'm sure it's not the first time you've seen it that way." Eric rummaged for a T-shirt and slipped the first one he came to over his head.

"Maybe, but not usually this high. It's cool."

"I imagine there are people living on lower ground who don't find it too cool. Do you always walk into people's bedrooms unannounced?"

"If I can get in."

Eric had to laugh. He felt a surge of affection and veered in Dillon's direction to tousle his hair. Then he took the rest of his clothes back into the bathroom and finished dressing.

Only when his shorts were halfway up his thighs did he think about the land immediately across the river. He zipped up and went back into the bedroom.

He dropped down beside his son and began to lace his shoes. "I wonder what's going on at the dig."

"I bet the river's almost up to the edge."

Eric thought about the metal object they hadn't been able to uncover. With the kind of careful digging Travis required, another hour would have been needed to free it. But surely now they would not be expected to exercise that much care. If the river spilled into the hole, who knew what could be sucked away? For history's sake, wouldn't it be better to simply remove the box, then fill in what they could of the unit and hope that other precious artifacts weren't lost forever if the river rose higher?

Adrenaline rushed through him, obliterating everything else. It was a familiar and welcome experience. "I'm going to call Mr. Allen." Eric tied the final knot in his laces and stood. "I know it's early, but I bet he's up."

"Nobody ever lets me use the phone this early." Dillon got up and followed his father to the door. "I can't wait to be a grown-up."

Eric thought of the talk he needed to have with Gayle. "It's not what it's cracked up to be."

"Yeah, well, nobody tells you what you have to do all the time."

"You'd be surprised."

"Why? By the time somebody's as old as you, they ought to know everything."

"Listen, champ, by the time somebody's as old as me, he just realizes how much he still has to learn. Sorry to have to tell you."

"Does that mean I don't have to try so hard in school, since it just gets worse?"

Eric punched him lightly on the arm. "No, it means since you have so much to learn, you have to get busy earlier."

"Noah has the right idea. I should have stayed in bed."

Travis wasn't home. Once Eric looked up his number in the inn's office and made the call, the telephone rang and rang. Dillon lounged in the doorway, his eyes bright with interest. Eric could hear the clinking of utensils and the soft padding of footsteps from the kitchen area, but he hadn't yet seen Gayle.

Eric hung up. "Either Mr. Allen is sleeping and doesn't want to answer, or he's already out at the site."

"How are you going to find out?"

"I'm going out there."

"Great, I'll go with you."

Eric put his hand on his son's shoulder. "No. I'm sorry, but no."

"How come?"

Eric wished he were better at this. "Because the river's high, it's rushing a lot faster than usual, and even though you swim better now and aren't as afraid of the water, you're still not good enough to take the risk."

"But I saved Reese! You know I did! I jumped in and saved her."

"I rest my case."

"That's not fair!"

"This has nothing to do with fair. It's all about taking care of you, which I am obliged to do as your father. Even if I understand perfectly why you want to go."

"You and Mom are ganging up on me. You sound just like her!"

Eric thought this might be one of those rare if unintended compliments a father received from his child. "Thank you."

Dillon did an about-face and stormed off. Eric was just as glad he didn't stay and argue, though if his son was going to his mother hoping for a reprieve, Eric knew Dillon was wasting his time.

He tried to think what he ought to take with him. He knew Travis had plenty of equipment, but it wouldn't hurt to bring some of his own. He would stop by the toolshed and see what might be helpful. He would wear one of the rain jackets and caps hanging on the back porch, change out of sneakers into his hiking boots, maybe get a Thermos of coffee and something portable to eat on his way out to the car. He needed work gloves....

Suddenly he realized Gayle was standing in the doorway, pretty and sensible in dark pants and a lavender blouse covered by a striped chef's apron with Daughter of the Stars stenciled on it. For a moment he felt like a car that had stalled in heavy traffic. He wanted to move on with his journey, but he was completely hemmed in. And terrified of what the next moments might bring.

Her eyes betrayed nothing. "You look like a man on a mission."

He had to clear his throat, although there was nothing blocking speech except words he didn't want to say. "I just tried to call Travis. He's not home, so I'm guessing he's at the dig."

"I bet you're planning to join him."

He searched unsuccessfully for recriminations or regrets in her eyes, listened for them in her voice. She gave nothing away.

"I am." He cocked his head. "Do you need me here instead? To entertain your parents, maybe, and keep Phyllis off your back?"

"I'll do that on my own. I may actually get the knack of it."

"Then you don't need me?" He almost winced at his tone. Relief was a good part of it. Excitement at leaving the inn made up the rest.

"I don't." She looked as if she wanted to say more but thought better of it.

"What?"

She gave a self-deprecating laugh. "Just that you look more like yourself than you have since you arrived. Your eyes are sparkling. You're looking forward to this."

She knew him so well. Sadly, she realized that if his eyes were sparkling, it was not because of last night but because of challenges he hadn't yet faced.

He didn't know what to say. She nodded. "I know, Eric. We'll have to talk, but not now. You go and rescue what you can, and please take my truck. The keys are on a peg by the back door. But be careful. The boys need you, and you promised to renovate my garden shed. So don't drown, okay?"

The boys need you. My garden shed. Eric wondered if he was reading too much meaning into the simple sentences, extracting it from an expression so carefully guarded that even a trained psychic couldn't gather clues.

When he didn't speak, she did.

"I don't regret last night, and you shouldn't, either." Then she turned and vanished back into the kitchen.

He was left to wonder exactly what she meant.

In the truck fifteen minutes later, he no longer wondered. His focus was on getting to the dig. He had a backpack of supplies, shovels and picks in the truck, and enough hot coffee for himself and Travis. But the moment the low water bridge was in sight— or, rather, *wasn't* in sight—he knew he had a problem.

The bridge had been transformed. Eric stopped in the middle of the road and turned off the engine, then got out and made his way to the beginning of the bridge. The concrete span was covered. Several inches of water rushed over it, carrying debris.

Branches floated by, a tire, then what looked like rusted bed springs. He rolled down his socks, although the gesture was futile, and took a step onto the concrete. Water pushed against his shoe and pushed hard, but he had no trouble maintaining his balance. He took another step, then another, until both feet were on the span. He remained poised there, ready to leap to safety if he needed to, but his feet were firmly planted.

Mind made up, he went back to the truck and took out the backpack, plus a long-handled shovel that would come in handy both as an ersatz walking stick and at the dig itself. Then he retraced his steps.

He waited until no large chunks of debris were in sight; then he started across in earnest. He was fine until the middle of the bridge, when his foot slipped as something moved beneath him and he nearly fell. In the time it took for him to regain his footing, he wondered if he had underestimated the strength of the current. But in a moment he was stable enough to take another step. Before long he was climbing along the opposite riverbank and heading to the dig site.

Although he had expected flooding, he was still surprised to see how far the water had crept up on this side of the river. The campfire site would be underwater soon, and Travis's carefully laid units would be puddles. Eric slogged toward the site, his hiking boots squishing noisily, and searched for Travis. Just as he was beginning to believe Travis hadn't come after all to see what he could rescue, Eric spotted him coming out from behind the trees that hid the unit they had worked on together.

Eric put two fingers in his mouth and gave a sharp whistle, hoping he would be heard over the river and the grumbling of distant thunder. Travis looked up, then responded with a quick wave. Eric started toward him.

He was surprised at how long it took to reach the other man. Rain had begun falling steadily again, and mud sucked at his feet. He used the shovel to propel himself along, and was more than a little glad when he and Travis were finally eye to eye. Travis wore a rain hat with a circular brim, and he had removed his glasses. He looked like a hunter on safari. In monsoon season.

"I thought I'd find you out here." Eric stuck out his hand.

Travis grabbed it for a perfunctory shake. "I've been watching the water. It's rising faster than I expected. If we're going to get anything out of there, we'd better get right to it. How did you get over?"

"I walked across the bridge."

Travis looked surprised; then he nodded. "Great. Glad that worked out for you."

"Yeah, well, it was touch and go at one point, but I managed." Eric peered over Travis's shoulder. "Have you made any progress?"

"We'll make more together."

"Are we going to observe the niceties?"

"There are no niceties. This has ceased to have any relation to archaeology. It's about folklore now."

"And treasure hunting."

"Afraid so."

Eric followed him back through the trees. "How much time do you think we have?"

"Not long. We don't want to be here if the water starts to rise suddenly. I've seen that happen, too. At the first indication, we'll have to get out."

Eric thought of the bridge and what it would be like if the water rose even a little. He had made it across, but a few more inches would make crossing back impossible. They would have to act fast.

"Let's see what we can do and get out of here." Travis stopped and stooped, and Eric looked down.

"How long have you been here?" The hole they'd been digging yesterday didn't look much deeper.

"Not long."

Eric took his shovel and began to loosen the dirt in front of the stones. Travis had brought a shovel, too. Both men were careful, doing a cursory examination of each shovelful of mud, but for all Eric knew, he could have been discarding Confederate gold. *Cursory* was unfortunately the operative word.

They stopped when the hole, which rapidly filled with water, was deep enough.

"Let's see if we can get those rocks out of the way." Travis stooped again, and Eric positioned himself on the other side. Together they tugged at two rocks that had once held up hardwood logs. Tons of logs, Eric estimated, although he didn't really know. The rocks had been here for centuries and had little motivation to be coaxed out of their home.

He sat back on his heels and rested. Rain poured off the bill of his cap and down the back of his neck. He was already exhausted, but he felt wonderful anyway. He was excited in a way that was completely familiar, though he had almost forgotten how it felt. He didn't even care what he and Travis discovered. The challenge was the thing that mattered. Pitting himself against the odds and, yes, taking risks to do it.

This was what Jared needed, too, he realized, and this was why his son had chosen to spend the next years of his life in the marine corps. Eric felt that revelation to his very bones. In this way his oldest son was just like him. Jared couldn't and shouldn't be talked out of being who he was, and Eric had been wrong to try. In the same way that Eric wanted to bring information and news, Jared wanted to bring justice and freedom. And both of them were willing to take the necessary risks to do their jobs.

"You okay?" Travis asked.

Eric gave a rueful grin. "Maybe I'm going to be."

"Glad to hear it. I think this stone's beginning to give."

Eric balanced his weight and leaned forward. He saw that Travis had indeed moved the stone. Now there was a slight gap that Eric could utilize.

Minutes passed, but in the end, the stone gave way.

"Yep, there's something behind it." Travis reached in, but the rusted black metal object wouldn't give. "We'll have to get the stone beside it, as well."

"Hey, Dad!"

Eric turned so fast he nearly lost his balance. "Noah?" He put his hand over his eyes, and tried to see through the rain and mist. Two shapes were coming toward them.

"Damn!"

Travis was peering through the rain, as well. "I don't think they should be here."

"Welcome to the club." Eric got to his feet and started toward his sons.

"I thought I told you not to come." He stopped Dillon with a firm hand on his shoulder; then, for good measure, gave him a hard shake. "Is this the way you listen?"

"I know, I know." Dillon looked genuinely sheepish. "But we, well, we were worried about you and Mr. Allen!"

"Great, and now we can worry about *you*. How'd you get over?"

"The bridge, of course." Noah looked perplexed. Clearly he thought the question was strange.

"You can still get across?" Eric didn't want to imagine that. If Dillon had been swept over and into the water…

"Yeah, the only time the bridge is ever spooky is when the wind's blowing real hard. It was just spooky enough to be fun."

Eric realized then that Noah wasn't talking about the low water bridge that *he* had crossed. Noah meant the suspension footbridge a bit farther up river. Eric hadn't considered using it. He would just as soon hurl his body into the rushing waters of the Shenandoah as climb those steps. But the boys had been crossing it since they were small children.

Travis hadn't interfered, but now he spoke from behind them. "Eric, if you give me some help here, I think we can move this and get to whatever's back there. Then we can all get out of here."

The wind was picking up, and so was the rain. Eric peered down at the river and wondered how quickly it was rising.

"Boys, you wait." He didn't want them going back alone now. Not with the storm picking up. Unfortunately, they were all going to have to stick together.

"We can help," Noah said. "That's why we came."

"Let them," Travis said. "It'll be faster."

Noah flanked Travis, and Dillon flanked his father. There wasn't enough room for four sets of hands to pull out the stone, but the boys grabbed trowels and shoveled dirt away from the edges to give Eric and Travis more room to maneuver. They were so busy working that Eric didn't register the cracking sound behind them. It was already too late to do anything when a limb from the nearest tree came hurtling toward them. Travis grabbed Noah to pull him out of the way. He almost succeeded, but the limb grazed Noah's arm as it fell.

"Are you okay?" Travis sent the limb rolling away from them with his heel; then, despite Noah's protests, he peeled back the boy's sleeve. A gash was bleeding freely.

Travis stripped off his windbreaker and tied it around Noah's arm as a bandage. He did it so quickly that Eric had no time to help.

"How does that feel?" Travis asked.

Noah looked pale. "I'm okay."

"You were lucky." Travis pointed toward the footbridge. "Okay, we're going back. That's all the warning we're going to get. It's not safe here. And we need to clean and dress that gash. You may need stitches."

Noah shook his head. "No, I'm okay."

"You'll be better when we get you home."

"Noah?" Eric asked. "Can you make it home?"

"I'm okay. I really am!"

"Right." Eric looked at Travis. "Do you want to go with him, or shall I?"

"We should all go."

"This stone's nearly out. If you'll be okay with Noah and Dillon, I'll stay and finish the job. But we've done this much. What do you think, boys?"

The boys looked at each other. "How will you get back?" Noah asked.

"I crossed the low water bridge before. The water wasn't that deep."

"You did what?" Travis looked grim. "I thought you came across the footbridge."

Now Eric realized why Travis had seemed surprised. Apparently he knew heights frightened Eric, and the suspension bridge wasn't only high, but, even under the best circumstances, it felt unstable, swinging and sagging with every step. Even the thought of it made Eric turn cold.

"The low water bridge was perfectly safe," Eric said. "I was careful. I'll go back that way. But you take the boys across the footbridge. As long as you think it's safe in this wind."

The two men stared at each other. Then Travis shook his head again. "It's too easy for you to get swept away."

"Then don't keep me here talking about it. Let me finish and get going."

"What if it's too deep?"

"I don't know. Maybe I'll just stay on this side and see if somebody will give me shelter."

"That's unlikely. The closest farm is for sale, and nobody's living there. You might have to walk as much as a mile to find somebody to take you in."

"Well, the water's definitely going to be too deep if I don't get moving."

Travis looked at the boys, then back at Eric. "I'm going to get them home. Then, if you're not on your way, I'm coming back for you."

"Dad, let me stay," Dillon said. "I can help."

"Go. Now. Before I do something a father shouldn't. You've disobeyed me once already. Get out of here."

Dillon looked as if he was going to cry, but Eric armored his heart with visions of his son in the swiftly moving current. "Now!"

Travis put his arms around both boys, and they started upriver toward the suspension bridge. The moment he was sure they were really going to leave, Eric went back to the hole. This time he didn't squat. He knelt, his knees and legs sinking into the muck. He had sounded more optimistic than he felt. The stone still didn't move.

He got up again and went for his shovel. Then he wedged it into the thin slit between the stone in question and the one to its left. He tried to force them apart, but the shovel slipped out, and he fell. He scrambled up, wedged it in again, and this time the stone seemed to shift. He wiggled the shovel, thrusting it in deeper and deeper, until the stone was at a new angle. Then he got down on his knees one more time and, with every bit of strength, hauled the rock out of the way.

Victory was his. He felt such a rush of pleasure that his hands shook. Or perhaps they were shaking from the unaccustomed labor. Whatever the reason, they were still plenty steady enough to grip the object the stones had hidden. And when he tugged it out, slowly and carefully, he saw that he was now in possession of a small rusty metal lockbox, exactly as Travis had guessed.

"Yes!" He was jubilant. He unzipped his jacket to see if the box would fit in the inside pocket, but it was too large. Instead, he stripped off the jacket and tied it around the lockbox to protect it. Then he slipped the box inside his backpack, removing some of the supplies to make room. The Thermos had a strap, and he slung it over his shoulder. Work gloves were tucked into the waistband of his shorts. He was ready to leave, and one glance at the river told him it wasn't a moment too soon. The water appeared to be rising. Soon the unit would be covered, and after that, perhaps the entire dig.

He grabbed his shovel and started back toward the bridge, hoping the water was still low enough that he could cross safely. But before he even got close, he saw that his luck had run out. The water was so high now that he couldn't even see the bridge, and when he was almost on top of it, he knew if he tried to walk across, he would be swept downriver.

The road behind him rose above the river and into the mountains. He tried to envision exactly what was on it. Travis had said the first house, the old farmhouse on multiple acres that Eric remembered, was vacant. And Eric couldn't visualize another house beyond that one. He knew that if he followed the road, eventually he would probably find someone to help or something he could use for shelter. But a new complication was on the way.

As they'd worked, thunder had steadily rumbled in the distance. Now lightning split the horizon, and the wind began to pick up. Getting to shelter immediately was critical, and there was no time to search for a house or barn on this side of the river. He thought of his boys and was glad Travis had taken them back. But that was his only consolation. Because there was only one choice left now. The suspension bridge.

In the distance, he saw the bridge swaying over the river. Once the lightning got closer and the worst of the storm closed in on him, the suspension bridge wouldn't be safe, either. He had to get there and cross, and he had to do it now.

He didn't move; he was paralyzed. He stood motionless in the rain and remembered a night in Afghanistan, a night when he had hovered on a ledge above an endless chasm and tried to make peace with his impending death. That night he had imagined many things, but never this. He wondered if the universe felt cheated and wanted another crack at him. Or perhaps this was a test. Face his greatest fear, conquer it, and he would be ready for almost anything again.

He told himself that he could change his mind, but he had to at least give the footbridge a chance. He forced himself to put one foot in front of the other, taking care to watch where he was stepping, until he reached the base of the bridge. He looked up and immediately suffered an attack of vertigo. He gripped the bottom of the railing and closed his eyes.

He reminded himself that no matter how he felt, he wasn't falling. He was standing on the riverbank, a bank that would soon be completely underwater. But he was not falling.

He opened his eyes and counted steps. There were twelve up to the bridge, and the railing was wide and sturdy. Twelve steps, his own personal recovery program. Then he would be on the bridge, putting one foot in front of the other. When he and Gayle had first moved to the Valley, he had crossed this bridge a dozen times for the sheer novelty of it. Once, when he and Gayle were crossing together, he had stood in the middle and rattled the sides to make it swing. She had squealed and threatened him. Laughing, he had chased her back to the other side.

Now he couldn't even climb the steps.

The sky blazed with another streak of lightning. He had no time to gather courage. This had to be done and done now. He took the first step, then the second. He thought he was swaying; he knew his knees were shaking. He took the next step, then the next. He didn't look any farther down than his feet. He forced the right one onto the next step, the left to the step above that. He gripped the railing and told himself that even if his knees gave way, his hands would keep him safe.

He was halfway up. If he could get this far, he could manage the same number again. Then, of course, he would be on the bridge. Not only was the structure swinging in the wind, but he remembered too well the way it had once felt under his feet. The walkway moved and dipped even without the wind. Nothing about the bridge was fixed.

But even if he fell, he would not go over the side. The bridge was encased in wire. He could pick himself up and try again. Hell, he could crawl if he had to, although somehow that seemed more dangerous.

He took two more steps, rested, then two more. He had two more to go and he would be as high as he needed to be.

Then he looked down. Below him, the river was white with foam, a turbulent, angry ribbon carrying everything it touched along with it. This was not the same body of water Dillon had jumped in to save little Reese. Even the strongest swimmer would risk drowning in this.

He swayed and closed his eyes. "You can do this, Fortman." In a moment he opened them again just as lightning split the sky. The storm was coming right at him. He had to cross and cross now.

"Dad!"

For a moment he thought he'd imagined Dillon's voice. Dillon was back at the inn with Travis and his mother. But even as he told himself Dillon was home safe, his son materialized on the other end of the bridge.

"Come on, Dad! You've got to get out of here!"

Eric gripped the railing. "What are you doing here?"

Dillon started toward him. "Come on, Dad. You can do it."

Eric didn't waste more time on questions. "Go home. Get off this bridge right now."

"Not until you get across!" Dillon was in the middle now. Eric couldn't see anybody behind him. He realized Gayle didn't know their son had come back for him. Gayle and probably Travis were seeing to Noah's arm. And while they were safely busy, Dillon had simply vanished back into the storm.

Dillon was three-quarters of the way across now. The bridge was not that long. The river was not that wide. Dillon stretched out his hand. "Come on, Dad. You can do it, I'll help you. Just like you helped me."

Eric's eyes filled with tears. Two more steps, then he would be on the bridge. Dillon's hand was almost in reach. Eric glanced down and saw water lapping at the stairs, and just beyond that, he saw the angry river.

Then he looked up and saw his bedraggled, rebellious son, eyes wide with concern, stretching out his hand. "Come on, Dad!"

Eric wasn't sure which convinced him: fear for his son's safety, or the rush of love and gratitude when he saw that slender hand reaching toward him to offer support.

Eric climbed the final two steps, then stretched his own hand toward Dillon's. Dillon took it; then carefully, slowly, they crossed the swinging bridge together.

Chapter 35

"I don't know whether to spank you or hug you." Showered and in dry clothes, Eric sat on the carriage-house sofa beside his youngest son. But to show his choice, he slung his arm over Dillon's shoulders and pulled him closer for a moment.

"Well, I'm not going to be so easy on you." Gayle refused to smile at Dillon. "The next time you deliberately disobey your father or me, kiddo, it's not going to end with a hug. I'm always looking for a galley slave."

"I just knew Dad needed help. Nobody gives me enough credit."

Eric caught Gayle's eye and saw she was struggling hard to be the bad cop. He added what support he could. "Credit or not, you're going to listen."

"I know. I know." Dillon aimed his most affable grin at his mother. "But can you get over it this time so we can look in the box?"

The lockbox sat on the table. Like his son, a shaken but intact Eric was anxious to open it, but they had promised to wait for Travis and Noah, who had gone to retrieve Gayle's truck. Noah's arm was freshly bandaged, and Gayle—who had apparently gotten good at this over the years—had determined it would heal without stitches.

The door opened with a bang, and the missing duo ran inside. Gayle handed them towels and hung up their rain gear. Noah went to his room to change, and Gayle provided Travis with a dry T-shirt and a pair of Jared's shorts.

Finally everyone was seated around the table. Gayle's parents hoped to fly out of D.C. in the afternoon if the storm passed through in time and had already left for the airport. The other guests were in Paula's capable hands. She was making popcorn and cocoa, and had promised to preside over a showing of *Shenandoah*, with Jimmy Stewart.

No one would disturb them.

"Who does the honors?" Eric asked.

"You." Travis leaned over and handed the box to Eric. "You're the one who risked your life to save it."

"That would be an exaggeration, even if it felt like it when I was crossing that bridge."

"Close enough. The lock's rusted through. It should give with a discreet yank. I'll look away."

Eric felt honored. He followed Travis's advice and jerked. The lock gave in his hand. "I guess this doesn't bode well for the contents."

"No guarantees."

Now that the time had come, Eric hesitated. "Remember when Geraldo opened Capone's vault?"

The boys looked blank until Gayle explained. "Geraldo Rivera is a television journalist, like your father."

"Not quite," Eric protested.

"Well, he's not quite as flashy as your father." Gayle laughed at Eric's expression. "Anyway, back before you were born, a station in Chicago announced they were going to unseal a secret vault that had supposedly belonged to Al Capone. Geraldo publicized the heck out of it. People thought there might be millions locked inside, maybe jewels, skeletons, who knows. They opened it on live television in front of a huge audience."

"And there was nothing in it except a couple of empty bottles," Eric said.

Noah was clearly not impressed with any similarities. "Why would anybody go to all that trouble to hide an *empty* lockbox?"

"Well, if it's empty, we can speculate. But let's see." Eric pried the top loose with his fingers. The rust didn't help, and for a moment he wasn't sure he could open it without destroying the box. Then the pieces popped apart.

The box wasn't empty. Inside was a small package wrapped in oilcloth and tied with string. Eric knew his duty. He'd opened the box, but this was Travis's find. He handed the package to him.

Travis's eyes met his. Understanding passed between them. They had been forced into becoming a team to rescue the lockbox. In years to come, they might well need to be a team again. There were three boys who counted on both of them.

Travis took out a pocketknife and cut the string. Then, carefully, he unwrapped the folds of oilcloth.

Everybody leaned over to see what he had uncovered.

"A book!" Dillon looked up. "Like the one in our play?"

"It's wet. And it's probably been wet more than a few times," Travis said.

Eric saw that the cover was leather, but it was shredding under Travis's fingers. There was an unmistakeable odor of mildew, and a powdery green mold bloomed in the leather cracks. If the volume had ever borne a title, there was no hint of one now.

"Can you open it?" he asked Travis.

Travis looked torn; then, carefully, he turned back what was left of the cover.

Everyone gathered closer. Travis shook his head. "There was writing on the flyleaf, but the ink is a blur. It bled into the page."

"Can you tell anything?'

"I think that's a *B*." Dillon pointed to what was clearly a signature of some kind. "Look, it *is* a *B*."

But even as they all craned their necks to examine the writing, the latest deluge sealed the signature's fate. As they watched, what was left bled into the paper and joined the other smears of ink. Had there ever been a chance of comparing this handwriting to any on record from John Wilkes Booth, it had disappeared forever.

"Is the book Shakespeare?" Gayle asked.

Travis turned the page and read the title. "The sonnets." He squinted at the small print. "Looks like it was printed in…1858."

Everyone was silent until Dillon spoke. "In the play, Blackjack told Robby he marked one of the poems with a leather lace. Did Miss Webster make that up?"

"No, that was the story I was told." Travis held up the book and peered at the top edges. Then he carefully opened the pages, and there, acting as a bookmark, were the remnants of a thin strip of leather.

"Can you read it?" Gayle asked.

"Not easily. It's in rough shape." Travis held the pages closer to his face. "It looks like this is number seventy-two."

"I can look it up online," Noah volunteered.

Gayle got up. "No, I have the sonnets. I'll get them."

"You read Shakespeare? For fun?" Dillon asked the question as if his mother had admitted to conjugating Latin verbs in her downtime.

"Not until recently." A moment later, she came back with a paperback volume. "I ordered this after your play was finished. I've been wondering which sonnet Blackjack marked. I thought it might be fun to read them all together and try to figure it out."

She found the correct page. "Shall I read it?"

"Please," Eric said.

Gayle cleared her throat.

"O! Lest the world should task you to recite
What merit lived in me, that you should love
After my death, dear love, forget me quite,
For you in me can nothing worthy prove;
Unless you would devise some virtuous lie,
To do more for me than mine own desert,
And hang more praise upon deceased I
Than niggard truth would willingly impart:
O! lest your true love may seem false in this,
That you for love speak well of me untrue,
My name be buried where my body is,
And live no more to shame nor me nor you.
For I am shamed by that which I bring forth,
And so should you, to love things nothing worth."

She looked up and shook her head. "Wow."

For a moment they sat in silence.

Noah was the first to speak. "We're never going to know who Blackjack was, are we?"

Gayle closed the book. "A man with deep regrets. And I bet that's all Miranda was ever meant to know."

Chapter 36

For the next few days, Gayle didn't avoid Eric as much as she allowed everything else in their busy lives to take precedence. Now that archaeology camp was over, Eric had three carpenter's helpers, and together the Fortman men made substantial headway on the Star Garden suite, coming back in the evenings sweaty and dirty, but, from all appearances, in harmony. Gayle stayed away from the renovations for any number of reasons, but at the top was a desire to let the guys have their fun without interference.

She spent time before the trip to Richmond catching up on all the things she had put aside during her stint as camp caterer. Most important, on Sam's recommendation, she hired a man who had participated in his prison ministry to cook breakfast at the inn five mornings a week. Gabe was intelligent and eager to get his life back on track. Just as important, he was a fabulous cook. So far the match was made in heaven, and she was afraid she could never go back to cooking breakfast full-time again.

On Tuesday the quilters put the final stitches in the breathtaking Touching Stars quilt. Helen insisted that Noah and Eric be there to help the women remove it from the frame. And when the quilt was off, she turned it over and told both of them to sign their names on the label alongside the names of all the members of the SCC Bee. Then she gave each of them a certificate of honorary membership.

Helen had taken the quilt home to bind it, but she promised it would be ready to hang next week.

Nothing could be put off forever. And late Wednesday afternoon, after the family came back from Richmond, where they watched Jared recite his oath of enlistment, Gayle asked Eric if he would like to take a walk along the river.

Eric looked as exhausted as she felt, but she hoped talking would make them both feel better.

They met on the terrace and walked silently down toward the water. The banks on both sides were still lined with debris. The flood had taken its toll on property, but the locals were philosophical. There had been worse, and there had been better. No one had died, and the water had receded quickly. Once the water was down, Travis had called to say that although there was substantial erosion, enough of the site was intact that, barring more floods between now and next summer, the camp could dig there again.

"How are you feeling?" Eric asked, when they reached the river. "I guess it went well today. Jared was certainly proud."

"I probably feel the way every mother of a recruit feels these days. But when I stood there, I understood exactly what Miranda went through when she watched Lewis riding off to war."

"But you weren't like Miranda. You supported him." He paused. "We both did."

"He'll be a marine to be proud of, the kind our country always needs."

"I hope he doesn't make the military his career. I don't know if my heart will hold up that long. It's going to be lodged in my throat until he's a civilian again."

"One day at a time." She pointed to their right. "Let's go this way. There's more of a path."

They walked for a distance before he spoke. "I remember plowing this trail the first time. I rented a tractor and nearly drove into the river."

"You left your mark on the inn." Gayle stopped and looked up at him. "And on me. But, Eric, this isn't where you belong. It never was. And I think we both know *I'm* not the woman you belong with."

He stopped, too. Then he took her hand and kissed it before he tucked it tighter into his. They strolled a little farther, like the old friends they were, and Gayle knew that this gesture of friendship was as much an acknowledgment of the truth as anything he could have said.

"What made you decide that?" he asked after a while.

"Watching you when the site was flooding. It was the first time since you came back to the inn that you really seemed like the old Eric. You glowed. You vibrated with energy. Your eyes danced with excitement. You were the guy we all know and love from our television screens."

"I guess that felt like old times."

She squeezed his hand. "I know. I think it's going to be time very soon for you to go back to your job. Maybe not exactly what you were doing before, but back into the world you love."

"Gayle, I'm sorry. Again. Forever."

She stopped and pulled him around to face her. "Don't be. This is best for both of us, not just you. I've been thinking and thinking about it. When we divorced, no matter what we told other people, each of us blamed ourselves. I wanted to be different for you, you wanted to be different for me. But that was never remotely possible."

"No matter what you might believe now, after all the times and ways I disappointed you, I did try."

She met his eyes, and her gaze didn't waver. "We can't change who we are, and blaming our basic nature is like blaming the sun for shining too brightly or the moon for not shining brightly enough. Our problems weren't about what we did to each other, they were always about who we are."

"I guess it's possible to fail, even when we try our best."

"And now it's time to let go of the guilt and the regrets, and let the divorce be final once and for all."

"Why does that sound so sad?"

She reached into her pocket and pulled out the velveteen pouch that contained her wedding and engagement rings. She put the pouch in his hand and closed his fingers around it.

"It's sad because we still care about each other. Maybe we even love each other. But I really don't want to be married to you again. Or anymore. Our marriage is well and truly over."

He smiled, too, but his expression was sadder still when he opened the pouch and saw what was inside. "I don't want these."

"Please take them and do whatever you need to. It would be a help to me."

He slipped the pouch inside his jacket pocket. "The other night? I wasn't using you. I really wanted this to work. I guess I was hoping that would be the final proof."

"It was an odd way to say goodbye, but I realized right away that's what it was. So we close that door forever and move on. We'll still be friends. I'll always wish the very best for you, and I know you'll do the same."

She stood on tiptoe and kissed him. Gently and finally. "And now, with no regrets in the way, it's going to be that much easier to do what's right for our sons. I hope you'll always feel good about coming here to spend time with them. You'll always be welcome."

"Gayle…" He looked away; then he looked back at her. "About the boys…"

It took her a moment to realize he was asking permission to speak. "What about them?"

"I want them with me."

For a moment she didn't understand. "You want to take them on a vacation before school starts?"

"No, I want them with me next year."

"But how?"

"I think I'm moving to Los Angeles. There's a job there, a good one, I know I'm ready to do. It means living there for at least the next year and setting up everything. After that I'll be traveling quite a bit, but next year I'll be stable and settled, and I can rent a place large enough for all of us."

"*Both* boys?"

He confirmed with a nod. "At first I thought maybe just Noah. The time left with him is so short. But Dillon's been shunted to the side too often when he should have been included. I can't leave him here alone again. Gayle, they both need this. They need a year with me. Maybe I'm not a perfect role model, but I can help them become men. They need an immersion course."

"But what about school?"

"I called their principal on Monday. We can make arrangements. They can go to school out there or follow lesson plans with me. I can hire tutors for the subjects I don't remember.

Noah can still come back and do his senior year and graduate with his friends, and Dillon will come and settle back in when the year is up. But let me have this time with them now."

She almost couldn't imagine it. Her sons, all of them. Gone. The carriage house so empty her footsteps would echo. Her life empty, even with an inn filled with guests.

"Oh, Eric, I don't know…" She shook her head slowly. "Are you sure?"

"Think of *them*."

Tears sprang to her eyes. Because this time Eric's instincts were right. This was exactly what their sons needed. And if they didn't take the opportunity now, it might never happen.

"Have you talked to them?"

"Vaguely. I couldn't come right out and ask without consulting you. But both of them are excited about coming to visit me in L.A. And I told them I want to take them to Texas first, to spend some time with their grandparents. I'm hoping we can all mend fences. We'll see."

Long moments passed as she struggled, but at last she gave a short nod, because how could that not be a good idea, no matter what came next?

He looked relieved. "I don't think they'll have a problem moving in with me for a year, as long as they know they can come back here if it doesn't seem to be working."

"You'll make it work."

"I intend to give it everything I've got."

"You'll be careful with them?"

His eyes softened. "I'll be careful. I promise. Precious cargo."

"Oh, I'm going to miss them."

"Of course you are. And you're even going to miss me a little, although the relief may get you through that part."

She laughed, even though her eyes were filling with tears. And when he hugged her, she hugged him back. Hard.

Eric took the boys out for an early dinner to talk about next year's plans. Gayle refused the invitation to join them, knowing that if she were there, her sons would be worried about her and wouldn't be completely honest. The moment they left, as if on cue, the carriage house grew two sizes larger and every sound echoed to torment her.

She tried to imagine life without teenage boys and simply couldn't.

She was forcing herself to eat a poached egg and an English muffin when somebody knocked. Glad for the interruption, she opened the door to find Leon, shoulders slumping, on the doorstep. Her heart sank when she saw a duffel bag at his feet.

She opened her arms, and he stepped into them for a long hug.

"Your dad's off the wagon?" she asked, knowing the answer.

He stepped back. "For a week now." He straightened his shoulders. He looked as if he had already cried the tears he'd needed to. "Mrs. Fortman, can I come back for good? I'm not going to be able to live there again. It's not right for him *or* me. If I leave, maybe he'll go back into treatment and maybe he won't. But I can't make him change."

"Of course you're welcome here. You're always welcome. You're part of our family."

"I know Jared's going to be leaving. I figure Noah will want the room over the garage all to himself. He deserves it. I'll move in with Dillon and—"

"Not to worry. There've been some big changes, but you're going to be the only guy in residence next school year." She explained the situation.

Leon considered before he nodded gravely. He seemed to understand everything she had and hadn't said. "You've always been there when I needed you. This time, maybe I can be here for you?"

She steeled herself not to cry. "Will you play your music too loud and make me remind you to do your homework? Oh, and leave your dirty socks on the rug every once in a while?"

"Sure, except that socks thing. Nobody should have to touch my socks."

"Are you trying not to cry just as hard as I am?"

"Pretty much."

"Go on and move back into your room. And Leon…" She swallowed. "Welcome home."

After he left, she finished crying; then she washed her face and combed her hair. There was only one way she wanted to end this difficult day, and one person with whom to end it. She put on her most comfortable walking shoes, checked with Paula to be sure everything was okay at the inn, then started down the road.

Travis was her closest neighbor, but he still lived a good distance away. As the sun slipped over the mountains, she admired fireflies and slapped mosquitoes. For a moment she tried to imagine leaving the Valley and pursuing a life somewhere else, but she knew she never would. She had everything she had ever wanted right here. And if someday the boys settled nearby, then this would truly be heaven.

Travis's Highlander was in his driveway, and he was alone. She hoped he wouldn't mind her company, because she was certainly in the mood for his.

She knocked and waited until the door opened. Something very much like butterflies fluttered inside her when she saw the look of surprise, then pleasure, on his face.

She had never been with Travis when she was a completely free woman. Now the change was resonating in every part of her.

"To what do I owe this visit?" He opened the door wider, then closed it once she was inside.

"Did you ever have a day when everything in your life did an about-face?"

"I think you're here to talk about yours, not mine."

"I'll give you a synopsis. Jared is now officially in the marines, and Eric is moving to Los Angeles and taking the other boys with him next year. "

He ushered her into the sunroom; then, without asking, he went into the kitchen and returned with two glasses of wine. He sat beside her and clinked his against hers.

"To moving on?" It was clearly a question. "At last? Or to regrets?"

She thought about it. "To moving on. To finally divorcing the man I divorced twelve years ago. To letting him be a real father for the next year." She clinked again. "Maybe to figuring out who I am."

"And figuring out what you want?"

She considered. "That too."

They clinked one final time. But she really didn't want to drink, and she really didn't want to sit. She stood and walked to the windows looking over the backyard stretching down to the water below.

He joined her, but they didn't touch. "You're sure about all this? You're okay?"

"I will be. This needs to happen. Every bit of it. I'll miss the boys, but they'll be where they need to be. And they'll visit."

"And Eric?"

"We'll still be friends, I think. If nothing else, we share three great sons and good wishes for the future."

"I see." He sipped his wine, and they stood quietly looking out to the river.

Finally he spoke again. "It sounds to me like you'll have a lot of free time."

She turned to look at him. She had always liked his profile. In fact, there was really nothing she didn't like about Travis Allen. The butterflies fluttered their fragile wings again, or maybe this time it was a showers of stars. She looked away.

Last week Travis had admitted he was in love with someone. She realized now, and would have known then if she had searched her heart, who that woman was.

For a moment she looked out over Travis's unadorned acres again, at the green stretch of grass just aching to be interrupted by carefully designed gardens. She thought of Miranda Duncan, who had realized too late that a good man who adored her was the real love of her life.

Then she turned back to Travis. Once and for all.

"You know, it sounds like I'm finally going to have time to put in a perennial bed for you. Maybe even two."

His eyes were warm, and so was his smile. "Why bother, when you have all that space at the inn?"

"Because when I stand here in the future, I want to see gardens stretching down to the river."

"You expect to be standing here in the future?"

She smiled back at him. "I can't imagine where else I'd rather stand."